# BESSIE'S MANDALA

## Mary Elizabeth Taylor

SARTOR PRESS

This is a work of fiction. With the exception of historical figures, all the characters appearing in the story are imaginary and not to be confused with real people, living or dead.

Cover art by Sabina Proulx, 1997
Cover photograph of Bessie, circa 1909

Canadian Cataloguing in Publication Data:

Taylor, Mary Elizabeth, 1916-
    Bessie's Mandala

ISBN 0-9681625-0-9

    I. Title.

| | | |
|---|---|---|
| PS8589.A912B48 1997 | C813'.54 | C96-901010-9 |
| PR9199.3.T36B48 1997 | | |

Sartor Press
5105 - 2829 Arbutus Road
Victoria, British Columbia, Canada
V8N 5X5

PRINTED IN CANADA

*for all my family*

*with affection*

# Contents

Mandala

1. a symbolic circular figure representing the universe in various religions
2. *Psychol.* such a symbol in a dream representing the dreamer's search for completeness and self unity
(Sanskrit, mándala — disc)

*The Oxford English Dictionary*

# PART ONE

# A SENSE OF DUTY

*Prologue...*

# Penny Farthing

May 1889

I'm running as fast as I can across the picnic grounds, threading my way in and out among the people, dodging around noisy laughing children with their hoops and their games. I'm jumping over a pile of gunny sacks lying ready for the races. I'm hiding behind a clump of lilac bushes.

"Bessie! ... Bessie!" The boy's voice rises staccato above the chorus of happy children sounds, disturbing the bright afternoon, the blue sky, cotton clouds, green, green grass, pink, blue, yellow flowers, lavender lilacs, and all the lovely smells. I listen and the voice grows fainter. Good, he's lost at last. I'll not let him spoil my holiday.

1

Only when I'm not near Martin can I think of him as a human being. Then, I can even pretend that under his ungainly exterior might lurk a few fine characteristics. As a good Christian — and I'm doing my best to be a good Christian — I might even lay down my life for him. But I definately don't like Martin.

He has bad breath. And the way he's been sidling up to me most of this day and thrusting his face close to mine, I simply can't stand it. Maybe he's short-sighted and I should be forgiving and not bothered by such matters. But I won't have him touching me. As a recent convert to the Christian faith I'm trying very hard to be charitable. But there are limits. Some things in life are too much for me to bear and Martin is one of them. I can't stand Martin.

Rising slowly from my crouched position I peek around the bushes and scan the nearby crowds. Martin is nowhere to be seen. Boldly I move towards the roadway that circles the picnic grounds, then stop delighted. A steam tricycle is heading my way, its driver proud and self-conscious. It passes. And beyond the fading steam I see a penny farthing, jaunty, by a box against an elm tree.

"Bessie! There you are." Martin comes all creaks and angles, his cry victorious. He's caught me unaware.

I must not be unkind. As a member of this Presbyterian Sunday School I must do my best to appreciate that Martin, too, is one of God's creatures. He takes my arm. I shake free and long to be back with my friends. I hear a whistle and a call. A new game is about to begin and I want to be there.

"Leave me alone, Martin," I glare at him. "Take your hands off of me or I'll scream. And don't you dare ever touch me again."

Martin turns red. Now he's angry. No doubt I've hurt his feelings after all my good resolutions. In an effort to

2

be pleasant and divert his attention, I point to the bicycle. "Look, Martin, have you ever ridden a penny farthing?"

"Of course not. They're too dangerous."

I didn't expect he'd have ridden one.

"They're only for grown-up people. For men," he explains.

"Why only for men?" His remark has nettled me, as do most of his remarks. The way Martin has always acted, I know he doesn't respect girls. And that's only one thing about him I don't like. I rise to the bait. "If a man can ride one why can't a lady?"

"Have you ever seen a lady ride one?"

"No, but just because we haven't seen a lady riding a penny farthing doesn't mean a lady can't — or hasn't."

"You're silly, Bessie. A lady couldn't ride one." He speaks with scorn.

"Don't you call me silly when you don't know what you're talking about."

"Well, anyway, *you* couldn't ride one."
"I bet I could. I've ridden a safety bicycle. A friend of mine owns one. And I didn't fall once."

"Well, that's different. A safety bicycle's different. I said you couldn't ride a penny farthing." He's taunting me. As he moves towards me, I back away.

"I bet I can."

"I bet you can't."

"I can if I want to."

"Then I dare you."

I turn and look at him with all the contempt I can muster, good Christian thoughts cast aside. "You steady it while I get on and I'll show you."

Now he's horrified. "You'll break your neck!"

"You dared me, so hold it."

No one's near. The lilac bushes screen us from view. I climb on the box and gather up my skirt, revealing my

3

lace and ruffled pantalets. But I don't care. I'll show that awful Martin that girls are every bit as good as boys at riding penny farthings. He'd be scared to even try. I knot the skirt about my waist and with legs freed, straddle the penny farthing.

"Steady it, Martin!"

Martin takes firm hold, straightens the bicycle, gives it a shove and lets go. The wheel wobbles. I tell myself to look straight ahead and not look down. Pedal fast. Keep going just as when you rode Tommy's bicycle. Only this wheel is a five-foot circle and I'm sitting high above the ground. Horses are more reliable. But I won't fall. I mustn't even think of falling. I didn't fall from the safety bicycle and I don't intend to fall now. Especially not with Martin watching.

The penny farthing moves along. Now past the bushes it is in full view of the Presbyterian picnic. I'm well on my way before I hear a shout: a man's surprised voice. "Hey, there!" the man's protesting loudly, "what do you think you're doing? Stop her, someone! That's mine."

Loud cheering from the children. I keep going. I have to. I don't know how to stop. Nor do I want to.

"Stop that girl!" An angry shout. I'm sure that's the Sunday School Superintendent. But I'm not turning my head to look. Beautifully balanced, my feet move rhythmically. I pedal on, half way around the circling road.

But, too soon, my ride is over. Two men run onto the road in front of me and, positioning themselves on either side, grab the penny farthing as it and I try flying by. As one man lifts me down I hastily unknot my skirt.

"You could have hurt yourself," says the older one, echoing Martin, but not unkindly.

The Superintendent, Mr. Clark, must have cut across the grounds, for he's approaching, red-faced and

4

puffing like the steam tricycle. With him is a young man wearing sports knickers. Mr. Clark, old, angular, and winded, is still able to take me by the shoulders and shake me.

"A girl your age should know better," he says in time, his hands biting into my shoulders. "Do you realize what a terrible thing you've done, taking what does not belong to you, making a shameless show of yourself...a brazen, unwarranted, impudent action..."

The men who "rescued" the penny farthing leave silently as Mr. Clark continues to scourge me with his tongue. I mean to listen but the success of my adventure has caught me as in an oyster shell and I, concentrating on my pearl, am sheltered from his wrath. His words merely intrude then fade from my mind like waves lapping on rocks.

"A shameful exhibition," he repeats. "No proper young woman would expose her limbs... I intend to report this incident to your parents and will suggest they see to it that you are punished..."

At last he lets go of me, and addressing the young man his voice is subdued. "I must return to my duties. I leave her to you. See that she apologizes." With that and another scowl at me, Mr. Clark marches off.

Torn from my oyster shell, I look apprehensively at the owner of the penny farthing.

"Well," he says, "what do you have to say for yourself, young lady?"

"I realize, Sir, that I shouldn't have taken your bicycle. But you see it was because of a dare and I wanted to get away from Martin." I pause, not knowing what else to say.

He stands, waiting.

Obliged to say something more, words come tumbling out. "Sir, it was an incredible feeling, the most exhilarating experience I've ever had." Again I stop. The

5

dapper young man is yawning. He's bored. I add lamely, "I'm sorry. In my enthusiasm I'm forgetting to apologize."

"Then don't apologize. Luckily, no damage has been done."

I'm relieved. "Thank you for being so understanding of my predicament. Those few moments will remain always in my memory as among the very finest..."

He interrupts. "No doubt, and it's quite possible you'll have a few more." He's uninterested, anxious to get away.

"I do hope so," I say feebly, my voice trailing off as I watch him roll the penny farthing to a nearby bench, mount, and ride away.

Still standing on the road, I close my eyes. Once more I'm clamped inside my oyster shell. Once more I revel in my triumphant accomplishment, totally forgetful of Mr. Clark's reference to the ride as a shameful exhibition.

When I open my eyes there before me on the grass is the prettiest girl, her eyes bright with admiration.

"Hello," she says, "I don't care what that awful old man called you. I watched you ride the penny farthing and I think you're wonderful. My name's Martha and I'm thirteen years old. What's your name?"

Thrilled that she observed and appreciated my undertaking, I say, "My name's Elizabeth, but almost everybody calls me Bessie. And I'm thirteen, too."

*Chapter I*

# Starting Out

Detroit, Michigan, August 1909

Standing on the verandah of Ma's house, I wait for the carriage Andy's gone to fetch. He offered to take me to Martha's in the family buggy, but, as it's a luxury for me to be alone, I declined. And I'm looking forward to the half hour or more it will take to cross town.

Here it comes, a smart victoria phaeton. Opening my parasol, I walk quickly down the steps to meet it. Andy, who has been talking with the driver, jumps down from the open carriage.

"Just what you ordered, Sis."

"Thank you. Indeed it is."

As he helps me to my seat he whispers, "You're looking grand today, Bess."

What an unusual compliment from my young half-brother, who is more apt to tease me! But then it's an unusual day. For I've made an important decision,

7

completed my plans, and I'm off to tell Martha that I've broken my engagement with Richard. I'll tell her also it's my intention to go to Winnipeg. That will surprise her! For there I mean to finish my preparation for the work in China.

I've dressed to please my friend, wearing the powder-blue suit she designed for me. It's of fine wool, with three rows of matching braid embroidery on skirt and jacket. Costume is Martha's interest, not mine. It was out of friendship she took me in hand, and has looked after my needs ever since. For that I'm grateful. Martha's been my good friend these many years.

The driver sits erect, eyes forward, waiting for his signal. I glance upward at the grey clapboard with its long row of steps and verandah with white railing, and notice someone peering through the lace curtains of the tall living-room windows. No doubt it's Belle. I wave, then speak to the driver, who flicks the reins. The bay moves briskly past newly planted trees and young lawns. I savour the clean atmosphere. The afternoon is near idyllic. I want to merge with the calm of the day and become one with it. But I can't. For a measure of unease remains. They are bittersweet moments that begin my memory in the year of Our Lord 1909.

I'm carried past vacant lots, some edged with wild rose bushes, their flowers long gone; some lots have bushes with ripening berries. The lots are part of a large tract of land that in 1894 was set aside so that the poor and unemployed might grow vegetables. But they've been abandoned in these days of industrial growth and activity and, over a year ago, the area was opened for development. The lots being close to the city centre, Ma immediately saw the advantage of investing and purchased three. On one she built her house. And she intends to build two more houses and sell them at good profit. She has also bought a large property in a

8

strategic spot in the city which, she maintains, will make her rich one day. Ma's doing very well financially and is no longer in need of my support. Andy, almost sixteen years younger than I and the youngest of her brood, will be graduating from high school this year. The thought of flight excites me — for, though I love my family dearly, I've longed to break the bonds and be free of the nest. I think that not unnatural.

Soon we are passing houses on smaller lots. Now houses can be seen closer together. And now they stand crowding one another as we enter the city proper. But even though small, the majority are neat and some have gardens. The streets are filled with people walking and people cycling. There are carriages with handsome horses. Tradesmen with wagons and weary horses. Some horses are stopped by watering troughs and some wear feed bags. Automobiles are honking, tram cars clanging. A man is calling his wares. A boy is whistling. It's an active Saturday afternoon in this prosperous city with a fast-growing population of over 400,000.

I'm proud of this city of mine, which extends for miles along the clear blue Detroit River and which is reputed to be among the finest of the cities in North America. Its wide avenues, accommodating the constantly shifting patterns of traffic and people, are paved with asphalt and brick. Over them the horses clip-clop, sometimes leaving behind them odoriferous offerings to the consternation of long-skirted women. Shade trees, maple and elm, line the streets. I'll be pleased to return to this handsome place one day when my work is done.

The carriage is nearing the City Hall as the clock strikes three. The building, of Renaissance style, has at each of the four corners by the clock tower a figure representing Justice, Industry, Art, and Commerce. Prospects for the expansion of industry seem especially good, thanks, in large measure, to Henry Ford, who has designed an automobile for the common man. "No longer," says Henry Ford, "are automobiles to be used only for the pleasure of the rich." Just this year he announced his intention to build the Model T chassis, which will require a minimum of upkeep and care. "Hereafter, any customer can have one painted any colour he wants, so long as it's black." The Model T will cost $840.00. But Ford is hoping that by raising wages more people will be able to buy it and, in time, even with improvements, the price of the automobile can be lowered. Henry Ford has a highly creative mind and has pioneered an assembly-line technique that no doubt other industries are already copying. Detroit leads all cities in the country in the manufacture of automobiles, having over twenty automobile factories. And, as a consequence, the volume of all related trades is increasing. Too, the real estate market is booming.

The carriage, turning off the Avenue, brings me soon to my friend's neighbourhood of older homes, the homes of a few of Detroit's well-to-do. I indicate to the driver where my friend lives: a large, red-brick residence set in beautifully landscaped grounds. He turns into the driveway, and brings the phaeton to a stop before the entrance. Martha has been watching for me. For no sooner have I stepped down from the carriage and am turning to speak to the driver, than she opens the door and comes rushing out to greet me with a hug.

"Bessie, you look wonderful!" She's pleased to see me in the powder-blue suit. "Don't ask your driver to come back — we'll look after you."

So after paying, I dismiss him.

Martha and I are both tall and slim — almost of a size. But there the likeness ends, for her hair is as fair as mine is dark. And our temperaments differ almost as much. For Martha's is a serene nature, while I — or so

10

I'm told and no doubt it's true — am somewhat tempestuous. Perhaps Martha might be likened to the calm of this summer day while my nature is more akin to a summer storm. We lock arms and walk together up the steps, talking nineteen to the dozen. And so, into the house.

"If you'll wait in the drawing room, I'll tell Anna to bring the tea. And I'll get Mother, she's looking forward to seeing you."

It's a gracious room, elegant yet comfortable, with mahogany furniture that glows, oak floors, and beautiful Persian rugs. A small table is prepared for tea and I note there are four cups! As I walk over to the window and stand admiring the garden I'm wondering who the other guest might be. But not for long. I hear a footstep, a footstep I know so well. Richard! I turn. He's standing in the archway, smiling. But I'm not happy he's here.

Before there's time to say anything, he's by my side, has his arms around me, and is kissing me. And I respond with warmth, for the truth is I love him. God knows it's not for lack of love I'm leaving him. My decision is quite apart from that.

"Why are you here?"

"Because Mrs. Schrieter invited me and I have an hour to spare."

"Did you tell Mrs. Schrieter we're no longer engaged?"

"No."

"Tell me, Richard, why did you come?"

"To see you. She told me you'd be visiting Martha and asked if I'd like to stop by for tea."

I frown. "You're not part of my plans today, and you're not making things easier." I'm adjusting my hat and no doubt look flustered as Mrs. Schrieter arrives with Martha.

"What's the matter with the love birds?"

11

"You and Martha may as well know right now that Richard and I will not be getting married and that I'm leaving Detroit. That's what I came to tell you."

They're shocked. But that's to be expected. "It wasn't my intention to break the news so bluntly. It's Richard's fault coming here." Martha, frowning, says nothing.

"A lovers' spat," Mrs. Schrieter brushes the announcement aside. "Sit down and have tea and we'll talk it over."

Anna, the housekeeper, is rolling in a well-laden tea-wagon. I nod to her from offended heights. I've known Anna for years. We're friends, but my mood at the moment won't allow me to unbend. We sit down.

"I don't wish to talk it over. Richard shouldn't be here, for we said good-bye over a week ago." I'm speaking as though he's not in the wing chair opposite me, still smiling, still treating the matter as though it were a silly game.

"You said good-bye. Not I."

Mrs. Schrieter turns to him. "But you'll not let her go, Richard."

"She won't go."

The arrogance! So sure of himself. Always expecting to have his own way.

"I have my tickets. Everything's settled. I'll be leaving in September about two weeks after Martha sails for Europe." And to indicate my composure, I accept a cup of tea from Mrs. Schrieter.

"I'm afraid I don't understand this. Whatever is the matter?"

Determined to hold on to what little calm remains, avoiding Richard's eyes, I say what I had carefully planned to say. "Richard is a very good lawyer, as you well know, and he intends to get to the top of his profession. And he wants and needs a wife..."

12

"And what's wrong with that?"

"It so happens, as you also know, I have plans to be a missionary in China. How can a missionary in China be a wife to a lawyer in Detroit?"

"Then stay here and do mission work in Detroit. That's what we all thought you'd do."

"Richard would be a very demanding husband, the kind that expects his wife to be on hand when he comes home, put out his slippers, and entertain his friends."

"And what's wrong with that?" Mrs. Schrieter repeats. "Richard, have some more tea, and help yourself to sandwiches."

It's obvious that Richard, if unhappy about our broken engagement, is not letting his emotions interfere with his appetite. I'm more than ever distressed.

I say, shortly, "It just won't work."

"I've never thought of Bessie as the domestic type, Richard." Martha speaks at last.

"Domestic! Who's expecting her to scrub floors? She'll have all the help she wants."

"Richard," I turn to him patiently, "it's important to save souls..."

"Save souls," he interrupts me. "You can save all the souls you want to right here."

"In my free time?" I ask, irritated. "When it's evident you no longer believe in the necessity of saving souls. Besides, I can see what will happen over the years — to my free time."

Richard has heard this all before. My words are for the benefit of Mrs. Schrieter, to whom I now appeal — not for Martha, for I'm beginning to think she has as little sympathy for my missionary work as has Richard.

"China is important to me. Since I was fifteen I've dreamt of going to China and having a mission school there."

13

"Then why did you become engaged to Richard in the first place?" It's a reasonable question from Mrs. Schrieter.

"Because I fell in love with Richard. One can't help falling in love — can one? Perhaps I thought there would be a way to reconcile the missionary with the lawyer. But now I feel that in all fairness to him I must go away. I've hung on to him too long."

If truth be told, I cannot trust myself to remain with him longer and not give in to his insistence that we marry.

"Richard knows I love him and always will. But I must pursue my higher calling and let him get on with his life." I say this reasonably coolly and with finality. But Richard snorts like a horse chafing at the bit.

Playing my game, he now ignores me and addresses Mrs. Schrieter and Martha. "I'm sure you'll agree with me that Bessie's too liberal in her views to be a good missionary. She's too tolerant, too understanding, and too interested in this diverse world of ours to be effective in such a capacity. After five years, I know her well. Granted she'll do her best to get people to turn to God, but will it be to a branch of the Protestant church? I doubt it. For what Bessie will do is fraternize with the enemy, very much as did the Emperor Frederick II when off on his Crusade. But instead of talking about astronomy and mathematics, as the Emperor Fred did with the King of Jerusalem, it will be about gunpowder, the I Ching, or whatever else they have in China. Then she'll declare the Mission open to whomever wishes to come to worship according to Tao, Buddha, Confucius, Christ — however anyone wishes to worship God. But remember," continues Richard, his voice acquiring an ominous tone, "though war had ceased, and Jerusalem made an open city, though the people were happy, the Pope was furious. Frederick, he said, has made a pact

14

with the Devil! Poor Frederick was excommunicated. Remember that, Bessie," he adds, turning pointedly to me, "the Emperor Frederick was excommunicated."

As I'm ready to flair up, he puts his arm before his face, pretending to ward off a blow. "Our Bessie may be tolerant but she has a temper too. As well we know."

Martha, amused by Richard's description of me, gets into the act.

"Remember the story David Brown told us of St. Francis visiting the sultan during the Fifth Crusade, thinking he might convert him. But instead, because Francis had so much love in his heart, he came away saying that God is everywhere and all religions must be respected? That would be like Bessie, now wouldn't it, Richard?"

They are laughing at me and have me on the defensive. But they'll not stop me. My love for Richard won't hold me. I'll not be prevented from doing what I believe is right. I have a goal in life and I'll pursue that goal no matter what.

My face must show my resolution. "I've bought train tickets and I'm going."

Richard, sobered, sits staring at me, then looking at his watch, he gets up. "I've a meeting and must be off."

He comes round to me and takes my hand. "You know where to find me. Anytime."

He kisses my flushed cheek. Then saying good-bye to Martha and her mother, he leaves.

Silence falls. Finally, Martha says, "I'm sorry for interfering. But you know we love you."

I nod. They're my good friends, and I can't take offense. But there's a ball of bitterness in my throat. I try to ignore the hurt and pass my cup to Mrs. Schrieter, who after pouring in the amber liquid, says, "We've known you for a long time, Bessie. You were twelve when Martha first brought you here and Mr.

15

Schrieter and I took to you immediately."

I'm glad of the change of subject. "Oh, no, I was thirteen, almost fourteen, and weren't you just a bit suspicious of the strange tomboy from the other side of town?"

"We met at a picnic, remember, Mother? Bessie rode a penny farthing and I became her great admirer. I was always such a timid mouse and there she was so daring and courageous."

I am able to smile a little, remembering. "You mean impulsive and foolhardy. That's what Ma called me when she heard what I'd done. She didn't punish me as Mr. Clark wanted her to, but she did give me a tongue lashing. It was all because of that awful Martin. It wasn't just his pimples. The way he used to sidle up to me! I would have done anything to get away from him. Then he made the silly remark that only men could ride a penny farthing. I told him he was quite wrong about that. He dared me and — what else could I do? I got away and can't recall ever seeing him again."

"Well I guess we must thank Martin for our meeting you," says Mrs. Schrieter.

"Even when you discovered I told fortunes and Martha and I began dabbling in astrology?" I'm teasing her now.

"I admit as good Lutherans that was hard for Mr. Schrieter and me, at first. But we recovered."

"Bessie," Martha speaks up, "your mentioning astrology reminds me of something I've been wanting to tell you for a long time, about my visit to my friend Emma in Zurich, last year."

Martha is about to tell me something, but Mrs. Schrieter, having thought of Mr. Schrieter, is no longer listening; she's launched on a discourse about her dear dead husband, dead this past year and a half. He was a husband who had loved her dearly and had in turn

16

been loved by her, had cared for her and spoiled her, allowing her everything her heart desired, who had, along with herself, spoiled their only daughter in turn. How unhappy he had been when that only child so stubbornly insisted on a career in fashion design. A career! Why should a woman want a career, of all things? Especially Martha, who would always be well looked after. He was horrified, for he had sent her to the most genteel of schools, and to France for language and art, thinking she would marry a man of good circumstance and that Mr. Schrieter and she would have grandchildren. And Martha had many suitors, as Bessie well knows. But his concern above all else had been for Martha's happiness. So in the end he had capitulated.

Mrs. Schrieter is growing tedious and Martha and I uncomfortable. For it's a story that's been told many times over. My mind retires until Martha's voice recalls me.

"You're rather unconventional, Bessie, you know. As Richard implied, you do have a knack for getting into trouble with authorities — sometimes. Admit it."

"If I'm not conventional, then all the more reason not to marry Richard. Who can guess, I might wind up by being a source of embarrassment to him. And I've been getting along very well with my church lately, thank you, and intend to continue to do so. Now I have more to tell you, Martha."

"And I have something to show you. So let's go upstairs."

"Run along then," Mrs. Schrieter sniffs, for the tears have been flowing. "But you must marry that handsome Richard, Bessie."

It's her parting shot. I give her a kiss and thank her for her hospitality.

"Martha," I say desperately as we go up the curving

17

staircase, heading for her studio-shop, "surely you understand why I can't marry Richard. If I don't do what I've wanted to do most of my life, I will always feel unfulfilled, and I've wanted to have that school in China just as much as you've wanted to be a fashion designer."

"Yes, of course I can understand that. But I've never had a love like yours." Then, perhaps feeling that she's said too much, she adds, "I really wouldn't mind getting married if it were to someone who would look after my accounts."

"Because you have no head for business. Which brings us to the matter I have to tell you. Can you guess where I'm going?"

"Not to China?"

"Not yet. But wait until we're in the studio and all will be revealed. And you can tell me about your time with your friend Emma."

On the second floor Martha opens a door and we proceed now single file up narrower steps to the so-called "Shop", which was once long ago the playroom, and after that the studio. It's adjacent to the caretaker's suite which Ludwig and Anna have occupied for the past twenty-five years, having come from Germany to join the Schrieter family. The large room, with skylight added during the studio period, is bright and cheerful. Martha has put long-stemmed fresh flowers before the fireplace screen. Along with her oil paintings and water colours of landscapes, flowers, and faces, sketches of dresses cover the walls. An easel occupies a prominent spot. There are bolts of materials on shelves, long tables, and two Judys — one dressed in a partially-made dinner gown, another in a grey-flannel suit. There are handsome mirrors, two sewing machines for the tailors who are employed during the week, and all the rest of the paraphernalia required by Martha. There are

18

high stools and two slipper chairs. I sit in one chair and Martha perches on a stool to face me. I wait for her to speak.

"First you tell me where you're going, to get away from Richard," she insists.

"The mission project requires a little more money — I'm pledged to contribute a certain sum. So here's a surprise for you. I've decided to go to Winnipeg, and probably will be there for a couple of years — at least until I have what's needed —"

"Winnipeg! You mean I can look forward to having you with me in Winnipeg? Tell me about it."

"When you got back from there this spring and told me it was the place you meant to start a business, I began to think of the possibilities from my standpoint. Winnipeg is growing at least as fast as Detroit at this moment, so I can as easily invest there. And I hope to add substantially to my bank account, and quickly. Mr. Jemmet has recommended me as personal secretary to a man in the spice import business, an old friend of his who happened to mention at a recent conference that he was in need of someone. I think it fortuitous. I'm to be there in September. So next year when you come to Winnipeg after finishing your business in Europe, I'll be there to see that you get a start with what you consider to be the boring end of it all. That is, if you'd like me to help for a while."

Slipping from her stool, Martha does a little dance. "If! Of course I would like. Books and money do indeed bore me to tears. Naturally, if all goes well I'll hire a manager and secretary. But to begin with...well, what a load off my mind! I do appreciate your offer."

"Your work is sure to be well received." I mean it, for Martha's work is outstanding. We chat about the things we'll do and the good times we'll have together. Then I recall she has something to say about her friend

19

and astrology. "Now tell me about Emma."

"You remember that when I was young, Mother and I would sometimes accompany Father to Germany on his business trips. He traveled around quite a lot and we would stay with a school chum of Mother's. The daughter, Emma, and I became great friends and I visited her occasionally while I was at art school in France. A few years ago Emma married. And this spring I went to see her at her home in Zurich for the first time since then, and met her husband, Carl Jung, who teaches at the university. He's a very clever man, a psychologist, who often works with mental patients. A most interesting man." Martha is talking hurriedly and enthusiastically, like someone trying to empty a bucket all at once. "I can't claim to understand everything he talks about.

"But Bessie, he uses astrology to understand his patients and claims there is a time-space link between a person and the planets at the moment of a person's birth. He calls it 'synchronicity', a word that seems to indicate that the pattern of the planets symbolically reflects the pattern of the person. It's macrocosm and microcosm — as above, so below — very much like a grandfather clock and your watch there which are keeping the same time. It's not the stars that force someone to do something. Astrology could be called a science inasmuch as it's based on observation and statistical evidence, and an art inasmuch as the interpreter must note relationships among the various aspects in a chart and consider all in terms of the whole. Which is not easy."

I interrupt. "Martha, you're going much too fast for me at the moment and I'm quite out of breath listening to you."

She pauses and laughs. This eagerness for knowledge that Martha has is one of the characteristics

20

about her I appreciate so much. Both of us have always been keen to discover as much as we can about life and living, and together we have peered down some unusual avenues — not always in agreement about what we have found. Some might think it strange for one like Martha, with such a studious turn of mind, to have an eye for fashion. But for my friend fashion is an art form that depicts and forecasts social trends and speaks of people.

I say, "I know almost nothing about psychology and I wish I knew more. And I'd like to learn all I can about your friend's work and his ideas on astrology, for I find his concept intriguing."

"Well, I won't continue about that now, but I intend to see Emma and Carl again in the next month or so and perhaps Emma will tell me more. I'll certainly let you know about it. Now before it gets too late, you must see my new fabrics. There, behind you on the table. Look at that beautiful delphinium blue silk. I thought of you when I saw it: the colour matches your eyes. It's what you'll need when the new boss invites you home for dinner."

"That probably won't happen. And I intend to be frugal. I certainly won't need it in China."

"But what about the next two years? You should be prepared, Bessie, you never can tell." Martha, as usual, is persuasive.

"It's beautiful... But, Martha, I think I should go now. The family are expecting me, though I probably won't be able to eat a thing after such a generous tea."

"I'm sorry about Richard. And I'm sorry about today, too. We had no idea you had broken off the engagement. Mother met him in town this morning..."

"Don't worry. There's no reason why lovers can't remain friends. And there's no reason why I can't see him in the future, is there, Martha? I truly hope I will."

21

"I'll ring for Ludwig."

Downstairs we unexpectedly meet Mrs. Schrieter arranging flowers in the hall.

"See, I've been in the garden while you two girls have been chatting."

"Girls! Mrs. Schrieter, I'm getting on in years. I'm thirty-two."

"Then all the more reason you should be married instead of going to China," she persists. Then she adds, "I do hate to think of you among all those foreigners."

I can't help laughing.

"In China, Mrs. Schrieter, I'll be the foreigner."

"Never," says Mrs. Schrieter emphatically. "Never will you be a foreigner."

There's stigma attached to 'foreign'. The Schrieters came from Germany years ago, but perhaps Mrs. Schrieter never felt alien in the United States. How much easier it must be for one who has money not to feel foreign.

I kiss them both. Then a bolt of blue silk flashes before my eyes and I tell the smiling Martha that I probably will see her about the dress in the next few days.

"Perhaps it'll be well to be prepared. Perhaps I might need it. But you'll be leaving so soon for Europe, Martha. Have you the time?"

"I'll design the dress and see it started. Mr. Miller can carry on. I trust him. And I'm so happy you're to have it: it's the perfect colour for you and I already know what I'm going to do in the way of a design."

"Well, I'll leave that entirely in your hands as usual, knowing the finished product is bound to be just right."

Ludwig is waiting in the driveway in chauffeur's uniform. He touches his cap and opens the door of the automobile.

Despite having made a difficult decision, despite my

22

carefully laid plans, an anticipated journey and adventure, the feeling that I'm pursuing the right course, the magic that was mine only a short time ago has been shattered. Clouds of uncertainty once more are gathering. And no amount of blue silk will cover them.

## 2

The front door of the Faris home is open as it's bound to be on a fine summer day like this. Walking quickly into the vestibule, I'm confronted with such quiet that I immediately grow apprehensive and pause. The family dines early and by now should be gathered around the big pinewood table in the kitchen. But mine is a noisy, talkative family. Has there been another argument? It's possible, for Ma's mood has been tense these past few days and I've caught snatches of talk recently about a real estate deal. Ma and Pa arguing. No, arguing is not quite the word — more like Ma lecturing poor Pa Faris. Well, I'll find out soon enough if that's what it is. No doubt about Ma being very angry. It won't be the first time lately I've had to play peacemaker. I'll change into a cotton frock and freshen up for battle; it's either war or everyone's out, which is unlikely. I listen. The quiet prevails.

I go up to my room where the fragrance from the wildflowers I picked early this morning greets me like a smile. The bed is covered with a patchwork quilt my grandmother made for me with bits and pieces from her rag bag, and lots of love, and expert embroidery. When I look at it I think of her. If it will fit into the trunk I'll take it with me. A bedside table holds my Bible, and there are as many bookshelves about as can be fitted

23

into the space available. Still there is not enough book space, for I've had to stack books on the floor along with papers and magazines. Ma gave up on me long ago. "Throw out what you aren't using." How can one throw out old friends? Besides, I never know when I might want to use a book or paper. Some books will go to Winnipeg, and I've told Ma everything else is to be saved against the time I return. Ma hates having "clutter" around her.

Having washed, I go to the dresser and quickly tidy my hair, which curls naturally about my face but is heavy and never dressed according to the latest fashion. I brush it and then do it up again the usual way, coiling and twisting it into a figure eight. Then, slipping into a cotton frock, I'm ready at last to face the family should they be in. I head downstairs to the kitchen.

There is indeed an air of gloom. But eighteen-year-old Isabel, looking up from her dessert, brightens visibly as I come in.

"Bess, can I get you something to eat?" It's a sigh of relief.

"No, thanks, Belle, I'd far too much to eat at Martha's. I was a pig. But I'll have a cup of tea with you. I was driven home in the Schrieter's automobile." I throw out the last sentence hoping to get a response, and as I do I take note of Ma, who's cleaning a pot at the sink. Ma looks at me and her eyes, which as a rule are full of good humour, are paled with anger, her mouth a grim line. Pa, in a rocking chair nearby, is woebegone. Andy, big eyes, big ears, tight curly hair, is sad and toying with his pudding, not eating. My apprehensions were well-founded.

They all speak at once.

"Did you have a nice time?"

"How is Mrs. Schrieter?"

24

And Andy says accusingly — for like most boys he's an automobile connoisseur — "You should have called me. I'd've liked to see the car."

Belle, trying to mollify him, says, "You've seen it before and you'll see it again."

"But it's a Packard!"

The conversation falters, fades away, and gloom descends once more. I wait for an announcement. But Belle, in an obvious effort to steer clear of any problem, says, "Bea's new beau was here today. He took her out to dinner and he's really sweet on her."

The new beau is the man Beatrice met when she went skating last winter. They have seen one another several times and recently he has started calling at the house, so I've heard. I've yet to meet him, but I am indifferent, for sister Beatrice has so many beaux that one more is scarcely a matter for comment. However, I play along with Belle's strategy. "Tell me what he's like."

"He's tall and thin and has horn-rimmed glasses and a long nose..."

"Now there's a man who's different."

"He's one of Henry Ford's architects."

"Ah-ha!"

"He has lovely dark eyes," continues Belle triumphantly, "and I think he's rather nice. And what's more Beatrice is rather gone on him, she told me so. But Ma says he's snooty — and she doesn't mean just because of his long nose." She flashes a bright smile and looks around, hoping that her joke will help Ma and Pa a little. But it doesn't.

Andy, obviously finding conversation about the new beau dull, asks to be excused, and picking up his baseball and mitt, heads out the back door.

Pa speaks quietly from the rocking chair. "Blake Arnold seems like a nice man. Comes from a good family in Chatham, Ontario. He's well-to-do and his

25

prospects for the future seem good. Our Beatrice is a beautiful girl and deserves a rich man."

Pa is not noted for tact. Belle squeezes her eyes tight shut and cringes, realizing the attempted diversion has failed. The battle is on.

"You," Ma turns on Pa. "You say she deserves a rich man? Indeed she does. Every member of your family deserves better than they've ever had from you. Your lack of effort, in fact your every effort, has led us straight to Poverty Street. Maybe they should all marry into rich families, for they'll certainly never get anything from us. After all these years of scrimping and saving and trying to make an honest dollar so they could have something, so they can hold their heads a little higher...."

She is going too far. I try to intervene. "Now, Ma, that's not right and you know it. No member of this family has any cause for shame."

But the tirade continues with both true and false accusations hurled at the hapless man.

Belle goes over and sits by Pa's chair, taking his hand to let him know he has a friend. Pa pats her hand in turn, and as the flow of words from his overly-vexed wife comes to a momentary halt, he gets up. "Well, I guess I'll go out for a walk."

"Off to find a little liquid comfort with your cronies. That's all you can ever think of doing when things go wrong." She hurls the parting shot as the door closes, then sinks, emotionally exhausted, into the newly vacated rocking chair.

It's time to say something. "Now, Ma, what's this all about? Goodness knows I've seen you mad before, but not like this. You've really been digging into Pa these past few days. What is the matter?"

"Bess, I've about had it with that man. You'll realize there's reason for my anger when I tell you what he's

26

done to us."

Rocking gently now, growing maudlin in her misery, memories crowding one another. "You know how I've planned to send Andy to university. How much I've wanted him to have the privileges denied my other children. Oh, how I've lain awake during the long hours of the night wondering how to make some money, unwilling to have my children brought up in poverty. How unhappy I was when you were forced to stop school and go to work. When I realized that Will Faris was no provider and never would be, I knew it was up to me to be the breadwinner. Despite all the opportunities in this city! The automobile industry alone." Her voice is rising.

This is not new ground. It's been dug over many times before. So I say, as I have said many times before, "Pa has neither interest nor ability to work with automobiles..."

And, as before, the same retort. "What interest or ability has he? And what ability, for pity sakes, is required with this new mass-production technique? Afraid to soil his beautiful hands is more likely."

"Don't be unfair, Ma. He's worked hard. People don't all have the same talents or breaks in life. You have more of a business head than Pa."

"And it was because you suggested I was destroying his masculine pride I let him get involved in my business again. Sakes alive! How stupid can I be. It was because I felt sorry for him in the first place I tried to teach him about investments and the real estate market. At least I had one good pupil in you. But to allow him near my money! I should have my head examined. All for the sake of that masculine pride!"

There is no doubt that everything that Pa does goes wrong. Trivialities and not such trivialities. Pa most certainly never did have the right touch.

27

"The one thing I can always count on him doing is the wrong thing." As long as I remember I could sense his unhappiness about Ma's easy superiority in the world of real estate, as well as his obvious sensitivity to her masked contempt of his many errors in judgement. Ma was never one given to needling her husband and sometimes I've seen her trying hard not to appear annoyed. But then there would be a certain coolness or, what was even worse, a tolerance which I am sure to him was condescension. "Well," I've heard her say, "try to do better next time." — much as she would talk to Andy.

Often Pa would tell the story of how something went wrong, a story told against himself, well embellished with Irish humour, that would set us all laughing, even Ma. But I knew that deep inside he felt only hurt, and that humour, that laughter, was camouflage. I was wrong in suggesting that she bring him back into the office. Indeed, it appears now to have been quite the wrong thing. Real estate is something else that's not his interest, especially when he's up against Ma. It is Ma's interest, something she can get excited about. "You have to have a sixth sense," she once told me. "It's not just a matter of reason." And Pa, though Irish, has not her kind of a sixth sense. The game holds a fascination for her. She can guess the way the wind will blow. Pa couldn't care less. But what has gone wrong now to bring down such wrath? Ma won't be rushed in the telling.

"He never was a Good Provider."

That always has been an irritant. The one thing that has grated over the years and brought on the rare but inevitable clash. Being a Good Provider is important to her.

"He has no gumption, no get-up-and-go!"

"Pa has a lot of fine qualities."

28

"Why do you always stand up for your stepfather? When you've had to turn over every pay cheque simply because he's had no initiative."

"Maybe that isn't the most important thing. You know he's been a good stepfather to me, treated me as if I were his own daughter. We've had lots of good times as a family, even though it was hard going for so many years. Ma, you know that. It hasn't been so bad. And, anyway, that was a long time ago. It's different now."

"Different, indeed!"

Now, at last, it's coming. Now the story will be told.

"He's taken every penny he could lay his hands on, without saying a word to anyone, and put it into some airy-fairy get-rich-quick scheme. And lost every cent. Real estate in Florida. Property that never existed."

"But how could he without your signature?"

"Don't ask me. Got that new simpleton of a lawyer to sign on some pretext or other. A slick deal. Turned over cash and lost every cent. Gone — along with the con artists. I swear, no one but the likes of Will Faris could have managed such a thing. And to be taken in by a scheme like that."

She has stopped rocking and is sitting bolt upright, her eyes flashing. "It was down at that saloon. A few drinks and he's an easy target."

Pa: frustrated in all matters relating to money, likely wanting to prove that he can handle a deal on his own, make a packet overnight and present it to Ma. "See what I've done." Even without a drink he never had any luck.

"Your money can't be all gone, Ma. What about your property on Gratiot?"

"No, not everything. That section out Gratiot is secure. And this house. But I'll have to liquidate a lot of my assets, maybe at a loss, just to keep going." Then she adds, more softly, "Bessie, there'll be no need for

29

you to concern yourself. We won't need your help. But it will be some time, a couple of years or more, before the Gratiot Avenue property comes into its own. If I can hang on to it and build some stores there, maybe I'll make a mint." Her spirits improve for an instant at the thought. Then, again, she is forlorn. "Just as I thought there was money for other things. The things I've always dreamed about. Now Andy can't go to university. Belle can't go to finishing school."

Belle speaks up. "Ma, I'm too old for finishing school. I'm eighteen. I really don't want to go. Remember, Samuel Johnson said an educated woman is like a dog walking on its hind legs." I recognize this as another attempt on my sister's part to cheer.

"That's not funny, Belle, nor was it clever of Mr. Johnson."

So much for Mr. Johnson.

"We're all grown up, Ma. You shouldn't have to worry about us anymore. Andy still has to complete his high school. And even if he has to work before going to university, work won't hurt him anymore than it has the rest of us. In fact it might do him a lot of good. And, Ma, you'll get along just fine."

Ma will get along, she always has. The times are with her. But another setback after all these years of struggling! She's fifty now. But she wouldn't give up her game for a hundred Good Providers! This I know.

"It still riles me that I must be both homemaker and money maker, while Will spends so much of his time drinking with his cronies, telling tall tales, and captivating the women." She turns to me. "Enough's enough. This is one woman who will not be charmed again. And enough of that biblical nonsense of yours. Forgiving is too costly. That man will never have access to my money again. I'll see to that." Another explosion.

She means it. But now she's a little calmer, putting

30

her mind in order.

"Well, thank the Lord I've got those lots." She wipes her eyes.

A relationship has blown up. Only the fragments remain, scattered and irretrievable. After all these years. I know my mother well: the episode is over. She packages the subject and sets it aside.

"What did Mrs. Schrieter have to say?"

I squeeze Ma's hand and give her a kiss. She'll carry on. She's a fighter, she'll make the best of things.

"She asked if you'd be sorry to see me leave."

"I hope you told her I'd be sorry. But I'll be glad, too — it would be wrong if you didn't leave. Of course I'll miss you."

Since Ma started to calm down, Belle has been itching to say something. I don't even have to look at her to see the wheels turning. But the tension has subsided now and I smile at her.

Belle, too, is relieved and her words come bubbling over. "Before Bessie leaves for Canada, let's have a party for her."

Now here's a complete change of subject! An oasis in a desert.

"I'm not doing very much at the moment. I'll prepare the food, get the house ready, arrange the flowers. I'd love to do it. Bess, who would you like to invite?"

In Belle's mind the matter is already settled.

But, before I can say anything, Ma speaks up. She always enjoys a party as does her gregarious family. A party might help tide her over this spot of trouble.

"I think a party's a good idea. Ask as many as you wish, Bess, there's plenty of space. Will Martha still be in Detroit? Do you think Mrs. Schrieter will come?"

Belle asks, "How about that good-looking, blonde man who brought you home last Sunday. He was fun."

So! My youg sister's thoughts are not just for me. I'm

31

amused and so is Ma. We both laugh, Ma shakily, but the laughter helps a little.

"You mean Joe Alexander. He's a member of my Bible class. Of course. I'll invite the whole class. And why not the Reverend Dickinson and his wife?"

"I can tell you why not," says Ma who it not the least attracted to the Dickinsons. "But, oh, of course invite them if you like."

"I think I should if I'm having anyone from the church, for he is our minister. And I'll invite my boss, Mr. Martin and his wife, and a few others from the office." I pause, then I add, "And Richard..."

"Do you think it wise to ask Richard?" Ma frowns, "I thought that was all finished."

The family is not happy about my decision regarding Richard.

I say stiffly, "Just because I cannot marry him doesn't mean I never want to see him again."

"Suit yourself."

"And don't forget Beatrice's young architect, Blake Arnold," Belle continues brightly.

"And Frances and Minne de Chêne and Winnifred de Chêne. And please, not so many that we'll have to peg them to the walls."

"And Bessie, you'll play the piano and we'll all sing..."

"Maybe, at first, to get the party going. But we should have some games."

"We should play Game of Ghosts. You know, where each player adds a letter to the word, and whoever completes the word is eliminated, but if the ghost can get someone to speak to him or her the person is back in the game."

"How about Geography? Naming towns beginning with a certain letter."

"How about Charades? That's always fun."

"Or Stammering? Naming all the words you can

32

beginning with a certain letter within one minute. And we'll have prizes. Just something simple like a handkerchief or a bookmark."

"Then we can have refreshments. People will want to talk a while. And before everyone leaves, perhaps a few more songs."

"It should be a very nice farewell party. Thanks for the thought, Belle. But mind you, I intend to be back home briefly before I go to China."

A thought strikes me and I want to share it with Ma, for my mind has not wandered far from the problems of the evening. "You know, Ma, 'All things work together for good, for those who love the Lord'."

"Yes, Bessie."

Is that all Ma can say! Another subject closed abruptly.

Ma gets up from the rocker. "I'm going out to see how the garden's doing. Think I need some fresh air. Finish cleaning up, won't you."

"Sure, Ma."

\* \* \* \* \*

She leaves her daughters planning and chattering. Bessie, who insists on trying to convert her, is apt to carry on with her religious philosophy for at least another half hour — given the opportunity. She doesn't intend to get into that now. But the thought follows her. She hasn't Bessie's faith, and finds it pretty hard to figure out how good comes out of bad in the space of just one lifetime. Her first husband, the man she loved so dearly, killed in an accident. Her father killed in the Civil War. And her brother Archie, whom she idolized, only eighteen years old when he joined the army. And eighteen when he was taken prisoner. Starved to death in Andersonville prison. Surely he has already been

33

through Hell. If he wasn't saved, will God say, "Sorry, Archie, why couldn't you believe as I asked? Andersonville was just a taste of what you're about to get." Trials and tribulations that seemingly strengthened her Mother McLeod's faith have made her doubt. When Judgement Day comes all she, Mary Faris, will be able to say is, "God, I've done my very best, and I thank You for my fine children. If I were to tell You that on earth I believed in the Lord Jesus that I might be saved, surely Your infinite knowledge would know I was lying."

After grade eight, at just thirteen, Bessie had to leave school to be trained as a typist. She worked long hours to help support the new family. She also helped bring up the children. Too much responsibility for one so young. Broken-hearted about having to leave school, she had carried on her studies with great determination, quite on her own, burning the midnight oil. Thank goodness she has spirit and lots of energy. Then, too, Bessie enjoyed the children, insisting they weren't work. "How can one not enjoy a child!" Bessie knows, too, how to play. But too much responsibility and her own father dead. Did that have something to do with the reason Bessie joined the church? Obviously the church filled some need. A support she longed for? For she had always to give support and was never like the other children. How Mary Faris wishes she could be sure about God and Heaven. Don't reason, just believe... God, that isn't so easy for the likes of me.

Suddenly she laughs. For a few minutes she has completely forgotten Will and the money. Well, there's one thing she's sure about. Will has gambled with her affections for too long. Now, half drunk, he has once again gambled with her money, sending her a way back down the ladder just as she was halfway to success. It's too much. When Bessie leaves, Pa will have a room of his own.

34

# 3

As there's no maid in white apron and cap at the Faris home to open the door to guests, young Andy has volunteered for the job and is directing those who wish to divest themselves of wraps, upstairs to the Master Bedroom. But as it is a balmy summer's evening and still light, most guests have come without coats or shawls and are moving straight to the living room, where the other family members stand ready to greet them.

Ma and Pa have declared a truce for the night, determined that it will be a pleasant evening for all, and are standing next to one another, as convention will have it. Next in line is Beatrice, followed by Belle, and then me. I can picture it all as though that party took place only yesterday. My handsome stepfather with his grey moustache and shock of grey hair. The four of us women: Ma, now beyond the prime of life; Beatrice, a beauty with her gold hair piled high on her head; brown-haired Belle with her almond-shaped eyes like Ma's, sparkling like her smile, frequently stealing a glance at the door, watching for a certain broad-shouldered, blonde man. And I, the tallest, all grown-up and just as foolish as Belle, for I'm glad to see my love who has just arrived, but from whom I'll soon be parting.

The room, large and unpretentious, is filling rapidly. By far the most important item of furniture in it is the grand piano, standing by the east windows, along with a large fern. Several years ago Ma insisted that her daughters take piano lessons, because knowing how to play a piano is a big part of a young lady's education. It was a great extravagance, for which she carefully budgeted. I know she thought it would be a source of relaxation for me; and so it has proven. And a source of pleasure for all, including friends, who would often drop by of an evening to gather round and sing, and sometimes, when rugs were rolled up, to dance on the polished floors.

Many of the guests know one another. They are laughing and chattering — old friends, most of them. Mr. and Mrs. Jemmet and the office staff are talking somewhat more sedately, as yet unsure of what to expect. Frances and Minne de Chêne sit together, as they always do, on the same sofa they always sit on. They are both slim and dark and look much younger than they really are. Winnifred de Chêne, an old friend of Ma's, is talking with Martha, who can only stay a little while as she is leaving on Monday for Europe. Blake Arnold, tall, stiff, and aloof, has never attended a gathering like this at our house. Beatrice is about to introduce him to the Reverend Dickinson and his wife, who also are here for the first time.

Mrs. Dickinson is a sweet and docile lady, quite in contrast to the Reverend, a large man of commanding presence. He has taken over the Presbyterian Church only within the past four months, and is much admired by the congregation, who seem to enjoy his fire-and-brimstone sermons — so different from those of our former minister, David Brown, my good friend and mentor. Ma heartily dislikes Dickinson's manner and seldom attends church anymore. "A fine excuse," I tell her. "You've said yourself it takes all types to make a world, and he does manage to pack the pews." Having said that, I have to admit that I can't really warm to the man either. But relating on a personal basis is one thing. I still must applaud his beautiful, rich, melodious voice and the fullness of his oratory. In that regard David Brown was no match for him.

Everyone has arrived, so I go to the piano and in order to get all involved I play a favourite, "Daisy, Daisy,

Give Me Your Answer, Do". And everyone joins in singing, even the severe-looking Blake. The party is off to a good start. I play another popular song and can hear Mr. Jemmet's voice blending with the Reverend Dickinson's fine baritone, for both can be heard well above the others. When I look up I notice Blake gazing into the depths of Beatrice's eyes, so on impulse I play "Drink To Me Only With Thine Eyes". Beatrice blushes, Blake frowns. Maybe it's his way of concealing embarrassment. I shouldn't tease.

After another song or two, I stand up to announce that Belle will take charge of the games. Pencils and paper are passed around for Geography. After that game, partners are chosen for Charades. The time passes merrily. Richard, who is usually the one to win the Stammering game, wins again, for he has a quick wit and an acrobatic tongue. The prizes are passed out and after rounds of applause it is time for tea.

Belle, with the help of Joe Alexander, who has not lost sight of her all evening, draws the curtains to the dining room. Flowers are bright notes of colour and so prettily arranged. And on the white linen tablecloth are plates heaped with small sandwiches cut in rounds, triangles, or rolled. There are, so it seems, an infinite number of Marguerites, Petit Fours exquisitely frosted, Swedish nut wafers, marshmallow mint bonbons, sugar almonds, and a variety of cakes. Sister Belle has quite outdone herself, and must have spent hours and hours in the kitchen. Ma, already seated at the head of the table, is ready to serve tea from a beautiful silver tea service, which I recognize as belonging to Mrs. Schrieter, who has not put in an appearance. "Because of father, you understand, Bessie," Martha had whispered. Absolutely delighted with the display, which really is a demonstration of love, I hug Belle, who is bursting with the pride of a master chef. Without a

37

shadow of a doubt the company too is delighted.

"As guest of honour, Bessie is to be served first."

While everyone is eating, reviewing the games of the evening, discussing the food and a dozen other matters, Richard, seeing that I have finished eating, puts down his cup and, taking me by the hand, guides me into the living room to a spot by the windows, as far away as possible from everyone.

Now taking both my hands, his eyes holding mine, all merriment gone from his face, he begs, "Change your mind, Bess. It's not too late. Stay here with me."

"I can't, Richard. My work is not here with you. Please, don't open the wound."

But he has opened the wound. And it is too late. And this farewell party has added finality. "I can't, Richard."

But, oh if I had.

Now I'm regretting I did not take Ma's advice and leave well enough alone. I had thought my emotions well under control, but they are fast surfacing.

"I'll never forget you, Richard. I'll always love you." I mean it. But perhaps men are different. They meet someone else and the past is forgotten. Foolishly I add, "But you will forget me, Richard. You will marry a very attractive woman, younger than I am. And you will be very happy." It is no prediction. I am saying it as a woman sometimes will, hoping it won't be true. Wanting the man to deny it.

As he does. "I'm not interested," he says flatly.

"But you will be." My words sound coy. But I am close to tears.

"I'm more interested in what will happen to you in China. Instead of telling my fortune, please tell me yours."

"I'm not fortune telling. And you well know I can never foretell anything about myself."

Someone is standing behind me. We have been

38

overheard. Flustered, I turn. It is young Bill Bates, a student from my Bible class, looking somewhat awkward in his dress suit.

"Hello, Bill. Sorry I haven't had much time to talk with you this evening. How are you? Have you met Mr. Richard Manners?"

They both nod.

"Miss Robinson, tell me my fortune. I've heard you're awfully good." The young man edges forward.

"No, indeed not. I'm not in the fortune-telling business."

"I know several people who've said your predictions have been almost one hundred per cent accurate. Please, Miss Robinson."

How I wish he'd just go away. This fortune telling started when I was in my late teens as one of Ma's parlour games when she had friends over for tea, encouraged by the de Chênes, who are clairvoyant, all three of them. But when I began to wonder where my so-often accurate answers were coming from, and whether I was tampering with something I would be wiser to leave alone, I stopped. For I believe there can be dangers for some people in such things. Besides, for me it was quite contrary to my interests as a future missionary. I haven't told a fortune for over two years.

I try to be offhand. "You want me to tell you that you'll fall heir to a million dollars and marry a beautiful woman?"

"No. It's just that for some reason it's important to me. I've been wanting to ask you for a very long time."

"I don't think it is important, Bill. It's not likely that telling you what is going to happen will change a thing in your life. Perhaps it's not good to know the future."

Bill is crestfallen and continues to plead.

I'm growing impatient, my thoughts are with Richard, wanting a few more moments with him.

"Really, Bill, I don't want to. Not tonight anyway."

"But I'm going away and probably won't have another chance to see you — you're going away too. I don't want to be a nuisance, but..."

It seems the only way to rid myself of him is to say something. Nor do I wish to offend my guest. "All right, Bill, let me see your hand." The lines in his hand mean nothing to me, anymore than do tea leaves. It is just something on which to focus.

But gazing at his hand I have the strange feeling of being somewhere else. As though the room has receded and there is no one around me. Only the pounding of waves...

I have no recollection of all I told Bill. All I remember is hearing myself saying, "You are going on a ship. There will be a storm. You will be drowned."

As if from a distance I hear Bill's voice as he withdraws his hand. "You're teasing me. You've heard I'm off to the lakes next week. I'm afraid I've been a nuisance." He is disappointed.

What a dreadful thing I have said to him! But I'm relieved that he doesn't believe a word of it, and is reading the anger I feel toward myself for allowing myself to be drawn in as annoyance at him. I can feel, too, my flushed face.

"I'm sorry, Miss Robinson."

I'm about to say something in an effort to ease the situation, when I become aware that there are others near us. I see Reverend Dickinson facing in my direction and wearing a stern expression. But he quickly turns to talk with Blake and Beatrice. Always attuned to my feelings, Richard takes my arm and says quietly, "It seems everyone has finished with the refreshments. So why not a few more songs?"

All have pronounced the party a great success. And

40

when I have said my final farewell to Richard, when the last guest is gone, the candles snuffed, and all that's left to do is to clear away, wash the dishes, and put the extra food away in the pantry — then I stand alone in the parlour amid the almost death-like silence that inevitably follows the leave-taking of guests. An aeon of time seems to pass, until Beatrice comes in. But it is not to add her congratulations about the evening.

"Oh, Bessie, how could you."

"Why, whatever is the matter?"

"Telling that young man's fortune in front of Blake. I was so embarrassed."

"Beatrice! Embarrassed! Why, I've told fortunes at Ma's tea parties for years. You've never said anything before. I had no idea it shamed you."

"It never has — before. But Blake is different. I could tell he didn't like it. He comes from a rather — well — superior sort of family, well-to-do, and well educated. His mother's a lady."

"Beatrice! Don't you consider your family every bit as worthy?" I'm shocked at my sister; I have never heard her talk like this before.

"Not worthy the way they are. We're just working class."

"Ma should hear that. Her grandparents looked down their noses at just about everyone. Maybe even the Arnolds would have been socially unacceptable to them. Personally I consider such snobbery a lot of rubbish."

"He said you were acting like a gypsy. I did so want him to consider my family above reproach."

"You shock me with your airs. Bea, it's not like you. I wouldn't give a fig for a man who considers himself superior to any other. All are equal in the sight of God. Why should a bit of spit and polish mean that one man is better than another?"

41

"For all your moralizing I haven't noticed you going around with an uneducated worker in tattered clothes. I'm going to marry Blake. I think he's a fine person, and he loves me. He's going to take me to Chatham in Ontario to meet his family — with Ma and Pa's permission, of course."

"What does he think of your having worked as a photographer's model — even if you were fully clothed? Might not his superior family put a model in the same category as a gypsy?"

"We have agreed not to say anything about that to his family."

"Well now, isn't that just a bit hypocritical? I wish you luck."

Then I relent. I have no wish for Blake's snobbery to get in the way of our relationship, especially when I'm about to leave my family. I put my arm around my sister. "I wish you every happiness. I'm sorry about the *faux pas*. I didn't want to do it. Bill Bates was so insistent. And what I said to him is really bothering me. But not because of what Blake thinks," I hasten to add. "Luckily, Bill didn't believe what I said; he thought I was just put out with him. Now let's go and help finish the dishes. Are you going to tell the others about Blake and Chatham tonight?"

"Of course. I'll have to. But we're not announcing an engagement until after I meet his parents."

I am about to ask, "And will that be only if they approve of you?"

But I hold my tongue. The edge of my evening has been blunted, but not for the world will I let on to my family. It was a good party and every one of them went to a great deal of trouble and too great an expense to express their love and give me a grand farewell.

42

**4**

Because the family stayed up well into the small hours of the morning, washing up, reviewing the party, talking about Beatrice's proposed visit to meet the Arnolds of Chatham, about my final plans to move to Winnipeg, and, of course not to be forgotten, about Belle's new friend, Joe Alexander, we all sleep in much later than usual. And it is Sunday morning and high time for me to get to church. Pa, it seems, has taken the buggy somewhere. So I must either ride my bicycle or be very late. Only Ma is wandering sleepily about. I grab a bite and rush out of the house.

Since wheels became cushioned with rubber, comfortable bicycles mass-produced, and in 1899 bicycle frames dropped so women could more readily cope with them, both sexes have taken to the roads, riding side by side — unchaperoned! What is more, roads have been paved to accommodate such "sinful" activity (as many ministers refer to it) and bicycle clubs set up which issue maps and indicate the location of inns. So on a Sunday (as this is the only day most people are free), equipped with puncture kits and tools and maps, men and women ride together. What's more, both gentry and working class ride together, talking and laughing and reveling in the sensuous pleasures of the countryside, instead of inhabiting the House of God where they belong. Challenging the very church itself. Upsetting the established way of life, a way that was good enough for our fathers and so surely is worthy of preservation. "O my friends, can you not see that a paved country road is but an easy way to Hell?" I heard those words only two Sundays ago.

The Reverend Dickinson has preached against the bicycle, calling it the Devil's tool, as so many youth of the land are showing a preference for excursions into the country. Besides, there is no doubt that in the past decade the bicycle has had a profound effect on women. All for the good, I say. Many, like myself, have given up waist-pinching corsets, cast aside extra petticoats, and even exposed a gaitered ankle. Just imagine the daring! Some women have even been seen to wear baggy pants called bloomers! According to the Reverend Dickinson, womanhood itself is in jeopardy.

In this, I fear, I am at odds with the man of God, for I cannot help but feel that God is to be found along the paved path and in the glories of nature as well as in the church. How I wish I, and everyone else, had more free time to enjoy both. And it is my opinion (and Ma's and Martha's, to mention but two more) that anything that brings women more freedom must surely be good! However, as one has to make choices, and because of my calling, I have settled for church on Sunday mornings. And out of regard for my new minister, I have made a point of walking to church in the past. Or, if other members of the family come along, we take the buggy, which has not been very often of late.

I pedal as fast as I can, then leave my bicycle almost a block away from my destination. Under the circumstances it is the discreet thing to do. So I am a little breathless when I get to my pew. But I'm on time.

This will be my last Sunday at this church for a while. I have always loved its simplicity, stripped of elaborate ritual and ceremony, and now I sit back prepared to enjoy the communion of like spirits. Friends turn in my direction and smile, acknowledging my presence, and I respond. They are all so pleasant. But how I wish David Brown were in the pulpit on this my last day. David, with his quiet and unassuming ways, well-educated, well-traveled, and well-read, preaching tolerance and understanding of all people — to the point where some elders in the church, and a few church

44

members, took issue with his liberal ideas and decided his quiet manners were uninspiring. It was seventeen years ago that the Browns first came to the church. It was pointed out that they were so likeable and warm-hearted that the congregation had not realized for a very long time the subtle ways in which it was being turned from the true teachings. Then, when it became obvious that David Brown's tolerance extended even to the prostitute, the drunkard, and the lax and ungovernable youth of the church, dissension grew. Finally he had been advised, because of his failing health — a good excuse — to give up his ministry and retire to a warmer climate. So four months ago, the Reverend David Brown and his wife, Felicity, moved to California and the Reverend Dickinson was called to take his place. The Reverend Dickinson is a very different personality: forceful, dynamic, of strong and certain views. He does not waffle, waiver, or waste time over another's viewpoint as did the Reverend Brown. Oh, dear! I won't for the life of me tell Ma I agree with her about Dickinson. I'm leaving and my tie with the church must remain firm. But how glad I am I'll be far away from his pulpit.

The opening prayer over, we rise to sing the first psalm. When the time comes for Dickinson to speak, we settle ourselves expectantly with rustle and coughs.

"My friends..." The rich, melodious voice moves on, coaxing his flock closer and closer to the throne of God. I am ashamed to admit that often my mind wanders to David and Felicity Brown and to the times Richard and I and others spent at their home. This is not a sermon with much intellectual content, but one that appeals to the emotions. But soon I am jerked out of my dreaming as his tone changes. He does it all so well. Whereas David Brown might send some people to sleep, Dickinson has many sitting on the edge of their seats as

45

he vividly paints a picture of Hell and describes graphically a lost soul pleading for water. If I don't like his style it is obvious the majority of people do.

At last the sermon is over, the final hymn sung, the benediction given. And when the time comes for all to leave, Reverend Dickinson stations himself by the door to shake hands and say a word or two as each person files past. Because so many of my friends have stopped to thank me for the pleasant evening and say such things as "We had such a wonderful time," "Enjoy your stay in Winnipeg," "I hope it won't be too cold for you in Canada," and "Come back soon," I am among the last to greet him.

I hold out my hand. But instead of taking it, he says, "Could you spare a minute, Miss Robinson? We would like to see you in our office. If you don't mind going there, we'll be with you soon."

I think, no doubt he has something to say about the mission. It is not unusual for me to sense a situation that lies immediately ahead. But not this time. I go into the office tranquilly and stand by the window, watching the last few people walking from the church. Then I turn as I hear him enter and close the door. He appears solemn and asks me to sit down by the desk. But instead of seating himself behind the desk in the high-backed leather-covered chair, he moves around the room with hands clasped behind his back, and looks out the window for a full minute or more until I grow apprehensive that something is amiss with the China project.

It is not a friendly face that turns again to me, regarding me silently before he speaks.

"To say that we were surprised at what we overheard yesterday evening would be understatement. That a member of this church would engage in such a deplorable, outrageous activity..." His voice drops. "Tell

46

us, Miss Robinson, how long have you been engaged in telling fortunes?"

My spirits, recently soaring, plummet. "Why, I..." I stop, shocked.

"When did all this begin?"

"Years ago...just as a parlour game."

"Are you not aware that you have been meddling with evil forces? Tempting the Devil himself? Tell us what other such activities you engage in. Are you unaware that meddling with the occult is condemned by the church? Do you not realize that you are engaging in something no better than witchcraft? It is not so long ago that witches were burnt at the stake, Miss Robinson. Mind you, it is not that we would burn witches. It is not that we would say that you, Elizabeth Robinson, are a witch. But you call yourself a Christian! What other occult arts do you dabble in? The ouija board? Tarot cards? Astrology? Tell us."

"No! I don't think it's like that..."

His voice rises. He is near now, leering at me. "Just a parlour game, indeed! You of all people. You — considering going out into the field to do the Lord's work! Do you really think yourself worthy of such a calling? Can you be trusted to help guide the souls of others — when yours, among all others, is so desperately in need of help?"

"But I don't consider what I have done is wrong."

"Then you are ignorant. And ignorance is not an acceptable excuse on your part. You in whom the church has placed its trust. Have you no powers of discrimination? Are you like a little child who knows not right from wrong?"

"I will never tell a fortune again." This I mean. Despite myself, tears are in my eyes, and my head is suddenly throbbing.

"We have respect for you, Miss Robinson. But we

cannot think of you engaged in such superstitious, soul-damning folly. Leaving yourself open to the forces of evil, the wrath of God, and the fires of Hell!"

"I said, not again." I have risen from my chair, angry. He is denouncing me and does not want my explanation, nor my thoughts.

"Miss Robinson," the voice is patient now, "let us kneel and pray that you will be guided to do only that which is right. That you will be cleansed of the satanic force that dwells within you. That such a power of evil will never again hold sway over you. That you might yet be considered worthy of the task that lies before you. Let us join hands and pray. Our Father..."

As he stretches out his hand, I move back in an effort to avoid him. But with a sudden lunge he grabs me. I abhor his hand, but out of respect for his position make an effort not to resist. We kneel by the chair. But I am so upset I scarcely hear the prayer offered for the good of my soul and the safety of all those who might come in contact with me.

As we rise at last, I attempt to shake myself from his grasp, but he grips my arm the harder, and his strong hand bites into my flesh.

"Miss Robinson, we feel constrained to place this matter before the elders. It must be given due consideration. To see if they — hmmn — with this new knowledge we have to present to them — will consider you a fit person — a suitable instrument — worthy of the trust that is to be placed in you. Far be it from us to shirk our duty as a minister of the church. There is church money marked for this venture in China. We are all aware that you have contributed and that the project was initiated to a large extent — or so we have been led to understand — by you. But it is the Lord's work, to be carried out under the auspices of this Presbyterian Church, and with it goes a great deal of responsibility.

48

The name of this church stands for goodness, righteousness, and truth, and must be protected in that heathen land. We must be certain that whoever is sent speaks only for the church. There is to be no weakness in the character, no flaw — no weakness that will cause one to fall into the sinful ways of the heathen Chinese. Indeed, we have heard of their superstitious ways. We have heard of their yarrow sticks and their fortune telling — just as you tell fortunes. We know about their oracles." These words are spat out. "What might happen, we ask you, with your wayward turn of mind? Would Presbyterianism be mingled and watered-down with the so-called religions of China: Taoism, Confucianism, Buddhism? Will this church find itself supporting Ignorance and Evil? Oh, no, not if we can help it. We know little of you, Miss Robinson. Only what our ears have heard..."

His grip is strong, but I am strong too, and at last I manage to wrench myself from him. I am horrified and trembling. My one thought is to get away. I back slowly toward the door. He is coming toward me, still talking. I turn, open the door, and rushing from the church I run the block to where my bicycle awaits me. Whatever else he says falls on unheeding ears and on an empty room.

Hardly have I peddled a block when a shiny black Ford starts to pass near me. It's too close. In it is the Reverend Dickinson, his heavy eyebrows raised, his grey eyes steely. He looks but does not acknowledge me. Surprised, off-guard, momentarily out of control, I turn into the back of the automobile and spill. Apparently oblivious to my plight, the Ford continues on its way. I pick myself up, dusty, hat askew, and walk my bicycle for a while, the film of tears making it almost impossible for me to see.

49

＊　＊　＊　＊　＊

When I tell my family about my trouble that evening, everyone hugs and kisses me and tells me I mustn't believe a word that awful man says.

"How shameful of him," says Beatrice, forgetting her own rebuff.

"You won't catch me going to that church ever again," says Belle.

"I think he's crazy," young Andy sums it up.

"Just the sort of bunk I expect from that man. Man of God indeed!" says Ma.

I should not have said anything. I knew they would support me. But are they thinking the matter through the way they should? They say what they do, not because it is necessarily true, but because they love me.

"I suggest you be yourself." That's the way Ma always talks.

Then Pa launches into a story about some Irish friends he once knew who had the second sight. And so it goes.

That night I have a dream I've had many times before. I am walking in the woods carrying three pennies in my hand. I hide the pennies under a log and go on my way. When I return and look for them, they are gone. I awaken, frightened.

## 5

The seat is of green plush. Well-polished mahogany shines bright in the day's light. The Pullman car is hastening north through southern Ontario along the Canadian Pacific line, swaying slightly, clickety-

50

clacking over the rail joints, moving at an incredible speed, maybe almost sixty miles an hour. Telephone poles — try to count them — are rushing by, fields of corn yet to be harvested, cows ever-nibbling in their pastures, a lonely farmhouse, a stretch of trees. I've never been this far from home; it's a great step into the unknown, and I thrill to the sights and the novelty of each new situation. I will refuse to allow the Reverend Dickinson to govern my days any longer.

So many friends were at the station to say good-bye. There were people from the church. The news about what happened had spread quickly. "Don't worry, I'm with you," "You have our support," they whispered, pressing my hand, giving me a hug, a kiss. "Forget it, Bessie. Just enjoy yourself. Do exactly what you think is right and don't let him upset you."

My last night at home Richard, to whom I have twice said farewells, made a surprise visit. He made light of the incident at church. "Just say the word and I will dispense with the monster." He didn't understand that it's not so easy. But all the support did help, did ease the tension. Even the heady perfume of Richard's farewell flowers brings comfort. It all made me feel much better as I stepped up into the train, following the porter with my small overnight case — Ma, Beatrice, and Belle trailing behind to say a last good-bye through smiles and tears.

I am thankful to have privacy, a double seat to myself, with the seats across the way vacant. Having specially chosen the longer route to Winnipeg through Ontario to see more of Canada, I am determined to enjoy the journey.

Two nights before my leaving, the promised message arrived from the Reverend Dickinson. The vote had been almost unanimous in favour of me. "You are evidently 'well considered' by the elders and members of the church," he wrote. "It is their opinion that the project should continue as proposed with no further concern or anxiety as to the character of Elizabeth Robinson, whom they all have known for many years. However, as minister and leader of the church, we feel it our duty to stipulate that, when the time comes for you to enter the field, you will be placed on a two-year probationary period under the supervision of others at the Mission." And he ended the letter by promising to be ever with me in thought and in prayer.

It is horrible. It is not a clean slate. Two years on probation and under supervision — when it's my project! Worst of all, to be the prisoner of his thoughts! I do not wish to have anything more to do with that man. Why wasn't David Brown there? How different it all would have been.

How can I repress these flashes of knowing? It is all so unsatisfactory. Keep on the go. Keep busy with mundane matters. I must write David Brown. Yes, I'll do that. He never seemed to find anything wrong with discussing Chinese philosophy, Chinese oracles, or any other kind of oracle. Indeed, he stimulated our interest in such things. Those wonderful evenings I spent with Richard, Martha, and others at his home. But is he too liberal and too broad-minded? So much so that he doesn't know right from wrong, as some church members say? I'm getting upset again, and I keep promising myself I'll forget the Reverend Dickinson. I will write to David as soon as I can, for he's the only one who will be able to see the full implications of the accusation, the only one who will be able to ease my mind in a way that Ma, with her obvious distaste for the Reverend Dickinson and with her religious doubts, cannot. And that all the others who speak and act wholly out of love for me cannot. David is the one to ease this recurring, gnawing tension.

52

Now I am trembling and feel very much alone. Richard! What have I done? I have dismissed him. If I had stayed with him I would not have this problem. Now I need him, but I have burned my bridges and now I'm alone. Alone with a shadow and stripped of what others call my "strength of character". Martha, you should see me now, my courage is just a facade. You are seeing yourself in me, Martha. It is you who have the strength. I really do want to be your wife, Richard. But not on your terms. Will the Reverend Dickinson's words pursue me, hound me? And for how long? Forever? Oh, do forget all this. I grow impatient with my circling mind. The problem will be resolved, in one way or another it will work out. It is a test. A two-year probationary period will also be a test. Think of something pleasant.

Unguided, my mind wanders back over the years to my first meeting with my love. A strange, instantaneous recognition. It was at the Jemmets. Richard smiled, almost as if to say, "Ah, there you are. I've been wondering where you were." We sat down together and talked so naturally, as if we had always been friends. Where? When?

He is a handsome man, my love. His hazel eyes, his pleasant smile, determined jaw — there lies the fault. He accuses me of being stubborn! He's impossible! A young, clever lawyer. Martha said, "Now, Bess, you must let me design you some clothes. Richard will like to see you well-dressed." He did. But Richard is easy to be with and not at all stuffy. We took young Isabel to Belle Island once. My young sister and I in our bathing costumes on the beach. Most appropriately dressed: bows, pantaloons, black stockings and all. Well covered. And the sun blazing down. Belle said, "It's so hot, Bess. Can't I take my bathing shoes off and my stockings and just let the sand and water ooze through

53

my toes?" And I said, why not. And took mine off too. And what would the Reverend Dickinson say to that? And to quite a bit more!

My head is aching. Stop thinking of the Reverend Dickinson. Stop thinking of Richard. It is all over. Bridges burned, no going back. I force open the train window and, taking the flowers, throw them away. It's over now. The tears come. Stop being childish. Get yourself a cup of tea. Pretend you're strong. Put on that mask. You're off to realize your dream, despite what's happened. You've had your time with Richard. And unlike Ma and Pa Faris, there will be no long years of pressure and problems, no accumulation of time to spoil the beauty of a relationship. Like my father, Daniel Robinson, for my mother, so Richard will always be the one true love.

The train is hurtling along — whoo-ooo-ooo — carrying me away from the Reverend Dickinson. But not away from myself. The fact that I had doubts about the wisdom of telling fortunes long before his condemnation, only makes it worse. Forget it. Concentrate on telephone poles, on fields of corn. Think of all the good things. No one else condemned me — why should he worry me so? Be-your-self. Be-your-self. Don't-be-a-fraid-to-be-your-self. Click-i-clack. Click-i-clack. But what gives me the right to pick and choose what I want to believe of my church's teachings? Surely I must accept them in their entirety or not at all.

The train is slowing down, coming to a station. It halts. The porter should be getting out his step stool, ready to help someone off or on the train. Someone is calling good-bye. I gaze out the window at a dirt road, at wagons moving. The town's postmaster is leaving with his booty collected from the train. An iron pump stands nearby, dangling its well-used tin cup. Honeysuckle bushes, soon to be clothed in autumn colour, discreetly

54

surround an outdoor privy.

Now the train pulls slowly ahead and stops with a lurch and the sound of cars jamming. Perhaps it is about to take on water from an ungainly chute extending from a water tower. I am alongside the little station, September's flies buzzing against its window pane. In the office is the telegraph operator with his green celluloid eye-shade and black sateen shirtsleeve protectors, tapping out a mysterious message in Morse code.

I'm startled by a movement beside me. I turn to see, across the aisle, the back of a large man with black hair and sideburns. The Reverend Dickinson! My gasp is a near scream. He turns, smiling. Pleasant dark eyes. How foolish of me. A woman is behind him. She nods in my direction.

"Sorry," the big man says. "I startled you."

"Yes, I was dreaming. I didn't hear you come up."

"Our name is Rand. We're on our way to Kenora." A kind voice.

"My name is Robinson — Miss Robinson. My destination is Winnipeg." Embarrassed, relieved, I keep talking. "I haven't travelled so far on a train before. I'm quite enjoying the experience."

Mr. Rand settles himself, then leans toward me. "For my part, I've done a lot of travelling. Within a limited area, that is. I'm an agent for a Toronto company. Men's wear. Sell to a number of small towns along the way. Our home is near Kenora: beautiful lake country, and very quiet. My wife travels with me occasionally, just to get away. Do you mind our talking, if it's not impertinent of us? Tell us if you would prefer to be alone. You see, we're country folk and always enjoy a visit."

Not so long ago I wished to be alone. But my mind will not let me be. "Yes, indeed," I answer, for a chat

55

might be the thing. And to be friendly in turn I say, "My father was a salesman. He was killed by a train. Toppled between cars when the lurching unbalanced him."

"I'm sorry."

"Oh, it was a very long time ago. I don't really remember him. I was only three."

"That would have been before they put in the vestibule for trains. It was dangerous to walk between cars then — quite a few people were killed or injured that way."

"It was 1878 when my father was killed. The trains were somewhat primitive then compared to now."

"Yes, the last decade and more has seen a great improvement in railway travel. I doubt if trains can be improved much more. Some have all the amenities. You lack for nothing — if you wish to pay for them, that is: barber shop, library with librarian. Some cars are luxurious rooms on wheels..."

"Where teas are served from fine silver service," Mrs. Rand adds with satisfaction.

"I've always found this train most pleasant. And the meals in the dining car could not be better. I marvel how such excellent food can be prepared in such a small space."

"With black-faced stewards moving effortlessly up and down the aisles even while the train sways and takes a curve. You admit it requires a bit of expertise." It is Mrs. Rand again.

"Yes, I can't help but wonder if they are paid a proper wage for their skills," I say.

Mrs. Rand continues, "I don't think automobiles will ever replace trains for comfort, do you? Not for long distance travel."

"I wonder. Maybe they will."

"Oh, no," protests Mrs. Rand, "the roads are so

56

dusty and bumpy, and there is always some trouble or another with an automobile. One can hardly drive any distance at all without a tyre blowing, the radiator boiling over, or the engine breaking down. There's always some problem."

We laugh. She is not far wrong.

The time passes quickly with my new-found friends. Soon the steward can be heard crying "Last call for dinner! Last call for dinner!" as he moves through the cars. The Rands invite me to sit at their table and I am delighted. We pass together through the corridors, Mr. Rand holding open the heavy doors to and from the vestibules. And soon we are in the dining car, being ushered to a table covered in white linen. The table is attractively set and there is a small cut-glass vase of chrysanthemums by the window.

After a good meal, we sit for a long time over our after-dinner coffee. The Rands tell me about the Dawson Trail, which was the route from Toronto to Winnipeg before the days of the railway. "It took ninety-seven days to reach Fort Garry from Toronto. Some people drove over that trail with their wagons piled high with baked goods and other stores. Brought hens to supply eggs, and a rooster. Even so, it wasn't an easy journey. Lots of people came over that trail hoping to make themselves rich by moving further west."

Both the Rands' parents pioneered in the Lake of the Woods district. The Rands talk about the beautiful water surrounding the island where they have their home, the fine trees, how they travel by boat to the mainland, about their log cabin, and how the coming of the railway changed their lives.

"Not at all primitive now," Mrs. Rand hastens to interject about their log home and the district. "We love it and our children love it. That's why we stay."

"It's a good community life. People help one another.

57

They had to, of course, in the early days. It was a matter of survival. It's a healthy life. But no real culture — have to provide our own entertainment. That's why we go occasionally for theatre and music to the big cities: Winnipeg or Toronto. But we wouldn't like to live in a big city."

The Rands do most of the talking. I feel I must say something in defence of city life. However, on the whole, I'm happy just to listen.

By the time we return to our Pullman car, it has been made up for the night, and the corridor is now marked by two walls of green curtains and quietly lighted. The green plush seats have disappeared, turned into comfortable beds. The hinged upper berths which hold the linen have been pulled down, and a man is climbing up the porter's ladder to his bed.

The Rands bid me farewell. "We'll probably be off the train before you are up."

With difficulty I manage to undress in the confines of the lower berth, then settle down between clean sheets and the comfort of such unusual quarters, the distinctive soot, oil, and steam smell of the train in my nostrils. How glad I am the Rands came to my rescue. They have invited me to visit them — that probably will not happen, but they are kind.

I lie awake reviewing the stories of the Rand's parents, who had pioneered a bit of Canada. Courageous people. But then, neither were my mother's parents and most of the other pioneers lacking in courage. As Ma always says, life is an uphill climb. Eventually I fall asleep picturing myself climbing the steep side of a mountain.

When I awaken I immediately reach over and pull up the windowshade. We have left shield country; the train is moving over flat ground. In the distance is a field of grain, ripe for harvesting. Nearby is a grain elevator.

58

Black, black soil! I must be close to Winnipeg. With a sense of excitement I throw back the covers and begin the awkward process of dressing.

# Chapter II

# Surveying New Land

September 30, 1909

*Dear Family and Dear Friends,*

*Thank you for your letters sent care of the hotel. I will answer each as promptly as I can. Please note the address on the back of the envelope for I am already settled. But more about that later for as I promised I will give you an account of my adventures from the beginning.*

*After a pleasant train journey my first impression of Winnipeg was, of course, of the C.P.R. depot heaped with trunks and boxes, for immigrants daily pour into the city from all over Europe along with mostly poor English, Irish, and Scots, all hoping to find work and a new beginning in life. For a few, or so it seems to me, a cloth bundle is the sum total of their worldly possessions. Many get off the train looking uncertain and lost. Many are not even able* to speak a word of English.

Having checked my trunks I took a cab to the hotel nearby, the Royal Alexandra, where as you know I had a room reserved at Martha's suggestion. What an immediate contrast! But then, I am quickly discovering Winnipeg to be a city of contrasts. The Royal Alex, as people call it, is about the finest hostelry in the C.P.R. chain and one of which there is every reason to be proud. There I dined and slept in luxury for three nights and two days. And had I remained within its walls, partaking of beautifully prepared food on excellent plate in a regal dining room, enjoying the comfort of my own room like an ostrich with its head in the sand, I would have gone away with a completely false opinion. But the short time I have been here has revealed something very different, and sinister. Something that has to do with the "haves" and the "have nots", something that deeply shocks and appalls me. And that is the extent of indifference, fear, and hatred that is shown toward the poor foreign immigrant.

But lest I give you concern about my new surroundings and be guilty, along with the Royal Alexandra, of conveying a wrong impression, let me say, without hesitation, there is a feeling here of hope, expectancy, enthusiasm for the future. And I have been caught up in that feeling. Hope is in the very air, and I am excited.

By the time I was settled, bathed, and had lunch, that first day was well on into the afternoon. So I decided to get a map of the city from the desk in the lobby, and set out for a walk, for I wanted to get my bearings and locate my place of work. This I did with little trouble. walking south along Main Street on the east side. In this area the street is lined with a number of substantial buildings of stone and brick. This is the core of the city, its business and banking centre.

61

*It was Saturday and a beautiful September day, a touch of autumn in the air. The street was filled with wagons, carriages, hundreds of bicycles, and some automobiles. The electric tramcars appear to be a popular form of transportation and I have since discovered the service is both excellent and inexpensive. Walking, it seemed no time at all before I caught sight of the City Hall across the way, a gingerbread edifice, typically Victorian, of red brick and stone, boasting a clock in its tower and a Union Jack flying high from its staff.*

*The City hall corners William Avenue while across from it on Main Street is what surely must be the tallest building in Winnipeg, the eleven-storey Union Bank. Tucked behind it, when I turned down William, I discovered a large and very active covered market square displaying a variety of fresh farm produce. And it was not far from there, among manufacturing firms, warehouses, suppliers, I found my place of work, in a brick building of unassuming character.*

*Having satisfied myself as to its whereabouts, and having located the office of Mr. Cedric Wilkins, my boss-to-be, my next thought was to purchase a newspaper and return to my hotel room to check for apartments available. For I had allowed myself seven days to get settled before starting to work one week from this coming Monday. I wandered slowly back to the hotel, familiarizing myself with the shops and their wares along the way until I found myself at a building called the "Crump Block", rather new-looking and displaying a sign at the door, "Apartment to Rent", which I decided to investigate — if nothing else, the place has the advantage of being close to work.*

*Sunday I retraced my steps and again walked south, this time beyond Portage Avenue, another wide thoroughfare, to the spot where Martha is renting her shop — an excellent location near the Hudson's Bay*

62

Company department store and Robinson's, another good-sized department store. Then I continued as far as the junction of the Red and the Assiniboine. That famous Red River — pooh! nothing much more than a muddy stream. As a matter of fact I walked for miles and turned myself into bed that night with such a feeling of pleasant weariness after a full day, that I never expected to be plunged into a horrible nightmare.

In my dream I could hear women screaming. Flames were everywhere. It was so real, so vivid! How can one's imagination create such horrid and unlikely scenes? Then, as though I were a witch about to be hurled into the fire, a large, strong man came up from behind and held me by my arms. I struggled, but it was no use. I was helpless. He grabbed my hair, which was loose and hanging down my back. He pulled my head back and the face leering into mine was the Reverend Dickinson's. Then I started screaming. My heart pounding, I awakened to the sound of a key turning in the door. I sat up and reached for my dressing gown. The door was opening slowly — it was the manager accompanied by a maid. I must have looked as frightened and shaken as I felt. The manager was relieved to be told it was nothing worse than a bad dream. My face was chalk white when I saw it in the mirror.

This will never do. It was a nasty accusation by Dickinson and it stays implanted in my mind no matter how much I try to rid myself of it. Maybe forgetfulness will come through work at my desk and, why not, maybe by way of social work — goodness knows, there must be need of it here. I don't know what I can do but I'll find out. Those poor unfortunate people I glimpsed at the station must need all the help they can get. Maybe now I too need help. And how better to help myself than by helping others?

Having made an appointment with the owner of the

63

*Crump Block for eleven o'clock Monday morning, I was thankful to get out, to clear my mind with good, fresh air and thoughts of a place I might call home. Well, the Crump Block is not the Royal Alexandra. Indeed, it can lay claim to little else than mediocrity. However, I discovered after a search through the newspaper and a conversation at breakfast time with the still-concerned manager of the Royal Alex, that construction can scarcely keep up with the scores of people infiltrating the city. Also, landlords are not loath to take advantage of the law of supply and demand. The Crump Block, as I said, is fairly new, the apartment clean and adequate, and the rent appropriate to my purse. It is within walking or cycling distance of my work, or an easy streetcar ride should the weather be inclement. Easy for groceries. Easy for everything. I decided to take it.*

*As one enters the building there is a vestibule with mailboxes, then a long flight of wide, wooden stairs quite bare of carpeting, which lead one to the second floor where there are doctors' and a dentist's offices. One more flight and there are the apartments, mine consisting of a large living/dining room, a bedroom, and a small compact kitchen off the dining area, and a good-sized bathroom off the bedroom with large clothes closet. It is everything I need. The windows of the apartment face east overlooking Main Street, which is noisy and bright during the long hours of the night as well as in the day. However, I'm a sound sleeper, impervious to most noises, and with dark-green blinds on the windows I don't think I'll have any trouble. Luckily I was able to move in right away. I quite like my new abode and I'm sure I will be happy here for the duration of my stay in Winnipeg.*

*The people, too, are friendly. On my way downstairs I encountered on the second floor, a rather rotund gentleman in a white frock. As he had stepped from the office with the gold lettering on the door's window*

64

*proclaiming "Dr. F.W. Fremming, Dentist", I assumed by his manner it was he. So I greeted him saying, "I am Miss Robinson, the new tenant on the third floor."*

*His round face was immediately wreathed in a smile. He bowed low and replied, "I hope you will be very happy."*

*It was fun searching for furnishings. By Friday afternoon the job was complete. There are now lace curtains at the windows in front of the dark-green blinds. A large patterned and rich-coloured rug covers most of the living/dining area, giving the place a warm and friendly atmosphere, while the furnishings, if sparse, are satisfactory — my one indulgence being a sturdy rocking chair which I have placed by the window where I can sit and read and view the passing parade. So you see I have done very well by myself. And when the bright morning sun floods the rooms, the place is cheerful.*

*Then my trunks arrived and I was able to adorn the walls with a few familiar pictures of family and friends, my map of the heavens and world map. Now there are books in the bookcase, and the handsome Martha-blue-silk hangs in the closet along with my other clothes and two old suits, which I am very glad to have included should I get involved in any volunteer work. And, regarding that, something unexpected occurred on Saturday.*

*At this intriguing point I will leave you, to continue with my story when I can next week.*

*Love,*
*Bessie*

65

## 2

*October 7, 1909*

*Dear Family and Friends,*

*Story continued. The Saturday after I moved into the Crump Block I went to the Hudson's Bay for a few personal items, and walking home slowly down the west side of Main Street, was almost to William Avenue and the City Hall when my attention was taken by a sign. It read, "Clements Realty and Investments, offices upstairs". It was almost one o'clock but I felt compelled to mount the long flight of stairs of the Clements Block, and without hesitation I opened the door to the office and walked in. It had not been my intention to make any investments until I had thoroughly canvassed the market, and I don't really know why I went up those stairs. But there I was, and across the counter, facing me, was a rather tall, slim, elderly man, well dressed and with a beautiful head of snow-white hair.*

*He examined me carefully from under bushy white eyebrows and then said, slowly, "Everyone's gone for the day." And he hesitated. I thought he was going to dismiss me, but instead he said, "But what can I do for you?"*

*I said, "I have rather surprised myself by coming up. I saw your sign. I have come to work in Winnipeg and want to invest some money. Could you advise me? Or maybe — another time?"*

*"Tell me what would interest you."*

*I hesitated. To tell the truth, I was a little embarrassed — not yet having studied the market in any depth and not wishing to display my ignorance. Finally I replied, "I expect to go to China in about two years time, and I was hoping to invest in something that will bring quick and sure results. I'm going to work in a mission."*

66

*I expected he might laugh. But instead those bushy white eyebrows simply rose, then falling knit together, while his mouth under a large white moustache displayed not the slightest emotion. His voice continued quietly as before, "Almost all investments — if made with discretion — are fairly sure to bring a return at the moment. Rather hard to miss. The place is expanding, rapidly. Bound to stop sometime, but not for a while."*

*He talked with me for a time, telling me something about the market, real-estate values, possible investments. He was very kind. Maybe he still had work to do, or wanted his lunch.*

*"I think I'm keeping you."*

*"Well, think of what I've said and come back again. If I'm not in, my son may be able to help you. I'm J.R. Clements, by the way. John Rickart Clements." I gave him my name, and was about to leave. He was stroking his moustache thoughtfully with a long finger. "Lots of mission work to be done around here, you know. Why not contact the All People's Mission — man named Woodsworth in charge. A good man."*

*Just what I wanted to know! I said, "I will."*

*He continued, "You mentioned you've been here only a week. If my wife's agreeable, and the weather too, how would you like us to drive you around a bit? Show you the Fort Rouge area and some property I have in mind."*

*I was delighted. His face for the most part is perfectly grave, almost like a mask, but occasionally a twinkle enlivens the eyes. I could not help but like the old gentleman.*

*So it was all set for next Saturday afternoon. He would ask his wife to send me a message.*

*I thanked him and once more started for the door, when a thought struck me. "Are you interested in this All People's Mission?"*

*"Decidedly not," he answered most emphatically,*

67

momentarily shedding his air of calm, "nor for the most part do I approve of the work of missionaries."

I was thunderstruck, and my annoyance must have been evident.

He went on, "I'm sure missionaries mean well. Possibly they do more good than harm. I do know there are lots of people who need help —lots of help. One can only do so much in one short lifetime. Everyone has a part to play in this world, and mine has been to make money. Help get a city under way. That's what I can do and what I do well."

Why was I distressed? After all I, too, am interested in making money.

His eyes were smiling again. "You see, by making money I can give to various institutions so that many of these unfortunate people, the kind that interest you, may benefit. But it's going to take a long time before some of these foreigners belong to this city. Three or four generations, maybe, before they'll even be able to speak the language properly and learn our customs. I won't be around to see it happen. But I think what my work and money has helped establish will prove at least as worthwhile as missionaries in China."

He spoke of "us and them". Instead, I think of "all of us".

Monday I reported for work wearing a navy blue suit and white blouse that revealed only a little lace. All stray curls were tucked carefully under. Presenting the proper secretary, so I hoped.

The new boss, Mr. Cedric Wilkins, friend and former college chum of Mr. Jemmet, is slight in build, slightly below average height, slightly balding, and wears spectacles. Being a friend of Mr. Jemmet, and being aware that Mr. Jemmet had written with enthusiasm about me to Mr. Wilkins, I had expected a more ebullient welcome than the one I received, which was reserved,

68

and strictly to the point. A manner which is not untypical of a certain class of Englishman, I imagine. And English he is. He said quietly and without a trace of a smile that the work would be demanding, and that after Mr. Jemmet's recommendation he would be expecting high standards from me. But he added that, though he expected me to work hard during office hours, it would be only on the rare occasion and only if absolutely unavoidable that he would keep me after hours or on a Saturday afternoon.

Demanding he is! He is tidy, efficient, and wants me to help him run a tight ship. I don't mind the work and manage to keep up the pace he sets. I even enjoy the challenge. Not only have I to cope with his personal secretarial work, interviews, calls, engagements — the sort of thing I did in Detroit — but more, I now have full charge of four stenographers, all young women who line the outer office and seem to enjoy intimidating Mr. Wilkins with the occasional flirtatious glance or word as he goes by. He refuses to take any notice and I think that to him, passing those young women must be like running the gauntlet, for I often see him averting his face as he hurries by.

Mr. Wilkins is not unpleasant for all his coolness, which could be simply a mask for shyness. It is my fond hope that before my time with him is up, his English reserve will thaw a bit and he'll bestow the occasional smile on all. But let me reassure you, we are getting along well. I have no complaints about him or the salary. He is most fair, and so far has kept his word about overtime. I appreciate this, for I well know his way is not the usual. Many clerks, typists, and other office workers are forced to carry on for long hours without compensation. I see lights in office windows late at night. Some, too, must work all day Saturday. Should they complain, they can easily be replaced. So there is much to be said in favour

69

*of this new boss of mine.*

*With love to all,*
*Bessie*

**3**

*Detroit, October 5, 1909*
*Dear Bessie,*

*All of us miss you but hope you are doing well. We are doing all right and I expect to recover my losses in time as the economy is doing so good. Henry Ford is moving right along with his mass produced cars and lots of people are coming to Detroit to get jobs. Blake, as one of Ford's architects, I expect will be making good money. He is already quite well off and plans to marry Beatrice before Christmas in Chatham. She was approved by his family! I don't much relish going there for the wedding but his family is insisting it should be held there as there are so many relatives and they want to put on a show. And it is all right with me if they want to look after the wedding arrangements. Beatrice would be hurt if I refused to go. Pa, of course, will be in his element. He is handsome and can manage to look like a millionaire and charms everyone. I find Blake a cool sort of fish, but he's a very capable person. He is fond of Beatrice and will look after her just fine, I'm sure. Maybe he's just not my type so I find him not easy to talk to. Beatrice would have liked for Martha to design her wedding dress but she's in Europe. Belle's all excited. Andy can't care less about weddings and is happy his school will keep him at home. Enclosed is a clipping about Bill Bates. They haven't yet found his*

70

body. It was a sudden storm on the lake, a bit of a twister. All our love,

Your Ma

**4**

Winnipeg, October 20, 1909

Dear Family and Friends,

No sooner had I finished my last letter to you than a message arrived from Mrs. John Clements to say that they would be able to take me for a drive Saturday afternoon. It turned out to be another beautiful autumn day. Promptly at two o'clock a handsome, chauffeur-driven automobile stopped under my windows and Mr. Clements came up to get me.

I was seated beside his wife and introduced. She's an attractive lady whose hair, emerging from under a fashionable hat, appeared as white and abundant as his. She put me at ease immediately with her informal and pleasant manners. Then almost at once my host announced that the automobile was not his. "Can't get used to these new-fangled horseless buggies. So I hired one for the occasion. 'Giddap'." This last word directed at the driver. "Straight down the road and slowly." And as we drove very slowly down Main Street he pointed out the various buildings, giving me a running account of the early days in Winnipeg. He spoke with such enthusiasm that I was fired with excitement.

"I think he's selling me the city," I whispered loudly to Mrs. Clements. "Unfortunately I can't afford it all."

"He's been one of Winnipeg's best salesmen since the day he came here," she whispered back.

71

"And may I ask when that was?"

"In 1874."

"A pioneer?"

"A late pioneer," Mr. Clements corrected.

"And what was the city like then?" Frankly, it looked still very primitive to the woman from Detroit. But before he could answer, my attention was caught by a couple of women sitting by the roadside, wearing long drab skirts and black shawls over their heads. They were clutching cloth bundles. One had a baby, and by them was the shabbiest of baggage. And they looked tired, tired to the point of exhaustion. A man dressed in shabby clothes and a black hat approached. I have noticed others like them. But here a woman's eye met mine, bewildered, frightened. It was as though I caught a glimpse of her soul. And in that moment my wish to help became a resolution. Perhaps, too, it was the obvious sense of well-being beside me that bothered me the more. My host had seen my head turn. He frowned.

"They don't belong here. Should be on the other side of the tracks."

And there they cast a shadow on that golden afternoon.

"Maybe he's looking for a job," I countered.

"He won't get one around here if he can't speak English."

"Then what can they and others like them do?"

"Huddle together with their countrymen. Some might make it, others won't." His voice was unconcerned. Then he continued with some asperity, "Shouldn't be here. Too many people being allowed into Canada. Immigration should be a little more discriminating. Ruining the country. Whoa — whoa there", he called to the driver when we were well out of sight of misery and misfortune, giving the driver a poke with his long finger. "Pull over here." Making it quite obvious he did not wish to continue

72

with that line of conversation.

So we passed the hopeless and the helpless as we went our happy way. And for me it was a delightful afternoon, the few hours I spent with my new friends, driving and stopping, and finally dining at the Royal Alexandra. I had posed a hundred questions and Mr. Clements seemed not at all loath to talk about "his" city. And though I'm sure Mrs. Clements must have heard it all a thousand times before, she gave not the least hint of boredom. She struck me as a most tolerant woman.

It was at dinner that Mr. Clements said with his usual humour — such relaxed, barbless humour, to which it is difficult to take exception —"My dear, this is the young woman who says she is going to China, but I've directed her to the All People's Mission instead. There she can be in every foreign country, all at the same time."

At this point Mrs. Clements told me something of J.S. Woodsworth who, it seems is a person quite well-known in Winnipeg. Mr. Woodsworth preached for a while at Grace Methodist Church and comes from a good Methodist family of ministers. But he was criticized by some for the emphasis he placed on the Social Gospel. This interested me, reminding me of David Brown, who too was condemned for embracing this popular movement that desires to establish God's Kingdom on earth, and emphasizes first the healing of the body. Evidently Woodsworth has written several newspaper articles that have caused a lot of comment and dissension.

"Woodsworth's a good man, means well. But he's a radical," interjected Mr. Clements, stressing the word.

After attempting to resign from Grace Church, he was given charge of All People's Mission in the North End, where he could try out some of his social missionary theories. "His wife, Lucy, is a well-educated gentlewoman who is unnecessarily putting up with a great deal of work and a lot of hardship for the sake of his ideal. But then

73

they are quite a pair." Mrs. Clements has met her.

"I have my doubts as to whether his work will do much good in the long run. I don't go along with it," was Mr. Clements' comment. "Still, something has to be done about those people. But I think he's wasting his talents. Means well. You can't make silk purses out of sows' ears. But if that's what he wants to try to do..." He shrugged. "Everyone must choose his own path."

I said, for I could not forget what we had seen earlier that day, "I know this is an old unresolved question, but tell me what you think. How much freedom has one to choose one's own path? Were those people by the roadside there through some fault of their own?"

Mr. Clements nodded. "No gumption."

Mrs. Clements shook her head. "Trapped."

I really had not expected anything else.

Of course I realized it was not usual for Mr. Clements to drive potential investors around town and dine them the way he had me. I was flattered and not too surprised when Mrs. Clements whispered to me in the washroom after dinner that her husband had taken quite a fancy to me. "Both of us have." She smiled. "And we would like to see you at our home before you leave Winnipeg." I, too, like the elderly couple very much.

When they had returned me to the Crump Block Mrs. Clements mentioned once again that they would get in touch with me. "As soon as we can. But I fear that won't be for a few months. Our daughter is getting married this spring and in the meantime Mr. Clements and I will be spending the winter in Tampa, Florida. We've a home there. We feel we've done our duty by Winnipeg winters. We're not as young as we once were."

"Speak for yourself, my dear," said Mr. Clements.

Having promised to look after my interest in a purchase of a piece of property in Fort Rouge, a new and growing district of better middle-class houses, and having

74

*advised me earlier on other investments, they left me feeling much more at home than I had ever dreamed was possible in this adolescent city. Determined, too, that on the morrow I would cross the tracks and explore the North End.*

*Love,*
*Bessie*

\* \* \* \* \*

Evening. I rock in my chair by the window, looking at the people in the street below but thinking of my newly-acquired friends. Mr. Clements must have both gumption and initiative, qualities that all self-made men and men of property seem to agree are necessary for success. The United States and Canada abound with rags-to-riches stories. The orphan cast out into the cruel, cold world — poor little ragamuffin — turns out to be not so helpless after all. By no means! He has inner resources known as "gumption and initiative", and though faced with one incredible problem after another, brick upon brick he builds his way to the top, becomes a millionaire, smokes Havana cigars, has two or more homes in various spots around the world where, depending on climate and inclination, he appears occasionally. Does he have to worry about dust accumulating in the corridors meantime? Not at all. His minions take care of all. And he suggests to the poor little ones who line the streets that they try the same thing. When one has managed to pull oneself up by the bootstraps from such beginnings, there comes a real sense of satisfaction and pride in self that outside help can never give. That in itself is reward.

There is no doubt that many little ragamuffins have managed to get to the top and no doubt others will yet.

But as I look around me, see that woman by the roadside, hear about the hundreds of people who are daily pouring into this country, I can't help wondering if the times are not changing — and if a few inhibiting factors have not been added to the equation. But today it's still the man who has succeeded in making money who is looked upon by the majority with admiration and awe.

Mr. Clements considers one other quality a help: background. He spoke of his father who had come from Ireland and settled in Ontario and married three times, each wife having borne several children and two having died in childbirth. He said his father loved his wives equally well and had remarked that they were such wonderful women, had he met them all at the same time he would not have known which to marry. Now perhaps that's just so much Irish blarney. Sounds like the sort of thing Pa would say. But discounting the Irish factor, from other things Mr. Clements mentioned I gather it was a large, strong, and caring family. So though he worked hard as a youth on his father's farm, his was probably a sound and healthy life.

Too, his father must have managed fairly well, for when John Clements came of age he opened a store in the village. But realizing that the store had little future, situated as it was far from the main stream of Ontario's life, John decided to leave. He got himself maps, and a little research convinced him that Winnipeg, with a population of around one thousand at the time, would one day be a great metropolis through which commerce, industry, agriculture would funnel. Well, today Winnipeg is called the "Bull's Eye" of Canada. 1874 was still two years before Winnipeg was incorporated as a city, but the map showed him a settlement situated at the junction of the Red and Assiniboine Rivers. It was the route from Minnesota to the north. And the Dawson trail led there from Toronto, while beyond Winnipeg was the great and sparsely populated west. "It had a potential, that town, I could visualize it, and it excited me."

He sold his store and with a capital of not much more than $350 bought a team of horses, fifty sewing machines, and two cabinet organs.

"But why sewing machines and organs?"

"Because my wife said every woman should have a sewing machine. And people need music. We were just married. To me she was the most wonderful girl in the world and I would have done anything she suggested — at that time," he added for her benefit. "Now she takes credit for our success. Sold every one of those things within three months for a lot more than was paid for them. That meant a little money to invest in real estate. That's what I was after, and that's how it all began."

Married life had just begun for them when they drove the merchandise to Port Sarnia and arranged for it to go by boat to Port Arthur.

"That was our honeymoon. That and the trek over the Dawson Trail."

It must have been a long, hard trek. I try to picture this very feminine lady with the cornflower-blue eyes dealing with the rigours of a wilderness the Rands described to me so well.

"When one is young, and strong, and in love, the world is there to conquer," was what she said. "John and I were from average Ontario farming families and didn't mind roughing it. We weren't counting on comfort when we set out on our adventure. So we weren't in the least disappointed."

And what was their first impression of Winnipeg? My own, much later, was of a rather primitive settlement and a muddy river. But they had seen it with different eyes. It was their oyster.

"In 1874 a row of low-standing buildings bordered a wide expanse of mud road. Some buildings were sturdier than others, but they were mainly of wood. There seemed to be endless flat land surrounded by the horizon and capped by the bowl of the sky."

"John had promised me the moon and stars if I would go with him. And that first night we stood under that sky it was easy to see we could reach them."

"Were there no trees?" There are a great many in Winnipeg now — but they spoke of the horizon.

"Not many. It appeared very barren to us from Ontario. There were some large, substantial homes — had been, along the banks of the Red, for almost forty years. And of course there were tall and pleasant trees around those homes. Planted not only for beauty but out of sheer necessity as a screen against the wild winds that sweep across the plains. These were the estates of retired officers and Hudson's Bay Company men who had money invested in England and Ontario. Very well-to-do: ordered their clothes and furniture and luxury goods from England for the most part. An order would take a year to deliver. Those folks were quite comfortable. They would have their dances and parties at the Upper Fort with menus that couldn't be outdone anywhere. Everything imported."

"The early Scottish settlers planted trees around their homes, too, and for the same reasons. But theirs was quite a different story. They built along the Red River, also, but to the north. Many had come from Scotland because they'd been forced from their homes to make way for sheep-farming. Most had next to nothing and suffered great hardships. They were a sturdy lot, they knew how to share and how to help one another. We knew many of the older people — still a few about."

Mr. and Mrs. Clements do believe in sharing — after

78

their fashion.

"The pioneers from Scotland took pride in their homes, though ever so humble. And later as the city grew, the people saw that the government planted trees along the streets. And you must see our beautiful parks. Have you not heard Winnipeg referred to as the City of Trees? A veritable oasis at one time."

They have watched their ugly duckling change over the years.

"I think I can honestly say," Mrs. Clements continued, "that as far as comforts were concerned, my husband and I were a great deal better off when we arrived than were those early Scottish settlers. But there were no trees around the small store we rented on Main Street. We lived in the back of it and, oh, it was so dreadfully cold that first winter. As bitterly cold as it was hot the next summer. All our food supplies froze and I along with them. Only the warm friendship of those early pioneers and the stories they had to tell kept me from running away home. And I remember in the springtime, looking out from the store across a vast expanse of mud to the ox carts lumbering slowly along, weaving from side to side so they would not get caught in the ruts."

"The ox carts had to go every whichway," interjected Mr. Clements. "Couldn't move along the tracks of other carts. You take notice of our special brand of mud: it's known as Manitoba gumbo and important to our agriculture. Yes, the carts had to weave back and forth, back and forth." He demonstrated with his arm. "Some went north, others came south on Main; some moved west on Portage and others headed east in that irregular fashion. And that is why Main Street and Portage Avenue are the widest streets in Canada. And why it takes so long to cross them — especially in winter with one of those blasted cold winds doing its darndest to

79

stop you. But those Red River carts, now they were really something. Built for the purpose. Heavy and lumbering maybe, and none too comfortable to ride in. But they were the only land transportation in those days. People would pile their bedding in and ride deluxe class on top, on the way to Minnesota. You see, the wheels of those carts were slightly dish-shaped — prevented them from tipping on uneven and slippery roads. And if a river had to be crossed those wheels could be removed, tied together, covered with oiled canvas, and used as rafts. Quite the right thing for those times. Used dog-sleds in winter. Of course, canoes on the rivers were faster when the water was free of ice, and water routes were used as much as possible. Oh, yes, there had been some progress by the time my wife and I arrived. Still, I guess, there were plenty of moments those first years when Mrs. Clements wished herself back east. But I never wanted to leave. No, couldn't rightly say we were pioneers, though the newspapers have called us that. You see, the groundwork had been laid by the time we arrived. We came along to help with the building. The first woman arrived about a hundred years ago. Quite a woman. Her daughter was the mother of Louis Riel. You've heard of Louis Riel?"

I had.

"He and many others were unhappy about an imposed government and he led a rebellion. Ended up being hanged. Maybe that was wrong, but I dunno. The man spelt trouble: wanted to take over the province. He wanted our land. Still, you couldn't help but admire him. A clever man, handsome and gifted. He'll be a hero one of these days. A half-breed: a Métis. Did you know those half-breeds were sometimes called Bois-Brûles? It's a nickname that means "burnt wood", after the colour of their skin. Some of those half-breeds have the

80

best of the white man and the best of the Indian in their blood. And they know it. They were a proud people in those days. But the notoriety of Louis Riel and the rebellion — that was big news. Excellent publicity for me. That and Manitoba's entry into Confederation resulted in a little land boom. Winnipeg took off in a hurry. And that's when my business took off."

"Winnipeg is located on marshland." It seemed Mrs. Clements had to provide a balance for her husband's enthusiasm. "Never knew such mosquitoes."

"I learned to smoke and the creatures avoided me. Some people become immune to them. Not my wife here. But she shared my view of the future. And I always had great faith in the place. I'll give you an example. That first year I contributed eighty dollars from my limited funds to the town's first waterworks. That money bought an ox to pull a water cart from the Red River. A barrel of water sold for 25 cents."

I couldn't imagine anyone drinking water from that river — ever!

"Typhoid —" began Mrs. Clements. But she didn't have a chance to continue. I wondered if she found it hard living with such an optimist.

"Fortunes were made and lost overnight in those days. Sure Lady Luck plays her part, but she always picks a partner with a cool head."

Is luck another part of the equation?

"A lot of men gambled their money away, spent too much on booze and women. But Ashdown, there" — he had pointed out Ashdown's Hardware Store on Main Street —"had his head screwed on right. He started with one thousand dollars in 1868, and was smart enough to stock what was needed. By the early eighties he was worth a peck of money. I didn't do too badly either. Then in 1884 the railways came, moving more goods and bringing more people. That's what we were all waiting for. Divided and changed the city."

Maybe there can be too much of a good thing. He doesn't appear to be so satisfied with all the people coming in now. But it seems life is never really hard when one is keen and has a philosophy like he has: "Never say can't."

<h2 style="text-align:center">5</h2>

Two letters in my mailbox, readdressed from the Royal Alex. One from David — no, it's Felicity's handwriting. The other's from Frances de Chêne. I'm thrilled. I've been anxious to hear from David who'll give me the advice I so badly need. I run up the two flights of stairs, unlock the apartment door, throw my handbag, gloves, coat and hat on the floor and fling myself into the rocking chair. Why Felicity's writing?

*Santa Barbara, California, October 18, 1909*
*My very dear Bessie,*

*I am sorry to be the messenger of bad news. Three weeks ago David had a massive heart attack and is now lying very weak in his bed. The doctor has insisted on complete rest. As, no doubt, the attack was brought on in no small measure through mental and emotional strain, I have taken it upon myself to answer his correspondence and do what I can to shield him from all worry and concern. I regret he cannot write to you as I know he would have wished. And I do not feel qualified to answer the very sincere and important questions you have raised dealing with theology and philosophy. It is unfortunate, but I feel it would be dangerous to disturb him at this*

82

*time. Knowing how fond he is of you, I am sure that knowledge of your ordeal would be cause for further anxiety which might prove too much for his weakened heart. It is, after all, a similar type of problem that he has been fighting, which has to do with the authority of those in charge of the church as opposed to the right to one's own interpretation of the Bible and other sacred writings.*

*I can only say these problems are sent to test us and we must carry on the best we can under the circumstances. It is God's will that these things happen. May He speed you in your work and bless you.*

*Felicity Brown*

I am shattered by the news of David's heart attack. I know I will never hear from him again and I had so counted on his counsel. He would have told me how to rid myself of the shadow of Reverend Dickinson. A shadow that so frequently envelopes me, suffocates me. Now there is no one I can trust. No one with the scope of knowledge and experience and love that he has. I need, want, a guide. For without such a one as David, I am afraid to step outside the bounds of the Church. I'm on my own and I'm frightened. I sit staring out of the window, seeing nothing.

I must write immediately. Just say how sorry I am.

Poor David. Poor Bessie.

I pick up the letter from Frances.

*Detroit, October 21, 1909*

*Dear Bessie,*

*Minnie, Mother, and I are pleased to be able to share the letters with your family. We are happy to learn that* you were settled so quickly. And, in our imagination, we can picture your new friends and acquaintances and the streets and life of Winnipeg.

But Bessie, we are concerned about your problem with the Reverend Dickinson. The three of us have talked about the matter so often. How can one be certain that his view of reality is any more than just that — his view? And no more valid than another's. After all there are so many views. Even men of the cloth differ in opinion. The Reverend Brown, for instance, whom we all liked so very much, had such different ideas from Dickinson. You know that Minnie, Mother, and I enjoy listening to a variety of opinions and then drawing our own conclusions.

Maybe you have heard or read that at one time most people believed in reincarnation. The early Christians did, as the Cathars and the Albigensians. And such a belief still predominates in this world. A lifetime is for experience, the purpose being the evolution of the soul. And, as in school, one moves from grade to grade, so to speak, as one learns and grows. When you see such inequality around us, it appears to be a most sensible theory to me. Sometimes, strong, traumatic experiences from past lives can be remembered by way of, say, a fear of heights, sometimes through dreams influencing one, as does all past experience. Bessie, we wondered if that awful dream you had about the Reverend Dickinson was a former lifetime experience, and that is why it haunts you and you continued to be so worried about him, because the horror still has a hold on you. We wanted to tell you about this because sometimes realizing the source of the problem will help dispel fears. I recall hearing you and Martha discussing Sigmund Freud and his work with dreams. But I don't know as much about that as you do.

We are all well. Your family, too. Last time we saw Bea and Belle they were really excited about the

84

*wedding. As perhaps you know, Martha will be back from Europe in another few weeks and we are looking forward to seeing her.*

*Anyway, we want you not to worry about the Reverend D.*

*Your sincere friend,*
*Frances*

**6**

*Winnipeg, November 2, 1909*
*Dear Family and Dear Friends,*

*A great deal has happened since I last wrote. My pleasant tour of the city with Mr. and Mrs. Clements saw about the end of the fine weather. Now when I step outside the Crump Block I'm clad in heavy coat, rubbers, spats and muffler. Snow has laid a light blanket over the city. It was necessary to put aside my bicycle and, though I often walk, on a few occasions when the wind has been sharp I'm happy to make use of street cars and glad to find them equipped with brushes for snow removal and, in each, a stove which the conductor can stoke with coal.*

*But the streets and walks were still clear the Sunday I crossed the C.P.R. tracks, now determined to get a better sense of the North End before visiting the Stella Avenue Mission — which I did that same day.*

*You should understand that it is only in the past three decades that the North End has become so congested, especially in the area around the tracks where it's an unplanned jumble of shacks and shanties and cheaply-*

85

built cottages of the working class. The North End also consists of older homes that existed long before the turn of the century. Once Point Douglas in the North End was the prestigious residential area. But by placing its tracks across Main Street, the C.P.R. changed the character of the city by dividing it into two distinct districts. And along with the tracks came the railway yards, the noise, the smoke, the soot.

The railway brought industry: iron works, machine shops, manufacturing of every kind. And it brought the immigrants, who included the "foreigners" (meaning those who are not British). Those who were needed by the C.P.R. found work and settled nearby. But there were those who had no trade and were seemingly untrainable — the "rejects" from their own countries, as I have heard it said. They, too, settled near the railway, or wherever they could find a spot, and they form pockets of hopeless poverty, the unemployable who, said Mr. Clements, should never have been let into the country in the first place. They are encumbrances and a source of embarrassment to the city. They create areas that can only be described as festering sores spreading disease, crime, and prostitution. And, resenting the presence of these "foreigners", the city offers little or no help.

When it comes to aid and public works (my information coming by way of Dr. Fremming and others of whom I have been asking innumerable questions, in my usual manner) preference is given to the South End and to other wards. Not all, but many of the City Fathers, so I am told, hope that by ignoring these despised foreigners they and their problems will go away. They prefer not to spend money to clean up the streets and provide sanitation. And typhoid is prevalent, endangering the whole of Winnipeg — one would think something would be done out of sheer self-interest! But evidently they prefer not to educate or care for these "dregs of humanity"

86

who in background and creed are "not like us". So it is left up to private charities and church missions to provide for them as best they can.

This particular day in late October being the Sabbath, there were few people about on North Main Street. But since then I have been there on a couple of occasions and find the small shops and the people pleasant and indeed fascinating. This is another aspect of the North End to take into account.

On the whole the stores are one storey, two storeys, mainly built of wood and unpainted. There are shop owners of many races and creeds, including the British of course. And a number of the owners are Jewish from eastern Europe, who can understand the many Slavic languages, so it is to their shops the majority of "foreigners" come. It's my opinion that those who speak out against these people are narrow-minded bigots. And they are many. The newspapers, especially the *Tribune*, appear only too willing to give voice to them. I say that Jew, Slav, and all add variety, colour, and character, and all have a worthwhile contribution to make to the community.

After walking along North Main a few blocks, I turned at random down one street and then another. Expecting to find dirt and poverty, I found it. Dirt roads and a ghetto quite beyond imagination. Despite what my new friends have said about "the other side", they did not give me sufficient warning. For here huddled what surely must be the worst of the city's rejects. Here was an atmosphere laden with despair.

Houses were the meanest of shelters, mere shambles crowded cheek to jowl and in more than one instance made from boards and banked with earth for warmth. Stovepipes were chimneys, and windows often had sections of glass replaced with cardboard. Any leftover space in those wretched lanes were dump heaps of *rusted iron, tangled wire, broken glass, trash. Trash everywhere. And there being no proper sanitation, the stench from the outhouses and littered garbage was foul. Drunks — but drunks are found almost everywhere in the city — further cluttered the dirt lanes. I was leered at, gaped at, whistled at, as I gathered my skirts about me and threaded my way along.*

*There were sorry specimens of women too, and children. Poor little tykes, some without shoes in this weather. All in filthy, ragged clothes. Malnourished. Their streaked faces pinched and sallow. Some had open, festering sores on legs and faces. I stopped to speak to a group of young ones who appeared to be playing a game with sticks. I tried to ask about the game but no one spoke English.*

*I continued walking and finally found my way out of that tangled web of dirt lanes. And breathing more freely, I walked between a row of tidy houses, small, still cheek to jowl. But here was a difference. Curtains hung on clean windows. The occasional flower bloomed on a window sill. Small front yards had grass, a few autumn flowers, a tree. These had to be the homes of men who work for the C.P.R., or in industry, or manufacturing. And that day I also walked past larger, better houses of clapboard or brick, some remaining from the district's more affluent days. Many are now being used as tenements, some have fallen into disrepair. Other more average homes still look as no doubt they have for years: settled, cared-for, and comfortable. It's a mosaic, this North End of Winnipeg, with its sections of ugliness and misery and its sections of lower-middle class comfort, its colourful stores and markets.*

*It was after four o'clock when I arrived at the house by the Stella Street mission and rang the doorbell. No one answered. By the hubbub that issued from within I could easily understand why. Glancing through the window I*

88

could see people standing about drinking tea. Cautiously I turned the handle and pushed open the door. There, close by in the crowded hallway, was a young girl. She greeted me with a wide smile and said immediately, "Let me take your coat. Go on in and I'll bring you tea."

I opened my mouth to apologize for walking in and tried to explain who I was. But she was already talking to someone else. Quickly I put my gloves in my coat pocket, gave her the coat, and walked into the large room I had seen through the window. People were buzzing and humming like so many bees. There was standing room only, and I was beside a man in a carefully-tailored suit, a fat man with heavy jowls.

Without the least idea who I was, he said in a heavy voice, "It's like pouring money into the ocean."

"What is?" I asked, feeling a bit like Alice in Wonderland as the girl with the wide smile handed me tea and a cookie.

"Trying to help the needy, that's what. There's no end to it. I believe God helps them as helps themselves."

"But some people are trapped and can't help themselves." My head was still full of ghetto scenes.

"So he says." The rotund man jerked his head to the left. "Finally dragged me down here to meet the working class. Wants me to contribute to the needy. I know him — there'll be no end to it."

"He" was Mr. Woodsworth. I talked to Peter Parker for sometime about the need to help the needy. Then, warmed by my tea, I talked with others, among whom were men in working clothes, many who spoke broken English, a few who ventured only a few brave words, and shy women in their Sunday best who stayed close to their husbands and spoke not at all. There, too, were other men and women well-dressed like Peter Parker from Grace Methodist Church. For I discovered Mr. Woodsworth wants South to meet North, hoping thus to

89

*improve conditions for the working class by creating an atmosphere of better understanding.*

*I stayed until the crowd thinned out. I met Mrs. Woodsworth, a charming lady. She was the one to whom I finally introduced myself.*

*"My name is Elizabeth Robinson. No one has asked my name or who I might be, and yet I've been given a royal welcome — after simply walking into your home unasked, for which I apologize." I wondered if she would be annoyed at my impertinence but she just laughed, took my hand, and added her warm welcome.*

*"We don't always ask people their names. In some cases we might be unable to pronounce them. Besides, we see too many people to remember them all. But Elizabeth Robinson I can pronounce. And I will remember you."*

*I told her of my intention to serve with a mission in China. And of my desire to help in Winnipeg for as long as I was here. I did not realize that the slim gentleman standing nearby was J.S. Woodsworth, and that he had overheard me.*

*He said, "When I hear people talk about doing mission work in foreign fields, I cannot help but think of the great need there is here at home." It was almost what Mr. Clements had said — and Richard about Detroit. And after my day's walking tour I could understand Mr. Woodsworth's point of view.*

*We talked. He is an idealist. Already I admire him and Mrs. Woodsworth greatly. It is their belief that the way to create a better life for the underprivileged is through cooperation rather than competition. And the underprivileged include the working man and his family, for the wages of the working man for the most part are so disgracefully low that mothers and children are forced to work in order to survive. Woodsworth also insists that cooperation is the only way to create a sound world:*

90

competition can only end in distrust and greed and lead to wars and destruction. With that too I agree, although I wonder if in a world such as this his dream can ever be realized.

Since that first visit I have been to the Mission on a few occasions and talked with Mrs. Lucy Woodsworth and a number of volunteers. I have learned that All People's Mission was formed in 1898 for the purpose of salvation. But in recent years, mainly under the directorship of Woodsworth, the mission has expanded to include among other things, kindergartens, boys and girls classes and clubs, night classes in English and civics, fresh air camps, swimming and gymnasium facilities, mothers' meetings, concerts and debates, and, of course, the dispensation of relief. But despite all that is being done by church missions and groups, voluntary organizations cannot keep pace with need. Churches are totally dependent on the affluent members, their Peter Parkers. Jewish and Slavic and other ethnic religious centres, although they do what they can to help their own communities, have few if any affluent people among them and therefore practically no funds to draw upon. Since 1874 the City has spent annually, on average, $6,200 on relief. All else is supplied by way of charity.

I hope all continues well in Detroit.

Love,
Bessie

91

## 7

*Germany, October 20, 1909*

*Dear Bessie,*

*It was a wonderful crossing and in the best of weather. I have wished, and more than once, that you could have shared it all with me. After accomplishing my tasks in Germany in double-quick time, I set off to see Emma. And without coaxing or pressure on my part, that very day I arrived we were engaged in matters astrological. Bessie, she's a person you would enjoy knowing. I can talk with Emma the same way I've always talked with you about religion, philosophy, and all. And it's rare to find a boon companion like that. We have promised to keep in close touch and she will send me books and information as she can. And as she is the wife of such a fount of knowledge as Carl, I feel I am very lucky and, of course, hope you will share the privilege with me.*

*She did your horoscope. But this and much more I will explain to you when I get home and have the time to write in more detail. Isn't the copy of your chart that I've enclosed an interesting-looking map? That's you, Bessie! Every individual is linked to the exact time and space into which he or she is born, so that each person is as different from another as leaves, or snowflakes — and is linked too in time and space to all else. He or she is limited in life by that chart, but has the ability either to fulfill the potential shown there or to let opportunities in life pass by. That's the free will bit. Of course, one must learn to read these charts properly, as every symbol is related to every other symbol, and a chart must be read as a whole. I shouldn't think that an easy job. Well, it's all very exciting to me the more I consider it.*

*Emma showed your chart to Carl at dinner time. He*

*looked at it with great interest. He said she had done a good job, and then indicated — and you can see from the red lines that he marked in — what he referred to as a Grand Cross, a rather unusual combination, which means, he said, you are a person who is always being blocked and must learn to deal with frustrations. So, Bessie, there are apt to be a lot of frustrations and trying times ahead for you in China, but nothing, I am sure, that you cannot cope with. You have always managed so well and have such strength of character — now don't deny it! Carl also said that no chart is either good or bad. It's the way one accepts situations in life, the attitude one takes that's important. For that is the way one grows — or fails to grow. It is the experience of learning that counts.*

*But I must leave all that for now. Let me know what you think of your "mandala", as he called it. Just think of the view of the world that could develop from a study of astrology! Carl believes it to be true because, he says, it works. And for him that is the test. And he said that even though he grew up in a family of ministers with a definite view of religion, he cannot deny what in his eyes has been proven. Most people may be sceptical about astrology, but I for one am fascinated, and intend to pursue the matter. And just think, you are the one who got me into this!*

*Well, Bessie dear, I must get on with my work in France, make my contacts, find my suppliers. However, I'm cutting my stay in Europe short as a note from Anna was rather disquieting. She said Mother is getting forgetful and unreasonable. It doesn't sound like Mother, though I think you too noticed that she seems to have undergone a bit of a change of personality since Father died. I feel she's dwelling far too much on his death. Nor is it like Anna to report such a thing. So I'll be glad to get home and see what it's all about. Besides, I'm such a*

93

*poor sailor that I'll be happy to be on my way before the ocean gets too rough.*

*My love to you,*
*Martha*

I hold my "mandala". The date in the centre reads, November 23, 1875, my date. I recognize most of the symbols, for Martha and I tried to learn something about astrology at one time, but I cannot interpret the chart. A part of me wants to say to Martha, "Let's discover all we can about astrology and decide for ourselves whether it has validity." Say to Frances, "Let's find out more about reincarnation." But I dare not engage in such activities. For, if I do, I will not be considered worthy of the Church and its trust. According to the Reverend Dickinson, my future is already in jeopardy. The Reverend Dickinson is never far from my thoughts. I cannot however hard I try prevent that, for I fear him. Though I realize it is my fear gives him a hold on me. Still I must respect him as the one who has been given authority in the church I mean to serve.

*Chapter III*

# Laying Foundations

*November 26, 1909*

*Dear Family and Friends,*

*How I enjoy hearing from all of you, for it brings you very near. I was delighted with the news of the wedding, and glad to know my gifts arrived safely and were acceptable. I look forward to receiving pictures of the beautiful bride and her husband.*

*Now let me tell you my news.*

*It was the Saturday before my birthday and not too cold an afternoon when I left All People's Mission, having spent a little while talking to the volunteers. There was a*

95

crispness in the air, the snowflakes falling lazily. My hands were warm inside my muff. The beauty of the white snow attracted me, and so I decided to wander a bit before heading home.

I had gone some distance, to a street with a few larger homes set on ample grounds — an area not yet destroyed by the speculator. I stopped in front of a three-storey house situated on a corner lot, a house with fine bay windows but badly in need of painting and, no doubt a great deal of repair. It was empty, and I stood looking and wondering who might have lived in this splendid dwelling, for there was a certain happiness connected with it that quite captivated me. I waited and as I watched, a man came through the handsome front door and tacked up a sign on the verandah pillar: "For Rent". So I walked up the snow-covered path and asked if he would show me around.

"It's not in too good condition," he warned. "But it's a fine house. Too much for the old folks to handle now. It requires a lot of domestic help. They've moved to Toronto to be near their family. But they're loath to sell.

It's a beautiful old house with oak floors and panelling, a wide curving staircase, a fine, large kitchen — a bright and cheerful house. Lots of space for classrooms. Two big bathrooms in which to polish grubby little children. A pleasant third floor for caretakers.

"It's exactly what I want," I said to the rental agent, surprising myself. For such a thing had not occurred to me before that moment, though I had been wondering since my introduction to the Woodsworths just how best I might make a contribution to the mission work here. My particular interests are, of course, Sunday Bible study and classes emphasizing English and civics for children and adults, including hot meals for children and adults when needed.

"But I would prefer to purchase," I said, "for there's a

96

great deal of work to be done to make the place suitable for my purpose. A lot of repairs, paint, wallpaper. And the grounds will have to be looked after. I doubt if there has been much work done here for years." I told the agent about my interests and his smile broadened.

"Would you care to put some money down — about the amount of a couple of months rent, as a indication of your intent — while I'm in communication with the owners? The Owens know the house will not sell as a single family residence in this part of the city. Nor are they happy about having it used by uncaring tenants. They've loved their home and have happy memories. They're old timers: second generation in the place. And they're not just being sentimental. They've fought a losing battle over the years for proper housing and sanitation in the North End and they have a certain hostility toward speculators who have their eye out for the three houses in this row. Want to break the properties into twenty-five foot lots and put up cheap housing and sell high. Place could have sold several times over, but they got this thing about it. Stubborn. I'm sure if I speak to them and let them know you intend to fix up the old place and care for it, and tell them the purpose you have in mind, they'll go along with it. Very decent people the Owens are."

I believe I was led there as one often is led to meet the milestones of one's life. And though at this moment I have little idea as to how I can manage such a project, as well as work for Mr. Cedric Wilkins, I'm every bit as sure that a way will be found. The means will manifest, all in good time. Of course, it's my hope that once the project is set up and running like clockwork, someone else will take charge when I leave. But one step at a time. It's up to me to make the start. And I can well afford it, for Mr. Clements appears to have the Midas touch just as his wife indicated. His stock market advice has even this

97

quickly brought me gain.

On my birthday I signed the papers and handed over the required amount of money. Now I have permission to take over the house December first. You can be sure I'm looking forward to that.

One last word. Please, please, stop fretting about my wanderings through slums and through the dark. It's the only way I can learn about people and understand their problems and their needs. Had I fear about such things I would not be going to China. My one gnawing worry relates to "That Man". I cannot understand it. Though I try, in every way I know how, to stop bothering about him, I cannot seem to rid myself of his presence. The de Chênes believe it's because of some far memory. Martha says because of some unfortunate square between our planets. Others of you have other ideas. I think that perhaps more likely my very dislike of the man is binding him to me, and in the end it is myself who is at fault. I'm hoping that by working hard in the area of my interests — giving service to others — he will simply cease to have any meaning. Still I dream of flames and fire.

Love to all of you,
Bessie

**2**

Winnipeg, April 15, 1910

Dear Family and Friends,

A little time at last to catch up on the diary. Forgive me for being so long about it but I'm sure you'll understand the reason for the delay as you read along.

Winter at long last is over and rains are clearing the

98

*snow and ice. People are chopping drains along the walks and roadways and the pavement is fast being uncovered. I'm looking forward to the first anemones, for once the flowers start appearing they come in abundance. Spring and summer are short and not being able to spread their offerings over a long period of time, heap them hurriedly under a hot sun. This is hearsay only on my part, for I'm still to meet with summer. But I wait expectantly.*

*But this I know. There is an intensity about everything in this city. Intense feelings, intense cold. There is an exuberance too and beauty in the Northern Lights that danced in the sky and held me spellbound on more than one winter's night, and in the Sun Dogs that brightened the sky in the early morning as I walked with my muff held to my face, while the frost formed on my cheeks and eyelashes and bit my fingers and toes. One hates the winter, which is colder but drier than in Detroit, and loves it all at the same time. It is clean and cleansing and devastating. Children in moccasins lie in the soft dry snow and make angels by spreading their arms and legs. They build forts and have snowball fights when the snow can be packed. They toboggan and sled. Children get ecstatic when the first snow falls, and maybe in a way I'm still a child.*

*The snow was falling the December day I took possession of the Owen House. Not quite sure where to begin, I had bought a bucket and cleaning materials, broom, dustpan, and a quantity of cloths for scrubbing and dusting; I drove over in a cab. Then having laid a fire in the fireplace of the large living room to take the edge off the chill, I was happily cleaning the inside windows, mentally making plans and pausing every so often to jot down notes. I looked up to see a tall, well-built man entering the room, smiling and urging ahead of him a woman and a little girl. I recognized them immediately as*

99

*a couple I had noticed that first Sunday tea at the Woodsworths. I remembered them because of his pleasant, strong face and because her eyes were dark and beautiful and her face so badly scarred and sallow. And the little girl vivacious and seemingly so sure that all is well with the world, dancing and bright-eyed. I loved the three of them there and then and I know I always will. Lucy Woodsworth had realized my need for help and they had volunteered their services for the day — and they have remained with me to lend the help and strength the project requires.*

*Mikhail Manekowski, Gedda, and little Lana — who else could manage the Owen House the way they do, with such good nature and efficiency? And in teaching them English and working with them I have grown very close to these three. Mikhail, Polish, is a mill worker and one of those rare individuals who is just the right person to have around for every emergency — highly intelligent, and much more than a handyman. Gedda is reserved but willing and capable. In the four months and more that I have known them, Mike's broken English has become good English and Gedda, who spoke only a few words and then hesitatingly, now speaks quite well and without embarrassment.*

*There is one problem: the Manekowskis are Catholics! Surprised, I wanted to know why they were at All People's Mission in the first place. The answer: because Mike is a great admirer of Woodsworth and his political views, and enjoys talking with him. I've already guessed that politics are more important to Mike than religion. They have moved from their small house to the top floor suite. Mike stokes the furnace and paints and repairs in his spare time. Gedda immediately drew on a group of her friends from the Polish community, organized them, and began a splendid job of supervising housekeeping tasks. But Catholics at my Protestant mission! At first I*

100

tried to rationalize that we all worship the one God, serving each in his own way, and why not? Isn't religious bigotry as bad as racial bigotry? But there was such immediate tension and trouble between Protestants and Catholics in the house that the matter was, in large measure, settled for me. Mrs. Woodsworth saw to it that I had more Protestant help and the Catholics left — all but the Manekowskis and a good friend of Gedda's: a nurse, Mrs. Poleski, whom the children love and whose services I value. It seems so right that they are there, it's as though it were meant to be. I can't turn them away.

Mike promised that Lana could attend my Sunday School class. How happy Gedda is about that I can't say. She is far more devout than Mike. I know a crucifix hangs above her bed and that she takes Lana to the Catholic church more than once a week. But perhaps in time they can be influenced to turn from the Scarlet Woman.

You no doubt have gleaned from my brief notes over the intervening months that all goes well. And you know, too, who was one of our benefactors. But I must tell you how that came about and the surprise I got the day before Christmas.

Mike, Gedda, Lana, and I were decorating a huge Christmas tree with sugar plums for the eleven children who already were attending Saturday classes. Lana had just handed me a red tissue-wrapped sugar plum filled with nuts, raisins, candy, and a little toy, after having so carefully licked and placed the Christmas stickers, and was indicating to me that she wanted this special one placed by the angel near the top of the tree, when I realized there were others in the room. Stepping down from the chair on which I was perched, I turned to greet a little lady who fairly glowed. Green eyes very much alive, and a mass of fuzzy gold hair under a purple velvet hat that matched her velvet suit. A decoration for our Christmas tree! So charming and so friendly was she and

101

so taken was I with this delightful bit of fluff that it was a moment before I realized that the man tucked behind her was Cedric Wilkins! A different Mr. Wilkins, flushed and proud, and introducing me to — guess whom — Mrs Wilkins! Proud as a peacock. I could see the tail feathers fan as I stared astonished and recognized too his enjoyment of my surprise.

"I'm Alexandra," said the little lady, with an engaging smile. "Do call me Sandy. Ricky's told me all about you and what you're trying to do here. And we are going to be friends." She made the announcement as though it were a *fait accompli*. But after all, I had felt the same way about the Manekowskis. (Indeed Sandy was right: we have quickly become the best of friends.)

I got a grip on myself finally and introduced them to the Manekowskis, whereupon Sandy immediately sat on the floor and made friends with Lana, who carried on an enthusiastic explanation of everything in Polish, the occasional English word, and pantomime.

As I watched them I wondered how Mr. Wilkins had found the place. Then I recalled the day I had received notice at the office that the Owens had agreed to sell, and in a burst of unrestrained pleasure had told him, simply because he was near. He had looked at me, frowned slightly, and said, "Now, Miss Robinson, will you take a letter. To J.H. Selby Junior, Esquire...."

I showed them over the house. Through the kitchen, scullery, pantry, dining room, and other downstairs rooms which serve as office and other community rooms, then up the curved staircase to the schoolrooms. Lana danced along with us, pointing out little details to Sandy.

"They get along like old familiars," I said to Mr. Wilkins.

"She's fond of children. We have three of our own — all girls."

This bit of information contributed further to my

102

mental spin. Well, family and friends, it seems I can be mistaken: I am not after all the one elected to make him smile!

"But where does everyone sit?" Sandy wanted to know, surveying a large bedroom, now classroom, with its well-worn carpet and shabby wallpaper.

"On the floor." And Lana, understanding, immediately sat down cross-legged to demonstrate.

"The floors are a little drafty. But the carpets have all been nicely cleaned. There are a few chairs for the adults and we'll get more."

"But you must have proper desks, the right size, and tables and chairs — and bookcases."

Some books and papers were stacked on the floor. (The usual, Ma!)

"Ricky," Sandy informed my boss with a wicked smile, "we'll send a carpenter up and have them made to order." It was the smile of one capable of twisting a husband around a finger.

"That's a big order." I hesitated, looking at Cedric Wilkins. "And a very expensive one."

He looked surprised, but as one not unaccustomed to such surprises. "We'll go home and discuss how big and how expensive."

Sandy winked at me. "What time after Christmas will suit you to see a carpenter?"

It's obvious he adores her. However did this man, seemingly so shy of women, find such a jewel? Fluff she is not. Her appearance is as deceptive as his. Now I am sure rather it was Sandy, realizing his integrity and intelligence, who found him.

The Owen House now has three handsomely outfitted classrooms, for thanks to Sandy there are a number of donors, close friends of the Wilkinses, committed to the upkeep and running of the House. And as of now there are all the children and adults we can cope with, including a number of Sunday School pupils. The Wilkinses head a Board of Directors and almost every Saturday Sandy comes around and brightens the place with her vivacity.

One of the members of the Board, and also a volunteer, is Ethel Reid, a grey-haired, rather toothy woman, one of the finest people I have ever known. She has a large home and a husband who can well afford to keep her, she tells me, so she insists on being a scullery maid four days a week, just for a change. She also looks after the kitchen staff and food, relieving Gedda of that.

"I've always had things so easy, it's about time I scrubbed a few pots. And it's a good way to get rid of a bit of pent-up anger."

"Anger! You get angry?"

"You'd be surprised. I'm angry about a lot of things. About the fact that women have so few rights. About the status of the working man."

I was properly surprised. Not so much about women's rights but at her concern for the working man. Interested, too. She can't talk to her husband about such matters, nor to his friends. So we talk a lot. She's given me more to think about.

Both children and grown-ups appear to love Owen House almost as much as I do, and for the most part are here because they are keen to learn. It is a place full of the happiness I recognized was just waiting to be manifested. Now there are lots of beautiful plants about, a tank of goldfish, a canary, and one special Siamese cat to take care of the mice, plus a big Collie dog. Soon in the garden there will be flowers and vegetables and many of the children and adults are already volunteering to help the Manekowskis with that.

Of course we have problems: mainly with parents, only minor ones so far with the children, and a few with volunteers.

104

*Once after Sunday School I was standing at the foot of the stairs with Doris Whiting, another Board member and volunteer, when down the polished handrail came eight-year-old Jay Goldberg. Our energetic Doris, whose motto seems to be "spare the rod and spoil the child", immediately took him by the ear. But I realized I had watched him sliding down the banister with a certain amount of envy.*

*"Don't you dare do that again," said Doris, shaking the culprit.*

*Jay winced, fright replacing happiness in big brown eyes.*

*"Please don't send me away."*

*After he had left to join the other children, I said to Doris, "I don't think he's harmed the railing."*

*"He's setting a bad example. The children will all want to slide down the banister, and we can't allow that."*

*"Why not?" I wanted to know.*

*So now there is a rule that children above a certain age can slide down the banister. We have rather strange rules that attempt to allow rather than forbid — something new in the lives of many of them and a manner of reasoning I developed from my tolerant mother. And, as Ma also taught me, human nature being what it is — perverse — having gained the privilege, not many always take advantage of it.*

*Though I now have a fair number in my Sunday School and Bible Study classes, Jay (as you can imagine by his surname, the only Jewish lad) is not among them. But I cannot insist on accepting only Protestants or those who do not have a religious background, and though I'm well aware that some come only for the food and education, if the need is there I let them come. Though it grieves me that I'm not being instrumental in the salvation of all, I cannot refuse any of these poor souls*

105

*and I hope that God through some special dispensation will grant them heaven — as I would were I God.*

[I lay down my pen, caught in momentary shock. Am I already making of Owen House an Open City? I sign my letter.]

*Love to all,*
*Bessie*

## 3

*Detroit, May 4, 1910*

*Dear Bessie,*

*This is a very difficult letter for me to write. For months I've refused to face the inevitable, refused to believe that life will not work out the way I want it. Like the spoiled one that I am, I've continued on my way day by day, planning and packing. I even purchased my train ticket, and yesterday filled the last trunk, knowing I was fighting a lost cause, but angry and determined to have my way. Then after I had padlocked the last bit of baggage, I went up to the Studio and cried. It's no use, Bessie, I cannot leave Mother at this time.*

*Anna came to me almost two weeks ago, quite distraught. She had received a letter from Germany asking her to go home. Her parents have both been unwell for a very long time. Now her father is invalided and they need her. What can she do but return? She is as concerned and unhappy as I. But not as willful.*

*I've not wanted to say anything to you, but when I arrived home I found that Anna had not exaggerated Mother's condition. Mother seems healthy enough but is unable to remember even little things. I caught her putting her arm in the wrong coat sleeve. Then she was unable to*

106

*figure out what to do. Little things like that. At first I was sure it was because Father's death had upset her so much. But Doctor Ralph says Mother will only get progressively worse. Doctors aren't always right, are they? But she does need so much help even with the simplest things. "Put her in a home," the doctors say. But Bessie, I've been to those homes and I can't do it. Nor, if I were to go away, could I count on home nursing, without Anna and Ludwig to see that she is well-treated — she's getting difficult to handle and even Anna and I grow impatient.*

*My childish demonstration is past. Anna, dry-eyed and tense, put her arms around me and promised to return as soon as she can. But I don't think she will return. I have decided to get a nurse to live in, who will help me. And I will continue with my studio-workshop a while longer and see how things work out. I gave the tailors notice some time ago. But they are still on back orders and though they have had offers of other jobs, I'm sure they will stay with me. I have also sent notice to Winnipeg of my intention to end the lease. It's an excellent location, but there will be another. But the years roll on, Bessie, and I was so sure this was the time for a move. I had so hoped to get to Winnipeg while you are still there. But were I to desert Mother I would hate myself. I'll keep hoping that she will get better.*

*Despite your warning I'm continuing with astrological studies, which I find a great form of relaxation and a comfort and help. Don't concern yourself about setting me on the "left-handed path". It's my decision. Like your mother, I look forward to discussing a few such matters with Saint Peter when I arrive at the Pearly Gates.*

*My love and good wishes to you, dear Bessie. In my thoughts I am with you at Owen House.*

*Martha*

107

## 4

The grand entrance is quite unintentional. It's Friday night and by the time I have left the office, gone to Owen House, written Saturday afternoon's lessons on the blackboard, seen to it that books and all are in order for my substitute this evening, dressed, and found a cab, it is already ten minutes past seven. I'm late and the other guests have already arrived.

I'm aware my cheeks are flushed from my exertions as the maid ushers me into the drawing room. Of course I'm wearing the Martha blue silk. The men stand. All eyes turn. (I must remember to tell Martha those glances are approving.) Mrs. Clements hastens forward and takes my hand.

"My dear, how lovely you are. We are just eight this evening. I do think eight or ten the right number for a dinner party, don't you? More intimate. I could have wished for ten for I would have liked you to meet my daughter and her husband. But they're still on their honeymoon."

By now Mr. Clements is at his wife's side, his eyes smiling. "As always I agree with everything my wife says. About you, that is. Now let me introduce you. Mr. and Mrs. Oscar Shaw, Miss Elizabeth Robinson. Our son, Ray, and his wife, Cora, and our nephew, Charles Clements — Miss Robinson."

The Shaws are stockily built and about fifty. Cora, a dainty blue-eyed blonde, is in white lace with a fresh rose by the neck. The two cousins are very different in appearance, but like the senior Clements both have a certain humorous expression about them, as though they regard the world as a bit of a joke. And why not? They are on top of it.

Mrs. Shaw, wearing the latest in fashion, a dress

108

with a hobble skirt, inches her way across the room, self-conscious and ungainly. But Cora has captured me. "What a beautiful dress! I can't believe you found that here.'

"No. But the person who designed it is a friend of mine. And Martha is hoping to set up shop in Winnipeg."

"How exciting. I'm so glad to hear that. When? For I will have to have dresses designed by her. It's exquisite."

"Thank you. I find your dress charming."

"It's the dress I wore to my sister-in-law's wedding. I'm glad you like it. But do tell me about your designer and when she is to come."

So some time is spent explaining to young Mrs. Clements about Martha and the unfortunate delay. By the time the subject of clothes and Winnipeg's need for good fashion designers has been exhausted, the maid arrives to announce dinner.

I am seated between Mr. Shaw, who is on Mrs. Clements' right, and Ray — while Mrs. Shaw is placed to Mr. John Clements' right, and the nephew to the left of Mrs. Clements.

The maid is placing vichyssoise set in ice before me, and already Mr. Shaw in a cultured English voice is directing a monologue at me, explaining how it was that he, a son of near-royalty, came to Canada a few years ago, explaining about his rewarding business deals in Winnipeg — all due to his own acute business sense. And on and on. I listen with one ear, hoping that I am nodding and exclaiming in all the right places, while my other ear is attuned to other conversations.

Cora and Ray are telling Mr. Clements about the mahogany furniture they are about to purchase for their new home, and Mrs. Shaw is explaining that oak furniture is by far the sturdiest and best. That is what she brought from England and that is what she advises them to get.

"Mahogany requires a lot of care and really is not the best to have with small children about. Are there small children?"

Ray is saying, "They're still a gleam in my eye. I'm doing my best."

Mrs. Shaw is appalled. "Rea-lly, Mr. Clements!"

"Yes, really, Mrs. Shaw."

By the exchange at the other end of the table it's obvious that the nephew is a favourite.

Mrs. Clements is saying, "Charles, I haven't seen enough of you lately."

"Lately you were in Florida."

"I remember that very well. But I've been back for some time."

"And busy marrying off a daughter. Concerning yourself with lace, and bows, and furbelows, so I imagine."

"Well, you were at the wedding. What do you think of the bridegroom?"

"A fine person as far as I can tell. A liberal-minded person."

"A friend of Laurier's as well as a staunch Liberal. But I want to know when you are getting married."

"I'm a confirmed bachelor."

"Don't tell me that. You were seen at the tennis courts again with that pretty Margaret Bradford. Now how about Margaret?"

"She plays a fair game of tennis."

"Don't tell me she beat you."

"She said I had the advantage of wearing trousers, and she wishes she could."

"Wear trousers? What a thing to say. Imagine women wearing trousers."

"I understand that after marriage a great many

110

women wear the pants in the family."

"Oh, Charles."

"Miss Robinson, I hear by the grapevine that Owen House is doing very well." We are well into the second course and Mr. J.R. Clements is finally plucking me from the eternal jawing of the boring, egotistical Mr. Shaw.

"Yes, we are doing very well. We are managing to look after over a hundred children during the week, preparing them for regular school. Adults come and go. For me it is a rewarding work and I want to thank you for directing me to the Woodsworths."

"I'd like to come and see your place. Do tell me where it is. Perhaps I could help." The English voice is Mrs. Shaw's.

"Woodsworth? J.S. Woodsworth? Is he that socialist?" It's my monologist.

"Preached a social gospel at Grace Methodist. Mrs. Clements and I met him some years back."

"I know about him. Writes for the newspaper occasionally, doesn't he? He's a dangerous radical, that one. Wants the working class to take over the South End."

"Oh, come now, Shaw." This time it's Ray Clements, at my side. "Probably just wants to improve their lot a bit."

"It's the City that should be trying to improve the lot of the working class and helping those who have no employment." I am more than a little annoyed at Mr. Shaw's remark about Woodsworth. "Charity is only a stop-gap. There must be better wages for the working man. And taxes should be used to help obliterate poverty." My last remark I direct at Mr. Shaw.

"Why? Isn't charity enough? We all give and give."

"Only if you approve of the politics of the situation or feel it's to your advantage do you give. The working man

111

should be organized against unfair working practices. I've seen —"

"I think you were annoyed, Miss Robinson, when I referred to Mr. Woodsworth as a radical. That, I believe, is just what he wants to do: organize the working man. And what do you think that would do to our country, pray? Is that what you, too, want done?"

"Oh, Shaw," a pleasant voice across the table is demanding his attention. To me it sounds like Oh, pshaw! "Miss Robinson will be going to China." Charles, the nephew, is changing the subject.

"Oh, no!" cries Cora. "To China? Aren't the most awful things happening out there?"

"Isn't that a good reason for going? I want to help — children especially. Through mission work. Something along the lines I'm doing here. But I would include a permanent home for orphans and unwanted children."

"Well, organize the Chinese, not Canadians." Oscar Shaw is insisting on a last word.

Now the conversation turns to China.

"What is happening in China now? What about the Boxer rebellion? Mrs. Clements asks.

"That, my darling, was finished years ago, in 1900."

"Officially, yes," I hasten to the defense of my hostess. "But missionaries still report trouble with antiforeign groups. It was always felt that the Dowager Empress sided with the Boxers while at the same time making conciliatory moves to Europeans."

"Now that the Old Buddha is dead," questions my host, "will there be more or less trouble for Europeans? What do you think? She died a year ago, or was it two?"

"You know about that? And that the Dowager Empress was called Old Buddha?" I am delighted. "I can find little or no news about China in the local papers."

"I guess the newspapers figure China's too far away

to be of any concern to Canadians. They only bother reporting if missionaries are killed or our trade is affected."

"So how did you know the Empress was called Old Buddha?"

"We have our sources," says Ray mysteriously.

"My husband means the Country Club. There's a retired colonel from the British Army here. He was in China all through the Boxer rebellion. And we know a Mrs. Campbell who lived in China for years. Her husband died there."

'What is the latest news you have, Miss Robinson."

"That a letter was sent to President Taft from the new emperor or rather from his government, since the emperor is only about four years old — to indicate the government's determination to carry out a reform policy. And that will mean cooperation with western methods by way of education through the missions. That's where I expect to be helping."

"I'm a bit dubious about that cooperation." It is the voice from across the table to my right. "From what I hear, the Chinese want the best from the West — and China for the Chinese, all at the same time."

"You can bet your bottom dollar there will be trouble again, and soon," Mr. Shaw prophesies.

"Wouldn't be at all surprised."

"Why do you think that, Mr. Clements?"

"Well, I'm quoting Colonel Marsh for the most part. But it seems there could be trouble from three sources. Japan could create a problem again. Russia will continue to force herself on northern China. And my guess is that the biggest source of all trouble could be from the Chinese people themselves: the reformists and the traditionalists."

"Oh, Miss Robinson," worries Cora, "I don't think you should go to China. You're doing such a good job of

113

mission work right here."

"There could be rebellions anywhere, you know. And danger..."

"But not in Canada. Not in Winnipeg."

"I can't imagine a beautiful young woman in such a beautiful blue silk dress being a missionary in China." This nonsensical remark comes from Ray.

"And why not? Dress hardly makes the person. Clothes are worn to suit the occasion. You will have to come and see me in China."

"I've always thought it terrible that Chinese women have to bind their feet." Cora has a soft heart.

"At least they can't run away," Ray tells her.

Both the Shaws have been irritating me and I can't help saying with feigned innocence, careful not to look at Mrs. Shaw, "The hobble garter that women affix to their legs to prevent them from taking more than a three- or four-inch step, lest they split their skirts — doesn't it remind you somewhat of the bound feet of Chinese ladies?"

A sudden quiet descends. I look at my plate. At least I have the decency to blush. Not only was the hobble-skirt reference in bad taste, but in polite society one does not mention women's legs. Looking up I see the men are smiling, and I respond by dimpling. Mrs. Shaw is not pleased.

However, instead of announcing her displeasure she says, "Pigtails. Why do Chinamen wear pigtails?"

And, after my rudeness, why do I take Mrs. Shaw's question almost as a personal affront? I make an effort at politeness. "The pigtail is also referred to as the 'queue'. And though it was once a badge of subjection forced upon the Chinese by their Manchu conquerors, it has become a feature of traditional dress, and now is cherished — like women's corsets in the West."

There I go again. Because I'm annoyed at Mr. and

114

Mrs. Shaw I'm being most unreasonable.

Ray is grinning broadly. Mrs. Shaw's mouth hangs open. But before anything more can be said, the nephew has whispered to his aunt and Mrs. Clements has risen. Dessert being finished, she is suggesting the ladies leave the men to their cigars.

So we ladies retire to the drawing room, where the maid has brought a tray with after-dinner coffee.

Holding her demitasse, Diane Shaw is forgiving. "Oh, Miss Robinson, I'm really intrigued by Owen House and your work there. Mrs. J.R. has told me so many good things about it. I'm determined to come and visit. And I can help. I have a reputation for being an excellent organizer."

"Thank you, Mrs. Shaw, but Owen House is already organized."

"Then I can be the efficiency expert."

"It is quite efficiently run." My voice is cold.

"One can always make improvements, you know. You can ask Mr. Shaw, I'm really very good at organizing." Then she adds a little coyly, "We might contribute monetarily, too."

"I certainly can't say no to that." Though I would like to.

Mrs. Shaw is forgiving, but I am slow in recovering my calm and Mrs. Clements is a bit put out with the two of us. I notice her frowning and looking at her daughter-in-law.

This time it is Cora Clements who decides to ease the situation. "Mother is an expert with roses. You should see them."

"Yes. Do step out into the garden while there is still a little light. The mosquitoes are a nuisance, but my roses have never been better."

The perfume from the flowers is heady, the garden a delight. The men, too, have come out. Enchanted by the

115

roses, I have wandered from the other ladies, and the nephew, his starched white collar bright in the fading light, is coming my way. A disarming, lop-sided smile distinguishes his rather remarkable Irish face. He plucks a rose and hands it to me.

I cannot help but smile in turn. "Bless you for rescuing me before I completely spoiled your aunt's dinner party."

"Always delighted to rescue a beautiful lady. Besides, Mr. Shaw was being a bit difficult. Hope I might have the opportunity to rescue you again."

"You've already missed your opportunity. I had to be rescued a second time over coffee. From Mrs. Shaw. I'm afraid I find her difficult as well. Perhaps I'm the one with the problem."

"Don't you believe it. They're good people but two of a kind. Oscar Shaw has been involved with my uncle in some business deals since they came to Winnipeg. So I know them well. Sorry I wasn't on hand to witness the fray. But perhaps another time?"

"Just hope there won't be another time."

"Well perhaps I can drive you home and we'll talk about it."

"I should like that."

Having blotted my copy-book, I doubt I'll ever see them again. "Mind your temper and watch your tongue," Ma so often has cautioned me. She should talk! But I really don't care. Though I find the Clements rather attractive, especially Mr. and Mrs. J.R., we have very little in common.

116

## 5

To put it mildly, I'm despondent. But let's face facts. I was the one to leave Richard. And I knew only too well that Lydia Gray was waiting in the wings. Waiting for me to depart the field. I have even said, and more than once, that Lydia would make Richard a good wife. She is attractive, small, with a trim figure, chestnut hair, and big brown eyes. Quite unlike me in every way. What can Richard see in her anyway? Sweet-tempered, feminine, home-loving, a good hostess, charming, docile, lace and bows. Ugh!

Ma has written to say they are married. And not even a year has passed since I left Detroit. How could he forget me so soon? How could he? He knew I wanted him and my mission all at the same time. And deep inside me I still hoped the unresolvable could be resolved. Now: never! I hurl a book across the room. Another. Then another. Then come tears.

## 6

*Winnipeg, October 2, 1910*

*Dear Martha,*

*In answer to your question, "What is he like, this nephew of Mr. and Mrs. John Clements?" Perhaps the best way to explain him is to say that he is someone very easy to be with. Kind, and rather persuasive. He managed to convince this stubborn individual to take a little time off from Owen House. And this I have been doing, Saturday afternoon or late Sunday afternoon and evening, or for the occasional dinner after work. Actually, it is not a bad idea to see how the place can function*

117

*without me — for it must get along without me entirely one of these days. And for the most part all goes well.*

*A problem is the Shaws who, to my horror, decided to volunteer money and their services. They have been intolerant of the Manekowskis from the beginning because of their religion. But I spoke to them sharply, saying that Owen House was the Manekowskis' home and the House was better for their being there. Frankly, I had hoped both Catholicism and my tongue would turn them away. But for some reason Diane Shaw seemed most insistent on being involved and said nothing more — she only raised her eyebrows. And now she has started to appear on a regular basis, and has taken things in hand despite my protestations. She is none too popular, except with Doris Whiting. But perhaps she means well, as Charles says. And of course money talks, and policies are governed by money, unfortunately. But we are doing our best to maintain our values and, with the help of Sandy and Ethel, so far we have held the line in all that matters.*

*Mrs. Shaw likes action and is a most determined character. The result: she is constantly stirring the pudding. Her first observation was that discipline at Owen House is slack and that lack of order is highly detrimental to the children's future. For instance, when Ethel or I sat down to the piano for a sing-song or music period — meant simply for relaxation — we would allow the children to drift in as they pleased, some first putting a last touch to their lessons or whatever project they might be working on. Or when a class began it was our habit to jangle a bell. Then they would come running from all directions.*

*"This will never do," fluttered Mrs. Shaw. "The children must line up in the hall and proceed in orderly fashion to their classrooms. Then before class they must be taught to first stand and sing "God Save the King".*

118

*They will be expected to do this at city schools and they must begin now!"*

*"The children are well-disciplined," I countered. "They do what they are required to do. What you want is not discipline but regimentation."*

*And so the fray went on until Sandy interjected, "Why not, Bessie? Having the children line up in the hall really won't hurt a thing. They might even consider it a game."*

*Mrs. Shaw got her way. But I remain the dissenter. and my annoyance with that woman, which began the moment I first saw her, has mounted. Reprehensible though it be, I feel myself grow taut every time she heaves in sight. House conferences have been held to deal with Mrs. Shaw's various points of discipline. (As you might guess, she has found a staunch ally in Doris Whiting.) So far her "organizing" has to do with just little things. But it worries me and I wonder if funding for such charities as ours should not go to one central bank and be impartially divided among the various mission projects. At the same time I realize it is because so many interested donors have put their money into Owen House that it is doing so very well, and I wouldn't like to see anything taken from my special mission.*

*But here I am going on as usual about my own pet interest when you asked specifically that I write about Charles.*

*Well, what more can I say about Charles? He has straight black hair, fashionably parted in the centre, light blue eyes, a long upper lip accentuated by a deep scar which he got when tossed by a bull or a cow on his father's farm years ago. His face is full of good humour. Average build, average height. I wouldn't say he was handsome, but he's pleasant to have around and I enjoy being with him - I find myself completely relaxed in his company. I've even been sleeping better and having fewer nightmares. And this I can only attribute to the*

119

*delightful outings and an abundance of laughter.*

*However, there is a flaw. He wants to marry me. It's a matter he has brought up on several occasions. If it weren't that he is such good medicine, I'd simply refuse to see him again.*

*Summer's weather was much too hot, relieved by the occasions when Charles took me on the river in a canoe or for drives in his Model T — to Assiniboine Park, once with his Uncle Walter and Aunt Josephine Clements. (Mr. Walter Clements is a younger brother of J.R. Clements, a carpenter by trade and doing very well with all the building that is going on in Winnipeg.) They had us back to their home for dinner. Charles appears to be very fond of his relatives. He is quite a family-minded person. Obviously the apple of his Uncle Walter's eye. W. and J. have no children of their own.*

*Charles was away on business for a few weeks and wrote to me. The letters — full of poetry and rose petals — made me feel rather special. He is a thoughtful and courteous person. I've noticed that he gets along well with both men and women. The fact that women like to be around him doesn't seem to bother him at all, and why he has chosen to give his attention to me I'll never know — our temperaments are so completely different. Why — when he can have any one of a number of young ladies, and Mrs. J.R. is frankly voting for someone named Margaret Bradford? Could it be because I am the one who is not available? Such is the nature of man.*

*He is practical. He is reliable. He is secretary-treasurer of the Clements Realty Company. A most eligible bachelor. Why, Martha, he is just the one for you! Your business manager and a very considerate person. You must get to Winnipeg this next year. I intend to start campaigning for my friend Martha immediately. I'll soften Charles up with sweet talk and ready him for the kill.*

120

*Love,*

*Bessie*

*P.S. When I told Charles about the Catholics and the Jewish lad, he laughed and said, "Watch out, Bessie, our Prime Minister, Sir Wilfred Laurier, once stated that he would not stand on grounds of Catholicism or Protestantism but upon grounds that can be occupied by all men who love justice, freedom, and toleration." At which point I interrupted him to say, "And that is as it should be." "But," Charles continued, "Laurier was cut dead by a great many of his friends both Protestant and Catholic." "It sounds like the case of Frederick the Second," I said. "Who?" asked Charles, puzzled. "A friend of mine," I said, unwilling to explain.*

*I approve of Sir Wilfred's statement and I mean to work for justice, freedom, and tolerance at Owen House.*

## 7

Flu. It seems half of Winnipeg is down with flu. The children brought it to the staff. First Diane Shaw succumbed, then Ethel, Doris, Sandy, and finally I, who so seldom get sick. Owen House was closed for almost a week. The others are back but I have yet to return. Mr. Wilkins' office is being looked after by someone from the secretarial pool. And yesterday Sandy telephoned to say "All is well at the House — don't rush back if you still feel under the weather." So I agreed to sleep in another morning.

It is Saturday, snowing and blustery. With just three weeks before Christmas, there is so much to be done. I intend to get to the House this afternoon. Perhaps if I get up, have a cup of tea, poached egg and toast, I'll

121

feel better.

I prepare my little meal, sit down to eat it, and find myself smiling at the basket of fruit on the table. Charles, so solicitous. And so persistent. There seems nothing I can say that will discourage him. Not even that I likely will be leaving Winnipeg before next summer is over. It will be good to be gone before next winter's cold sets in. I don't really mind the cold, but I want no more flu like this lot, thank you. I am still weak as a baby and light-headed. Almost everyone else I know had flu but Charles, who remains perfectly well: as impervious to illness as to my rebuffs. Maybe a bit of a Christian Scientist like his Uncle Walter and Aunt Josephine. Said he doesn't believe in being ill. A case of mind over matter, no doubt. Well, I believe that the mind has a lot to do with one's state of well-being. But it's a sure thing I went down in a heap when this particular brand of flu came to town. I'm feeling a bit better already with that tea. What if I were to make a good hot bowl of barley soup with plenty of carrots and cabbage for lunch? That should help get me to the House.

\* \* \* \* \*

I'm dressed warmly and on my way downstairs. I open the vestibule door and — stand transfixed. I want to turn and run back upstairs. But I cannot. Already so weak. Now I have to steady myself against the door. He is apparently looking for my apartment number. Now he sees me and I'm trapped.

"Miss Robinson, we've come to visit you and here you are!" Big teeth show in the heavy face.

"Reverend Dickinson, I'm just on my way out. I'm sorry." My voice is scarcely audible.

"But you are not well?"

"I've been sick but I'm better now and I must go." I

122

want desperately to push past him. But he fills the doorway.

"We can see you're not well. Let us help you back to your apartment."

"No! I must go." I want to shout but the words hardly form.

"We have a message for you. Something you'll be glad to hear. Surely you'll grant us a few minutes of your time when we've come so far. We'll not keep you long."

"You haven't come from Detroit just to see me?" The situation is unreal.

"No, of course not. We were invited to speak in Winnipeg. Did you not know?"

I've been too ill to read the papers. I shake my head.

"Under the circumstances we thought it would be much better to talk with you rather than write."

There is nothing I can do but turn and climb unsteadily upstairs, he following. But I won't let him into my apartment. I must think of some way to keep him out.

Mrs. Jones from the next apartment steps into the corridor and nods. Can't make a scene. I'll open the door, step in quickly, say, "I'm ill. Write me."

I fumble with the key in the lock — and drop it. Before I can do anything, Dickinson has stooped to pick it up, forcing me to move back. He opens the door, takes my arm, and steps inside with me.

"It's not proper for you to be in here alone with me." This as an afterthought. I do not as a rule concern myself with such propriety.

"It's all right, Miss Robinson. We are your minister and will only be a few minutes. See, we'll leave the door ajar."

I try desperately to get a grip on myself. It is wrong to hate a person so. Or is it fear I feel? Shame takes

123

over. My lips are dry, but I make an effort to speak.

"How did you know where to find me?"

"You sent a generous cheque for our China Mission Fund — from your office. We telephoned and were given this address."

Of course. Or he could have had my address from any number of his church members. After all those dreadful nightmares! Now a visitation by day. Try to keep calm.

"Tell me why you are here. Then you must go."

He is staring at me.

"We have come as your minister and your friend."

"My friend?" My contempt is not hidden.

"We regret — what can we say? — a difference of opinion — that slightly disagreeable episode when we last met. You appear to have taken our remarks in the wrong spirit, from what your friends have told us. We spoke as your counsellor."

"Indeed! You implied I'm a witch, in the clutches of Satan, damned to Hell..."

"Now, now. We did and said what we considered right. We spoke as a minister to a member of his flock who has gone astray. Our admonitions were meant to help, not to anger. It seems you have taken our words amiss."

"Amiss? You wrote to me. If those who know me well had not come to my defence, you would not have agreed to let me —"

"Now, now. That happened a long time ago. It is the Christian way to forgive."

"Are you asking my forgiveness?"

His tongue is moistening the thick lips. "You have donated a considerable sum towards our project in China, Miss Robinson. We have come to inform you that sufficient funds are at last available and it is felt that the work can now go ahead as planned."

124

"I have already been apprised that is the case." Surely he is aware that I know. "I mean to leave for China from Detroit in late summer." This, too, surely is common knowledge at the church. "Now I must get to my work. Thank you for coming to tell me."

His eyes flash, then narrow. He is no longer smiling.

"We have a surprise for you."

"A surprise! What surprise?"

"This particular project has aroused a fair amount of interest in China. The Chinese are anxious for reform and are relying heavily on our mission schools for western education. We intend to set up an outstanding science programme."

"I'm well aware of all this."

"And to prove our goodwill towards you, not only have we personally donated a sum of money to match yours, but we will be taking a sabbatical so that we will be there, with our wife, to help you initiate the work. To see that all goes well."

He is regarding me shrewdly. Are those last words meant to taunt me? He is playing with me: cat and mouse. He must realize now that I can scarcely abide being in the same room with him. Right from the beginning he has meant to be guardian of my every move, of my every word. And he plans to be there beside me! How impossible that will be. A living nightmare.

"It is impossible. I don't think I will be able to go this coming year. Maybe the following year."

"But you have just said you are going this coming summer."

"I have important work here. A mission school in the North End of the city. And I have been thinking it might be wiser for me to remain here a while longer."

"We are sorry, Miss Robinson, but we must know, and immediately. It was our understanding that the

125

matter was settled." He pauses briefly, as though in deep thought. "However, if you feel you cannot go, there is someone who is interested in taking your place. A Dr. Gerald Foster, a man of science. He has the right background, a university degree."

The words sting me. My lack of formal education has always been a deep wound within me. Maybe this is what he wanted all along: to have Dr. Gerald Foster. Yes, of course!

I know I am no longer functioning rationally. Even though uncannily able to look down upon myself with distaste, to condemn my action, yet my feelings take over.

"Then why not let him go?" That is what Dickinson wants. To replace a witch with a scientist. "And now, you go. Get out of here." I am screaming as loudly as my weak condition allows.

Now his voice comes soothingly, low, musical. "Miss Robinson, surely you don't mean that. You're not at all well. We think you should take a day or two to consider this very important matter. Don't throw away in a burst of anger — or because of illness — a goal you have set for yourself these past many years. We can come back Monday evening. We leave for home Tuesday. We think you should realize the consequences of such a decision. Dr. Foster cannot be expected to go to the mission for just a year or until it's convenient for you to take over, since it means giving up his present position. If he goes — then you do not."

Of course I want to go. I have always wanted to go. I do not require more time to think about that. But how can I go if Dickinson is to be there supervising my every move? I haven't changed. I can't change myself — not from the self I basically am. He'll provoke me. I'll refuse to condemn the Chinese for their philosophy. Whatever it might be, he'll still consider me a witch in

126

league with the Devil.

"It seems Dr. Foster is much better qualified than I."

"Yes. But you have priority. You have donated a great deal of money. Your friends at the church have made it abundantly clear that your are their first choice."

The elders must realize Dr. Foster's superiority but do not want to hurt me.

"I will not go to China."

"Give yourself some time. You might reconsider."

"No. I cannot change my mind."

"You are so sure?"

"I am very sure."

"Then, if that is your carefully considered opinion, would you be so kind as to type a letter to that effect?" He is looking at my typewriter and the clutter of papers beside it. "We know you can type most efficiently."

A petty insult.

"State clearly that as you have undertaken important mission work in Winnipeg and feel you cannot leave it at this time, you'll be happy to see someone else take over the post proposed for you at our mission in China. But you'll know how best to state the matter."

I move toward the table. Slowly I remove my gloves, hat, scarf and place them on one chair. Slowly I sit down by the typewriter.

I insert two sheets and a carbon.


### 8

At last he is gone. I remain in the chair, unmoving. For how long I cannot tell. My mind is clouded, circling in space. Then, at last, I feel my head throbbing.

127

How did this happen? The project in China is my dream. My purpose in life. My reason for being. For this mission I have given up the man I love. And now, in but a split moment of time, all is changed.

Where lies the fault? Am I my own worst enemy? Did I invent the monster, Dickinson? Make a monster out of the man of God? My life in ruins because I cannot tolerate the Reverend Dickinson for just one sabbatical year. I have given up my love. Can I not give up my hate?

Run after him. Tell him I've changed my mind. Perhaps it is not too late.

But I cannot. I cannot let go of my pride, or my hurt, or let go of my fears. Nor can I put up with humiliation for just one year. And I am ill.

It isn't fair. If God is testing me, then I have failed. It isn't fair. It is too much to ask of me. After all these years of working late into the night to educate myself, to prepare myself to help others — for just this particular cause. Years of being the big sister, the one relied upon, the strong friend! I'm not really strong, Martha. I'm really very frightened: of Dickinson, of life, of myself. I've always wanted someone with whom I could talk over my problems. I want Richard to look after me. I want a little girl like Lana...

Without warning, without reason, like a tornado the moment has come and gone; and in its wake, destruction.

\*　\*　\*　\*　\*

A knock at the door rouses me. A voice is calling through the door, still ajar. "Hello! Hello! You there, Bessie?"

Charles! The door is pushed slowly open. Charles, hat in hand, a sprinkling of snow on hat and coat,

128

holding a box of flowers.

"Something to cheer you. Sandy said I'd probably find you still here."

He is good medicine. Charles with his smiling eyes and lop-sided grin.

"Just what I need." My voice finding its way up from the depths of my being is wavering but certain. "You are just what I need. I've come to an important decision, Charles. I'm not going to China. Instead I'm going to marry you."

## 9

I sit alone on the bank of the Red River, my wide-brimmed straw hat on the ground beside me. Yesterday evening Charles took me to visit an old pioneer by the name of Bannatyne and I was entranced by the stories he told of his youth in Winnipeg. So vivid were his descriptions that now as I look down the river I can almost hear the voyageurs of those bygone days singing as they heave round the bend. I imagine I can see their long canoes, their colourful costumes and bright headbands. They paddle vigorously. They have great energy. Then they are gone. And now is the year 1911. They had their time, their reason for being. I stare at the grey water. No one is near.

By me is a flower. I pluck it. It is a bright yellow flower with six petals. Once the secret of its unfolding was held within a seed. I look into its dark heart, imagining my name written on it. The petals are twelve instead of six: the twelve houses of my horoscope. My mandala. "Bessie, that is you!" Everything is right there. Within me, the seeds of my unfolding, my destiny and death. Is my patterning a caprice of God, of nature, or of my own making over many lifetimes? Is it one or all? Moodily I tear away a petal. That is the childhood that never was. Another petal. The life with Richard I threw away. Another. The life in China that is not to be. A feeling of utter despair engulfs me. Impatiently I tear away the other petals, and into the flowing river I throw the flower's heart.

# PART TWO

# ACCORDING TO ONE'S LIGHTS

## Chapter IV

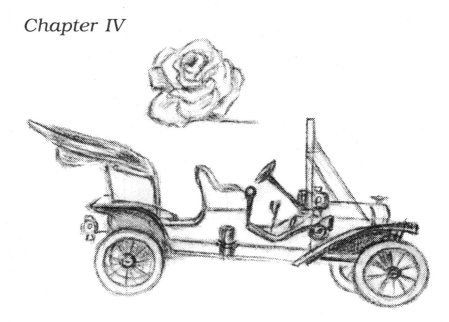

# Building

The J.R. Clements family. As so often is the case on a Sunday evening, the family has dined at the parents' home and is now relaxing in the drawing room. The men are smoking: cigars, pipes, but no cigarettes for those are considered rather effete. The women are talking over the week's events, household matters, affairs at the Club, people in general, and so and so in particular.

"Charles and Bessie will soon have returned from their honeymoon," Cora remarks, hiding a yawn behind a dainty hand.

"I'm so looking forward to having Charles back," says Mrs. Clements senior. "Don't we all miss having Charles around."

"Mother, were you surprised that he married Bessie?" The query is from Sarah, the recently wed.

"Yes, I'll make no bones about that. I like Bessie

131

very much, but..."

"But you can't picture Charles hitched to a woman so Hell-bent on saving souls, eh Mother?" interjects her husband, pouring himself more port.

"Heaven-bent, Father," corrects Ray.

"Maybe that's about it," agrees his mother. "Charles has always been so easy-going and she is so — well, so intense about everything."

"Maybe that means they'll be a good balance for one another," suggests Sarah.

"Or get on one another's nerves."

"Charles has no 'nerves', Mother. He is absolutely unflappable."

"Maybe 'nerves' is the wrong word for Charles. He's certainly not high-strung. I don't think I ever remember seeing him in a temper since he was a little boy. But stubborn — yes, he's stubborn. You can push Charles too far and he'll get as stubborn as a bull. I admit I was so sure he'd marry Margaret Bradford. They are very good friends."

"He was besotted with Bessie from the moment he set eyes on her, you know that," explains Ray. "Never looked at Margaret again."

"But I was so sure that when Bessie left Winnipeg, he'd be back with Margaret."

"What are you all carrying on about anyway?" Mr. John Clements says grumpily, setting his glass of port down on a side table and running his fingers over his drooping moustache. "Charles knew who he wanted to marry and he's got the woman of his choice. And Bessie's got a good head on her shoulders and likely knew what she was doing. Damn good-looking woman, too. You've got no right to shop for a man's wife, Elmira. Don't know anything about how she and Charles will get along. That's their business. All I know is that they are two fine people. I like her blue eyes and I like her

132

spunk. And I wish them well. Handed them $50,000 as a wedding present. That should give them a good start. They can build a nice house in Fort Rouge, Bessie can have a little money for that Owen House, and there will be money to invest. Can't see how they can go far wrong with a sum like that for a nest egg. A lot more money than we had when we got married, eh, woman?" Mr. Clements reaches over and pats his wife's hand. "And the times were a lot harder then than now."

"I would have liked to have been at their wedding," reflects Sarah.

"She just wanted a quiet wedding at her home with her family. She definitely did not want a white wedding."

"How strange," says Sarah, who married in a beautiful white lace gown and veil.

"I thought it odd," Cora agrees, "especially when her good friend is such an excellent fashion designer."

"You and Ray were away, Cora," explains Mrs. Clements. "Her friend did design a wardrobe for her. She sent sketches and fabric samples for Bessie to choose from. They're really beautiful. You'll see the clothes when she returns."

Behind her hand Cora whispers to Sarah, "What do you think of Charles taking her to visit all the friends and relatives in Michigan and Ontario?"

Sarah whispers back, "I found it quite enough to see the relatives at my reception. You wouldn't catch me visiting Fred's family on my honeymoon. I'd be bored stiff. How horrible of Charles."

"I know Bessie would have preferred a trip to Europe, but Charles said they could go another time," explains Cora. "He felt he couldn't take so much time from work."

"Of course he could have taken the time." Ray has overheard. "But can you imagine our cousin Charles,

133

hot-footing it all over Europe? Wanted to show his beautiful bride to his relatives."

"How perfectly awful," Sarah is whispering to Cora again. "Worse than displaying wedding presents."

"That's enough, Sarah," Ray is frowning at his sister. "It's just that Charles is very fond of his family, and he's proud of Bessie."

"On about Bessie and Charles still," growls Mr. John Clements. He turns to his new son-in-law. "Pass me a cigar, will you, Fred."

"Now, John, you know your doctor said you shouldn't. You're not as young as you once were."

"No, he didn't say I shouldn't, woman. Said I should use a little discretion and I'm using it. Besides, I'll never be any younger than I am now. Pass the box of cigars, Fred."

"You said the cigar you had after dinner would be your last one."

"It was my last one. This is the next. Stop worrying about me. Nothing like a worrying woman to drive a man crazy."

His wife, trained in knowing when to change the subject, turns to her son-in-law, whose large and handsome frame fills to capacity the well-cushioned chair. "Sarah had me over the other day and showed me that fine full-length oil painting of Sir Wilfrid Laurier you have hung in your sun room."

"Yes, when I first saw it I said it was a fine painting, and Sir Wilfrid gave it to me."

"He must have thought you deserved it. You have done so much for the Liberal Party."

"Only because I believe in it."

Fred Hamilton draws long on his cigar and then, exhaling, says, "Sarah tells me that one of her father's brothers is an inventor and will be coming to Winnipeg soon."

134

J.R. Clements, by now puffing contentedly on his cigar, has been listening in. "That's my brother Ben. Always was good at fixing things from the time he was a young'un. Always wanted to know how things worked. Anything went wrong at the farm it was always 'Get Ben, he'll fix it.' And Ben always did. Great imagination, that one. Always managed to get it together when no one else could. Always figuring out new gadgets. Now his latest invention is a road-building machine. Managed to get a patent for it and he's bringing his machine to Winnipeg. Guess he won't run out of roads to build around here."

"He's Charles' father, did Sarah tell you?" puts in Mrs. Clements.

"I told you, Fred, remember?"

"And you said Charles' father was younger than your father."

"By twelve years. He's still only in his sixties."

"A young man!"

"And still able to smoke a cigar without his wife nattering at him."


2


September 1911

I sit in the rocking chair I purchased for my old Crump Block apartment, looking out from the verandah over an expanse of green lawn decorated with the first bright leaves of autumn. Charles is off in the Model T to visit Uncle Walter and Aunt Josephine. I baked an apple pie and sent it along in my stead. I simply have to have time to myself.

"Have a good rest," Charles told me affably.

So many relatives. All pleasant. But I've had just

135

about enough of them for the time being. Maybe because I so often can't agree with their views, and then too I'd prefer to be at Owen House. And I wish I had more time to read and study. It depresses me to think that since my marriage I've had less time than ever to pursue my own interests, even though I'm no longer working at Cedric Wilkins' office. When I quit work I thought I could give those hours over to the Mission. But it hasn't turned out that way. I miss Wilkins' office and the staff. Housewifery bores me. Housewife! Married to a house. Ha!

I'll not be tied to this house on Church Street any more than I can help. Luckily, Charles is not a demanding person. He's easy, he's pleasant, and he's good about helping out in the kitchen when he has the free time. For which I'm thankful. And he does take me places other than to his relatives. "Anywhere you'd like to go, Lady." He has started calling me "Lady" lately, his term of endearment. I find this amusing, given that I was once referred to as "that tomboy from the other side of town". Maybe I should give Martha's fashions a bit of credit.

So we go to the Walker Theatre, or to the Bijou Theatre (which is in the Clements Block and part of the Clements domain) to see the pictures, with a pianist in the pit playing appropriate melodies, and to watch vaudeville. We spend Sunday afternoon in the parks and sit on a bench listening to a regimental band in an ornate octagonal bandstand as it plays marches, waltzes, and classical selections. Or we go for a picnic in the country, I wrapped in my duster, the picnic basket in the back of the car, singing as we bump over the rough gravel roads, Charles off-key as usual, but vigorous. Then it's "Let's drop in on Uncle Will and Aunt Kitty, or Cousin So-and-so." "Or it's "Let's have them over." There seems no escape. But I must figure out

136

some way to get to Owen House more often without having to bake too many apple pies. Owen House is where my mission lies, and I will not be sidetracked — not that Charles means to sidetrack me. I was aware there were a few relatives around when I married. But heavens! Why does Charles feel it his duty to keep check on all of them and act as intermediary? He's like a mother hen! "I'll make a bowl of onion soup and take it over to Cousin Jane; she has a heavy cold and lives alone. Onion soup is good for clearing a cold.

"Why, Charles, I didn't know you were such a good cook."

"I have all sorts of hidden talents. Just hang around and you'll see."

Funny how little most women know about the men they marry. Surprise, surprise.

As well, he is apt to slip a little money to someone. He will explain if he thinks I've noticed. "Bill's just had an operation and they're a bit short of cash." He is that way with his relatives. But I have no reason to complain. His relatives, in turn, have been generous to me, showering me with goodwill and friendship, always putting out what they have to offer in the way of tea or food, always making me feel welcome.

Generous! Uncle John giving us $50,000 as a wedding present! That's a huge sum of money. Charles and I spent a long time discussing just how it should be used. Charles wanted to spend about $5,000 to build a house in the Fort Rouge area near Ray and Cora. The houses on Wellington Crescent, the holds of the ultra-rich, are worth more than $10,000 apiece and are like palaces, surrounded by their own parks. But I don't want to live in Fort Rouge — not now, and preferably not ever. I prefer a place closer to Owen House, where I can concentrate on what is important to me rather than on furnishings and all the distractions associated

137

with higher living, such as formal entertaining, clubs, and other things which, frankly, bore me to tears. I favoured buying a large lot to the northwest of Owen House, where there are a middle class of people of mixed origin. There a pleasant house could be built for two to three thousand dollars. But Charles is dead set against that. So finally we agreed to settle here for the present, renting a very ordinary but bright and sunny house a fair distance from the mission, but close enough for me to cycle over whenever I choose. Which is far more often than Charles wants me to. He is always saying, "I'll take you in Black Beauty." Black Beauty being the new Model T, named after a favourite horse he had as a boy. Why he has to name his car and put a nameplate below the windscreen, and treat it as though it were alive, I don't know!

"There's no need for you to cycle to Owen House."

"But cycling keeps me slim, Charles."

I'd prefer to see you safe. You know the North End is full of crime, disease, and prostitutes."

"I'm quite healthy and I have nothing to interest either criminals or prostitutes."

"You are a little naive..."

"Oh, do stop worrying, Charles. I'm rather well known in that part of town, and if anyone were to lay a finger on me I'm sure half a dozen people would come to my rescue."

"One might hope so."

Charles is overly protective, and that annoys me. But I know he means well.

No money was put into a house. But as Uncle John had winked at me in front of Charles and mentioned that he hoped some of his gift would be used for my mission, it was agreed that I would have a share for my interests, and Charles an equivalent amount to use as he wished. So I plan to use most of my allowance for a

138

badly-needed renovation of Owen House, including new roof, new windows and storms, new plumbing, new heating system, and playground equipment. Mike has looked after the place quite magnificently to date, but he almost danced with joy when he learned of my plans. New carpets, new draperies: quality that will look good and last well. Practically a new Owen House!

Of the rest of the money I intend to present the Woodsworths with a sum, as a contribution to their many projects, and to send a sum to the mission in China. China — a feeling of guilt remains, for it was my failure, my inability to overcome my hate and my pride... Guilt can be tiring and depressing.

But Owen House is flourishing. There is a large Sunday School class now, and after all, a soul saved in Canada is as valuable as a soul saved in China. Admittedly, part of my desire to go to China arose from my longing to see and learn more about that country — it holds a fascination for me. Perhaps it is not God but myself I have failed. And what was given up was a selfish desire. Or so I rationalize. But if that is so, then why does this feeling of guilt persist?

Charles, with great faith in his father's machine, has invested his portion of Uncle John's gift in the new road-building enterprise. So neither spouse, now or ever, can complain of the other's extravagance in matters of faith. Of course, most of the common portion of the money has been turned right back into Company shares, for after all it is the Company that supplies us with a living.

I was introduced to my in-laws when they arrived in Winnipeg from Minnesota two months ago with the invention. At his father's request Charles had looked around in an attempt to find and ready office space for him. But in the end it was I who located an excellent spot at 840 Notre Dame Avenue — Notre Dame being an

139

important axis road. Little did I guess at the time that I had begun to mark the confines of my future territory, much as does an animal. What can I say but that in the patterning of my life I am a chief conspirator.

Within a few days of the parents' arrival, Charles' father purchased a house on Langside Street. "Because it's just off Notre Dame and handy to the office."

Before they were moved in, Charles drove me by.

"Not too desirable as a home for them," I commented.

"Why not?" he countered. "Too many people of British background on Langside?"

I ignored his jibe. "The houses are too close together, on very small lots."

"No different from most city houses."

"But your parents have lived in the country so much. I should think they'd have preferred a little more space, as I do. It certainly is not what I'd like."

"Well, it's their choice and it's only for a little while. Father has sunk all his money into the machine and places are not only difficult to come by, but this one was a bargain."

After his parents moved in and we went to visit there for the first time, I found myself holding back, reluctant to go in.

"What's the matter, Lady?" Charles was impatient to see his folks.

How could I explain my feelings? I just shook my head and stood by the gate until he took me gently by the arm and guided me up the short walk.

Later I tried to interpret my action to him. "It's so depressing. How could your father have chosen such a place?"

"It's not that bad, surely! I didn't find it so."

"I think your mother's very sweet about it. She's already looking forward to a brighter place where she

140

can have a nice garden. She told me so. And I can well understand that."

"And that will be as soon as Father makes his money — which won't be too long." Charles spoke with some exasperation.

"I think he purchased too hastily. Your father isn't in the house all day long the way your mother is. A longer street-car ride wouldn't have hurt him. I'm sure a brighter, better place could have been found with a little more looking." That was criticizing his father's judgement, and I'm quickly learning that criticism of relatives, especially his father, is not tolerated. I can always tell by the change in his voice when I have made a wrong remark.

"Mother's never one to complain. Besides, what's it got to do with you?"

Why should that house on Langside Street bother me so? I persisted in talking about it. "Imagine building a house six feet or less from the next one and then placing the dining-room window directly opposite the neighbours' window."

"Where else could a window have been put in that room? Mother didn't say it bothered her, did she? Maybe she considers it rather friendly. Townhouses have only a wall between them. Surely you've seen a similar type of house in Detroit?"

No use talking to Charles. Maybe it's something else that distresses me.

Before the parents arrived, Uncle John referred to his brother, Ben, as the little fellow who was a bit of a mechanical genius. So it was somewhat of a surprise to be introduced to a man over six feet tall, broad-shouldered, with a walrus moustache — the only likeness between the brothers being a smile in the light-blue eyes and an almost constant bantering humour that seems to imply that life is not to be taken too

141

seriously.

Once again I was made most welcome, this time by the big man and his wife, who could not be much more than five feet tall. After dinner, and still at the table, while father and son were planning a demonstration of the Clements Road Builder, I sat having a second cup of tea with "Mother". (How strange to say that word.)

She had known Ben since they were children in Ontario. "We lived on neighbouring farms not five miles apart. We grew up together."

"Chris, that's not right. You never grew up." Ben had evidently been listening with one ear.

Then Chris blinked both eyes at me as if she wanted me to understand that this was an old joke between them.

"I never had time to grow up. There was far too much to do. There wasn't such a difference in our heights to begin with. But Ben really got out of hand. We were good friends then. And we're good friends now." She spoke with pride.

The parents-in-law are fine people. But I am always glad to get back to my home on Church Avenue — there's something about that house on Langside Street... Not that my house is anything very much. Just all that I want. (For Charles' sake I must get around to buying more furniture, and decorating. One of these days. Owen House is taking all my attention at the moment.)

No, my mother-in-law is not the complaining type. And I really like her. But I find her devotion to housework downright irritating. Thank goodness for Amy, who comes to look after my cleaning. And my house is simple to clean: no lace doilies, and the few knick-knacks received as wedding presents will never see the light of day if I can help it. Knick-knacks and doilies just make for a lot of unnecessary work. Too bad one just can't live in a tent all year round and cook out-of-doors. But I must consider the uncomplaining amiable Charles, who is more concerned about appearance than I am. At least he was willing to postpone purchasing fine furniture, the "doodads" and the "gee-gaws", until we are both ready to choose a home on "the right side of town".

But I do try to see that good food is prepared for Charles. And I am determined to be a good wife to him. For Charles is a dear and obviously happy with me both in bed and out of bed. And whenever I have a bad dream now, I just snuggle up to him and he puts his arms around me. He knows I have nightmares, but I've never told him about Dickinson or my terrifying dreams of fires, or the pennies I hide under the log and lose. And I doubt I ever will. I can't talk to him the way I could talk to Richard. He is so — well, down-to-earth. Somehow he wouldn't understand. Oh, Charles is a sympathetic listener about some things — people, mainly. And of course I would never tell him about Richard.

Also, though I'm quickly finding out how much I have in common with the Woodsworths and their political views, I have to be very careful what I say about that to Charles. I discovered that early on. Already I've opened my mouth too much in front of relatives and friends who I can plainly see are attempting to be tolerant and who regard my ideas as a bit of a joke. I grow warm just remembering some of those moments. Sometimes I wonder if Charles ever takes me seriously when I talk about things that are happening in the North End. Last time I mentioned the need for a workers' union he immediately put an end to the conversation by saying, "I really don't like your cycling around the North End. You know the place is full of criminals and prostitutes. The Reverend Dobson said Winnipeg could claim title as vice

143

capital of the country, and the North End is where it can all be found."

I've heard it all before. "That is not the point I'm making."

"You worry me."

"Well, stop worrying, for you'll not stop me."

And he settled himself behind his newspaper, rustling it to indicate displeasure.

When we were married in Detroit Ma said, "I'm glad to see you've got such a good man and you're able to do your mission work in Winnipeg. Still, I'm a bit sorry you won't be in China — I'm looking forward to travelling there one of these days."

And I said, "Maybe we can go together in a few years.

And Ma said, "I'd like that." She meant it.

Oh, Ma, let's not let anything stop us!

Everyone in Detroit thought Charles wonderful. Ma talked real estate and development with him. Andy had great fun with his soon-to-be brother-in-law. Beatrice and Belle were charmed. And Martha found him so delightful that I wondered if she secretly wished he could have been her husband-manager-secretary-accountant. Martha. There was so much entertaining, so much to do, so many friends and well-wishers about that we managed only an hour alone together. I wanted to say so much and tell her the thoughts I could not commit to paper. I wanted to explain that I married Charles out of need if not love, because I felt my action required an explanation — and because I needed to unburden myself. And I wanted to tell her that I was truly fond of him, that he was my good friend. But she started off almost immediately with a most ridiculous remark.

"Do you realize there are still people in this world who believe the earth is flat?"

144

"So I've heard, but—"

"It's odd, isn't it, with all the evidence to the contrary."

"Seems impossible..."

"Isn't it the same with evolution? One just has to observe to see that the earth is much more than four thousand years old."

Was she trying to trap me?

"Please don't get into that, Martha, we have so little time together."

"I don't want to get into that. What I want to say is that there are such widely different points of view that we shouldn't get caught with one idea and say that's it. We should be always searching for truth."

"So?"

"If one were forced to live permanently in a certain part of the Canadian prairie, say in a part of Manitoba, and were never to read a book or hear anything to the contrary, one could easily believe the world to be flat. But try to reach the horizon, say in a ship the way Magellan did, and the world one discovers is round."

"What are you trying to get at, for pity's sake? If one lived on the prairies, one wouldn't be near an ocean-going ship."

"That's only an example. Another is that for ages people believed there was a consciousness, or God, in everything..."

"That's pantheism. A pagan belief."

"Many Christians believe that God created a world apart from Him and that is why souls have to be saved, as you believe. But what if a transcendental Being is not only above, but also part of, all? As some Unitarians believe. Then it is likely right that all creatures of His creation will ultimately reach a fully enlightened state and there is no need to save souls. Just guide people towards the good. Understanding and loving one

145

another, as Jesus said..."

"Another one of your long speeches," I said coldly. "You've been talking to the de Chênes and I've no time for that sort of thing today."

Martha was taken aback by my attitude and looked crestfallen. I didn't care; she had no right to say such things.

"But Bessie, I've been waiting to tell you something about what I've read, and the conclusions I've come to. I thought you'd be interested."

I wasn't interested. What was she trying to do? Make chaos out of my already upside-down world?

"What would you think if you were me?" I asked her. "I don't care to hear you say once again that missionaries are unnecessary and that I'm wasting my time, and souls are not in need of saving and all I believe in is wrong. Let's just leave the subject by agreeing that you have your opinions and I have mine."

"And only God knows who is right and who is wrong," Martha added quietly. "I am certainly not saying that everything you believe in is wrong, Bessie. And it probably does no harm to save souls. In some instances it might even be helpful. At worst I'd say you were wasting your time."

My perspicacious friend and I have had many arguments over the years. Indeed, pitting my wits against Martha's was something I once looked forward to. And we would leave the battleground laughing and ready for the next fray. But this day it was different. I was on edge and her remarks were upsetting and alien. I was properly miffed.

"Perhaps you have another long speech ready for me on the subject of astrology?" Having written suggesting it would be wiser for her to forget such matters, I hoped she might recognize my sarcasm. But she was unheeding.

146

"No, but I thought you might like to know that just about now Saturn has come into a position that means responsibilities for you."

"I thought Saturn was the symbol for restriction." I was still being sarcastic — or was I?

"That too."

"A fine thing for you to say when I'm marrying Charles tomorrow. And what would it be if I had gone to China?"

"No different. Maybe Carl would have recognized in your chart the fact that there was to be a sudden change in plans and you would not get to China."

"Well, I've had quite enough of this astrology nonsense about restrictions and frustrations. I'm marrying a fine man and I'm enjoying my work at Owen House and I don't believe Charles is a person who will ever interfere with my plans. He is a most helpful and kind individual. Not at all authoritarian like Richard..."

Richard. A spasm of pain grips me as I recall the night before the wedding and the almost uncontrollable desire I had to go to him. How impossible. Charles is a fine person. I must not let him down. Then at the reception a friend of Ma's mentioned that Richard and Lydia had a son — a beautiful boy, the friend had added, looking obliquely at me to get my reaction. How appalling the wave of jealousy. Ma must have known about the baby and hadn't told me. Belle hadn't told me. How dare Richard! Lydia was one thing. But a son that should have been ours! My passion on my wedding night was anger turned against Richard.

I get up and pace the verandah, an unconscious attempt to get away from myself, from a situation and my thoughts. I'm shivering. The days are drawing in, the nights growing cold. I must go in and make a cup of tea.

147

**3**

July 1912

Sunshine brightens the room and sparkles on the brass bedstead. In camisole and petticoat I open the closet door.

Charles is suddenly alert. "Why not wear the blue silk?" He is referring to the dress I wore when we first met.

"Much too dressy for the occasion. And don't you dare think of wearing your morning suit, or anything like it. I'll wear the old powder-blue skirt with a ruffled blouse. That's the thing. I don't want the Manekowskis to feel out of place.

"They'll be at the reception?"

"But of course. It's their home and they are my special friends. Besides, Mike has done so much. He's supervised the remodelling and repairs, as well as working hard in every way. I wouldn't dream of holding a reception at Owen House without them. If I had my way the entire staff would be in the reception line instead of serving. It's a big day for them too. They've all worked with such enthusiasm to make our Open House a success."

Charles says, hesitatingly, "It's not done, Bessie, to invite caretakers. There will be a number of people from Fort Rouge and Armstrong's Point and ~

I interrupt. "The Manekowskis are different. And the Woodsworths will be there along with some of their co-workers." No doubt I sound the way I feel: defiant.

He ignores my tone. "Who will be receiving besides yourself?"

"Only the directors: the Wilkinses, the Shaws, Doris Whiting, Ethel, and myself. Why? Are you worried that the Manekowskis might insist the South End bow and curtsy?"

148

"It is not appropriate for the caretakers to be among the guests. I'm surprised the Shaws approved."

"They didn't. There is very little that 'Oh, Pshaw' approves. I insisted. And as I was the one who had put up the money, I got my way. Money is power, you know."

"He has contributed a great deal of money and time to the Owen House project."

"That he has and I've often wondered why."

"Because it's the thing to do to take an interest in a charitable organization. Haven't you noticed the write-ups about Oscar Shaw in 'Town Topics'? 'His selfless style of life, his liberal offerings to the poor.' Didn't you know Owen House was mentioned as one of his chief charities?"

"I have little time to read that magazine. It just tells about the social whirl of Winnipeg's elite. Who's left for Florida. Who's returned from Europe. Who wears what to the theatre. Who cares! Oscar likes to get his picture about. I might have guessed."

I pause as a thought strikes me.

"Charles, do you think he's doing all this for Oscar Shaw?"

"In large measure."

"He should be working at Owen House for God, or for people and children in need, which is the same thing. 'What you do unto the least of these my brethren you do unto me.'"

"Probably that too, but my guess is, the underlying motive is a personal one. However, he is a good person and I do believe Diane, especially, is sincere about her work — and a hard worker."

"The two of them are constant problems. But I'm still managing to control matters of importance with the help of Ethel and the Wilkinses. But the Shaws are trouble I could well do without. God works in mysterious ways,

149

but I'm still wondering why He sent those two to Owen House."

"Oscar went there because of his image as a public benefactor. It could be that one of these days you'll see him running for public office."

"Well, he can't run fast enough for me. You see, Charles, I've been tainted by your humour! If anything happens to spoil our glorious hour this afternoon, you can be sure who'll be the spoiler."

"I can imagine who might spark the spoiler."

"I promise I'll try one of Ma's methods today. I'll acknowledge his presence with a nod and keep my distance. I've already taken the precaution of asking Ethel to stand next to me in the reception line."

"And after the reception let me take you to dinner at the Fort Garry. You were up at dawn and off to the House. You've been working too hard."

"I like your idea. I'm half dead on my feet, actually. But I'm so pleased everything is turning out well. Hasn't it been a good year for us in so many ways — even the weather?"

"In every way. A good spring. A good summer. And here's another bright and sunny afternoon."

"It couldn't be better for the reception."

"Well, if you're ready, let's go. Black Beauty's been groomed and awaits us at the curb."

Outside, Charles opens the black and brightly polished car door; I step on the running board and then in. Charles closes the door, moves to the front of the Model T, smiles and pats the hood, acknowledging Black Beauty as he might a horse. Then he cranks the car: one-two-three turns. One-two-three turns more. One-two-three again — and she starts! He jumps into the driver's seat, and we're off with a toot of the horn for whoever might be watching. (After all, there are not many automobile owners on our avenue.)

150

As Owen House comes in sight I can't help saying, "Please, Charles, park and let's sit and admire the House a bit. Do you realize the last bit of paint went on just yesterday?"

"Yes, I think I heard about that."

"If you could have seen the house that winter's day..."

"I saw it last year looking a bit dilapidated."

"When Mike had already done so much work on it. Wouldn't you agree we've awakened a Sleeping Beauty?"

"It's a fine house. Stands out like a sore thumb in this neighbourhood."

"Like a beautiful flower, Charles. Charles, I have an idea."

"Oh, not another!" He strikes his forehead in mock surprise.

"I want to buy the house next in the row and turn it into a home for unwanted children."

"Sufficient unto the day is the evil thereof."

"You said sore thumb and you said evil. And you're wrong on both counts. Let's go in. I want to see that the tables are set and everything is properly arranged. How many guests do you think there will be ?"

Charles thinks that most invited from the South of Winnipeg will be on hand. He's right. But I would not have been so pleased had I known the reason, which I learned later from Ethel. Charles knew, but wisely refrained from telling me. Luckily I had not read the write-up in "Town Topics": "Thanks to the good will and generosity of one of Winnipeg's well-known entrepreneurs, Oscar Shaw Esquire, a mission building in the North End, known as Owen House, has been completely overhauled and refurbished. It stands as a model of enterprise and charity to all who will be fortunate enough to view it this coming Saturday. By invitation only."

151

Women, *haute couture*, are arriving, carrying parasols of light flowered fabric to match their soft, clinging, floor-length dresses, accentuated by over-tunics in contrasting colour, with low necklines and sides curved and cut to meet trim-belted waistlines. Small head-hugging hats on well-groomed hair. Tall plumes standing high. Women in white with white hats and men with white starched collars and imported custom-tailored suits. Just the thing for the North End ghetto! All out to view the newsworthy charity. Rather, to view one another and, above all, to be seen and to be seen associating with that charitable and outstanding business man, Oscar Shaw Esquire.

Ethel, next to me in line, whispers, "One might think the ladies are attending a royal garden party."

"Was it the word 'reception' that confused them?"

"Maybe they never heard of the North End."

"That's my guess."

Also mingling with the fashionable is that controversial character, J.S. Woodsworth — radical, socialist, lecturer, journalist — accompanied by his wife and a couple of other family members. To be gawked at, if not always talked with, by the many here who disagree with his sentiments. But always worth a few whispered comments (if not now, then later over a hand of whist). And quite a few of Woodsworth's socialite volunteers are among those present.

"Look, just imagine," I overhear a lady of high fashion say, "there's Sandra Butler. She told me just now she's working with That Man at All People's Mission. And would you believe it! Of all things: Daisy from the shirt-manufacturing Wilsons of Wellington Crescent. Believe you me, one might do well to speak to her. And Ethel Reid in the reception line. One of the directors, evidently. She's a strange character — looking a bit dowdy, as always. Everyone knows she doesn't get

152

along with James. They say he has a paramour. And who is that young woman with the dark eyes? See — over there, with the chestnut hair and scarred face. Wearing that embroidered blouse and the awful brown skirt. Rather attractive if it weren't for the disfigurement. A bit haughty in her bearing — doesn't match the clothes. Whoever can she be?"

I look at Gedda. Maybe she's feeling out of place with so much focus on fashion. Mother Clements is nearby, chatting to a group of ladies. I move aside briefly and whisper to her. She nods, excuses herself, and in short time is talking to Gedda, whose face brightens perceptibly. Lana joins them and it's obvious immediately that Mother is as charmed with the golden-haired girl as Lana is delighted to be with the little lady. Another conquest. Conquest comes easily to both: they are completely unselfconscious. Will Lana's beauty spoil her in the future? I hope not. She has taken Mother's hand. Mother has no doubt introduced herself as Auntie Chris; she's Auntie Chris to almost everyone. Lana is pointing upstairs, apparently wanting to show her something. And as the three leave the room, I breathe a sigh of relief for Gedda. What if they found out she's the caretaker's wife?

The guests are wandering about, taking a tour of the house by themselves, or with a director or friend of Owen House. Some are taking tea, talking in groups. Fred Hamilton approaches, holding a cup and a sandwich.

"Bessie, a beautiful job. Congratulations. Now, I've heard you before and I'm sure I'll hear you again on the subject that education should be looked after by the City, and that people should not have to rely on charity."

I laugh. "That's correct. Are you aware that there are almost ten thousand children in this city between the

153

ages of six and sixteen who are not attending school? Charity can try all it might, but only compulsory school education and laws forbidding child labour will take care of the problem."

"Well, Bessie, that's the hope of the Liberal Party."

"I know Sir Wilfrid Laurier is your friend. A fine old gentleman. Too bad he was voted out of office last year because of his stand on the naval bill. I agree with him that Canada should have her own navy, independent of the Motherland."

"That's right. Laurier is seventy-two years of age, but in my estimation a far better man than our Conservative Robert Laird Borden — who I fear will get this country into a real mess in double-quick time. It's a common belief that the Mother country can be counted on to look after the best interests of Canada, that as the King's government and Foreign Office are all-wise and all-knowing, Canada will stand behind any decision made in London. But I think these can be dangerous assumptions."

"My feeling about Sir Wilfrid has been that he is something of a pragmatist, trying to please too many people." But not wanting to get into a long political discussion, I change the subject abruptly. "Well, anyway," I say brightly, "so far all is rosy. Real estate is selling as it's never sold before. It's been a good year in almost every way..."

"Bessie, how can you say it's been such a good year?" Doris Whiting is standing by my elbow with her husband. "Don't forget the Titanic went down in April!"

"I hope you don't mean it's a portent of further disaster, Mrs. Whiting." This from Fred.

"Those poor souls," she says. "I can't help wondering: was it everyone's destiny on that ship to drown that day — I mean, those who did drown?"

I am thankful that Fred replies. "That would mean

154

that life is planned for each of us from birth, and I can't go along with that."

Doris is about to start up again, but her husband intervenes. "I'll never forget it. I was heading to the office when I heard a newsboy yelling, 'Extra! Extra! Disaster at sea!' I couldn't believe my eyes when I saw it meant the Titanic. Unsinkable. They swore it was unsinkable."

"It was terrible," Doris continues. "We had a friend on board. Or rather, a friend of a friend..."

I leave them discussing the tragedy that no one can forget and move on to mix with the other guests. I wave to Sandy, who throws me a kiss. She is doing an excellent job of making everyone comfortable. Her soft-yellow dress is charming without being overdone. Sandy has a way of always striking a balance.

After more than an hour of talking and explaining, I move to the dining room for tea and am selecting a watercress-and-egg sandwich when I hear two women talking behind me.

"Over there. Mr. Woodsworth talking to that Manekowski."

"Handsome, isn't he?"

"Manekowski? Handsome, maybe. But handsome is as handsome does. And my husband said that an international workers' union was formed in the United States just a few years ago and is starting to organize in Canada. I wouldn't be surprised at all if that Manekowski were involved. You just wait and see. My husband says that Manekowski spells trouble."

"My husband thinks Woodsworth is every bit as bad."

Without turning I leave the dining room. Charles will be proud of me. But then maybe it would be wiser not even to mention this to Charles.

In the large drawing room the incessant din of a few dozen conversations is overwhelming. But by now some

155

people are leaving. I pause to bite at my sandwich and notice Father Clements with a group of men. I draw near, then hesitate. Of course they won't be discussing Owen House. I catch snatches of conversation. I might have known, it's that all-consuming topic: the road-building machine.

" The initial demonstration out Pembina was a great success."

It is the proud inventor speaking, glowing and expansive.

"...ploughing everything right back into the business...can hardly keep up to work requests...can't build the machines fast enough."

"Is ploughing it all back in wise?"

"Sure. Can't lose. The city's expanding in all directions..."

I've heard it all before. Mother's planning her new home the other side of the Osborne Street bridge. Everyone is riding high. Well, at the moment so am I, with Owen House moving along the way it is. To each his own.

A lady in white is saying to a lady in blue, "I'd say a lot of good money has been wasted on this place. If people are poor it's God's will, and this won't help them — only make them envious and greedy."

"Dissatisfied is the word. I say charity begins at home. God helps those who help themselves."

"Did you see the way those classrooms are fixed up? About as classy as a private school. And notice the quality of the cloth in the draperies..."

"And the carpets. Imagine! And there's even one of those new electric vacuum cleaners. I saw it."

"It's much too posh a place for a lot of good-for-nothing immigrants. They'll not get a penny from me."

"Shush! Look who's here."

I allow myself a cold stare before moving on. Hardly

156

satisfying when there is so much I'd like to say to them. Does inaction make me canny or a coward? Eager to enter the fray, yet determined not to upset other potential donors, I turn away and head for the kitchen.

Sitting — or rather, slumped — at a well-scrubbed harvest table, as far as possible removed from the clatter and chatter of cleaning up, is Ethel Reid, sipping coffee. She looks up and gives me a wide smile.

"Just had to rest my tootsies. But whatever is the matter with you? Has someone been giving you a bad time?"

Having noticed Ethel's coffee, I sniff and follow my nose to the sideboard. After helping myself, I return to sit by my friend.

I point to my cup. "Maybe this will help, but I'm not sure. Ethel, I think I've heard just about the most ignorant, thoughtless, selfish statements imaginable." I explain at length, mimicking and gesturing for emphasis.

Ethel laughs. "What did you expect? That the fashionable set would all come out and line up behind Woodsworth? If some pledge a little money, that is all that can be hoped for. Let me tell you what I heard. I was giving Sally Prince and Sheila Lang a personal tour. They're friends of Diane Shaw's. You don't know them and wouldn't want to. I was explaining about the new bathroom and doctor's office off the kitchen here, telling them how the children have to be checked, deloused, and cleaned. Sally wanted to know what I meant by 'deloused', and I had to explain about lice. Don't they ever read the papers?"

"Probably only the social column."

"After shrieking a bit, as though they expected lice to come popping out of the corners, Sheila wanted to know why the foreigners can't take baths in their own homes. When I said it was unlikely they had bathtubs, she

157

suggested they use washbasins."

"Reminds me of Marie Antoinette. If the poor have no bread, 'let them eat cake'. It seems a lot of these people have come out because of Oscar Shaw. Ethel, why didn't the Shaws set up their own charity when they can well afford it?"

"That's easy. The groundwork was already laid at Owen House and the place running like clockwork — though Diane would never admit that. Besides, there are not many locations around here quite like this."

"I'd be willing to help them look for one."

"You know, I was wondering before you came whether I could afford to take a holier-than-thou attitude towards Sally and Sheila. I give a little help and enjoy every moment doing it. I give a little money I can easily afford, and at the end of the day I return to all the comforts of a fine home with servants to cosset me."

"Enough of this self-analysis. And don't feel you have to apologize to Sally and Sheila. But, you know, that makes me wonder. Perhaps you're right, Ethel, perhaps we have little reason to feel superior to the Sallys and Sheilas of this city. Where do you and I really stand? If it came to a showdown, would we line up behind Woodsworth and Mikhail?"

"Speak of the Devil. Here comes Mike with a cup of coffee and a broad grin. Welcome, Mike, and join the weary crew."

Mike straddles a chair. "The Woodsworths and most of the people from the missions have left, so I thought it time for me to leave. Mr. Woodsworth is a wonderful person. A real saint."

"Tell me, Mike," I ask, "do you belong to the International Workers of the World?"

"That I do. And I belong to the Labour Party. Why?"

"Because your name is being bandied about. You're considered to be a dangerous man. So is Woodsworth."

158

"I'm honoured to have my name linked with Woodsworth. But I'm afraid I'm not very dangerous — unfortunately. The Labour Party members insist on fighting among themselves, and until they can hold behind a single purpose, they will never be very effective."

"And what single purpose would you wish on them?"

"A stand for decent wages. With decent wages child labour would no longer be required to help provide food for a family."

Ethel speaks up. "I've seen it with my own eyes. I went visiting with Mike and Gedda just last week. Some of the shacks we were in were appalling. Dimly lit, and children of six and maybe eight years of age doing piece work or sewing buttons on dresses. Wearing out their eyes, the poor, white-faced, skinny little tykes. Slaves, that's what they are. When they should be playing in the sunshine."

"It's only a strong union that can take a stand against the business class, which keeps forcing wages down," says Mike. "And I intend to do what I can to unite the workers."

"Mike," I ask, "are you aware that the business community will consider any interference with their established practices heresy?"

"I can't worry about what they think. I must do what I can to change a sorry situation. And I can't figure another way out of this mess except through the unions." Then anger leaves his voice. "Have you heard Woodsworth is planning a survey of the working man's budget? He intends to let the government know how much the workers make and how they spend their money. I hope it will shock a few good people into action. No grass grows on that man Woodsworth."

Mike's English is now very good, but not his English sayings. Ethel and I laugh and say in unison, "You

159

mean, 'under his feet', Mike."

Mike turns to me, concern in face and voice. "Would you go along with a heretic?"

"Yes, Bessie," Ethel says, half teasingly, half seriously, "that's what we were talking about just now. Which side of the fence are you on? Business or working class?"

After spending so much time in my North End mission, I know Mike is not wrong. Looking him straight in the eyes, I say in a firm voice, "I believe that now is the time for heretics."

He returns my steady gaze. Mine falters. I look down at my beautifully-tailored four-year-old suit skirt, still good style. "My sympathies are with the working class, Mike, you know that. But still I live with the business world — and engage in business activities. It seems that the truth of the matter is I'm right in the centre, hoping the day won't come when I have to stand up and be counted."

"Ah, there you are." It's Charles. "I've been looking in all the corners. Thought you'd be curled up fast asleep by now. How are you, Ethel? And — Manekowski?"

"Sir." Mike stands up.

Charles continues, "The afternoon has been a great success. Congratulations to all of you. I believe Owen House and the other North End missions will be getting a fair amount of help as a result of this day. I've heard nothing but admiration for the work you've done here."

How like Charles to emphasize the positive.

"Are you ready, Lady? Shall we go? You've scarcely eaten today." Concerned, as ever.

"Yes, do go, Bessie," Ethel urges me. "I understand you were here long before me this morning. I'm happy to stay and see that everything is looked after."

Mike is still standing. "I'll see that all is in order for your Sunday School," he says. "Don't worry about

160

another thing."

"Thank you, Ethel, and thank you, Mike. Your offers are gratefully accepted. All right, Charles, let's go. I am hungry, so hungry I could eat your Black Beauty."

## 4

*Detroit, September 15, 1912*

*Dear Daughter,*

*Pa, Belle, and I saw Andy off to his University the other day. He's tickled pink. He got into the State University with good marks. I'm tickled too. I didn't have much education — I had to help my mother with her work just like you had to work. And just like you I would have liked to have been able to study more at school. But girls in my days weren't expected to know too much — just how to cook and sew and look after children. But now Andy's started thanks to you and my hope is that an education will broaden his mind and make his life easier. It was good of you to send the money to get him started. Andy says that when he becomes a lawyer and making money he means to help fund that Mission of yours. I know he's written to you some but I'm to tell you he will write again once he gets settled. Martha was over the other day. We hadn't seen one another for some time and it was good to have her. She wanted to know the latest news about you and I told her you haven't been writing so much lately guess you've been busy with married life and everything but that you was doing splendid. You got yourself a good husband and was doing what you want to do at that Owen House Mission. It's all good except that you are not in China where you want to be. So then I had to make a thrust at Martha — in fun of course as she knows I'm so fond of her — I said, so much for Grand Crosses and*

161

*frustration, what do you say to that, Martha. Maybe our Bessie got herself out of a fix and fooled the stars by staying in North America. So Martha had to tell me all about how symbols like Saturn could be interpreted in two different ways. Like nothing is ever bad or good she said, it is just the emphasis that is put on something. Responsibility for instance is always a form of restriction and if you can accept and enjoy responsibility it won't appear so restricting. So we had a laugh when I said it was a fine way of wiggling out of a mistake. Then she said it is probably all happening as it is supposed to happen which sounded to me like we are so many cosmic puppets. To which she replied quoting her friend Carl, that free will is simply the choice to accept cheerfully the situation we find ourselves in. Which doesn't seem much of a choice to me. And when I put that to Winifred de Chêne, Win said that is why reincarnation is necessary so that souls can build on many different experiences. If I was God — if there is a God — I would not have left so many dratted riddles for people to solve. I would have written the rules so there wasn't the least doubt in anyone's mind as to what course to take. I find it all very untidy. But I had a fine time with your friend with all the talk. I wished you had been there, you would have enjoyed it.* [Or would Bessie? She would have before that run-in with Dickinson when he put the fear of the Lord into her. Well, I'll find out for she won't mince words in her reply. She's a strange one, my well-beloved daughter, with her liberal ideas and her boxed-in beliefs.]

*Martha is not having an easy time for Mrs. Schrieter is getting harder to manage. But she doesn't complain — just admitted she's had some bitter moments because of her dreams gone wrong. She has good help now and is managing all right and getting out more though her life can't be too lively. However by nature she's a*

162

*contemplative person though I don't have to tell you that. She says she had her fling when she was younger, says now her life is a challenge, but that's not so different from most people. That's just life.*

*Love from your Ma*

"Humph!" Ma thinks as she signs the letter, "I wonder if the church wouldn't consider Martha and her friend Carl's ideas heretical. But then wherever would we be without heretics! If God is on the side of progress — which I sometimes doubt — then He needs such people to keep the world going. He needs undertakers to clear away the deadwood and heretics to sow new ideas. Why should people have to stick to the established party line or be damned?"

## 5

April 1913

Winter's snows, reluctant to leave, are piled in dirty patches at the roadsides throughout the city and show white in the fields beyond. Though it's still somewhat cold, spring is determinedly on the way. The sun is shining, the sky blue, and Black Beauty bumps happily along with top up and eisenglas fastened securely in place. Winter has done its usual damage. Potholes are everywhere and cannot be avoided, while ruts and depressions, filled with water beyond the reaches of the pavement, keep us dancing from side to side. It is hardly the weather to picnic.

"A bit coolish, don't you think," was Charles' comment.

"The warmest day since winter. Put on your long johns and a warm sweater, and I'll take a couple of extra blankets. We both need fresh air."

"You mean you need fresh air. You always need fresh air."

"It'll do you good. You're looking a bit pale. And I feel fine."

"If it's an excuse you're looking for to get me out, you don't need one. I'm game for a drive."

He is always game for a drive, if not for a picnic on so cool a day.

So we go. Searching for signs of spring. Stopping to pick crocuses near the Mennonite village with its picturesque white-washed houses and flat fields of rich black soil. Noting the birds and the occasional wild fowl. Stopping to buy a bucketful of gasoline at a grocery store. Taking pictures with our new accordian Kodak camera, for we belong to a camera club and Charles has built and equipped a darkroom in the basement of our home. It really is his hobby, for goodness knows I have little time for such an activity, enjoyable though it be. The drive to St. Andrew's Locks is a favourite outing. Built only two years ago, the year we were married, the Locks have made navigation possible by way of Lake Winnipeg and several rivers to Hudson Bay and west as far as Edmonton. Already 99,000 tons of freight have passed that way. The province is rightly proud of its acquisition. The day brings colour to the cheeks of the present explorers, colour to the trees. And the water in the Locks sparkles. And our spirits rise.

*     *     *     *     *

Home again.

"It's been a wonderful day, Charles. I don't want it spoiled. I'd far rather stay home and develop our pictures." I mean it.

"Anything but go to the Shaws'."

164

"They bring out the worst in me. I can't help it, Charles. I look at them and get prickly all over."

"That's obvious to everyone, I'm afraid. Why can't you make a point of talking to the other guests? There will be a number of people for dinner and it was good of them to invite us."

"They only invite me because I'm your wife and you because you're Uncle John's nephew."

"Oh, I think there could be other reasons why they invite me. Try not to be so negative."

"Whenever I meet them socially, it seems impossible for them not to make some inane, insane, inept, incorrect, ignorant comment about China or the Chinese. Almost as though to barb me."

"Now you are just taking personally what probably is not meant as such. Promise me you won't get prickly about any comment they might make that has to do with China - or anything else for that matter."

Taking me by the shoulders, he looks seriously at me. I know, only too well, that he has been annoyed and embarrassed by my frequent flare-ups. I don't plan them. They just happen.

"I promise, Charles." Attempting to be the demure wife is so unlike me; I doubt if Charles is fooled.

"Well, get yourself dressed, we should leave within the hour." He gives me a kiss before releasing me.

"You know," he continues conversationally, upstairs now and turning to his closet, "the Shaws have had their new home on Wellington Crescent completely redecorated. And I understand this to be the first time they are entertaining since it has been completed."

I can't help sighing, "I know only too well. Diane has hardly been able to think of anything else but that house for weeks. And she's been so coy about it all. It's to be a great surprise. Like the opening night of Grand Opera."

165

"Well, be nice to her. It's her dream house. One of these days we'll have ours. Tonight she is the prima donna. Give her her due. Compliment her on the decorations. There — that is something you can talk about with her."

And not being able to leave well enough alone, he adds with great indiscretion, "You know, you've been prejudiced about the Shaws right from the beginning."

I'm indignant. "You said yourself that very first evening I met you, that they're not the easiest people to get along with."

I'm angry. "And I am not a person given to prejudice. You know that. Prejudice has nothing to do with the matter. They have been a source of trouble and difficulty..."

Charles has evidently decided now is the time to shave. I hear him close the bathroom door gently behind him.

I hurl my bathrobe on the bed. Tears come to my eyes. He has left to avoid an argument. Coward! Anything to avoid an argument. Too nice to slam the bathroom door. Too gentle a person to shout at me. Well, I'm not such a nice person. I reach into the closet, remove my dress, and slam the door with a resounding bang.

\*    \*    \*    \*    \*

Charles has no idea how strong have been the tensions at Owen House since a few days after the reception when Oscar Shaw called for an extraordinary meeting of the directors. Sandy phoned me. It was on a Saturday when no activities were scheduled at the House.

"I don't know what it's all about, Bessie. Mr. Shaw asked me to call a meeting for tonight. Said it's

166

important." She sounded worried.

"Anything wrong, Sandy?" I was surprised at the tone of her voice. The Reception had been pronounced a great success by one and all. "Has it something to do with money?"

"I haven't the least idea, Bess. He didn't say. Just sounded more than usually perturbed — to put it mildly."

Oscar and Diane, the last to arrive for the meeting, entered like a threatening storm. Shaw's brows were drawn, his eyes glinting. Scarcely waiting for all to be seated, he turned to me and said, bluntly, "I want that Manekowski fired. I want him out."

I was thunderstruck. I looked around at all the startled faces, noticing that Doris, alone, was smiling, evidently already in the know and agreeing it seemed, as usual, with the Shaws. In the complete silence that followed his request I asked, "Why?"

"Because he's a dangerous man. That's why. He's a Labour man, a member of the International Workers of the World. I've had him checked out and he's doing his best to stir up trouble in our city. He's a radical. He's been caught talking to the men in a factory I own..."

"It's a free country and Mr. Manekowski has every right to do what he wishes — without your interference."

"He's insolent and sometimes doesn't even bother to acknowledge us," put in Diane with more than a little heat. "And besides, he's Catholic..."

"Keep to the point," her spouse interrupted. "If Manekowski treads on my rights as a businessman, I'll interfere in every way I know how."

"Perhaps as a labourer he feels you're not allowing him his rights."

"This country, Mrs. Clements, in case you are unaware — and certainly by your attitude you appear to

167

be ignorant of the matter — this country stands for free enterprise. This country and this city is as great as it is today because of business. And we'll not have any bohunk like Manekowski upsetting the order."

"Mr. Shaw, let me point out a few errors in your last statement. Let me point out that free enterprise at the moment has value only for the few and not for the many, and the country belongs to all of its citizens, who have every right to share in its wealth. The city would be great if it were not that a large part of it is rotten because of poverty and neglect — due to the fact that free enterprise allows the wealthy to prey on the defenseless. Free is only for the affluent. Workers are forced to accept long hours and unfair wages. Farmers accept prices as though set by some divine authority — an authority they feel they have no right to question. Most women are second-class citizens with no rights whatsoever, no right to vote, no rights either in, or to, their home. Some work unbelievably long hours and are little better than slaves. They are slaves! Only the rich get richer while some, Mr. and Mrs. Shaw — because I believe it is you who are ignorant of the situation, though this surprises me because you are connected with this mission — some people are starving. To make this city great there is much that has to be corrected. Mr. Manekowski, who is Polish, might be trying to help correct some wrongs. In that you could be right. But the derogatory term you use is a reflection on your own self..."

"Oh, Bessie," it was Sandy who stopped me just as I was wound up and in full oratorical flight. "We won't let Mike go. I'm sure that isn't what Mr. Shaw means."

"You bet that's what I mean." Shaw, turkey red, fell into the error of his wife. "Having that man standing around at the reception — a common labourer acting as though he were one of the directors..."

168

"He was a guest and he is a very important part of this mission project." Shaw was going too far. The impertinence of the man! "He was my invited guest and you well know it. That was all settled before the reception."

"The point today happens to be his politics."

Here Ethel put her oar in thoughtlessly: "The Woodsworths knew Mike for a long time before he came to Owen House and they get along well together."

"Of that I have no doubt."

"If the Manekowskis go, I go." By this time, along with the Shaws, I had lost my temper. Would I actually have resigned, falling again into the same error I had with Dickinson? This time not out of hate but because of my fondness and admiration for Mikhail?

"Now let's have a little order in this meeting. It's nothing more than a shouting match." Cedric Wilkins, the present Chairman, in turn shouting from the end of the table. Bringing me to my senses.

"Bessie, we couldn't do without you, you know that," Sandy whispered loudly down the table.

"But we could do without the Shaws," I said in a voice that carried well in a room that had finally fallen silent once more.

"Order, order," Cedric Wilkins called. "Come now. Let's get on with this meeting properly. Mr. Shaw, please present your reasons for wanting the dismissal of Mikhail Manekowski. Then we will have a civilized discussion on the subject and call a vote according to the rules."

In the end, though the Shaws lost their case, the incident did not serve to improve matters between us, and for some weeks our relationship was strained to the breaking point. Though well aware of my feelings toward them, Diane now has invited me to her home. Is it a Christian attitude on their part? Forgive and forget.

169

Charles says so. Says that even though I might not agree with some of their values, they are fine people. My attitude toward them is not so charitable. Sweetness was never my strong point.

But Charles must go to the Shaws' and I must go along for his sake.

By the time Charles emerges from the bathroom with a patch of shaving cream showing near his left ear and an apprehensive glance in my direction, I have recovered and am into my dress.

* * * * *

The Shaw house is a splendid piece of architecture, surrounded by trees still void of leaves, their branches tracing pencil-like patterns against the stone work. As we walk towards the door, Charles turns to me, face long, lips tight.

I answer to his unspoken words. "Yes, Charles, I'll do my best to behave."

And taking my hand, he tucks it through his arm.

Upon our knocking, the door opens to a blaze of light. As the maid takes our wraps, coming toward us with arms outstretched is Diane herself, dressed in slim black pantaloons which show beneath a knee-length tunic. Oh my! And in that instance my eyes have taken in not only Diane Shaw in pantaloons but two tall Chinese vases which grace the wide entrance to the drawing room, and beyond the entrance a painted Chinese lacquered screen, a large Chinese rug, and Chinese furniture.

"How do you like me?" Diane sings out. "It's designed by Paul Poiret of Paris." And with hands in the air she pirouettes. My eyes are open wide, I feel like laughing. Looking at Charles I can see he too has caught the joke, for his eyes are twinkling: Admire the

170

decorations — but promise, don't talk about China or the Chinese.

"Beautiful," I say to Diane, my voice controlled. And looking into the drawing room, I sincerely mean it.

"Thank you, Bessie dear," says Diane unexpectedly. And as the bell rings to announce more guests, I am saved from further conversation for the time being and, turning, move into the drawing room away from Charles. Our little in-joke unexplainable to our hostess.

The drawing room is elegantly and not overly furnished. A delight to behold.

"I'm glad I'm here," I say honestly to Uncle John and Aunt Elmira, who are standing between the fireplace and the painted screen, talking to a couple I have met before, a Mr. and Mrs. Casper Holmes. "I don't think I have seen or ever shall see a room so handsome."

"And did you know," says Uncle John wickedly, knowing well my feelings regarding the Shaws, "Diane was her own interior decorator."

"Well, one can't always be wrong," I laugh with him.

"She's wrong about those trousers. Awful!" Mr. Holmes speaks vehemently. "'What are women trying to do anyway, nowadays? Trying to pretend they're men, that's what. What with those suffragettes running wild all over the place. Grabbing the votes in the States. It shouldn't be allowed. Put them all in prison, I say, and let them rot there. Don't know what this world's coming to!"

I'm staring at him, flabbergasted. My mouth opens. "Mr. Holmes, do you believe a woman's costume makes a political statement?"

Mr. Holmes turns red. J.R.'s eyebrows shoot up. And beyond him, not too distant, yet close enough to catch the drift of my words, is Charles, a disapproving expression on his face.

Good Lord, why do these people afford me such

171

wonderful opportunities to disgrace Charles and his family? Martha, of course, would have answered my question to Casper Holmes in the affirmative. I would love to hear what he has to say and debate the matter with him. But in the midst of his sputtering reply I interrupt with "Please excuse me. There is someone I must see."

Cora has just appeared, thank goodness. I make a hasty retreat.

There are not as many guests as Charles had led me to expect. Sixteen sit down to the long dining-room table with host and hostess gracing the ends. The centrepiece of flowers (all from the florist at this time of year) is a work of art, as are the candelabra: masterpieces in silver. All in excellent taste. Another "gloating party", I can't help thinking. Everyone still oohing and aahing, everything meant to be admired — all the newly-acquired booty, the silverware, the oriental rugs, everything. There have been so many gloating parties in Winnipeg these past few years. People becoming rich overnight and stuffing their houses with everything and anything. But no. Stop being unfair. Wealth is not new to the Shaws and they have shown impeccable taste. Even Diane's clothes are exquisite — or would be on someone with a figure like Sandy's. Sandy would look delightful in pantaloons and embroidered tunic. The Reverend Dickinson would be preaching about the Satanic ways of fashion designers were he back in the States where, like Casper Holmes, the Established Order is deeply shocked at the sight of pantaloons and women's ankles — where bills in more than one state have come before the House in an effort to prevent females over fourteen from wearing skirts that do not "reach that part of the foot known as the instep". Pantaloons are a religious as well as a political issue. Well, and what next? I'm all for them. Here at the

172

Shaws pantaloons and decorations both appeal to me. I turn and smile involuntarily towards the end of the table and find Diane Shaw is regarding me with a bemused expression. She returns my smile.

A truce? No doubt I've been responsible for exacerbating problems and never attempting to ease that last hassle. That isn't Christian-like. What really is at the basis of my constant irritation with the Shaws? Sandy manages very well with all sorts of irascible people. Even Ethel knows how to keep her calm far better than I do. After all is said and done, the Manekowskis are still at Owen House and nothing more is being mentioned about firing them, though it is obvious Oscar Shaw has no liking for the caretakers. And the Shaws, even though defeated, have continued to help monetarily and with the planning. A truce? I'm willing to go along with that. And tonight I must be good. Tonight I must. For I have been placed halfway down the table and across from me is Charles, who will continue to keep his eyes on me — without a shadow of a doubt. Across the bowl of hothouse roses I catch his ice-blue stare. He's still apprehensive! Why, I've just been sitting quietly, I've hardly spoken a word.

"You're back from Florida early, J.R...."

My attention is taken by my neighbour, who is calling down the table to Uncle John, seated to his hostess's right.

"A few business matters. Loans not flowing quite so smoothly. Get things in order and then my lady and I will move permanently to the land of perpetual sunshine."

"We'll miss you, Mr. Clements," another man with a diamond sparkling from a tie pin remarks. "The city will. You've had a hand in its growth and witnessed a long and splendid period of expansion."

"That's so, and it's been great fun for me.

173

Population, only one thousand when I came. Shacks mainly and mud road. Now Winnipeg is the third largest city in Canada. And our dreams of making it the capital of Western Canada have been realized. But I'm thinking my career climaxed last year," Uncle John adds thoughtfully.

Mrs. Holmes speaks up buoyantly, "And now over a great area of this wonderful province there are villages and farms. And there are railways everywhere.

My neighbour adds, "Amen. Railways even where they are not needed. Do you know that it has been said that the U. S. lays tracks in order to develop the country, Germany builds railways for purposes of war, and Canada builds them for fun."

Everyone laughs.

"Now isn't that so, Mr. Hamilton?" The neighbour is following up his advantage. "Didn't the Liberal government build a third transcontinental railway? And was it necessary? Did anyone bother to ask that question?"

"The Liberal government has been out of power for over a year," says Fred Hamilton quietly. "And railways are still being built at the rate of two miles a day."

"Whatever," says Mr. Holmes, obviously a Tory. "I blame the Liberals more, for they were in power for years and started the racket. For years now the immigrants have been sold wilderness areas. A few shacks spring up and it's called a village. And then the government arranges for a railway station with some foreign name. And more tracks. You can't deny it, Hamilton. You're in real estate and you know 'demned' well that every gambler from the U. S. has been up here buying land — even where there's none to buy. Why, soon there will be no more open areas left on the map of Canada."

"Don't be too sure," Oscar Shaw's compelling voice

174

sounds from the head of the table. "Perhaps those days of fast real estate selling are over. J.R. mentioned that his career had peaked. And, I'm thinking that could be true of Winnipeg's as well — for the time being, anyway."

Heads turn.

"What do you mean?" Mrs. Holmes' voice is suddenly deflated.

"Some of us at this table are well aware that London has been lending Canada huge sums of money to build and expand. And London has suddenly decided to use its money for internal purposes. Money is no longer forthcoming."

"A temporary slowing down of construction only," says Charles, hopefully.

"Maybe, but you can imagine what will happen if money is withheld from London and other sources even for the space of a few months more. Already credit is tight. Interest rates have shot up. We all know that."

"What about it, J.R.? What do you think will happen?" The appeal is to the eldest business man at the table.

Heads turn again. As at a tennis match. Ball again in Uncle John's court.

"Well...I've been thinking about the matter for some months now, as a matter of fact. The signals have been coming through from the Old Country low but clear. And I don't like what I'm thinking. Haven't said much, for I've had my day and I've had my fights and I'm getting too old to start getting all steamed up now about the economy and a possible collapse. But I can't see anything ahead but trouble in the immediate future. I've played the game and I'd like to retire from the arena just as soon as I can."

Mrs. Holmes gasps and dramatically claps her chest. "It can't be that bad, surely. Mr. Shaw, tell us. Please!"

175

All heads turn once more. And Mr. Shaw, having been given the opportunity, launches into a monologue that continues the length of three courses — through soup, salad, and entree. However, for once I listen, for he is confirming my own apprehensions of this past little while.

His voice drones on. "Over the past few years foreign loans have been rolling in by the hundreds of millions, the largest amount coming from the Mother Country. And Canada has been spending recklessly, without giving proper study to the various projects it has invested in, or to where those projects might lead. Easy borrowing, big spending, for projects beyond the needs of the country. Well, now the loans are drying up and British interest rates have increased. Farmers are finding it harder to get credit. And for many, little if anything they have belongs to them. Wheat prices are falling. All they need is a year or two of poor crops to place them in serious debt. Most of them already are mortgaged to the hilt. And as good crop years and poor crop years seem to move in cycles, I'd say they are about due for a bad time."

"Let's hope you're wrong, Oscar," my neighbour is speaking. "For if what you say is true, it won't only be farmers who will be in serious trouble."

"Fraid not. Could be true of all public works, real estate, everything. And Winnipeg is going to hurt the most in this country because Winnipeg has been expanding like a balloon."

"A balloon about to bust?"

"Maybe, although I hope not."

"Now surely you are painting too gloomy a picture." Charles, never wanting to believe that anything could possibly go wrong. "It's a great country with great resources."

"Oh, Mrs. Shaw," the woman who has been doing

176

most of the oohing and aahing is fluttering. "Mrs. Shaw. How awful it would be if there were a bust. And just after you've got this beautiful home and all this beautiful furniture, and...and everything."

"Mrs. Shaw won't have to worry much," Mr. Shaw reassures her. "We can ride out a recession for a year or so. But there are a lot of little business men who can't." His laugh is bitter, not unkind.

"It would be tough on more than the farmers and the little business men if a recession continued for even a few months," Ray, who probably has been talking with his father, says morbidly.

"Oh, please, please," Diane raises both hands in an effort to stop the conversation. "Please don't spoil this evening with any more such depressing talk. There has been far too much already. Let's talk about our new Legislative Buildings. Don't you find them elegant? Don't you think they set quite the right tone for our fine province?'"

But although Diane tries her best to lighten the mood, there is no doubt that the men, mentally, are busily reviewing their assets and reckoning their chances. A problem that all, very likely, have been doing their best to keep in abeyance has now surfaced, is out in the open, and from now on will rule conversations and override all else for a very long time to come.

Charles is silent as we make ready to drive home. He quietly lights the lanterns and cranks the car. And he does not comment on the Packards and Lincolns that are lined up with the Model T. Nor does he say, as so often he has before, "I'm thinking of getting a better motorcar one of these days. Just hate to give up old Black Beauty here. Think we could stable two horses?"

Partly to break the heavy silence, I say, "I did behave, Charles. I didn't say one thing that could have

177

disturbed you or anyone else. Though, you can be sure, I was given plenty of opportunity to do so. Just imagine all that talk about our beautiful and prosperous city. The city masks a great deal of ugliness and no one so much as mentioned that. Just imagine all the money that has been pouring into this country to be spent so wastefully. No long-term planning. No thought of what might lie ahead. It's sinful. Governments simply live from one election to the next. High living. Big projects. Just a bit of the money that was wasted so thoughtlessly could have been used for long-term gain to clean up the slums, to provide education for all children. Don't you think if you were Prime Minister, you'd consider that the wise thing to do? Why, you would win the respect and adulation of the majority of people in this country. Then, more than just the flabby rich could speak with pride of Canada."

But Charles is not listening.

The night is cold and I am glad I left the rugs in the car. "I find it hard to understand why Oscar and Diane have gone out of their way to be so nice to me. She actually smiled at me at the table. I mean, a sincere smile. To even consider there must be an ulterior motive for the change of heart is probably being very un-Christian, so I have decided to try and forgive and to smile at them a bit more. You'll approve of that, won't you? What do you think, Charles? Do you think they've decided they made a mistake and Mikhail is not a subversive as they thought? Or could it be that, with the approaching recession Oscar is talking about, they feel that cooperation with Labour is the best way to help us all out of a bad situation. I hope that last is the case. Do you?"

But Charles is not listening.

"Charles, you are not listening. You're not irritated with me, are you? You can't be. I did behave. You know

178

I did, when I was just dying to tell a few of those stuffed peacocks a thing or two. Some of them can't see beyond their moneybags and are truly very ignorant of the long-term problems that are brewing for us all in this city. They'll have to wake up one day. If not on their own, they'll be forced to."

But I can draw no response. So I, too, lapse into silence.

## 6

July 1913

Disgusted, I push the papers away from me and lean back in my chair. I have been working over accounts for the better part of the morning, and now I gaze morosely at the littered desk. Owen House is getting along — but barely getting along. Charity, it seems, has dried up as government loans from overseas have dried up: overnight. Owen House will have to get along on a shoestring from now on until the recession is over — if the shoestring be forthcoming. What to do? Where to cut corners? I would like to talk the matter over with Ethel, but Ethel has gone home to take care of a few housekeeping details. Having been forced to get rid of most of her household staff, Ethel, dedicated though she is to the mission, has less time to spare for volunteer work. It's the same with many of the volunteers from the south side. The recession has hit almost everyone, and is hurting. Overnight. It happened overnight!

"Believe me, Bessie, this is the work I love. I could scrub pots here from morn to night and enjoy it. Working on my own at my place doesn't have the same meaning. There it's a chore, and I hate it. But it has to

179

be done. To add an untidy house and poor meals to a lack of communication could overbalance an already very shaky marriage."

"Then why do you stay with James?" I blurted out, and was then appalled at my question.

Ethel shrugged. "It's hard to say. For a multitude of reasons, including my losing all the money that originally came from my family and was used to build James' business. At my age, where would I go? And besides, though it's hard for anyone including myself to believe, I still love him. You see, I have a lot of wonderful memories. We've just grown apart, I guess — or something. Whatever it is, I won't let him down now that the going is rough."

"I shouldn't have asked. I'm sorry, Ethel. It's none of my business."

"Oh, I don't mind telling you, of all people, Bess. I've never said anything before. Thought everybody knew about his lady friends and everything else. Besides, there was no reason to burden you with my problems. Just another marriage that has soured."

Problems. Everywhere there are lots of problems. Personal problems. Economic problems. I open the gold engraved watch case that hangs around my neck on two strands of fine gold chain threading through a gold bar set with seed pearls. A gift from Richard. Always a reminder of Richard. Almost twelve-thirty, it tells me. Why not have lunch put on a tray and take it upstairs for a chat with the Manekowskis? It's usual for Mike and Gedda to have their meals in their third-floor apartment, as it's an opportunity for them to be alone with Lana. I haven't seen enough of Lana lately, what with all the concern about money and service.

Lana is six years old and will be starting to regular school next year. Seeing Lana will chase the gloom away. Lana is a bright spot in my life. Right from the

180

outset it was as though I had known her forever. Like Richard. I feel about her the way I have always felt about Richard: almost a part of myself. A child of my own could be no closer.

I head for the kitchen, where Mrs. Critchley does the cooking. Expertly sidestepping the chatter and complaints of Mrs. Crutch (as she's called by the children), I collect my lunch amid kitchen steam and clatter and go quickly up the back stairs.

Tray in hands, I call through the door, "Company for lunch. May I come in?"

"Of course." Gedda has jumped to open the door and then calls, "Lana, it's Robin."

Robin has been my special name since the time I was first introduced to Lana as Miss Robinson, when after a few attempts at pronunciation the little girl decided to settle for just two syllables.

Lana comes running, and scarcely have I put my tray down before I'm being hugged.

"Look, I'm putting my new doll to bed."

It's one I have given her.

"And what have you named her?"

"Her name is Elizabeth. That's your name. And she's a very beautiful doll."

After talking about dolls and the school she will be attending, Lana says, suddenly contrite, "But your lunch is getting cold. I'll tell you more about Elizabeth and everything another time."

"And I want to talk to your parents. But before I go, would you like me to read you a chapter from *Alice in Wonderland*?"

"Oh, please, Robin." Lana claps her hands. "I like Alice because she's almost the same age as me and meets lots of funny animals." Lana loves animals; the Collie especially is her friend.

"You spoil her, you know," Mike grumbles as Lana

181

returns to her bedroom and her doll.

"Well, let me try. With the loving discipline you give her, I don't think it will be possible."

"We're doing our best. It's difficult with only one child. I was one of a large family — no chance of being spoiled."

"We want another child," says Gedda. "You know I've lost two since Lana. But I keep hoping. But please begin your lunch and we can talk business later."

She picks up a piece of fine embroidery that is near at hand and begins working it. She, too, knows that I have carried a child for three months and lost it. Gedda is much younger than I.

"We'll both hope."

The third floor apartment is bright and cheerful. Originally servants' quarters, it consists of two bedrooms, the larger displaying the crucifix over the bed — which I have chosen to ignore — a large dining-sitting room, a fair-sized kitchen, and ample closet space, one closet now serving as a bathroom since the recent remodelling. Gedda has turned the apartment into a home, making it special with her colourful needlepoint, petit-point, and fine embroideries. She designs her own work and wall hangings.

I push aside the tea tray and turn to Mike.

"Mike, we'll be running this house on a shoestring soon."

"And where will we get a long enough shoestring?"

"That I don't know. Can you think of any way we can cut down on expenses?"

Mike shrugs. "We won't get more equipment for the playground as was planned. Lucky the house is in good shape, though there are a few things still to be done which are essential. We can make rules about turning off lights and things like that. Cut out most paid services. Gedda and I can take a cut in wages and still

182

manage — I have other work."

"I can hope that last won't be necessary. You get little enough as it is. Let's see first what else can be done. We can't get along without Crutch and Pole. Some of the others, maybe. By the way, did I ever tell you what Charles said when I told him what the children had nicknamed Mrs. Critchley and Mrs. Poleski? He said, 'Crutch and Pole — how appropriate. How can they be other than excellent staff?' I assured him they are among our best support. The children love them, especially grumbling old Mrs. Crutch. Those two do so much more than just cook and nurse."

Gedda says, "Perhaps we'll have to give out smaller amounts of food. And, of course, cancel excursions."

"Oh, Gedda, that I don't like to do. Excursions if we must. But let us try every other thing first before we cut down on the food. It's about all some of those children get. Yes, we'll have to let most of the paid help go. And that means relying more on volunteers."

"Mrs. Stainton won't be coming again. Said she's needed at home."

"Let's hope we can find replacements. I'll call a meeting of the Directors immediately. Please list all the points you can think of. Perhaps this recession will end soon." A pause. "I think I say that as often as I say 'good morning'!"

Another pause. Then Mike speaks.

"I think it unfortunate that Mr. Woodsworth resigned as superintendent of All People's Mission last month, even in order to become secretary of the Canadian Welfare League. Of course, the League is much needed, and he did help establish it. Still, he'll be hard to replace. Quite a number of people stopped working at the Mission after he left."

"Perhaps there's no connection. Perhaps the help left for the same reason they're leaving us. Everybody's

183

being affected."

"And most of all the labourer, who is out of work with nothing laid aside for wet weather."

"You mean 'a rainy day', Mike," I say absently, out of habit.

"Even before this recession the picture was bad for the working man. You've read Woodsworth's analysis of the working man's budget?" He points to a stack of papers on the floor. "Mr. Woodsworth figures that a decent annual wage for a family of five is $1,216 with rent of $240 and food $424. That rent is if the house is five rooms without bathroom or furnace, but with water and sewer connections. But do you know that most working men are paid under $600 a year and many much less? How are they expected to get along?"

"And," says Gedda, snapping at a thread with her embroidery scissors, "a lot of mothers and children have to work to help pay for that food and rent. And that is only one of many reasons why children drop out of school even after they have found their way in."

"Think of how many families are getting along on so much less that what he calls decent." Mike persists in emphasizing the point. "And how many are out of work now and have nothing."

"Woodsworth is getting himself deeper and deeper into trouble with the business community for advocating a legal minimum wage."

"That's so." Mike is enthusiastic, for to him J.S. Woodsworth is a man, ready to stand up for his principles, ready to put his head on the chopping block for the sake of the underprivileged. "Just imagine," he says sarcastically, "a legal minimum wage could mean curtailing the right of the business man to make a big profit from the labour of his workers."

"Business men aren't having a very good time, either, at the moment." As usual I have the uneasy

184

feeling of sitting right in the middle.

"Don't be fooled. For most of them their troubles are only for a little while. I'm talking long term. And if something isn't changed for the workers their lives will continue always on the edge of disaster. You've read the *Free Press*." Mike points to his stack of newspapers. "That good man, Mr. Woodsworth, has also suggested public ownership of land as a way of protecting the poor against the exploitation of the rich."

"Then do you wonder why the landowners are down on Woodsworth?"

"I don't wonder at all. But change there must be for the greater good of a majority of people."

"Doesn't government support of people and public ownership go against Darwin's concept of survival of the fittest? Protection of the poor, to some business men, means condemning their God-given right to make a profit — but it also means that those who are least fit to face the struggle for existence would be propped up at their expense, only in the long run to weaken the whole fabric of society. Now you answer me that one, Mike."

"I would say along with Mr. Woodsworth that one of the first conditions of being a Christian is to be humanitarian. I would say that one might be surprised how many of these people, who are considered subhuman by so many in this city, when given half a chance with an education and a fair wage, would prove themselves and do a lot of good for this community. Some of the most courageous and finest people I've known since I came to Winnipeg, have been called the dregs of humanity, called people who should be left to die for the sake of the human race."

"I can't deny what you say, Mike."

Mike's face is grim. "You should see the fine men and women and children I know who are being forced into poverty and near-starvation because there are no

185

checks on this capitalist system." He bangs the table and the dishes rattle. "Woodsworth is doing all he can with his articles, 'Canadian for Tomorrow'. But I wonder when the tomorrow he writes about will ever come. There's too much selfishness and too much apathy. He's trying to present to his readers, in a most reasonable way, the problems you and I have talked over so often: the need for community action, broader school programmes, assimilation of the immigrant into the life of the whole community — all this with provincial support. He writes what he has said for years, that the immigrant who cannot speak English, who has no work, and who is left to his own devices, is a threat to the community."

"And for saying what he has," adds Gedda, "Mr. Woodsworth's life has been threatened."

"Do you realize," asks Mike, "that this year immigrants are coming like a flood into Canada — and more than ever are settling in Winnipeg? And nothing is being done."

"But help to the immigrant is what we have been trying to give through Owen House. What All People's Mission was doing for years before our time. And we have been encouraged by all sections of the larger community." No sooner do I say this than the naivete of my words hits me.

"But what we have been doing is on such a small scale it never could be life-threatening to the capitalist class. It is even something that men like Shaw can get involved in and turn to profit — not only by way of publicity but tax deductions. But Woodsworth is suggesting that what is now charity be people's rights and that it be carried out on a big scale by the government. Then every pocketbook will be touched and no one will get the credit. A new way of life for all. There's a big difference. Let me read this to you. You get the *Free Press* but maybe you haven't read the *Tribune*."

Mike thumbs through a newspaper. "Here it is. This fine city newspaper has labelled Woodsworth's articles as 'the most all-embracing succinct and nefarious libel on Canada ever printed.' And I have the idea about what it all means even before I used the dictionary.

"I would say that is strong language."

"Woodsworth has always had enemies."

"Good men always have enemies. But now he is so openly publishing his opinions, and at a time of crisis like this. Do you think he is wanting matters to come to a head? Asking for trouble?"

"No. I think he is trying to make a solution."

"And it is unlikely that many will listen. Mike, if this situation continues — this recession grows worse — what will you do? Or maybe I should ask, what are you attempting to do for the working man?"

"I wish I had our friend's background. But I can only work in my corner and that is a corner in the working force that I know better than Woodsworth. The working man can bargain only by withholding his labour. Labour members are badly organized and cannot agree among themselves. So now is not the time to strike. It's time to consolidate. And that is my interest at the moment. It's not now that I am a dangerous man like Woodsworth. But later when we are organized and when the times improve. Then I will be a dangerous man."

He says it lightly. But I can see that Gedda is not happy; she looks down at her embroidery to hide her eyes.

Lana can be heard in the bedroom singing to the doll, Elizabeth.

I say, "Sometimes I prefer a fantasy world. Where is *Alice in Wonderland*?"

187

# 7

August 1913

Lana has a dog and calls him Marx. Actually, the Collie was my dog in the beginning, or perhaps to be more exact, I just thought he was. I got the Collie, a Siamese cat, and a canary because not only am I fond of animals, I thought they would be good for the children. They are fine creatures, and the Collie, a real beauty, is intelligent and good-natured. When I was first introduced to him, he already had a name, Maximilian. But as that was a bit of a mouthful for the children, many who are still finding their way in the English language, I called him Max.

The cat has work to do about the house and does it most ably. An excellent mouser is Simon who, when not on the job, can usually be found on tabletops, on top of cupboards, or at the top of other high places, often to the consternation of Mrs. Crutch and to the delight of the children. The canary, who sings and sings, had to be put under the watchful eyes of the kitchen staff, well out of reach of Simon — almost an impossibility. But we hope that Simon is learning that the canary, formerly called Birdie, is a member of the family and not meant for assassination. Birdie! What a horrible name for so heavenly a songster. Charles changed that, thank goodness. When he was first introduced to the household he renamed Birdie "Onan", after the Biblical character who scattered his seed on the ground. Trust Charles.

I'm not sure whether it was Lana who adopted Maximilian, or Maximilian, Lana. They have become the best of friends these past four years. And I'm sure she has been saying Max. But the other day I distinctly heard Lana call "Marx". Marx? And then I realized the other children were doing the same.

I corner her. "Lana," I say, "His name is Max."

"Marx, Robin, his name is Marx."

Where did Lana pick up that name in the first place? My guess is that she has heard Mike and his friends discussing Karl Marx, and my instinct is to stave off trouble. I've had my fill of problems with the Shaws because of their antagonism towards the Manekowskis, and I can do without more.

"No, Lana, the name is Max, short for Maximilian."

"No, Robin, that won't work."

"And why won't it work?"

"You see, I've written a poem to Marx. Do you want to hear it?"

"Of course, but —"

"It goes like this:

*I have a dog, his name is Marx*
*He's very good, he seldom barks*
*I call him and he stops and harks."*

Then she adds, "Papa said I could say, He's clever and he almost tarks. That's silly!" She makes a face.

"It's a fine poem, Lana, but you can just as easily write a poem to Max.

"Oh, no, I couldn't make up a poem about Max!"

"And why not? I'm sure you can do it, and very well. I want you to try. His correct name is Maximilian. That is the name on his papers, his birth certificate."

Later on in the day Lana recites a new poem to me:

*"I have a dog, his name is Max,*
*My patience he does often tax*
*My training of him is too lax."*

"I like it."

189

"But it doesn't work. That's not my dog. My dog is good and obedient. His name is Marx, he seldom barks, I call him and he stops and harks."

"All right, Lana. I want you to test that. There he is. Call Max."

Lana calls, "Max, Max. Come here, Max. Come right now, Max."

But Max pays no attention, not the slightest.

"Now," says Lana, "I'll call him by his proper name and you'll see... Marx!"

The big Collie lifts his head, wags his tail, and comes running.

They're in cahoots!

Of course I let the matter slide. And of course the time comes when the matter surfaces at a Committee meeting.

"I hear the name Marx being bandied about here and it's getting on my nerves. It seems to refer to that dog, whose name I thought was Max. And I think someone should put a stop to it."

"What's in a name?" I say airily.

"Quite a lot, when the name is Marx."

And so it goes.

Diane speaks to Lana rather severely. It's really a way of getting at Mike. But Mike refuses to enter the fray, and like the Collie pays no attention to what he doesn't care to hear. He lets Lana handle the situation, and Lana finally agrees with Diane that the name is Max — Maximilian.

But what can one do when all the children insist on calling the dog Marx? When Max will only answer when Lana says "Marx"? The cards are stacked against the Shaws.

The next thing I hear from Lana is, "Robin, don't you think Marx should come to Sunday School?"

"Oh, I don't think so, Lana. I don't think that's

190

necessary."

"Why not? Don't you want Marx to go to Heaven?"

Immediately I'm in deep water. I've been having lunch with the Manekowskis and Lana's parents look at me with great interest, wondering how I'll handle this one. I haven't the faintest idea, so finally I say what my heart tells me.

"Of course, Lana, I want Marx to go to Heaven."

"Then why shouldn't he be taking classes with me?"

"Because I'm sure he wouldn't understand about things, the way you do."

"Oh, but he would, Robin. He understands a lot, maybe even more than you and me. Papa says Marx has better hearing than we have. You know how he pricks up his ears and knows about something before we do. And he has another sense too. What did you say, Papa? He's aware in a way we aren't." Lana continues, uncannily perceptive, "Maybe it's like his name. Remember when you and Mrs. Shaw wanted me to call him Max? But Marx knows exactly what I mean, not because of what I say but what I mean. He gets the message."

I raise my eyebrows at Gedda, as if to ask, where did she learn that? And Gedda, catching my meaning, shrugs.

"Wherever did she learn so much about animals?"

"From Saint Francis," answers Mike.

"We've told Lana the story about Saint Francis and the way even the most ferocious, man-killing wolf would listen to him and meekly follow him," explains Gedda. "And about his love of even the least of God's creatures."

"I don't think it's only that," adds Mike. "Lana just came this way."

And I believe him. But Lana is growing impatient, wanting to get back to the point.

191

"Marx is one of God's creatures," she insists, "and cats and birds and elephants are too, so why wouldn't He take them to Heaven?"

"Maybe He will. Yes, I'm sure they'll be in Heaven with us." I'm feeling uncomfortable. Animals aren't supposed to have souls, according to church teachings.

"Then Marx had better come to class with me next Sunday. And I'll give him a few lessons before so he won't feel too far behind the others."

Cornered, I laugh. "But really, Lana, I've never heard of a dog attending Sunday School!"

I appeal to Gedda.

"Gedda says, "I'm sorry to have to inform you, Robin, we were telling Lana that in the Middle Ages people took their animals to church — their dogs and pet falcons, too."

I'm astounded. I'm getting no help from either Mike or Gedda. I say, uncertainly, "Come to think of it, I've heard of that."

My remark is unwise: Lana jumps up. "Then I can take Marx to class "

"I didn't say that, Lana. Can't you just picture the racket and confusion that must have gone on in those churches?"

"I really have no idea about that," she says in her very best grown-up manner. "Maybe yes and maybe no. But Marx will make no fuss. And if he does, I'll just ask him to leave."

Now, when Lana attends Sunday School, Marx comes with her. She sits on the floor with one arm around him, and the children vie to be close. Lana tried to get Simon to attend as well. But Simon would have none of it. Well, some people are like that!

I'm forced to admit that Marx is good and quiet and quite a drawing card. Once, for fun, I accused the Collie of sleeping and not being attentive. He opened his eyes

192

and regarded me long and sorrowfully, as if to say, "You humans really don't understand animals — I'm absorbing every thought."

No soul? Saint Francis might have said that all of God's creatures are evolving — every last one of us.

*Chapter V*

# A House Divided

August 1913

I am seated at the piano. Standing in the doorway and staring at me is a gawky, hollow-chested girl of about fourteen with stringy hair, her dress clean and well-patched. The high voices of the Sunday class children sing out. The girl appears to be waiting for the song to cease.

> *"Jesus loves me this I know,*
> *For the Bible tells me so.*
> *Little ones to him belong,*
> *We are weak, but He is strong."*

My playing ends with a thump and the children's singing changes to chirping, like so many birds.

"What is it?" I ask the girl. "What is it you want?"

"It's my turn," she informs me flatly.

194

"Your turn for what?"

"That's Bobby's sister, Jean," a youngster from the back of the room shrills out by way of explanation. "Jean Simpson."

"Oh, Jean Simpson. Bobby's not here today. Is he all right, Jean?"

The girl, obviously none too bright, ignores the question.

"Is there something I can do for you, Jean?"

"Ma said it's my turn," she persists. "I should come instead of Bobby today."

"Instead of Bobby! But everyone's welcome. Except that this is a class for younger children. But come in if you wish — though the class will soon be over. Let's see where you can sit. Do you mind sitting on the floor with some of the little ones — over there?"

It is a large class and getting larger all the time. Twenty-three today. "Hmmm. But how's Bobby?"

"I don't want your class. I just want my tea."

Well, that's a blunt statement.

"Ma said it's my turn. Wouldn't be fair to take two of us."

"Hmmm. Of course. That was thoughtful of your Ma."

I'm really under no illusions. A majority of the children come for the tea, not for the teaching. But I can only do my best and maybe souls will be saved after the tea. I look at the thin children, the eager faces, and my heart responds.

Turning to Jean, I say, "You'll find a chair in the room on the left. We'll only be another half hour. But look around if you prefer. I'll come and find you."

I have already asked Mrs. Crutch to add a bit more water to the soup. It's getting to be an Oliver Twist drama when I would prefer it to be the loaves and the fishes. I must give more of my own money and ask

195

Charles to give as well. The City should try to do more. But people are pouring in from outlying districts — from everywhere, so it seems — adding everyday to the long breadlines. If this recession is not over by the time winter sets in, and people no longer have produce from their gardens...

"Now, children, I'm going to tell you a story." I bring the piano stool to the front of the class, sit down, and fold my hands in my lap. "This is a story about Jesus and his twelve disciples. First I want you to tell me the names of some of those disciples. How many names can you remember?"

An arm shoots up. "Peter," an excited voice calls.

"You're right, Joey. Peter. That's one. And who else was there?"

*     *     *     *     *

Riding my bicycle home, I'm heartsick. Without a doubt Mrs. Crutch's watered-down soup and sandwiches are the reason for the swelling ranks of the Bible classes. Poor Jean Simpson. I found her in the kitchen, awkwardly filling soup bowls.

"Want to help," Jean explained. "Not just take your tea for nothing."

So before the afternoon was over Jean was invited to come again next week to help put out the food and serve the little ones. And she repeated in her honest way, as if to make sure the signals between us were correct, "I can't abide your classes, Missus, but I'm glad to pitch in and do you a turn for a wee bite."

"That's fine, Jean. And see that Bobby's here too next week."

My mission is to save souls. Surely it is of first importance to save souls. But I can't ignore the needy! Remember the story of the Good Samaritan. That's

196

Woodsworth's social gospel, and David Brown's. I simply can't turn away the hungry. If it were not for Mrs. Crutch's crusty approach to the reality of the situation—"Don't expect me to turn water into wine!" — the house would be swamped.

There is a rule that Charles lives by. I'm not sure, but maybe it was Abraham Lincoln who said it first. Anyway, Charles believes that one must do one's best in whatever situation one finds oneself, though it can be only in the light of one's understanding. To do right as one sees right. But surely there lies a problem, for each of us has a different perspective on life. So who has the right answer? I say that is why it's so necessary to have the Divine Word for guidance. Martha has a different idea. She says universal knowledge can be found within oneself because one is part of God, that God is within and not outside us. But I know Martha's ideas are not those of the church. And surely church teachings are the only secure basis for belief.

Maybe I can persuade Charles to take a walk so I can talk to him about the situation at the House. Just a little walk out of doors in the good fresh air. Everything seems clearer out of doors. I'll broach the subject of money as we walk. It's another lovely summer day. But as I pedal I notice storm clouds are forming. Winnipeg has lots of sudden summer storms: this could pass.

Charles is in the parlour. His long face is drawn and as dour and foreboding as the clouds.

"Charles, whatever is the matter?"

"Sit down, Lady. I have something to say to you."

"Charles, I thought we could take a walk before supper. I have something to say to you."

There is a flash of lightning, a clap of thunder, and the rain descends.

"Well, we can't take a walk. Sit down."

I sit. I wait for him to speak. Suddenly he blurts out,

197

"Father's broke. Lost everything." Somehow the statement is not unexpected.

"So... "

"So we'll have to help him"

"We?" I say weakly. "What do you mean? Help in what way? You intend to give him more money? Of course..."

"I have no more money. That is, no more funds that are available. All I have is now tied up in the Company. I tried to pay off a few of Father's creditors. He was overextended. We decided he and Mother will do best to leave the country — for the time being, anyway. They're not young and I don't want to see them hounded in any way when there is absolutely nothing more that can be done, that any of us can do. Father has given me the house on Langside Street. He insisted on doing that in exchange for all I sunk into the project. And I've found them a farm in Wilmot, Michigan. Heard about it through Mother's brother, who lives near there. I telephoned him last week and got a telegram back today. There will be relatives nearby to give them a hand."

"And why wasn't I told about this conspiracy? When did all this happen?" Come to think of it, I haven't seen his parents for over two weeks.

"Just in this last week and a half. You've been so concerned about your Owen House, I haven't wanted to bother you. It's been touch and go for months. Kept putting money in and hoping the situation would change for the better. That we could bail him out. But it's hopeless. It's best that they go. They're old and Father is taking it all pretty hard. He had such high hopes and was doing so well. Just went too far, too fast, at the wrong time."

"With your help."

I am bitter. There have been plenty of warnings. I

198

advised him not to sink so much money into one thing. Oscar Shaw told him to pull up short.

"When will they be leaving? Perhaps it's better they go."

"As soon as possible. As soon as the farm in Wilmot is purchased. I thought, perhaps..." He hesitates, his voice taut, his face pale. "Perhaps we could use your money."

"What is left of my money is for Owen House."

"You are using it to feed more and more of those foreigners." His voice is suddenly changed and slightly contemptuous. "And the more you feed, the more will appear on your doorstep. They're coming to the city in droves for handouts. Why should you feel responsible for them? Charity begins at home."

"It's God's work and I am committed to the cause."

"Come now, Lady, is it less God's work to help my parents? Would you refuse help to your own mother under similar circumstances, giving preference to foreign hordes?"

"Your parents are your concern." I throw the words at him angrily.

"And that is why I'm humbly asking for your help — because I have nowhere else to turn." He pauses, then adds, "After all, the money you are spending on Owen House — at least a considerable sum of that money — did come from Uncle John."

I am beaten.

"Maybe this recession will soon be over and then we'll be able to get back on our feet," says Charles, always the optimist.

"Maybe." My voice is dull. I no longer am optimistic.

We visit the parents that evening to bring them news of the impending purchase. I am sorry for my father-in-law, who looks old and defeated. Not even one attempt at a humorous remark. Very quiet. When he does finally

199

speak to me it's to say that the house on Langside Street is in exchange for the farm in Wilmot. Had I not been feeling compassion, it is likely I would have burst out in anger. Instead, saying nothing, I turn to Charles' mother, who is busying herself preparing tea. I cannot but admire the little woman. Always upbeat, like Charles. Able to look on the bright side of every situation — even this disaster, it seems.

"I'll be so very glad to see my brother and his family, and there are quite a number of relatives in that part of Michigan." (How well I know.) "Haven't seen any of them for years. And we're very good friends. And, do you know, it will be good to get back on a farm again. I really do miss the farm and the animals and having a real garden. Ben will like it too." And shaking the hot water around in the teapot to warm it, she moves closer to me and whispers, "Best thing in the world to rid him of his troubles. There's nothing like working in the good earth and being around animals."

There could have been no other decision. But I am left with very little money now, and if the Shaws and others are forced to stop contributing, Owen House will be lost.

\* \* \* \* \*

It is not until the next day at supper that I think to ask Charles about the house.

"What do you intend to do with the place on Langside Street?"

He hesitates. "What do you think I should do?"

"Get rid of it as fast as possible. Then maybe I will have a bit of money for my work."

"I thought we might move in and save the rent on this place."

"Never!" Involuntarily I bang my knife and fork on

200

the table and sit bolt upright. "I hate that place."

"Oh, come now, Lady. Hate is a rather strong word. You can't mean that. It's just a house, nothing special, but nor is this place. I'd put them in the same category."

"Stop saying 'Oh, come now, Lady' to me. And let me tell you something. You're quite wrong. It is not the same as this one at all."

How can I tell him why the other house repels me? Perhaps it has to do with something that happened there long ago. (Or will happen there?) There is something very wrong about it. It is not a rational feeling, so how can I explain?

"I like this place and you agreed we could stay here until we build a home of our own — and that can be as soon as the economic situation allows, if that is what you want. I'll move any place you want as soon as we can — to the South End, if you like. But please, not there."

His voice has a note of sarcasm. "I'm not in control of world affairs. I'm not responsible for the economic problems of this province."

"Oh, indeed! But you did have something to do with putting so much money into your father's stupid machine. That was not the decision of the federal government or the provincial government, to say nothing of the world." I am shouting.

"And you were not loath to spend lots of money on your pet project. Get hold of yourself. It does no good for either of us to throw accusations at the other. We'll do the best we can. I'll try renting the place."

"Renting! Sell it. Please, Charles, sell it."

"You know very well houses are not selling at this time. But we'll do what we can."

\*　　\*　　\*　　\*　　\*

201

The parents move out, leaving the furnishings behind. After several weeks of trying to sell the place without one offer being received, the house on Langside Street is rented.

But the tenants pay no rent. After three months Charles stops by, only to find they are gone, having left behind in fair order all that did not belong to them.

"Well," he says, probably thinking of his father, "when you haven't got the money, how can you pay the rent? I think they were good people."

"It takes a hard-nosed business man to squeeze water from a stone," is all I have to say.

So the house is rented again. And the same thing happens. And in the early spring of 1914 we give up our home on Church Avenue and move to Langside Street — just until the recession is over. Which surely must be in the near future, says Charles. Otherwise everyone will be bankrupt, everything will be lost.

I reason with myself that my attitude towards the house is simply irrational. Psychic feeling is the deep-seated, sinful problem within me that I am striving so hard to change. To live in that place for a time, to face my apprehensions and discover they are pure illusion, is perhaps the best thing for me. It is what may free me. After all, as Charles insists, it is just a house and surely I, witness to such poverty and pathos in the North End, should not complain. Surely I am strong enough to put up with this, especially as it is an opportunity to change myself. I will be diligent in prayer and logical in outlook. After all, it is not meant to be forever.

Surveying the many boxes and our nondescript furniture now crowding the pieces left by the parents, I do my best to see the bright side of the situation.

"I'm afraid we won't be able to entertain the Shaws

202

here."

"Did you intend to?"

Daylight is fading. I give him no answer as I gaze at the darkening room.

## 2

1914-1915

The recession deepens and becomes a depression. The great Canadian dream of getting rich in land becomes a nightmare. Land cannot be given away.

On June 28th, in the obscure Balkan city of Sarajevo, a place few Canadians have even heard about, the Archduke Francis Ferdinand is assassinated.

The summer is an unusually hot one, unusually quiet. Anxious, sad weeks. A time of waiting — waiting in long lines at soup kitchens, waiting for handouts, waiting for something upon which one might vent one's anger.

Then, on August 4th, German troops move into Belgium. Bold headlines in the *Free Press* and other Winnipeg papers announce Great Britain's declaration of war. And a cheer goes up for King and Country, and for release from boredom. God Save the King! The Mother country is at war and therefore so is Canada.

For many men, that year of the depression, it means free room and board, a chance to see the world, a bit of excitement. Pay: a dollar a day for privates. Canada's standing army consists of 3,110 men. Hardly anyone has any expertise at war games. Hardly anyone knows how Canada should go about preparing for war. But the young men join by the hundreds anyway. And with only a smattering of training and with the most inadequate of equipment, they are sent overseas to fight under British command.

That year a poor prairie crop adds to the country's problems. And as international trade has been disrupted by the war, the loss of markets compounds the difficulties and threatens total disaster.

The winter that follows the hot summer is bitterly cold, and people are desperate now not only to find something to eat but some way to keep warm. The banking of fires and removal of ashes is a constant chore for the householder — a matter of survival in Winnipeg. At six o'clock every morning Charles heads down the basement stairs, shakes down the ashes, and removes them into a pail. Then he shovels coal from the bin to get the fire blazing, controlling the draught so that the fire will burn until he returns from work. He sets the pail of ashes outside the kitchen door on the back porch, to be carried to the backyard dump by the wooden fence that opens to the lane.

Whenever the coal bin is filled it sends soot through the house, so that a special cleaning of the place is necessary. But this is not the year to complain, for whoever has coal is among the fortunate. While smaller homes may have pot-bellied stoves, most of the poor have very little in the way of heating facilities, or coal or wood, and must depend upon what they can pick up along the railways or find in backyard ash heaps. But too often ashes are put through a fine sieve before being cast out, and the pickings are lean. Still, scavengers are everywhere. Frequently Charles and I see men and children searching through the dump.

"This can't keep up, and won't," Charles insists. "Europe will soon be crying out for both food and war supplies. And they will have to turn to Canada."

*     *     *     *     *

204

The faithful Jean Simpson does not appear one Sunday. Her cough has been worsening of late. Guessing she is ill, I get hold of some goose grease for her chest and a pail of soup, and along with Gedda set off to visit. Jean, in a narrow cot pulled close to the stove, is very sick.

"Missus," she addresses me, her voice feeble, "I didn't mean to let you down."

"Don't you worry one bit, Jean. When you get better you'll be back with us and then you can do double duty to make up for missing time."

Mrs. Simpson, standing nearby with Bobby, looks frightened and says very little. It is young Bobby who is voluble, pleased to see his teacher.

Before we leave I promise Jean that we'll be back to see her. "Mrs. Crutch can do with your help, so you get better as quickly as possible."

Outside I say to Gedda, "Did you notice that though the place was spotless it was almost barren of furniture?"

"I'm not surprised," Gedda responds. "If they ever had any furniture it has probably been used for firewood."

*     *     *     *     *

I am there when Jean dies, her Ma kneeling by the cot to hold her hand. Before drawing the cover over the quiet face, the mother kisses her daughter's forehead. Then, as though she must excuse such a display of affection, she says, defiant and dry-eyed, "She was not a bonny lass, but she was a good girl and she was my Jean."

It is I who shed the tears.

Not a bonny lass and not one I had known long. Plodding, awkward, dull, honest, loyal, determined.

205

After Jean's death Ethel Reid and I spend much of our spare time carrying food and medications to the absentee pupils of Owen House.

"James doesn't know, but I fudge on our food budget — and on a few other things as well."

We have been getting acquainted with the many small, inadequately heated shacks and their occupants, some of whom have been forced to drop what pride they had to become scavengers and beggars, eking out their lives in a state of uncomplaining desperation.

"How do they stand it?" I ask Mike one day after returning to Owen House to thaw my frozen fingers before setting out for home. "Why don't they scream?"

"They don't know how. I'm trying to teach them. Besides, just now they haven't the strength. And it's much too cold."

Owen House has found another use this winter. Quite a number of working men are crowding into the Manekowskis' apartment on certain evenings — slipping quietly up the back stairs. I often work late at the House, and certain faces are becoming familiar.

"Good friends of ours," Mike explains to me with a wink.

Oscar Shaw, happening by one evening and noticing a group on their way into the kitchen, questions me, wanting to know who the ruffians might be.

"Friends of the Manekowskis," I reply offhandedly.

Oscar Shaw is angry. He's not a stupid man.

"Without their wives? It's possible. But more likely they're a pack of troublemakers."

Although he allows the incident to pass, I'm positive he will be checking on Mike's activities, and I tell Mike of my fears. But Mike simply shrugs off the warning.

"The gentleman can't prevent me from having visitors to my own home." And saying that he gives me another one of his wide white grins.

206

Food has become so limited that the government, through the press, is constantly warning people to conserve. So bad is the situation that in late winter a woman is arrested for feeding crumbs to the birds.

The depression, the scarcity of food, all the problems the city has, are blamed on those damned foreigners, who from the outset have been the cause of Winnipeg's overcrowding and slum conditions, the cause of disease, of everything that has gone wrong. It is the Germans who started the war and are killing our young men: therefore every German in Winnipeg is regarded with suspicion and hatred. Not one is allowed to join the army. Winnipeg, so full of racial tension at the best of times, is now in the grip of madness.

In 1915, with the depression seemingly at its ultimate, the economic situation abruptly changes as the Allies' needs for food supplies and war equipment increase. Once again Canadian farmers are in demand. And once more their wheat is being bought at inflated prices. Once more they are purchasing farm equipment on credit and going deeper and deeper into debt.

With the country at war and now half a million men in uniform, there is scarcely any building taking place. There is a housing shortage, a shortage of building supplies — and no prospect of change.

3

April 1916

Having arrived early, I manage to find myself an aisle seat half-way back in the Walker Theatre. Soon the place is packed. People are even standing, and many have been turned away. With waist enlarged and belly full, my mind is concentrated on the

207

speaker, in total agreement with the speaker's words. As usual, Nellie McClung has completely captivated her audience.

"Now, some of you were with us last year when we staged that mock Parliament." She pauses.

Some hands shoot up. Some voices call "Yes!"

"Well," the lilting, taunting Irish voice goes on, "you will recall it was all because of our Premier, Sir Rodmond Roblin. It was he himself who said that woman's suffrage would be a step in the wrong direction for this province. Giving women the vote would break up the home, he said, for a woman can't vote and put dinner on the table on the same day, so he implied. The majority of women are emotional, he said, too often swayed by misdirected enthusiasms, and if possessed of the franchise would pose a real menace to this fair province. It would be unwise to introduce such uncontrolled temperament to our form of government."

A loud hiss is heard throughout the theatre.

Nellie McClung laughs. "We replied to that right here in this very spot. We turned the tables, pretending that it was the men who are the second-class citizens — the poor, down-trodden, put-upon men who are the ones seeking the vote. It was only a play, mind you. It was just a game. But it was as true as every word that Sir Rodmond spoke to us. And what was the result? Some men were properly shocked. You'd have thought they'd have been well over their shock by that time, wouldn't you, with all the talking that's been going on these past two or three decades. Mind, the Conservatives burned me in effigy. But don't feel sorry for me. I want you to know I didn't feel it at all. But did it do them any good? Not them. It got us a lot of publicity. And that's just what we needed."

I cheer along with the others.

"We got the support of the Liberal leader. And now

208

the Conservatives are out of power and the Right Honourable T. C. Norris and his Liberals are governing this province. And what does that mean to us? He promised to help us. Yes. But what has happened, my friends? Not much. Are you aware, dear women of this audience, that you are not persons in the eyes of the law? You have been ruled to be persons in matter of pain and for reasons of penalties. But you are not persons in matters of rights and privileges. You are owned by your husbands. You have no legal rights where your children are concerned. Are you aware? Yes, I see you are. Well, do something about it."

Her audience is with her every word of the way.

"The law says no woman, idiot, lunatic, or criminal can vote. How do you feel about being classed with idiots, lunatics, and criminals? I say, do something about it. On one hand woman is placed on a pedestal by men and idealized. On the other hand she is treated with the utmost contempt. Some women, that is, are placed on pedestals."

She pauses.

"Now let me tell you a story that some of you may not have heard. Our former Premier was finally persuaded to go with us to see some factory workers. We went in his beautiful automobile, and a red carnation reposed in each of two cut-glass vases, hung on either side of the plush interior. And when he was told the factory 'hands'—you realize these women are not people, let alone persons, just 'hands', for that is the only value they have to their factory owner — when he was told they work — I say slave — from 8:30 a.m. to 6 p.m. for six days of the week under the most appalling conditions for little return — much less than men would get for the same work — he answered, 'No doubt they get used to it. They want their pin money, and if they're sick they can always quit.' Pin money indeed! What they work for are the staples of life — for bread and butter. Sorry: no butter, no jam. Bread and rent.

"May I add that though shocked, and it was obvious the gentleman was shocked by what he saw, he still refused to appoint a female inspector, a reason we had asked him to go there. Couldn't wait to get away. And his final words were, 'Nice ladies should not involve themselves in such disgusting affairs.

"Now I have been referred to as a hyena in petticoats. I am called 'Calamity Nell' and 'That Holy Terror', and a score of other such names. I don't care what I'm called. In fact I'm rather proud of those names. I say I am, or you are, not a 'nice' lady unless I, or you, get involved in such 'disgusting' affairs and try to change such inhumane conditions.

"There are those who say, roll bandages, knit socks, be like the women who fill in for our men while they're at war, do what you can, but stop haranguing and carrying on about votes for women. Ladies, and gentlemen too — those of you who support us — we have a duty to the country to which our sons and husbands will soon return, God willing, and a duty to the world into which our children will one day enter. This is a province, this is a country, it is a world that needs the compassionate help of the woman voter. And that is why I am here on this platform tonight. Help me help this land. I beg you, one and all, to help keep this matter of votes for women foremost in the minds of everyone. The Liberals are in power and said, prior to the election, that we have their support. But don't forget that was prior to the election. Have you heard anything mentioned since the election? Keep at it, friends, keep at them, keep the fires stoked, don't let them die down for even one minute. Wishing will get you nowhere. This is the time for action more than ever before.

210

"Now, when this meeting is over, please, as you go out, take the pamphlets which are by the doors, as many of you possibly can, and distribute them along the streets wherever you may be. Don't just leave them on the doorsteps. Ring doorbells. Talk to the women. Do your utmost. We will get the vote. We will be persons!"

When the vivacious Nellie McClung steps down from the platform, it is to a standing ovation and a rousing cheer.

Passing through the hall I commandeer several large bundles of pamphlets. Then, realizing the folly of trying to carry them all the way home, I hail a cab.

* * * * *

Charles is home before me. I hadn't expected that. It seems he has been pacing up and down the street and is by the house as the cab draws up.

"For God's sake, Lady," he calls to me. "Where have you been? I've called everywhere. I've called Owen House. I've even called the hospital. In your condition couldn't you at least have had the consideration to leave me a note?"

Deciding the best thing to do is to ignore the perturbations, I hand him a bundle.

"Good to see you, Charles. Here, help me with these."

Noticing the bold words on the pamphlet, he mutters, "Nellie McClung. That woman." Then, "What is the point of all this waste paper?"

"My war effort, Charles. Let's go in and I'll tell you all about 'Our Nell'."

"She's not my Nell. The woman's no better than a rabble-rouser."

"Charles!" I frown as I remove my coat and hang it on a large hook.

211

"What do you intend to do with these, for heaven's sake?" he asks, dumping the bundles under the coats in the already-cluttered hall.

"I thought you voted Liberal, and Norris indicated his support of women's suffrage."

"Has he? Then what is the purpose of this? That woman simply can't stop talking. I've heard her tongue is hung from the centre and wags at both ends."

"She's interesting, she's funny, and she makes sense. We don't have the vote yet, and she's right when she says we mustn't stop working until we get it."

"I thought you had more than enough work to do at Owen House and here. More than enough to keep you occupied."

"There is always time to do what is necessary."

"In my estimation what is necessary is looking after yourself. You've had three miscarriages, and if you're not more careful you'll have another. Lady, take it easy, if not for your sake then think of the baby. What has all this got to do with the baby?"

"That's the point. I want our child to be born into a better world. I want a better and safer world for Lana and her generation. For all of us."

"And you think women voting will result in a better world!" His mouth curls as though he were about to laugh.

"Don't you tell me men have all the answers. Look at the mess men have managed to get us in. Depression! War! Because women have a compassion and understanding that most men lack, I believe that when women are allowed to vote they'll vote against ignorance and injustice and will bring a measure of sanity that this country has not known before. That is what I am fighting for."

"Well, let me suggest you let other women do the fighting and you look after your home for a change. The

212

washing's not done. The supper dishes were left in the sink. There are papers everywhere. The place is one awful mess."

"It's not easy to get help nowadays..."

"My mother never had help. Her house was always tidy. Never a pin out of place..."

"Your mother! I'm not your mother." This record has been played before. Too often. The conversation is quickly getting out of hand. I take a deep breath and speak more quietly. "Tell me, Charles — for I don't think we've discussed this in all the years of our married life. What do you think should be the role of women? Stop pacing! Sit down. Just wait. I'll put the kettle on and we'll have a nice cup of tea while you talk and I listen." I think, as I head for the kitchen: And it will give both of us a chance to cool down.

With tea hot and tempers cooler, we sit across from one another in the parlour, I in a green oak rocking chair and Charles in matching arm chair with its seat cushioned in soft red Spanish leather — remnants from the parents.

"All right now, I'm listening. What is your ideal of womanhood?"

"Well, I've been thinking while you were making the tea."

Obviously he is pleased to have been asked, and settles himself more comfortably in the chair, resting on the tip of his spine, his legs outstretched, long fingers linked, head thrown back, a beatific smile on his face. Two light bulbs, surrounded by frosted fluted glass hung from a decorative metal holder, are strengthening the corner shadows and casting bleak light on husband and wife. And, no doubt expecting to mollify and dignify his spouse, Charles opens his mouth and puts his foot into it.

"I say a woman is the pivot and mainstay of the

213

home. And the home, in turn, is indispensable to the well-being of the country. For the home is of utmost importance to the emotional, mental, and physical development of the children. When a mother is uncaring, or not at hand, then the home is not sound, the grounding for the child is insufficient or wrong. The child lacks a feeling of security, has no sense of direction, no knowledge of what is right and what is wrong. Without proper homes children lose their moorings, they come adrift, minds and bodies become warped. They become problems to society and are an economic drain. So, in the last analysis it is the woman who sets the pace, rules the home..."

"And brings the slippers, embroidered by her own little hands, to her husband when he returns from work," I mutter — but to myself, for Charles, eyes turned ceilingward, hearing me not, plows manfully on.

"In the last analysis it is the mother's teaching in the early, formative years that determines whether the child becomes a proper citizen and fit for this great country of ours." Charles has really become expansive. "It is in the home where a healthy morality is rooted —"

I interrupt. "And what, may I ask, is the role of the man — in your opinion?"

"It is the duty of the man to be a good provider — and I hope I will always be that. But it's the duty of the woman, primarily, to be a good wife, housewife, and mother to his children."

His eyes are half closed now. He sees me not, and so continues unabashed.

"I believe a woman should have ample education." This is for my benefit. He knows full well how keen I am on education and that I have already insisted that our son, or daughter, will have the best.

"But," he rambles on, "if she intends to be a homemaker, it is unnecessary for her to be trained for a

214

lifelong career. If she intends to be a homemaker, then training in a career would take her outside the home and could mean division in the home, lack of care for home and children. A career is a full-time occupation. So too, in my estimation, is homemaking a career — an honourable career, and a most worthy and rewarding one. This does not mean inequality between husband and wife; rather it means dissimilarity — complementarity — instead of what could become competition between the sexes. Perhaps a woman's role is the more difficult one. But, if so, it also can be the more creative one. A wife has often been referred to as her husband's helpmate. But, as you know, I believe a man should be a helpmate as well. For the woman's task is not an easy one and great demands are made on her time, her strength, and her skills, every hour of the day — and sometimes well into the night when there is a young family."

As he pauses for breath, his helpmate once more interrupts. For though no doubt it might have pleased many a woman, this verbal package has been sent to the wrong address.

"Does this mean you intend me to stay cooped up in this miserable hole after our baby is born, giving of my time and skills every hour of the day and possibly of the night? Just here?"

My tone is icy, and a surprised Charles bumps hastily to earth.

"Now look here, Lady, I don't mean altogether. But I should say that with the child more and more of your time will be centred in the home."

"You mean me to give up my work at Owen House?"

"I didn't say that. But if it takes up too much of your time — yes."

He is quickly becoming exasperated, probably because what he considered to be a compliment to

215

womanhood has not been accepted as such. How little he knows me.

"Frankly, I was hoping a child or two would put a stop to some of those shenanigans which I have always considered a bit dangerous. And your chumming around with those North-End Bolsheviks!"

"Bolsheviks! So that is what you think of the Manekowskis. I can't believe it!"

"Damn it, Lady, you don't seem to realize the embarrassment you've been causing me. I've tried to put on a good face. And I'll not let you down. But the things you've said in front of my friends and relatives! Sometimes it's been almost too much. I'm sure they often wonder whose side you're on."

"Must one take sides? I'm all for improving social conditions. If your side is for getting all it can at the expense of the underdog, then let's say I'm on the other side."

"Lady, calm down. I thought we were talking about something else. I didn't mean to get into an argument with you In your condition —"

"In my condition! That again. What do you think I am? A China doll?"

"No, not a China doll. You have never impressed me as being that."

"Then stop treating me as that. I want you to know I have no intention of ever giving up my work in the North End. And I have every intention of handing out those pamphlets. The fresh air and exercise will do the baby and me a lot of good. And don't you dare refer to my friends the Manekowskis as Bolsheviks just because Mike happens to have a social conscience—which, it seems, is more than you have. If you think the most important thing in life is to make money and more money, then I say: Bah! Besides, you haven't done too well in that respect. As far as I can see you are a

216

marvel at always doing the wrong thing." My emotions must be getting the better of me, for I am equating Charles with Pa — I'm talking like Ma. "Look where you and your investments have brought us. To this dump."

I can see that my accusation is like a slap in the face. He does want to give me a nice home. He wants to be and is a good provider, considering the circumstances. He works hard. Why did I have to say that everything he does is wrong? There is that in me that stands back and regards my every action. What is this part of me that deplores my more unfortunate roles? Who is this Watcher, so dispassionate and detached? I know it. Yet I am unheeding and unable to prevent the oncoming storm.

Hurt, Charles hits back. "It wasn't a dump when my mother lived here."

"Your mother again. The perfect model of womanhood."

"That, at least, is true."

"Yours is the second talk I've attended this evening, and my preference is for the first."

I flounce out into the hall, slamming the door behind me. At the same moment the doorbell rings. About to climb the stairs, I hesitate, then go to the vestibule and open the door.

It's Cora, smiling, something in her outstretched hand.

"Ray is waiting in the car... Why, Bessie, whatever is the matter?"

So the matter is showing in my face. I may just as well admit it.

"I've had a disagreement with Charles. He's being miserable."

"Well, for what it's worth, I gather he reported to the recruiting depot and he's not wanted for the time being, anyway. Maybe it was not nice to be told he's too old,

217

like Ray. And besides, Charles has flat feet."

I am unsympathetic. "I'm sure he must have known about his feet. But does he know he has a flat head?"

Cora changes the subject. "I understand you want a layette pattern and I thought you might like the one I used for my baby. Take a look at it anyway. I think it's attractive and it's been so practical."

She offers the pattern.

I am about to take it, but I start to cry instead as Charles, likely having heard Cora's voice, comes into the hall. Turning, I run up the stairs.

But I can still hear them. Charles is speaking to Cora. "I'll take the pattern. She'll be all right tomorrow and I'm sure she'll phone to thank you and apologize. I understand women can get a bit strange when they're in that condition."

"Really?"

"She's not herself. Just a bit upset."

<br>

## 4

*Winnipeg, September 4, 1916*

*Dear Martha,*

*It has been a very long time since I last wrote and you have had only the telegram sent by Charles to say the baby arrived and all was well. I know you have been anxious to hear from me about everything but there hasn't been a moment until now to write. it has all been very trying and exhausting.*

*The baby was born at home — a wrinkled, red-faced creature with a hank of black hair, looking for all the world like a little old Indian and not at all like my beautiful Lana whom, I confess, at first I hoped she might resemble. Now I'm glad she's different and I'll love this*

218

*little creature because she's mine, and will try to do my very best by her. Charles adores her, and with delight and blind folly showers her with the most ridiculous presents. He hugs her, cuddles her, plays with her. Then he is off and I am left to take care of the problems, for she has been a colicky little one right from the outset. Looking after her I do not mind, for I love children and have had a lot of experience with my brother and sisters, as you know; but it's all the other work as well that tires me so. A night and day ordeal. I pray the worst is now over. With this war, decent help is hard to come by. We managed to find a nurse for a while. One which I don't believe had her head screwed on properly even on her best days. She more than once arrived smellng of alcohol (and where she got it, with our new prohibition laws, I have no idea). I dared not question her, for I was desperate for sleep and frantic for help. But when she dropped the baby — who yelled harder than ever, but appeared to be all right — I fired her. At Charles' insistence I tried a couple of young girls, but both proved more trouble than they were worth. Since then I have been on my own. Of course it would be different if we could afford higher wages, which we cannot.*

*There, I have let my hair down a bit as I used to do with you. And, as ever, it has done me a world of good. Now I'm ashamed of myself for being so caught up in my petty problems when there is so much horror taking place in the trenches in Europe. Our men continue to contest the same few miles of "no man's land", over and over. One day we hear that the Canadians have won a little ground and then the next day it appears that the enemy has recaptured the same few acres. On and on the struggle goes, and thousands die. And to what end? It is said the purpose is to make the world a better place. But I wonder, and find it hard to believe that the right way to go about improving the world is through horror and*

219

*suffering and by way of the ruined minds and mutilated bodies of those who are our country's strongest and finest. Though the fighting is bound to end one of these days, I am sure it will be but a respite, a period for regrouping and refurbishing the arsenals. War and hate can only breed war and hate. I feel that the only way countries in the future can have real peace is for them to very deliberately prepare for peace. Charles does not agree with me, nor do his relatives, that there will be just a period of rest before another great war. I hope they are right and that I am very wrong.*

*Ma wrote that Andy intends to volunteer should the U.S. enter the war. And she has not taken to that very well. She begs him to finish his studies, for he is doing so well and it won't be too much longer before he will be qualified. But youth is impatient for action. Andy says when — not if — the U.S. enters the war, the balance of power will go to the Allies and the Germans will soon be forced to capitulate. He is probably right. And he is not the only one saying that. We in Canada all hope the U.S. will enter and help put an end to all this bloodshed. But at the same time I want to see our Andy safe.*

*About the dress you sketched for me: it is handsome, and under different circumstances I would love to have it. But no, Martha, I really have no need for it, and besides would feel it quite out of place in my situation at the moment. It's a fashion for the South part of Winnipeg, I'd say. There lawns are tended by gardeners who keep every flower and blade of grass in perfect condition — skilfully and unobtrusively. Should the owners come out of doors, it is to balconies or verandahs away from the street, or to have garden parties hidden from the common eye by high walls or hedges. While here on Langside, in the core of the city, it is on the front verandah or on the front steps that people sit, talking, arguing, singing, strumming guitars or ukuleles. Children skip on the*

220

*sidewalks, play hopscotch, ride their wagons* or *tricycles, play jackknife on the grassy verge. The street is full of vitality and altogether it is a pleasant, rollicksome, hazardous walk that one takes along the way. A healthy outdoor atmosphere that I rather enjoy.*

*But back to the dress. Thank you Martha, but I think I'll wait until we are settled in our home and the chaos of baby and war is over. I'm so glad hems are a good eight inches off the ground. At least the women's war effort has created fashions that are more practical and comfortable, and I hope fashion will never again make mandatory the binding, suffocating clothing of the past. Diane Shaw is not the only woman wearing trousers now. Though Charles would never want to see me in trousers (and I feel I must give in to a few of his harmless wishes), at least I can enjoy the freedom vicariously, and will no doubt in time see my daughter in quite "outrageous" outfits should this trend continue. The thought delights me!*

*And thank you again, Martha, but no horoscope. If you must cast one for her I do not want to know about it. I made a pledge not to get caught up in such matters ever again, and I do not mean to break that pledge. And in answer to your next question, I would not, even if I could, attempt to predict the future for her. You must remember that when one is emotionally involved with a person there is no longer the required detachment — desires and emotions take over. I wish little Martha all the best. Please tell the de Chênes, much as I love them, if they send me any more news from the spirit world I'll not open any future letters. That's harsh, but Minnie wrote that "there are those on the other side who wish to make contact with you." And I am constantly fighting myself and trying to snuff out these tendencies within me which are condemned by my church. Even though I did not like what Dickinson said to me, I now realize he said what he* had to say. It is not an easy battle, for it seems as though it is my very nature I am attempting to overcome.

I can tell you, Martha, this house depresses me. I try to close my ears and eyes but still it seems to whisper, and often I see shadowy, restless forms moving about — nothing harmful, but it troubles me. The place is haunted by a memory. It isn't only ancient castles that have ghosts, Martha. This place cannot be more than three decades old, but something went very wrong either in this house or on this spot before the house was built, and these troubled souls cannot rest — and I am kept on edge. The de Chênes could be right: it is as if these souls want to get through to me. But I'll not have it.

Of course I cannot speak to Charles about such matters, Charles who is too well-grounded to notice anything. He wouldn't understand about such phenomena and might send me to a doctor. But we'll be gone one of these days when the war is over. For now, the housing shortage remains. There is even a scarcity of rooms for people coming to the city. And no building proceeds — all effort goes into the war.

Forgive me, but I feel better as I continue to scribble my thoughts to you. And I'll feel even better when I'm out and about a bit more and back at Owen House. Ethel and Sandy came by with presents and their good wishes. They phone occasionally to keep me up to date and ask advice. It makes me feel good to know I'm still needed. Diane and Oscar sent a present via their chauffeur — and the great shining motor car caused quite a stir in the neighbourhood.

By the way, I don't want you to think that Charles is oblivious to all the work I have to do with the baby and the house. He's always kind and helps in his way when he can with the dishes and meals, and he does the shopping. But, of course, he has to be about his business. He says, "We'll get a nanny for the child when we can."

222

*And just when will that be? He has such grand ideas! And for Martha he has such big ideas. He's already wondering about the best of private schools and talking the matter over with his cousins. He's also a very sensitive person and sensitive to my moods. I must try not to hurt him with my quick words and temper, which I'm afraid I do all too often. We'll manage somehow.*

*Love to you from me and your* namesake,

*Bessie*

*Chapter VI*

# Tinder Box

Autumn. Another gratifying day full of golden sunshine, with just a slight and pleasant nip to the air. Sweater weather. Members of the Clements clan, including now small children, have been invited for a picnic at the Hamilton's cottage by the river. Having lunched and walked along the bank and through the bright fallen leaves — the children revelling in them, kicking them high, throwing them, rolling in them, playing and laughing — all are now resting on the large screened-in verandah. The little ones, covered with a warm blanket, are sound asleep on a couch — except one-year-old Martha, who is asleep in my lap. The men are indulging in pipes and cigars. Thank goodness there's a slight breeze to carry the smoke away. Up to this point the conversation has been pleasant but rambling. Now Fred Hamilton directs a question at me.

224

"Charles here tells me your young brother has joined the U.S. army?"

"Yes. And my mother, especially, is none too happy about that. She remembers all too well what happened to her father, and to her eldest brother, whom she adored, and the price the family paid as a result. Both my grandfather and uncle were casualties of the Civil War."

"I am sorry."

"Mother wanted Andy to complete his law school first. And I know she was hoping the war would be over before he finished and was called up — like all mothers, I imagine. But Andy joined despite all protests. Said he wanted to get into the fray and help finish it off.

"Well, the consensus of opinion is that the war will be over in a few months time, now that the U.S. has thrown its weight with the Allies. So perhaps it won't be long before your brother and all the other brothers will be back home and at their studies again."

"Let's hope this war will not go on much longer."

"Bessie, I should have thought a young man like your brother would have opted for the flying force?" It's Ray, with a twinkle as usual.

"But Ray," Sarah shudders, "Flying is very dangerous. Those machines are so flimsy. They can't stay airborne very long and most pilots are killed sooner or later. I shouldn't like to see you in one of those things."

"You just might if this war goes on. War is dangerous, you know, wherever one is, and I for one would prefer to be above the ground and go to certain death than be maimed through trench warfare."

"Ray!" Sarah is cautioning him, looking at me.

"I'm sure Bessie knows just what her brother has gone into. It takes a lot of courage and he'll be the better man when it's over." Ray goes on heedlessly, "If I

225

get to go I'll try to get into a flying machine..."

"Well, you're too old," Cora cuts in, "and Fred was just saying the war will be over soon. So there."

"I hear those flying machines can go at something better than 80 miles an hour," Ray continues with enthusiasm. "And they're equipped with machine guns where the rate of firing is synchronized with the revolutions per minute of the propeller. So the men are no longer shooting off their own propellers as happened before. It's much safer flying than it was at the beginning of the war."

"And those machine guns are a great improvement over what the men used for attack in 1914," says Fred. "They only had pistols, bricks, and chains. Besides, fly men are a sort of elite group. they live in comparative comfort and are not forever wallowing in mud."

I can see that Sarah, always empathetic, is anxious to change the subject for my sake.

"If flying machines are improving all the time, Father, what do you think they will be like after the war ends — in a few years?"

"Don't ask me. I'm strictly a horse-and-buggy man myself. You wouldn't get me up in the air, not for anything. Your mother neither — eh, Elmira?"
His wife agrees.

"I say the air was meant for birds. Put your question to Charles here. He's the son of an inventor."

"Well, what do you think, Charles?"

"I think we'll all be flying over the Atlantic one of these days — and the Pacific. All around the world."

"Really, Charles? I can't imagine what it will be like."

"Oh, I can," I say for fun. "I read an article in the *Ladies Home Journal* not so long ago. Sarah, you and I will walk up to the ticket office and say, 'Two tickets for London, England, please.' And the clerk will say, 'Step up on the scales with your luggage. One at a time,

226

please.' Then for me he'll read, 'Two hundred pounds exactly.' For I'll have seventy pounds of baggage including Martha here — I won't leave her behind."

"At least seventy pounds, if I know you women," cries Ray, entering the game.

"At three dollars a pound, the price of my ticket will be six hundred dollars..."

"Oh, you're wrong there," Charles interjects. "I'm sure you'll not be allowed to carry more than about thirty pounds of luggage. It won't be like going on a steamer, you know. Enough fuel will have to be carried to get across the Atlantic, and weight will be all important. Just consider the number of hours it will take. Our flying machines can now stay up for only an hour or two at the most. But if machines can be designed to stay up in the air long enough, you'll get to Europe much faster than by steamship."

"But you won't be able to walk around inside a flying machine. And think how cold it will be up there." This from Cora.

"Flying machines by that time will be like small airborne rooms. You won't have to wear goggles and a helmet, Cora, the way the men do now."

"Do you think so, Charles? What fun!"

I hold up my hand for attention. "The airborne room will be like a luxurious drawing room designed by one of North America's outstanding decorators. There will be a crystal chandelier, mirrors, plants, oriental carpets on the floor — floor and walls being heavily padded to help deaden the thunderous noise of the engines —"

"I disagree about the chandelier," interrupts Ray. "Much too heavy. Remember, weight is a consideration. So we get rid of the plants as well. And there will be Philippine or Japanese stewards to show you to your seat, do the cooking, serve the meals, and make the beds..."

227

"There will be beds?" questions Charles. "One can't expect to sit up for the thirty-six hours or more that it will take to cross the ocean."

"'Why Philippine or Japanese?" Fred wants to know.

"They will be chosen because they are light in weight and short in stature. Everything has to be considered with a flying machine."

We all laugh.

"Well, be careful," cautions Uncle John. "I hope your flying machine company doesn't hire a Japanese for a pilot or he might take it right into China."

"Don't worry," laughs Sarah. "Surely those machines will never fly that far, Father."

"I don't know about that. Those Japanese are an ingenious lot and they are doing all they can to force themselves into China."

Trust them, the men are back to politics again.

"At least that doesn't concern us," says Aunt Elmira in a vain attempt to ward off the inevitable.

"I don't know about that, Mother," says Ray. "There's been some talk about the Allies having agreed to support Japan's claims on China after the war in return for concessions from Japan. China, you know, has been doing all it can to oust foreign investment and foreign governments."

"One can hardly blame them when you consider how the imperialist powers have been encroaching on China," I say shortly, immediately on the defensive.

"And the awful things the Chinese have been doing to foreigners and especially to foreign missions," says Aunt Elmira, ignoring my remark. "My dear," she continues, leaning slightly towards me, "I'm so very happy you didn't get to China. Things always work out for the best, you know."

"Yes, Bessie." Sarah has been listening while the men continue with their politics. "We heard your

228

mission was wiped out. So many killed — and horribly, too. I'm so sorry."

"I wish I'd been there."

"But Bessie, you can't mean that!" Sarah frowns at me.

Martha stirs. I lift her up and hug her, hiding my face. Head down, I quiet the child and rock her back to sleep. How can I explain my feeling of guilt for not going? The man who took my place suffered horribly, but managed to return to tell the story.

Along with Dr. Gerald Foster, the Reverend Dickinson entered a small shop one day, only to discover two Chinese men concentrating on yarrow sticks — oracle divining. For moments Dickinson stood transfixed. Loathing anything to do with the occult, he vented all his pent-up hatred against the unsuspecting pair, thrusting aside the yarrow sticks with his walking cane, shouting at them as he had shouted at me. But to them it was incomprehensible. Their surprise slowly turned to anger. Only too happy to make an example of him, a gang of Boxers sought out the mission, tortured and killed the man of God before the terrified mission people, then horribly maimed and killed the missionaries and set fire to the buildings.

True, such things are happening elsewhere in China. But would it have happened to my mission had I gone to China? I could never have instigated such an incident. What if I had gone to China with Dickinson? Would he even have thought of going there had it not been for me and had I not told Bill Bates's fortune that fateful night? When was all this misfortune set in motion? Why must I feel I am in part to blame for what has happened on the other side of the world as though I possess tentacles capable of reaching over great distances? Do one's thoughts, words, and actions go on and on, encircling the earth forever, affecting everything and everyone? If

229

that is nonsense, why must I feel so guilty because I erred? After all, I am only human.

"China doesn't worry me at the moment, but Russia does." Fred's voice breaks through my unhappy thoughts. He is talking between puffs at his cigar. "Those Bolsheviks are getting altogether too strong for my liking."

"The Tsar never was in control of his country's affairs — a weakling from the outset. That mad monk, Rasputin, who had the Tsarina hypnotized, is the one who gave the orders, or so it is said."

"Ineptness, whoever the fool, has resulted in a form of revolution since the workers' strike in Petrograd in March. Workers' councils have been set up all over the country. Now with Lenin spirited out of Switzerland and back in Russia to lead his Bolsheviks, you mark my words, that revolution will turn to violence."

"Unless the British and Americans can help the moderates hold the line."

"Let's hope they can. Those Bolshies are going around stirring up the people and shouting for Peace, Land, and Bread."

"And what's wrong with that, Fred?" I can't resist asking quietly. "Haven't people the right to Peace, Land, and Bread?"

"Perhaps, but for one thing they won't get their Land and Bread with Peace."

"For another thing," adds Charles, "those Bolsheviks have no intention of containing their communist movement. They mean to infiltrate the Western world. As a matter of fact they're here right now."

"Why worry?" Uncle John speaks up after a period in which the company has time to digest the awesome words. "Communism will not come here. This is not a country of peasants and slaves."

"Maybe not peasants," I say. "But I beg to disagree

230

about the slaves."

The sun has gone down. The conversation, earlier so filled with laughter, is changing, growing heavy, and I am not helping to keep it in its former channels.

Charles is frowning pointedly at me, saying with some exasperation, "Conditions are improving here all the time, Lady, and will continue to improve. I say keep the Bolsheviks out of this country."

He exasperates me, always expecting me to flare up. If he is expecting me to say something, maybe I just will. I turn to him. My words are measured. "I hope you are not, as usual, about to equate communism with strikers, Charles. Workers should have the right to strike for better working conditions and higher wages."

Fred, in an all-too-obvious attempt to avoid argument, speaks up quickly. "I, for one, can't wait to see how women's votes will change all that's wrong in this country and get it back on even keel. How about it, Cora dear, how do you intend to use your vote next election? For Grit or Tory?"

"Fred, you know I don't understand a thing about politics. And truly I don't care. It's all I can do to cope with the house, the children, and all. I guess I'll vote the way Ray does."

"That's my sweetheart," says Ray smugly. "And my guess is that's the way most women will vote—the way their husbands do. How about you, Sarah? You'll vote Liberal?"

"Just you wait and see. I don't altogether agree with your thesis. What about the women who'll vote to cancel their husband's vote — to spite them?"

"That's one more reason for women voting. And how about you, Bessie, can we count on your voting Liberal?"

I realize the remarks are meant simply to recapture the day's light motif. But what with my unhappy

231

thoughts of China and a surfeit of Charles' frowns, I am already out of humour.

"Only for as long as I continue to agree with the Liberal platform will I vote Liberal." I pause briefly, then plunge carelessly on. "I intend to vote for the party that gives help to the underdog and not to the one that aids the slave-driver." Then, knowing only too well I shouldn't, I add, "Like your friend, the money-grubbing Oscar Shaw, with his inhumane factories. Should he attempt to become the Liberal candidate for Premier of this province — as I know he would like to — or to run for any other important post, I'll do all in my power to stop him."

Through the ensuing silence Sarah's reproachful whisper to her brother comes to me clearly: "You know you should not have asked her." As though all are aware of my temperament and tendencies and none agree with me!

I turn defiantly to Charles, heedless of the fact that his face is hardening, the hurt look in his eyes giving way to one of stubborn anger. But before I can speak, he says coldly, "So, you would support these workers in their unions and their strikes?"

"Yes." Maybe at last I know where I stand.

"Are you aware of the Bolshevik intention? Have you ever read the Communist Manifesto?"

"Yes, you know I have."

"Well, just in case your mind has become somewhat clouded, let me recapitulate the essence of that document."

His eyes and words are directed at me. While the others sit in uncomfortable silence, he bites out his words with precision.

"Communism is a threat not only to Russia but to Europe and our country as well. Communists have never concealed their aim, which is the overthrow of

232

existing society by means of violent revolution. And, should they succeed, it would mean the end of our free enterprise system. An end to our freedom." He continues. "There is little doubt that a violent revolution is about to break out in Russia, because since the abdication of the Tsar in March, the Bolsheviks have been shouting for blood, accusing Nicholas of attempting to regain his throne by betraying Russia to the Germans. That is nonsense and simply an excuse for violence. And now that the Romanov family have been moved to Siberia under the pretext that it is for their safety — but more likely to isolate them from their followers — the cause is in danger."

"Whose cause?" I ask, warming to battle.

"Damn it, Bessie," Charles explodes. "The cause of freedom. The Manifesto has called for the workers of the world to unite. These Reds have infiltrated into factories all over our country and are just waiting for the right moment for revolution. Aren't you aware that the trouble in Russia began with a workers' strike in Petrograd?"

I can feel the muscles in my face stiffening. "You are surely aware that I know as much about this as you do. But you are a fool if you think communists will take over this country. The workers only want a fair deal. If they were fairly treated there would be no need for strikes."

Charles has no right to direct his words at me. How dare he talk to me like this in front of his relatives, treating me as though I were an ignoramus.

"Bessie," Uncle John now cuts in with an air of infinite patience, "Charles is simply trying to explain that there could be serious consequences if this Bolshevik revolution were to get out of hand. And it is well for us to be on our guard. I was talking to Rockefeller last winter in Florida. Said the place is

233

crawling with communists. Said the thing to do is round them up and jail them or ship them out of the country. I don't agree. Don't think this country would ever go for communism. Ours is a land founded on freedom and opportunity. But be on guard, I say."

"Shaw's been warning us for a couple of years or more now. These unions will turn into something ugly one of these days." Fred has turned to his father-in-law and to Ray, ignoring me. "These unions are a threat to free enterprise. And that Pole, Manekowski, is a ringleader..."

They may ignore me, but I do not intend to let that one go by.

'My friend Manekowski is no Bolshevik," I interject hotly. "He has no desire to see communism implanted on this soil. All he is working for is a bit of bargaining power. All he is asking for is a decent life for workers, the ability for them to share a bit in the bounty and goodness of this country. You consider yourselves compassionate people. You give some money, you smoke your fat cigars, and are complacent with your riches. You have little idea of the misery that is the lot of a majority of people in this country. Mikhail Manekowski knows only too well what workers have to contend with. And I admire what he is doing. When you call him a Bolshevik it only goes to show your ignorance, your complete lack of understanding —"

"That's enough, Bessie." Charles stands up. I am no longer Lady, I'm Bessie! Well, it's about time he found out about me. "I think we should get Martha home, fed, and to bed. Besides," he adds to the others with a bit of misplaced humour, "Bessie has a long day ahead of her tomorrow. After her Sunday School class she has a conference with Comrade Manekowski."

Fighting back tears, I reach for the baby's fallen shawl. Nodding briefly to the silent company, who

234

return my nods, I move towards the door. Only Sarah walks outside with us to the car.

Finally, on the way home, numb and despairing, when able to speak I ask, "Why did you have to humiliate me like that in front of your relatives?"

"Damn it, Bessie, why are you always, always, blowing off your mouth? Always on the other side of the fence. Always making such stupid remarks in front of my family."

"Why is what I say considered 'blowing off my mouth'? Why can't what I say be accepted as one person's honest opinion as opposed to another's opinion? Mine are not stupid remarks. Besides, I thought Martha and I were your family."

"Then act like my family."

"Must I agree with everything you and your relatives say in order to belong?"

"It would help." As he viciously accelerates the car, an unnatural silence descends.

## 2

The hours go by. The chasm widens. Tensions heighten. After Martha is fed and put to bed, I place on the table a cold supper which Charles eats, newspaper in front of him. Usually after supper he offers to clear away, but tonight he moves to the parlour and continues his reading. Without comment I clear the table and after finishing the dishes go silently upstairs to bed. I've been sent to Coventry! I'll teach him a thing or two. And turning away from the centre of the bed I cling to the edge, determined not to make up with my errant spouse. Always in the past after little tiffs, he rolls over and puts his arms around me. But tonight, when Charles finally comes to bed, he turns his back on me. Tonight I need have no fear of reconciliation.

With hurt in my chest, I sleep fitfully. And all the repressions and frustrations and now the resentments that are mine rise to the surface and over and over they go in my mind like a giant ferris wheel, each chair holding a Shaw, a Dickinson, Charles and his rotten investments, Charles and his too many relatives, this house I don't want to live in, its dark basement where I have to wash the baby's diapers, the clothes, Charles' dirty handkerchiefs, his smelly socks, his heavy winter underwear — rinsing everything in two tubs of water filled by way of a hose, everything having to be fed through an electric wringer, once from the washing machine into the first rinse water and then through the wringer swung ninety degrees into the second rinse water, then through the wringer again into the basket to be carried upstairs and outdoors to be hung to dry. Some might think I should be thankful to have an electric washing machine and wringer. But if Charles had only taken my advice about those investments — I have far better knowledge and intuition than he apparently has — none of this would be necessary. And making me put up with all this in order to provide for a second cousin's mother-in-law — or somebody — to say nothing of everyone else, when charity should begin at home. Not that he seems to know where home is. There was absolutely no good reason why we could not have stayed in that bright, comfortable house on Church Avenue that I liked so much. Because he just had to show that he had all the answers. If he had only listened instead of being so pig-headed. That's what he is: pig-headed!

I twist and turn and doze, and finally when dawn comes wake up, startled, my mind still a whirl of

236

resentments. Martha is calling from her crib. Charles is already gone from the bedroom.

Breakfast is a repetition of solitudes. Charles, who no doubt has slept soundly, is dressed for church in a dark suit, white shirt with starched collar, silk tie, and well-polished shoes.

Prayer book in hand, he says, "Well, I'm off to church." It's a half attempt to be pleasant. "Martha's my charge this afternoon and I'll take her to visit Uncle Walter and Aunt Josephine after depositing you at the House. I'll give her toast and milk if she gets fussy. She'll be fine, so don't you worry. When will you want us to pick you up?"

Unwilling to give in, I reply coldly, "Ethel has something to do in the kitchen this afternoon. She has already offered to bring me back — probably about six."

"Very well then." He stoops to tickle Martha, who is playing on the floor. She gurgles happily. He turns and leaves.

I watch his back receding through the doorway. So!

It has become the custom in the past few months for Charles to attend St. Stephen's Anglican on his own Sunday mornings, while I stay home with the baby and prepare the Sunday roast and vegetables. Then, after Martha is fed, napped, and dressed, it is my turn to be off to Owen House to take my Sunday School class and do whatever jobs are required of me there. To date the arrangement has worked well. When I go to the House during the week, I take Martha with me, Ethel and Gedda sharing the care of the child when necessary. Time at Owen House for the most part constitutes the high moments of my week.

When he returns, Charles recounts the sermon; but this gesture of reconciliation is met with cold indifference. If he wants to, he can just try a little harder. So once more there is silence, a silence that

237

continues until I am left at the steps of Owen House.

Walking in I experience, as ever, a sense of relief. I take a deep breath and some of the dullness and anger dissipates. I exhale and walk quickly to the kitchen, calling hello to Ethel, who is seated at a table, busy with her market lists.

"See you about five-thirty, Ethel? I have a bit to do in the office after my class. Will that be all right with you?"

"Just fine, Bess." Ethel lifts her head from her work and gives me a smile. "I've a few things to do too, and if I'm through with my bits and pieces before you, I'll be happy to put my feet up, sip some tea and read." She points to a book resting on the table near her. "I'm in no hurry to get home. James is away. So take your time."

"Thanks, Ethel, you are a dear as usual. But I must be back by six, because of Martha. So you can count on me by five-thirty. See you then." I give her the brightest smile I can muster and disappear towards the staircase.

Already I feel better. This is the place where I belong. This is my place. Why ever did I marry Charles? Much better we had remained good friends — good friends and lovers. The rest of the marriage bit is not so good: the housework, the cooking, the never-ending responsibilities — most of such little consequence. Responsibilities, too, to people who could get along very well without me. People with whom I have almost nothing in common. How much do I have in common with Charles for that matter? Not much. Petty responsibilities, when there is so much of greater importance to be done in the world. Matters I could cope with much, much better. Here in the North End are the people who need me. Here are my interests and my friends.

"Good afternoon, children." The children are all bright and responsive. All so eager to learn.

Three-thirty and the class is over. After exchanging

good-byes, chatting a bit, I counsel an older child who has turned to me for comfort. And when she leaves she is more at ease because of my words. The incident only serves to underscore how much more important is my time spent at Owen House, how comparatively worthless the life on Langside Street.

Downstairs in my office a fire burns brightly on the hearth and gives a lift to my spirits. How like Mike to think of building a fire for me on this cool autumn day. I take note of the large hearth rug with its rich reds and blues, golds and browns, the colours highlighted by the leaping flames. I turn on the desk lamp and with a sigh settle down in the familiar chair. From a drawer I pull a file marked "Current — Maintenance". Sunday. But almost the only time Mike and I can meet to discuss maintenance problems and costs.

The door opens and Mike walks in. Without warning my anguished heart responds to my friend. He is my friend and perhaps the only one who really understands my political views. Better than even Sandy or Ethel, who live in posh houses and whom I have seen very little of since my move to Langside Street and the advent of the baby.

"Please sit down, Mike. Pull your chair closer and we'll go over these costs together."

"Today, Robin, I have a request for something that to me is important. Something that was overlooked at the time of remodelling. I've taken the liberty to check details and costs and feel the matter should be taken care of as soon as possible." As he pulls his chair close to mine he places a sheet of paper before me. I glance at it briefly and slip it under the other papers requiring attention.

Heads close, minds concentrated, we set to work. It has happened so often before. But today is different. Today I feel his closeness and am aware of his

239

masculinity as never before.

I stop talking and look up, thinking about him. Like Richard he is a leader, so sure of himself. Even his hair, with its dark-copper curls, is almost the colour of Richard's. Strange I haven't thought of that before. More powerfully built than Richard. Impulsively I reach out and put my hand on his. He looks up, surprised, then takes my hand in both of his. His eyes look into mine, questioning but not reproving.

"Mike, you know I'm with you."

"I know that, Robin, bless you. It takes courage."

His sympathy breaks down what barriers remain. I blurt it all out: what was said at the Hamiltons', my unhappiness, my alienation. He understands. He knows enough about the family I have married into. He certainly knows the Shaws. He understands my problems. I knew he would. As he strokes my hand, my face, tears of self-pity flood my eyes. Then it is oh so natural to rest my head on his shoulder. So natural the feel of his arms around me, his face in my hair.

"Mike, oh Mike."

But this must not happen. Pushing him away and shutting the file in a hurried effort to gain composure, I get up from the desk and move quickly to the door. But there I stand, head bowed, hand on the doorknob. But I don't want to leave him. I want him to hold me again and give me that sense of security I need so badly.

"Robin, I'm..."

His voice trails off. It seems to me it holds a plea. In my need I think that plea is for me. I turn the big key in the door, locking it. I face Mike. Reaching behind me I unfasten my skirt and, letting it drop to the floor, step out of it. I unbutton my blouse, take it off, and throw it to the floor. Then I raise my arms to receive him. Responding, he embraces me, picks me up and carries me gently to set me down on the rug before the fire.

240

And there we make love, giving expression to the harmony that has existed between us from the very beginning.

And at last I am at peace.

It is the clock striking the half hour that recalls and cautions me. It is five-thirty.

"Mike, I must go."

No need to say that we will meet again.

How tenderly he helps me dress, helps me arrange the long dark hair, and after one last kiss releases me.

I unlock the door and run to the kitchen. Ethel, lost in her book, whirls around at my breathless call. She looks at me carefully over her reading glasses.

"Bessie, whatever has happened to you?"

"Why, what's the matter?" I'm immediately on the defensive.

"You're excited."

"Just been busy." I am no good at dissembling. But Ethel has no right to question me, no right to interfere in my private happiness. "I'll wait for you outside."

Outside the air will cool my hot cheeks.

When Ethel appears I can tell she hasn't believed me. She frowns deliberately, indicating disapproval.

*   *   *   *   *

At home deceit is easier. I can ignore Charles, with whom I am not being friendly anyway. Hurriedly I pick up Martha, take her to the kitchen for her supper, then rush her upstairs for a bath and a story before bed. Later, when Charles and I have our meal, he does not bother to look at me directly. Just as well, for my secret has warmed me and surely must show. Finally, giving up on his few attempts at conversation, he leaves to find comfort in his pipe and book. Leaves me to the joy of a memory and the anticipation of future assignations.

241

**3**

*Winnipeg, April 7, 1918*

*Dear Martha,*

*There is something wonderful and special I must tell you — you who are my confessor and who have shared my past moments of joy and grief —so that you may also share my present happiness. I have found a true love. When I am with Mihkail it is as though all the years since I left Detroit with their problems and frustrations have dropped away into a bottomless abyss. My life began again one Sunday last autumn. Mikhail is Richard — and more, for there is nothing egotistical about Mikhail. We love and are as one. We talk and agree absolutely on the subject of social justice and the role of women in the work place. The short stolen hours I have with him are pure bliss. So don't tell me it is wrong. How can something so very beautiful be wrong? Charles has never really understood me as a person. Nor can he tolerate my political views. And he has so obviously been unhappy, and even angry, over the years when I've stood up to his relatives and friends. My life and work are at Owen House with Mike and in the North End, and though Charles and I will continue together, most especially for the sake of little Martha, because of my lover nothing can bother or hurt me again. Wish me well, Martha, my oldest and dearest friend....*

*Bessie*

242

## 4

Spring 1918

If Charles has noticed a change in me, nothing is said. If I do not reply when he tries to make overtures, he says nothing. If I do not respond when he holds me in bed, he is adjusting, it seems. He does not shake me, chide me, or show anger in any way. That would not be like Charles. He can get angry, but for the most part he is a mild man. When it becomes obvious that his pleasantries are proving ineffectual and his love-making is being rebuffed, he can still remain civil. Which is more than I can manage.

One day in early May I am shopping in town and have Martha in her cart, when I notice Charles coming out of a restaurant. Surely this is his time to be at the office! Ah! With him is that woman, his old flame, Margaret Bradford. So that is what it's all about. Unobserved, I stop and watch from a distance as they chat and laugh. Then Charles, removing his hat, leans forward and, holding the hat so that it shields their faces, kisses her. There is no doubt about that! So obvious. As though his little trick would fool anyone. Miss Margaret Bradford is holding his hand, saying something. Something sweet, sugary sweet, cloyingly sweet, sickeningly sweet. And then they part, looking back at each other, waving. Acting like a couple of silly adolescent sweethearts.

Why should I care? All the better. Takes the pressure off. So much for that. The Clements clan at least should be pleased about Margaret Bradford. She was their choice from the outset — I know that all too well. I'll say not a word to Charles. I'll give no hint of what I've seen. But I can't help it as the weeks pass and it's necessary for husband and wife to talk, if my voice is just a little sharper, my tongue a little quicker,

243

my temper showing to disadvantage. Charles has remarked on the fact — and with some amusement. But why should I care?

And what about Gedda? I can't quite picture Gedda anymore, not the way I used to. Looking a little strained, maybe? Gedda with her sallow, scarred face. I haven't had much time for Gedda lately, except to leave the baby with her occasionally. Time only to pass a few brief impersonal words. But perhaps Gedda by nature is a somewhat strained, worrying type. Her nature is not my fault. I can't help what happened between Mike and me. After all, how can one help falling in love? It's not as though it had been planned. It just happened so naturally, and so beautifully. What right has Gedda, or Charles, to make me feel guilty? Just because at some ill-conceived emotional moment we made our vows — to the wrong partners. How did we know what lay ahead? How can we be blamed? My head is aching.

* * * * *

One Sunday while Mike and I are making love, Gedda comes to the office door.

"Mike, Mike, are you there?"

Mike does not answer. But I am sure Gedda knows he is in here with me.

"Mike?" She pauses, waiting.

We know she is standing there outside the door. We scarcely breathe, holding tightly to one another, conspirators against a world that cannot understand.

"Mike!"

The door handle turns. But the door is locked. And after a few moments Gedda's footsteps can be heard receding.

Mike is a bit rough and brusque after that. But I can understand he would be upset.

244

We avoid one another as much as possible when there are others around. When it is necessary to speak we are purposely brief. So why does Diane look at me archly, as if she shares my secret? It cannot be that people know Mike and I are lovers.

Everyone knew about Richard and me, once upon a time so long ago. Everyone was happy for us. It was so very good and right... But that was long ago.

\* \* \* \* \*

It is toward the end of May when Sandy approaches me and announces that Cedric has been transferred back to Ontario and that they will be moving in a couple of months. I'm surprised and shocked, but then I haven't been seeing much of Sandy lately.

"I'll send you our address, Bessie, as soon as we're settled. In case you need us for anything."

"Sandy! I'll miss you. How can we manage without you and Cedric? However will I be able to keep the other members of the Board in order without your help?" I say the last lightly but I mean it.

Sandy, her eyes narrowing, looking straight at me, retorts sharply, "You'll manage. Why not put Mike on the Board? He's sure to support you." And with a toss of her bright head she turns on her heel and walks away.

I am badly shaken. Sandy knows. Does everyone?

\* \* \* \* \*

The morning of June first as I'm entering Owen House, I almost collide with Ethel, hurrying to get outside. She stops abruptly.

"Wonderful news, isn't it?" she says, her eyes searching my face.

245

"What wonderful news, Ethel? Do tell."

"Oh, don't you know? About Gedda having a baby. You know she's having a baby..."

"No... No... I didn't..." My head is suddenly spinning, and in an effort to hide my feelings I turn and carefully close the door behind me.

"She's almost four months along. You know how much she and Mike have wanted another child. I'm surprised you don't know."

Fighting for self-control, I can say nothing. Why have I assumed that Mike was all mine?

Still watching me closely, Ethel frowns, then says, "Don't hurt her anymore, Bessie. She's a wonderful person and deserves her happiness."

Why can't Ethel, who has had so many problems with her husband and so much unhappiness in her life, understand my desire for happiness? Ethel is my friend. Why does she, of all people, expect me to turn my love back to Gedda? Why Gedda and not me?

"Good-bye, Bessie."

Another cold good-bye. But Ethel, having opened the door, turns to say more gently, "I'm heading home. See you tomorrow perhaps."

But I've been shocked and I'm trembling. Why have I thought that Mike was my exclusive property? Because I love him and need him and thought that he returned my love, and that my love was sufficient for him. I take a step towards the hall, my feelings naked in my face. And there is Mike coming towards me.

"Mike!"

I'm sure he sees me. But he turns and walks away. Didn't he see me? How could he not have? Why didn't he stop and say something? It isn't right of him, it's so unlike him. Maybe he didn't see me. Going to my office, I shut and lock the door, and sitting down I put my head on my desk. What have I done that is so wrong?

246

Why must I always be made to feel guilty? Why is everyone against me? Why should it be Gedda who deserves happiness and not I? Why should there be such insistence that old-fashioned, primitive customs of marital fidelity be maintained?

Again the Watcher. I look at myself and see myself and know the answers but refuse to acknowledge them.

Maybe Mike didn't see me. Surely the next time he will speak. Everything will be all right. He won't desert me. He can still have Gedda as his wife. After all, I wouldn't expect it to be otherwise. I wouldn't have Lana upset for anything. Mike can still be my lover.

But there is guilt that cannot be dispelled as time goes by and Mike no longer comes to me, avoiding me in the house and in the garden and taking a most business-like approach toward me in regard to all House matters. It is no longer play-acting for the sake of others. His actions are meant to tell me what I am not willing to hear. A deliberate coldness in his voice. A coldness tinged with sadness. How can you expect me not to be unhappy, Mike? I'm unhappy and very, very lonely.

Finding him alone in the kitchen one afternoon, I confront him. 'Why are you avoiding me? Why are you treating me like this?" No doubt these are questions women have asked over the centuries.

"I think you know. I have a responsibility."

"But surely I, too, am your responsibility. You love me. I know you do."

"I love Gedda. I always have."

"You don't love me?"

"I didn't say that. It's different. I admire and respect you."

"Indeed! Then why are you hurting me?"

"I'm sorry. It never should have been."

"How can you say that? Our love is beautiful."

247

"Now it is over."

"How can love be over?" I speak contemptuously. And the next moment I am pleading, "Mike, it doesn't have to be."

"It has to be." His eyes, looking into mine, are severe. "I've hurt Gedda and I didn't want to."

"Why didn't you think of this before?"

"I should have." "

What you mean is that it's all my fault."

"No, I didn't mean that. I love Gedda."

"You've already said that."

It is a tragicomedy played the world over. Personalized for me. And I am the one who rang up the curtain and opened the act.

In my bitterness I repeat, "You have already said you love her."

"Then let's stop talking in circles and get on with our work."

"Now you are angry with me."

"With myself." He turns from me and walks out of the room. It is over.

Desperate, I rush past him, out into the street. He does not follow. It is over. I wander, hardly seeing, shrouded in my own confused thoughts. Once again frightened and unsure of myself. I want to run away. But there are people dependent upon me. And there is Martha. The thought of Martha brings a measure of sanity and I start on my way back to Owen House and my office, by now emotionally drained and scarce able to walk.

Unable to work or even think, I finally take a street car home to face Charles and Martha. Warily watching me, Charles asks no questions. Probably he knows like everyone else — like Ethel, Sandy, Diane, Gedda. All of them. Saved by Martha's prattling and needs, I hug the child to ease my pain. The curtain has been rung down.

248

**5**

Diane, it's so wonderful to come to your beautiful home. How clever of you to have suggested these *kaffee klatsches*. It makes the war seem a universe away. At least for a couple of hours."

"Oh, you mustn't use that horrid word. Don't you know it's German?"

The usual half dozen or so ladies, having arrived sharp at 10:30 a.m., are gathering in the hall.

"It's a happy respite for me too," smiles Diane. "My uniform awaits me, and after this I'm off to the hospital again to empty bedpans and take temperatures."

"Make beds, too, and do a lot of other menial tasks," Sheila Lang chortles on. "I think you're so wonderful — a woman in your position."

"I don't mind in the least. I'm glad to help out. It releases the few nurses still on staff for more important work."

"You have so much energy, Diane," says Cora, taking over from Sheila. "I quite envy you. I wanted to assist in a hospital, but as you know, I was already doing canteen duty and then after my second baby came along, Ray wouldn't allow me to take on another thing."

"Well, Cora, my children are all grown up and away from home and, yes, I have energy to spare. Here's Sarah. Ladies, come this way. I thought we might have coffee on the sunporch this morning. It's such a marvellous day. Do be seated."

"Bessie coming?"

"Let me pour you some coffee, and help yourself to a biscuit.

Haven't you noticed, Sally, that Bessie hasn't been with us for a very long time? I ask her occasionally. But perhaps she just doesn't want to come. I know she never has favoured me exactly."

249

"She's never been at my house and I've invited her."

"Nor at mine. Do you really think she's purposely avoiding us?"

"I think she's just keeping very busy," says Sarah, accepting a digestive. "What with the baby and all. She hasn't the help at home that we have."

"I don't care what her reasons are, but frankly I'm just as glad when she doesn't show up. She doesn't seem to realize how obnoxious she can be sometimes with her Mr. Woodsworth ideas."

Sally corrects her. "You're too kind, Sheila. Bolshevik ideas, I'd say."

"At least, thank goodness, Woodsworth is no longer in Winnipeg to keep stirring up trouble here. My husband says he's a menace."

"Yes, thanks be for that." Sally refuses a biscuit but picks up the thread. "None, Diane darling. But think of Bessie's poor husband, Charles. I do feel sorry for your cousin Charles, Sarah. He's such a dear."

"Why must you feel sorry for Charles? He's a man perfectly capable of taking care of himself. Why must you be sorry for Charles?"

"Someone told me Bessie has a crush on that fellow what's-his-name — Manekowski? But I don't believe a word of it, not really. Bessie is a very honest sort of person. I've always rather liked her, despite her strange ideas."

"I think Sally, and you too, Sheila, are both being rather silly." Sarah is annoyed.

Diane stops pouring herself a second cup of coffee and puts down the pot.

"You may as well face it, Sarah. It goes much further than a crush, if you want to know. Believe you me! I wasn't going to say anything, but now that Sally's mentioned it... Don't tell anyone I said so, but —"

"Far more than a crush? You mean all...the way?"

250

Sheila, fluttering her eyes, is delightfully titillated.

"Just that, my dears."

"No!" breathes Sally, excited. "But now that I think of it, she has changed somewhat in the past year or so. I knew she was different, but I couldn't have said just how."

"Well, I can," says Sheila. "For one thing she's not nearly as fashionable as she used to be. Not at all the way she was when we first knew her. Neat enough. But remember how beautifully she used to dress?"

"That was because of that friend of hers in Detroit who designed for her. Now she doesn't seem to care. Must just pick her suits and dresses from any old store."

"After all, there is a war on," Cora reminds them. "I think she looks just fine. And I think what you're saying about her is just so much gossip."

"Diane should know," says Sheila hopefully. "You are positive, aren't you, Diane?"

"Positive." Diane is enjoying herself. "Everyone around Owen House has known about it for months. I've held my tongue for I didn't want to do her an injustice. But everyone seems to know..."

"Oh my dear, now I am so glad she doesn't come to our coffee parties. I don't think I'll ever feel quite the same way about her again."

"For my part I don't care if I never even see her again. How horrible of her. For a Christian, especially, it's a deadly sin. And isn't she the one who wanted to go to China or someplace and convert the heathen?"

"Hardly Christian of you to talk like this. I think it's your gossip that's the deadly sin." Sarah has found her voice. "What you say is probably not true, but even if it is, though I don't condone infidelity, I've often wondered why society must condemn the woman, yet looks with such tolerance on the man." Clearly Sarah is upset.

251

"Bessie is Ray's cousin's wife, and I've always liked her." Cora is bravely following Sarah's lead. "And I mean to treat her just the same as ever, no matter what."

"Perhaps Charles should have married Margaret Bradford. And I know he would have married Margaret if Bessie hadn't come along just when she did," insists Diane.

"That's none of your business, Diane."

"Margaret is one of us. You know that, Sarah. Right from the start one could have guessed Charles was going to have trouble with Bessie."

"Don't you think quite enough has been said about Bessie?"

"I'd just like to know however in the world she could have been attracted to a foreigner like Manekowski."

"And a Catholic as well. One might have guessed there'd be trouble. Why ever was he allowed at that mission in the first place?'

"He's quite a handsome specimen, Sally. Haven't you seen him?"

"Only at that Open House, and that was years ago. I really didn't pay much attention. If I'd know what was going to happen... But surely the man has no money. Isn't he just a worker? Why," — Sally's voice rises in astonishment — "isn't he the janitor at Owen House?"

"Caretaker, my dear," Diane corrects her. "He is referred to as the caretaker — at Bessie's request."

"How insulting it all is — to all of us. Diane, why do you and Oscar continue to contribute your time and money to that place? Especially now that the Wilkinses have gone."

"Oscar has his reasons," Diane says meaningfully, eyebrows arching.

"I think it's time for me to be getting home." Sarah is plainly disgusted. "If you would like to come now, Cora, I can drop you off.'

"Of course, Sarah, if the others will excuse us."

"Cats!" Sarah tosses the words over her shoulder as she leaves. "Sorry, ladies, but I consider you a bunch of cats."

Her pronouncement does not in the least disturb Diane who, accompanying her two guests to the door, looks like the proverbial creature who has swallowed the canary.

## 6

July 1918

Charlie and Emma are two very fine young people." Charles is patiently explaining his latest protégés.

"I'm sure they are."

Cousins from the west. More cousins. And as usual, no doubt very nice .

"Well, what do you expect me to do, Bessie? It was only right of me to offer hospitality. There's not a decent place in town available for them. You know that. It will only be until they can find a place to stay."

"They will be here a year, at least." I know very well that will be the case. Returning veterans are finding it difficult to get housing.

"They can have the back room upstairs. It has a balcony and a private staircase to the back yard."

"And they'll need a bedroom. Why not let them have the master bedroom, it's closest to the back room. We can take the front room." I am resigned. I haven't been treating Charles too well and he deserves better. Besides, he's right. There probably is no other place for the young people to go.

"Maybe Emma can help look after Marty," says Charles.

253

'Why must you always call her Marty when her name is Martha?"

"She calls herself Marty. The decision was hers."

From the beginning there has been a conspiracy between father and daughter.

I shrug. "So. Martha already has an east room and we'll move next to her, which won't be a bad idea as she's still waking up at night." Or am I the one who is still waking up at night?

"I'll fix up a double burner and an oven for the room. They can get their water from the bathroom. I'll make the rooms as comfortable as possible for them."

He is already planning to make their stay a happy one.

"It certainly won't be the Ritz," he adds.

"No, it certainly won't be." I can hear my voice — discouraged — and recognizing that, I go hastily downstairs, fighting back the tears that are always with me.

"I forgot to tell you," his upbeat voice continues, "Charlie's brother's in town with his wife."

I stop on the stairs. "Oh, please, you can't expect them to stay here too."

"Oh, no. Syd has been in Winnipeg for some time. He wants Charlie to start a tire business with him: 'Curtis Tire Service'. There will be more automobiles than horses in town one of these days. Charlie and Syd will do well."

There is a buoyancy to his voice as he talks of the happy young couple. He starts whistling off key. Putting my hands over my ears, I continue on my way down.

*     *     *     *     *

They are an attractive couple. Glad to have a place. Eager to fit in and be as helpful as possible. Emma, a

254

second cousin of Charles, seems always on the edge of laughter. Whatever did God do to so many of the Clements clan? Tickle them at birth, that they insist on having such an odd slant on life? Her husband calls Emma "Queenie" and adores her. One can't help but like them. They take my mind off some of my problems. Actually, it is like having a younger sister around again. I get along very well with Emma and Charlie. We play whist, ride, and walk together. They are the tonic I need. I find myself laughing, forgetting myself. And because of them, Charles and I are talking more easily again.

Forgetting myself. It is right and high time that I should. There are others to be concerned about. My charges in the North End, for instance. My problems are petty compared with those of others. Soldiers. Discharged soldiers are returning to fill the hospitals — amputees, soldiers gassed, with permanent lung injuries, many who will remain in hospital for the rest of their lives. Will they be remembered by those for whom they sacrificed themselves?

## 7

One afternoon I plan to take Martha in her cart to the store. But, instead, I sit on the verandah — waiting. Martha plays with her dolls. The postman hands me a letter from Ma.

A numbness sets in. I've thought so often of my young, curly-haired brother with the big ears. The love I have for him. The love returned. The many jests. The teasing that levelled our ages.

255

*Detroit, July 15, 1918*

*My Very Dear Bess,*

*The house is empty. there is no one to talk to and I wish you was here. It seems not right just sending a telegram. I got mine today and it was cold. It's about Andy. To the War Office he's just another number and people are getting telegrams all the time nowadays. But Andy's our boy and he was doing so well. I know he could have helped people if only he'd had his chance and hadn't gone off to war. Just like my brother Archie. Andy was so sure he was needed to send those Germans packing. Maybe he wouldn't even have been called up. But he just had to volunteer. He was so sure he'd be all right and he'd be back home in no time at all. We both had read all about trench warfare and what is happening over there with the shell fire, the barbed wire, the mud and all. But that didn't stop him. He must go. And he'll not be coming back, Bessie. It must have happened about as quick as he got out there. I can almost hear those guns blazing, shells exploding, the screams of the maimed and the dying. And then too there's the stillness of the dead. And mud everywhere. Mud covering Andy's boots. That all must be Hell, Bessie. No chance for Andy to be a hero. Just another number. What good was it all? He could have done good here. It seems he was blown to bits and there will be nothing of Andy's to send to me. It is not that I need any trinkets of war or anything else to remember my son so that doesn't matter. But it is such a cruel waste. Don't you write and give me that nonsense about God being love and all is well with our Andy. Today, for me, for sure there is no God. Pa and I aren't close any more so I'm glad he's not here. Pa once told stories about the Irish Wakes he used to attend when he was a boy and said it was good to keep the dead near and dance and sing and feast with the family and friends all about so the grief is not held in. But we can't do that here. I know when Pa comes home and hears about Andy he'll go out and get drunk and get himself a woman. For me, I just want to have a good bawl. But I'll wait until I mail this for I want you to know. Andy was like a son to you too. The others I'll tell after.*

*Your Ma*

## 8

E xtra! Extra! Read all about it! Tsar and family assassinated!"

Charles, Charlie, Emma, Marty, and I are on the verandah in the early evening, welcoming a cool breeze after the day's heat. A newsboy is making his way down Langside. Rushing to the gate, Charles signals to him and buys a paper. He glances at the large print as he returns up the walk.

"I knew it would happen." Satisfaction with his own perceptiveness is apparent. I' knew it would. Those Reds could not afford to keep the Tsar around. Had he been freed he would have become a rallying point. Those damn Bolsheviks have shot the entire family."

Charles looks pointedly at me.

'Why look at me like that? Are you implying that I, or my Bolshevik friend — quote, unquote — pulled the trigger?"

"Don't be ridiculous, Bessie." Charles is plainly disgusted with my outburst. So he turns from me to his cousins and continues with a summary of the article.

"The royal family, so it seems, were in a town in the Urals, called Ekaterinburg. Kept prisoners in a place known as Ipatiev House." He squints at the paper in the fading light. "On July 16th they were herded into the basement and executed. Without a doubt at the order of

257

the Soviet in Moscow."

Emma is upset. "There were young children."

"Charlie," Charles goes on, "do you realize what this could mean?"

He hits the paper with his hand. His back is to me now; he is completely ignoring me.

"Our only hope is that the Allies stand firm alongside the White Russians. Should those Bolsheviks take over Russia we could all be in trouble. Russia is just the beginning. Communists have already infiltrated our country. Their goal is world domination. Should we for one minute let down our guard, what is happening in Russia could happen here."

In full swing now, Charles is expounding and expanding his theories.

"This city is doing what it can to keep check on the extremists. Bessie knows I was sorry when Woodsworth was dismissed as Director of the Bureau of Social Research. I was sorry he felt compelled to leave the city. I agree with a great deal that he was doing to help people. He's a fine man. But in times like this we can't be too careful and there is no doubt he was stirring up dissent and playing right into the hands of the Reds."

I hold my tongue. I have already made one silly statement this evening. I am so on the defensive lately that I have done and said a great deal I regret.

However, unable to resist, I say in a voice that Charles is bound to hear, "Bedtime, Marty. Come along, little one, and I'll tell *you* a story."

258

# Chapter VII

# Conflagration

Autumn 1918 - Spring 1919

I lift the receiver from the wall-phone in the hall.

"Hello."

"Robin. It's Mike"

He hasn't called me Robin since that day. But now his voice is light and happy.

"You all right? And Mr. Clements?"

"I'm fine, Mike. And Charles refuses to be ill. Tell me, how is Gedda?"

"That's why I'm phoning. The baby has arrived. A beautiful boy. Healthy. Gedda's fine too."

"I'm so glad for you — for both of you. But Mike, do be careful. Both of you must be very careful."

259

"Don't worry. Gedda had the baby at home. The midwife was our Mrs. Pole. I checked to be sure there was no sickness at her house. Otherwise I would have delivered the baby myself. But all is well. Now I'm insisting Gedda stay home with the child until this flu epidemic is over."

"The right idea. Lana — how is she?"

'Lana's okay. Her school is closed, of course. And I intend to isolate her too, and that will be tough on our active young lady. But she'll have her mother and little brother to look after, and she's very pleased to know she's a necessary part of it all. Wants to help."

"Isolation. That's the best thing. Clean all food well. And get some lysol, Mike, and see that the rooms are washed down."

My voice trails off. I am thinking of death and birth.

"Robin?"

"Yes?"

"Perhaps the House should be closed. Until it's all over.

"As a matter of fact, Charles has already suggested that."

Charles doesn't want me travelling to the North End as long as this epidemic lasts.

"He intends to speak to Oscar Shaw today. But I've no doubt Oscar will agree. It's the wise thing to do. I'm so glad all is well with Gedda and the baby, Mike. Nothing must happen to that baby. And I know you'll take every care."

"We will see to it that all goes well."

"With you too, Mike." I can't prevent the catch in my voice.

A laugh at the other end of the line. "Strong as an ox."

"I'll call when I have a message for you. Also, just to check in occasionally. And I'll want to speak with Lana.

I miss her. Good-bye, Mike."

"Good-bye, Robin."

I hang up the receiver and return to the kitchen, where Emma and I have been chatting over a cup of tea.

"Gedda's baby has arrived. It's a boy. And all is well."

"Thank goodness." Emma knows about the Manekowskis. "They'll have to take special care of their newborn. Babies are so vulnerable."

My mind is elsewhere. "I've often wondered if a baby, or anybody for that matter, dies only when God decides that is what has to be. Some soldiers, some people manage to go unscathed through such terrible ordeals: it's as though they're shielded. While others... My friend Martha says that the time of death is decided prior to birth. The Bible says there's a place and time for everything: a time to be born and a time to die. Martha says her ideas do not deny God — far from it. It's an intelligent universe and astrology, when properly examined, is one intelligent approach to the study of the universe. She believes that one's whole life is pretty well mapped out and it's only one's attitude towards situations that one can control. Attitudes, she says, are what counts, for one grows through experiences — as though our attitudes are about the only free will we have. Opportunities and problems are shown in one's horoscope, and if one is clever enough to read it..."

I straighten up. How thoughtless of me. Why should I be quoting Martha and talking on about astrology? Emma is not interested in astrology and ignores my remarks. Emma's mind is on the vagaries of God.

"Then God has chosen to end the lives of thousands of people by way of this epidemic. People are dying all around us. Bessie, I'm more than a little frightened, though I try not to be."

261

"We all are, Emma."

"It's awful to think of men having gone through that terrible war — why, some of them were in it for the entire four years — only to come home to die of Spanish influenza. I consider it most unfair."

"Emma, maybe we shouldn't have started talking this way. After all, God knows best. But it's being reported that this is well on its way to being the worst epidemic since the Black Death in the Middle Ages. So very many countries are affected. And if it's as bad everywhere as it is here..."

"Charlie told me there are not enough coffins for the dead. It was in the paper."

"Nor are there enough undertakers to bury the dead. Charles thinks the high rate of mortality is due, in part anyway, to the fact that so many soldiers and civilians had such poor diets during the war that they have little resistance."

"Well, Charlie and I are a couple of healthy country bumpkins. We'll survive." Emma's natural optimism is already bubbling to the surface. "Bessie, I meant to tell you. I went to the drygoods store on Notre Dame yesterday for a spool of thread. And as I was leaving the store, there was a man shovelling snow from the sidewalk. He coughed, then he spit phlegm, just as a policeman turned into the Avenue from Furby Street. He's to be fined fifty dollars, and I doubt if the poor fellow has anything like that kind of money. I've read that people are being fined that amount for even coughing or sneezing in the open. How can people help coughing and sneezing?"

"I doubt if everyone's fined, but perhaps it's an attempt to force people to use handkerchiefs and containers so germs won't be passed on so readily. Perhaps it will mean the end to spittoons. I hope so, anyway. There must be blessings that come from bad."

262

\* \* \* \* \*

Two weeks later Charlie arrives home sick. Then Emma, nursing him, falls ill as well.

Standing at the foot of the stairs, I am hesitant to go to them. I, who have never been apprehensive about entering the disease-ridden homes of my charges in the North End, am apprehensive now.

I tell Charles. "I thought of our Martha and I didn't know what to do. I started up the stairs, then went back down to the kitchen. I started up the second time and halfway up I sat down. I was a coward."

"But you finally went."

"I really wanted only to shut their door and put a blanket soaked in disinfectant over it. I had to talk to myself and force myself to go into their room. You know there are neither doctors nor nurses available. Emma is still crawling around a little. But she can't really cope."

"I'll do what I can, Bessie. They're my cousins and my responsibility."

"But you are away most of the day."

It was just a fortnight ago that I talked to Emma about everyone having a certain scheduled time, a time to live and a time to die. Does death await me upstairs? Or will death inject me with the lethal virus when I go to Corneil's corner store for supplies this afternoon?

\* \* \* \* \*

Pulling Martha on the sled onto the snow-banked road — for the walks are impassable — I wonder how disease can survive this sharp cold. The weather must surely kill some bugs. But influenza is a problem every winter, though nothing as bad as this has ever been known. It is difficult to manoeuver the sled even on the road, for the road is not properly cleared. Unusual.

263

Winnipeg is dependent on its snow-removal crews, but now too many men are off ill.

Martha looks happy and cozy, a long white scarf wrapped around her toque, then around her neck, across her chest, and tied in the back. With mitts pinned on and a blanket over her coat and boots, Jack Frost will have a hard time getting at her.

Once on the road I half turn to find my neighbour, Mrs. Beggs, waving to me and smiling. I wave back and wish her good afternoon, the words almost printing themselves in my frozen breath. Mrs. Beggs is already putting out her milk bottles. Now that we have a bedroom facing the street, I often hear the milkman before dawn, the runners of the wagon crunching in the snow, the horses stamping and neighing, bells tinkling. Pleasant sounds. Though Charles and I get up early, often by the time I collect the milk it is frozen, with the cream pushing its way inches above the bottles, their little cardboard caps resting jauntily on top. Mrs. Beggs, poor soul, her husband returned from the war with an injured spine — though not enough to prevent him from working. How much compensation would they — and other couples like them — get, I wonder. Mr. Beggs' injury causes him to walk like a drunken man, and I have heard the children teasing him. How cruel in their ignorance some children are. Mrs. Beggs, a war nurse, keeps her place immaculate, inside and out. The Beggses supplement their income by taking in roomers. Mrs. Gillis, who lives in the attic rooms with her little girl, Nancy — just about Martha's age — is a war widow and gets $300 annually. Not much to go on.

Neighbours to the other side of us are the Duncans, an attractive looking couple with a pretty daughter. The parents are both deaf and mute. So they are known as the Dumbies by almost everyone in the neighbourhood. Will all the suffering that the world has gone through

264

and is still going through, bring a little more tolerance to this intolerant city? One can hope so.

Marty laughs as the sled lurches and slides. We pass the Lee On Laundry where Charles has his shirts washed and collars starched. I can picture the brown paper parcels with black Chinese markings, standing neatly on the shelves in the front room waiting to be collected, while steam mingled with the odour of bleach fills the air. The Chinks, the owners are called.

Before Corneil's store at Sargent is a vacant lot sporting a billboard advertising Palmolive soap and advising, "Keep that schoolgirl complexion!" (Charles says he's sure a lot of schoolgirls don't want to keep theirs.) Across from the billboard, an old barn. Perhaps that's where the Dacolas stable their horse and keep their wagon. In summer horse and wagon, with Pete or Mike in charge and filled with luscious fruits and fresh vegetables, stop along the street for the benefit of housewives. A fine industrious family, the Dacolas, but not British. Foreigners: Italians. Referred to by the local bigots as the Dagoes.

Maybe I should go first to Dacola's Fruit and Vegetable Market at Furby and Sargent. A fruit salad with oranges, apples, bananas, and figs might be good for Charlie and Emma. Good for all of us. Will it be at Dacola's Market that Martha and I meet our fate? A time for everything. Sargent Avenue is busy with traffic and streetcars. Better get off the road. The snowbank is hip high.

"Hold on there, Marty. Heave-ho, over we go."

How cruel this world when that young flyer came home to die of influenza. As Emma said. That young McLeod — Ma's family name — had, somehow, managed to climb onto the wing of the plane when his pilot was shot and guide the machine safely to earth. Then, instead of thinking of saving himself, he had

265

dragged the wounded pilot from the cockpit and carried him to safety, hiding in foxholes and braving enemy fire. Why should someone like that come home only to die? God surely must be as proud of young McLeod as is the whole of Winnipeg! Was his life, like Andy's, wasted in that terrible, senseless war? Maybe one is born for a certain purpose, and when the work is done and lessons learned, one dies. Maybe death is not such a bad thing after all — no worse than birthing. Strange how one's life impinges on the lives of others. One might set an example like that young McLeod, or start something going for good or for ill. So many spin-offs, one might never even be aware of all or any of them. How can one guess the effect McLeod might have on others? Because of one act of valour. Martha would say that his experiences will make him a better and stronger person for his next time around. While the coward returns to earth a coward. Well, carry on, Bessie, you in your little corner , in your little way. You aren't being asked to crawl out on the wing of a flying machine, or carry Emma and Charlie through no-man's-land. Just get a little fruit salad up to them and make them as comfortable as possible. Charles' motto is 'Do what is right as you see the right.' And one can do no more. I agree with Charles there. Too bad he too often sees like a man with astigmatism.

*     *     *     *     *

We survive. The country cousins and Charles and Martha and I. Though Marty and I also come down sick, it is with comparatively mild attacks of flu. Before the epidemic even begins to peter out it is the spring of 1919 and 65,000 Canadians are dead — more than the number of Canadian soldiers who died in the war in Europe.

And what about those soldiers being demobilized so slowly, though the Armistice was signed last November 11th — slowly returning to find there are no more heroes' welcomes. There is no place for most of them: no housing and no jobs. Most have returned to find they are as unnecessary and as unwanted as the "foreigners" who "clutter up" the city.

"What does the city intend to do for these men?" I ask Charles one morning, the aroma of coffee filling the kitchen, perking on the gas flame as I make toast, using a grilled screen over another burner, flame turned low.

"What are they going to do for themselves?" Charles replies hesitating over his next mouthful of cereal. "If there is no work available, maybe they should try creating jobs for themselves. Like Charlie and Syd here. They showed a bit of initiative, and they're off to a good start with their tire business. Now when I left high school in Crookston I started up a candy and ice-cream parlour. Invited a friend to be my partner. But I found I was doing all the work while he spent his time out front being friendly with the customers. So I closed out. I say every man must pull his weight. Workers, not shirkers. Then I started a chicken farm. When things go wrong, a little initiative is all that is needed. That was just before Uncle John invited me to join the Company."

"And what happened to the chicken farm?"

Something is bound to go wrong where Charles is involved — though, to be fair, not necessarily through any fault of his own.

"The weasels got the chickens." Charles is laughing. "Crafty little creatures, those weasels. I did everything I could think of to keep them out of the chicken run."

"Can't you draw a parallel?"

"What?"

"Between weasels and capitalists."

"Damn it, Bessie, why do you always have to twist

267

my words to suit your theories?"

"Oh, sorry. Sorry I asked."

I should know better by now. I mustn't get into another argument. It does no good. Charles and I have been getting along better lately, what with Charlie and Emma about. Besides, Charles was wonderful all during that awful flu crisis. Cheerful and helpful in every way.

Thinking of the flu, and wanting to say something positive, I remark, "At least the flu epidemic appears to be pretty well over. We can be thankful for that. We're all healthy again."

And Lana, and Mike, and Gedda, and the baby, they are fine too. I kept in touch with Lana by telephone all those months. Now she's back at school and doing well. I'm proud of my protégée and I've promised to put her through university when the time comes.

"I'm so glad, Charles, that you suggested Owen House be closed last fall. That area was rampant with flu virus. More deaths reported there than anywhere else in the city."

Charles knows how much I love Lana and approves of my plans to help her. He is fond of her too.

"Lana and the baby weren't even a bit sick, even though Marty and I were. It was worthwhile keeping people away from the House."

"It wasn't as though no one was allowed in."

"Whatever do you mean? A notice was posted saying no one was to go in."

"The House was closed as a mission for reasons of health. But that didn't stop Manekowski from entertaining his friends. With the mission not functioning it was an excellent place for him to hold conferences with members of the workers' unions and other malcontents. Something's brewing."

"That's not so. Mike wouldn't have put his children at risk."

268

"It's true."

I stare, unbelieving.

Having finished his breakfast, Charles gets up and leaves, scarcely bothering to glance at me.

## 2

May 1919

It is not often that I've been to Ethel's. Ethel does little entertaining, and when she does it is usually for her husband's business friends and their wives. Ethel and I, for the most part, do our chatting, serious and otherwise, in Ethel's pleasant kitchen at Owen House. The kitchen has always been referred to as Ethel's, for almost from the outset she has been in charge of all culinary matters, Mrs. Crutch and her volunteers carrying out the orders.

Today, however, I feel it imperative to talk to Ethel, who is at home. So having dressed Marty in a pretty blue frock to match her eyes and put a blue bow in her dark hair, I'm off with her to Ethel's.

The house is spacious. Generous, like Ethel. Homely, like Ethel. And like Ethel, nothing seems to quite come together. Sofas, tables, lamps, draperies, though of good quality, are a hodge-podge — but a pleasant, comfortable hodge-podge notwithstanding.

Having settled Marty with cookies and milk, a blunt-ended pair of small scissors to suit her little hands, and some old picture magazines she can cut up, Ethel pours tea.

"How lucky you are, Bessie, to have a little daughter. I've often thought how different my life might have been if I'd had a child. But I mustn't complain. Life has been

269

better for me since the moment I started in at Owen House. Lana, too, is a bright spot in my life. She spends a lot of time in my kitchen, as you know, helping out and talking with me. She's a ray of sunshine — but no angel: Gedda has to be quite firm with her sometimes. There is just that something special about Lana. If she were older I would call it charisma. Everyone is attracted to her. I just wish she could stay with us always, just as she is, and never grow up."

"Yes, Lana is someone special. I recognized that right from the beginning. I love that young girl very much too. But I guess we'll have to let her grow up."

"Well, Bess, what's on your mind?"

"Mike. Ethel, it seems Mike had union members meeting at Owen House during the time it was supposed to be closed...

"Who told you that?"

"Charles, by way of Shaw of course. Shaw via Shaw's agents, no doubt. Charles thinks trouble is brewing. More strikes, and this time perhaps violence. Revolution, no less! I'm worried. Why didn't Mike tell us? Why so secretive? That's what makes the statement about trouble plausible."

"I've wondered for some time whether I should say anything. But I've hesitated, not wanting a witch-hunt on our hands. When I first returned to the kitchen it was obvious quite a number of cups and other utensils had been used. You know how some men scarcely wash things? And they were carelessly put away. Not the way Mrs. Crutch and the girls do things. The floor was not as clean as when I had left. Some spilled tobacco ashes around. Quite a number of little things like that. Seemed a bit off, if you know what I mean. Even an odour of tobacco about, as though men had only recently left and had not aired the place."

"Why would they have to meet at the House, Ethel?

270

There are other places, surely."

"Maybe because it was officially closed. Maybe they felt it safer for some reason. Though Mike is quite aware that Oscar Shaw has been checking on him for years."

"Mike's had his friends there often before. And I've always championed his right to do so."

"Maybe that's partly why. What do you think?"

"But Mike's made no bones about those meetings before. We've always been told about them. And he's had every opportunity to say something to us these past few months and hasn't. I phoned during the epidemic — often."

"I called too. This strike has been going on since May first: strikes are not unusual in Winnipeg, but this time there's a great deal of tension."

"The reason is that Calgary Conference, I'm sure."

"I may as well tell you, Bessie, I'm not just a little upset. Since that Calgary Conference in March, I've been seeing everything through a different lens. And not a very clear one."

"A red lens, perhaps? You too?"

"I've heard James talking with his business associates on three difference occasions, and they're convinced the Labour Conference in Calgary was for the purpose of hatching a revolution as terrible as the one in Russia. They talked about the labour members who attended as being either communist or socialist — and according to them there's little difference between communism and socialism. Both 'isms' are out to get the business men."

"You can be sure Charles and his cousins are saying the same thing. It seems that fraternal greetings were sent from the Conference to the Russian Soviet government, which hasn't soothed anyone's concern."

"Do you think Mike is involved?"

271

"As far as I know he had nothing to do with that conference. He's a socialist — a Woodsworth-type socialist. And Woodsworth has a well publicized aversion to violence. I can't imagine Mike changing his ideas overnight; he's always had such a great admiration for Woodsworth. Since J.S. has been in the west he's continued to develop his socialist platform and wants to see a social democratic party formed in Canada. Of course that frightens quite a lot of people."

"But Bessie, social democracy is not the same as Russian communism."

"Just try to get that through the thick skulls of some people in this province — like Oscar Shaw and his ilk. Woodsworth has said that 'they who possess superfluity possess the goods of others', and there are a great many people who insist on the right to keep what they neither need nor can ever use. So such words are frightening to many affluent people in this city."

"It's unfortunate that there is such a lot of muddled Marxism in the mixed thoughts of those labour groups. And with their stated approval of the Russian experiment, there could be danger."

"How many people in this country do you think can separate the ideas of Woodsworth and his followers from the muddied ramblings of the others?"

"Not many, I'm afraid."

"From what I read, J.S. is more and more convinced that a just social order can only be achieved through political action. But I've never once heard or read him say 'violent action'. Rather, it must be peaceful evolution, even if it takes many years. That's quite the opposite."

"Woodsworth has too much appreciation of, and regard for, Canada's cultural heritage. Still, it's all a little scary, Bessie. The government is so nervous after the takeover in Russia. And it's obvious that some plans are

272

afoot."

"And Woodsworth and Manekowski are being dubbed Bolsheviks."

"That's nothing new, of course. They've always been called that."

"Woodsworth has said, 'Let us forget the precise phrases of Marx and let us solve our own problems.' And that's the way it should be."

"Where is Woodsworth, by the way, Bessie. Do you know?"

"Still in British Columbia, I believe. But one of these days he's to begin a speaking tour. And can you imagine, some people are suspicious even of that. 'What's that man up to? Stirring up trouble as usual! Be on your guard! He's heading our way!'"

I came over to Ethel's hoping that a talk with her would settle my fears. On the contrary, I feel worse than ever. For my concerns about Mike and his undercover plotting are confirmed.

## 3

May-June 1919

The day the mouse ran along the wainscotting in the kitchen, frightening Marty so that she vomited up her milk, is the day the strike that had begun May first became a General Strike. And ever since I have associated the General Strike with mice, spilt milk, and fright.

Charles, arriving home at noon that day, made the announcement. For days now he has been going around with an I-told-you-so look on his face. Rather pleased with himself, it seems, for having predicted what is soon to be upon us. This is it, folks. Harness the horses and into the fray!

Why Charles always has to act as though he is one of the Big Shots in this city, I certainly can't say. He acts as though he still has that $50,000, when almost every penny of it is either gone or shackled. Because he is part of the Company, he thinks he is right in there with his Uncle John, Oscar Shaw, Fred Hamilton, and the rest of them. A Big Shot! As though if he hasn't got it today he'll have it together tomorrow, as long as those Bolshevik labour unions can be kept at bay. Well, we'll see. Unless things look up in the future, he blew his chances. Just look at the poverty up and down this street. You'd think by looking around he'd have a little more sympathy for the working man.

Charles, and the three tiers of government, as well as most of Winnipeg's press, are positive the strike is part of a great revolutionary plan which, starting on the banks of the Red River, will spread throughout the country. A *Tribune* editorial states that, for all practical purposes, Winnipeg is now under a Soviet system of government.

"Just you wait, Lady. Aren't you glad I saw to it that we are well-stocked with food? Knew something was brewing even before the first of the month. I won't have Marty suffering."

"How about all the other Martys in this city?"

"First we look after our own. Joe Blow looks after his. I look after mine."

My temper is about to flair. He is wearing his stubborn look. Soon we'll be at it again, and nothing will be gained. Forget it. Why bother to explain, even once more, that is exactly what Joe Blow is trying to do.

Each day advances the play. Tensions increase. Positions become polarized. The Strike Committee is matched by a Citizens' Committee of One Thousand which includes Fred Hamilton and Oscar Shaw — and

274

not one returned soldier among the lot of them! The two groups come to an agreement to continue essential services such as milk and bread deliveries, and newspapers, so the people can be kept apprised of events. The head of the Crescent Creamery Company suggests that "By Permission of the Strike Committee" placards be placed on wagons and other conveyances that must continue to operate. And, although the police force favours the strike, some of the force have been persuaded to stay on duty. For its help in these matters the Strike Committee gets no credit from the Citizens' Committee. And so the days pass, filled with tension but with very little violence, as the Strike Committee has asked the strikers to remain home as much as possible.

Ivens, editor of the labour newspaper, writes that the aims of the strikers are better wages (necessary because of inflation and the otherwise high cost of living), improved working conditions, and a better attitude on the part of employers towards collective bargaining. But the employers are convinced that such statements are just attempts to fog the real aim, which is the overthrow of government authority. It is not only the Citizens' Committee that believes this, but the provincial government and the federal government as well. Watch out for what is happening by the banks of the Red River! There communists are in control of the labour movement — witness the Calgary Conference. Violence is imminent. The real danger comes from the alien element in Winnipeg, in particular from the North Enders. If the strikers really mean what Ivens says they mean, then let them return to work and their employers will try to negotiate with them in a civilized manner.

On May 22 emissaries from the Canadian government — the Minister of Labour, the Honourable G. D. Robertson, and the Minister of the Interior, the

Honourable A. Meighen — arrive from Ottawa, ostensibly to act as impartial mediators. They are met at the train by members of the Citizens' Committee. And immediately the labour leaders are alienated, and any possible usefulness of the mediators is lost.

"Why, they've already made up their minds who is right and who is wrong. If Ottawa believes the strike is just a cloak for revolution, why bother to send them in the first place?"

I am on the phone to Ethel. James is also a member of the Citizens' Committee and Ethel has been hearing a few things.

"For one thing they came to let General Kitchen, the commanding officer of our Winnipeg militia, know what Ottawa wants him to do in case of trouble. The North West Mounted Police have been alerted and reinforced. Quantities of machine guns and rifles are being sent here. That's about all I know and none of it is pleasant."

"There's a real bias against the Strike Committee. I've been speaking to Mike and he says definitely no violence is intended. He swears to that. And labour is doing everything possible to prevent it happening by insisting that the strikers stay home. I know Mike's telling the truth."

"You've been speaking to Mike? I haven't seen him lately. Did you ask him about those meetings at the House?"

"I did. But he was rude and only laughed. Said, 'Ask me no questions, I'll tell you no lies.'"

"And what did you say to that?"

"I told him it was a childish reply. Something that Lana might have said. And he agreed. He said he had learned it from her."

*     *     *     *     *

276

On May 25 Senator Robertson calls a meeting of various representative workers and issues an ultimatum: strikers must return to work and sign agreements to sever relations with the Winnipeg Trades and Labour Council or they will be discharged with loss of all rights including pensions and any future government employment.

A number of already hungry and frightened strikers return to work. Still the majority stand their ground.

On May 27 a statement from the House of Commons by Prime Minister Sir Robert Borden makes it absolutely clear that Ottawa is on the side of the Citizens' Committee. As a conciliatory gesture he also says that the government will respect the right of a man to a living wage and will aim for an eight-hour work day and a forty-eight hour week.

The strike continues.

On June 6 Mayor Gray bans all parades and forbids the gathering of crowds.

On June 8 J.S. Woodsworth arrives in Winnipeg. And the following day, with paper in hand, Charles is reporting the news.

"Woodsworth's here. Well, that's not unexpected. He could be the catalyst for a lot of trouble. He should have been stopped before he started on that tour of his. Should have been picked up by the police long ago."

"Why? This is supposed to be a democracy. Can't he say what he wants?"

"It's a democracy and we mean to keep it that way."

The Curtises have been invited down for coffee and Emma speaks up. "I quite like Woodsworth and his ideas, Charles, if you don't mind my saying so. I consider him a real Christian, though Charlie and I aren't church-going people. After all, if Woodsworth is thought to be dangerous, so was Jesus."

It is quite a statement, coming from Emma, and

277

everyone is astonished — even Emma, who blushes deeply at her boldness.

"Whoa, now! Remember, I consider Woodsworth to be a fine man. But his social Christianity is playing right into the hands of the wrong people. We can't have that at this time."

Charlie, coming to the defence of his young wife, says, "Emma has an older brother out west who idolizes the man. He even repeats the Woodsworth Grace to his family before meals."

"The Woodsworth Grace? What's that? I've never heard of such a thing. Have you, Lady?"

I admit I haven't.

"I'll get it," says Emma eagerly. "Douglas sent it to me, hoping we'd use it." And rushing from the room, she goes upstairs.

Charlie asks, "Isn't it the same Ivens who has the labour newspaper who was expelled from his church as minister because of his social gospel teachings? And did he found the Labour Church?"

"Yes, I think so. But I gather the expulsion was because his preaching was more about social economics than biblical matters," Charles answers.

"The Labour Church is based on the Fatherhood of God and the Brotherhood of Man. Undoubtedly opinions are divided on its purpose. No doubt a lot of people have thought it just another cover for communism and revolution."

I am surprised. "Charlie, I had no idea you were interested in church and politics."

"No more than I have to be. I'm starting up a small business and I don't want anything to happen to destroy it. My information comes from the Woodsworth fan, brother Douglas. He keeps sending us tract literature. Douglas wrote that Woodsworth is involved in this Labour Church and is a good friend of Ivens'."

"That follows." Charles knocks the ashes from his pipe.

"It goes right along with Woodsworth's desire to secularize religion," I say. "And I'm not altogether in agreement with him there, for I believe salvation is of primary importance. But inasmuch as he thinks brotherhood should be part and parcel of everyday life, I'm all for it."

Charles opens his mouth and I know it is to air his ideas on welfare. But Emma has returned holding a letter, and considerately he puts his pipe back in his mouth.

"This came some time ago — back in April," Emma says breathlessly, opening the letter. "Here it is. Woodsworth's Grace Before Meat. 'We are thankful for these and all good things in life. We recognize that they are part of our common heritage and come to us through the efforts of our brothers and sisters the world over. What we desire for ourselves we wish for all. To this end may we take our share in the world's work and the world's struggles.'"

I look from Emma to Charles, wondering how he is taking that.

Charles says, "Hmm... I'll think about that. Anyone for more coffee?" He doesn't want to offend his young cousin and speaks with a touch of humour in his voice, almost patronizingly.

A moment later, returning from the kitchen with the coffee pot, he says, "Tell me, Emma, what do you think of that man's social gospel?"

"Well, really, I'm no authority. I think perhaps I've already said too much." Emma is a bit flustered and appeals to her husband. "How about you saying something, Charlie?"

"Go on, Queenie. You've been reading your brother's literature and know more about it than I do. Don't

279

worry, I'm here to defend you."

"I don't know as much as Bessie about this, but I think that Woodsworth is concerned with salvation too. But he thinks people have to be cared for first. I think he believes capitalism can be carried too far if it puts too much wealth in the hands of the few..." Emma gulps.

"Monopolists, you mean," Charlie helpfully supplies the word. I for one, have no desire to be a monopolist. All I want is to provide a service and be able to take care of a family. And I think that is the desire of the majority of people."

"Amen," says Charles. "That's the right idea."

"Woodsworth feels that individualism can get out of control and lead to wars..." Emma stops.

"I see cousin Douglas writes long letters. I don't disagree altogether with Woodsworth. But tell me. Are strikes what stop wars and rampant individualism? How about Petrograd?" Charles is talking down to his cousin, but kindly. "And do you think what Woodsworth is supporting will prevent another Red revolution? That is the question."

No one answers. No answer is expected.

"Well, we'll see. We'll see what happens."

"A thief sees only pockets on a saint," I say.

"And what's that innuendo all about?" Charles is miffed.

4

June 17.

The North West Mounted Police arrest ten men, including members of the Strike Committee. Four are "foreigners". The *Free Press* reports that the

280

federal government will make use of the newly amended Immigration Act to deport these four without trial, while an amendment to the Criminal Code which has increased the maximum penalty for a seditious act from two to twenty years will deal harshly with the others.

The Strike has been dealt a heavy blow.

Worried, I telephone Owen House. Mike is not there but Gedda comes to the phone.

"I don't know where Mike is." Gedda also is concerned. "He refused to tell me in case I'm questioned."

Veterans, facing hardship and unemployment since their return from the war, have decided on an illegal parade. They are furious because they consider the arrests unwarranted, and furious too that Senator Robertson and Meighen have associated almost entirely with the Citizens' Committee since their arrival in Winnipeg. Claiming that the ban on marching is an infringement of the civil rights for which they have so recently fought, it is their intention to confront Robertson. They mean to march from the City Hall to the Royal Alexandra, where the emissaries have been staying. The march is planned for Saturday, June 21.

Tensions are at their height and nerves taut the night of June 20. I sleep fitfully, only to fall into a sound sleep at daybreak. When I finally awaken it is to discover Charles already up and gone.

Arising, I check my watch on the dresser. It reads almost ten. Emma must have Marty. I pick up my comb to run it through my hair — and stop. There, lying among my ebony-backed brushes is a large sum of money. How careless of Charles, and how unlike him, to leave money lying around. Over a hundred dollars at least! I slip the bills into a drawer and continue dressing.

Once in the kitchen I can hear Marty laughing.

Emma is playing with her on the back porch.

"We're having a good time," Emma explains. "You were sleeping so soundly, I thought you wouldn't mind if I took charge."

Martha loves Emma.

" Thank you. I needed that sleep. It seems Charles left a long time ago."

"And my Charlie left early too. He and Syd want to be at the shop to make sure there's no vandalism. Bessie, I do hope there will be no trouble over that parade."

"If there is, it won't be the fault of the veterans, for I know their wives and children will be there. And they wouldn't allow them to be there if they intended any trouble."

"Then why did Charles insist we stay home today? I would like to see the march. And why are Charlie and Syd worried that something might happen to their shop?"

"Just precaution on their part. You know Charles and all this silly talk about a Red revolution in Canada. It's because of such stupidity that so many women and children in the Fort Rouge area are locking themselves up in churches. It's all so ridiculous. Others are guarding their homes with rifles and even machine guns. They've been frightened silly by all this prattle about revolution. I know for a fact that the strikers are holding revival meetings and praying that God grant them the strength to carry on. All they're asking for is a little humane treatment and a little more bread on the table. So don't worry. Then I add, "But it does bother me that the Citizens' Committee and the government are expecting trouble."

"Why?"

"Because there is such a thing as wish fulfillment. Because they expect a revolution, they just might hate

282

to be proven wrong."

My thought upsets me.

Time drags. Just after the noon hour Charles telephones.

"Just checking in, Lady. And another warning to both of you: stay home. I don't know whether you got the news, but the mayor issued a proclamation this morning to say that women or children who are involved in the parade are there at their own risk. The crowds are beginning to form outside the Clements Block and around the Union Bank, centering in on the City Hall. I've been watching them from the office. I guess you know the veterans intend to march from there to the Royal Alexandra. But Mayor Gray will read the Riot Act if there is the least sign of trouble. And there could be, because there are more than veterans gathering here."

He emphasizes the last words. His voice sounds ominous.

"Why should the Riot Act be read to veterans who are making a simple protest..."

"Bessie, — exasperation now — "I'm just telling you the facts. Another fact is that there is a warrant out for the arrest of your friend, Manekowski."

I don't answer. It's always "your friend, Manekowski". After a pause he asks, "Do you know where he is?"

"No. If I did I wouldn't say."

"Didn't think you would. The police are looking for him." It sounds like a chuckle.

My dander is rising. I still do not speak.

"Well, I don't know when I'll be home. Remember, stay put." Again his is emphasizing the last words. And now, without a doubt, comes a laugh.

He hangs up.

As the minutes go by, my concern for Mike increases. I am distracted. My thoughts are for Mike

283

during lunch; I hardly pay attention to Marty's constant questions or enter into Emma's quiet conversation. Then in a flash the answer comes. Of course!

"Emma, I know where I can find Mike."

"What? Why do you want to find Mike?"

"Never mind. I'm sorry if I sound rude, but I'll explain later. I must go out right away. Will you please look after Marty a little longer?"

"Bessie, you're not to go out!

"I must go."

I go to the desk in the dining room, my cherrywood desk, and take out two envelopes, carefully writing an address on each. Then, running upstairs, I remove the money from the dresser drawer, count out a sum for each and seal the envelopes, marking them "1" and "2". Putting them in the deep pocket of my skirt, I leave the house.

Few people are visible as I head for Notre Dame and William Avenue. It's almost two o'clock. As I near Main Street I can see hundreds of people, including women and children, milling around the City Hall. How ever will I find Mike?

Mike will be up in front. If the men from the factories are there as Charles suggested, then Mike will be to the front. And if I have been able to make that simple deduction, so will have the police. I must get to him first.

Elbowing and pushing my way through the crowd, I near the front of the City Hall where the men are readying themselves to begin the parade scheduled for 2:30. My first frantic search brings no result. Then I see him near the monument, capless, his bright hair showing inches above the men who surround him.

I get as near as I can, then call, "Please, please, I have a message for Mr. Manekowski."

My voice commands attention. The men make way

284

and Mike sees me.

"Robin!"

"A private message," I say grimly, handing him an envelope. "They mean business, Mike. You have no choice but to leave. I'll see that your family get to you. It's now or never. So go."

"Bless you," Mike says tolerantly, smiling at me. And remains where he is, turning away from me to continue the conversation I interrupted.

Angered by his lack of regard for my concern and warning, I can feel my face burning. I frown and his friends who see me return my frown with brief, amused smiles.

Why is Mike so stupidly heedless after the arrest of the other strike leaders just four days ago? What more can I do?

Protesting shouts are heard from the crowd on Main Street as the pounding of hoofs sound more and more clearly, coming towards the City Hall. Well trained military horses: the North West Mounted Police, and dozens of them! They must be nearing the Union Bank when I hear a shouted command. The horses break into a trot and come into view. And as the crowds give way, the street is cleared. Not far along North Main the Mounties swing about and now, unobstructed, continue on their way back towards Portage.

As they disappear people once again surge into the street in front of the City Hall, blocking the way of a clanging southbound streetcar. A few streetcars have been allowed to run. But the crowd, angered by the charge of the Mounted Police, now refuse to give way. One man pulls down the trolley from the overhead wire. The crowd cheer.

I climb up on the steps of the monument to see better, as has Mike, recklessly, along with his friends. A number of men and boys are pressing around the

285

streetcar, attempting to rock it. The doors open to disgorge the frightened passengers, and as they tumble out men and boys, encouraged by the shouts about them, once more start rocking the streetcar until it almost keels over.

"That's it, Joe, take it off the track."

"Bully for you. Heave it!"

As it is derailed another loud cheer goes up.

I can hear the sound of breaking glass. Smoke is rising from the car. Someone has set it on fire.

And now horses can be heard again — this time galloping. The Mounties are returning. But the people remain on the street. So absorbed are they by the car that they appear to give no attention to the oncoming horses. And this time the police have clubs, and as they charge they are flailing this way and that, seemingly heedless of women and children.

Panic ensues. Women are screaming, attempting to get their children off the road. In their fury men hurl rocks and bottles, anything at hand, at the Mounties. Two are unseated, obviously hurt. City police rush to their rescue and carry the injured men out of the fray. Then, as before, the North West Mounted Police proceed southward.

Behind me, faintly through the din, a voice is trying to be heard. I turn and find myself staring at Fred Hamilton. The doors of the City Hall are open, and Fred and various officials are on the balcony, accompanied by a number of policemen. Mayor Gray is reading the Riot Act. Fred is looking straight at me. Then he turns to speak to someone at his side. And now the police are coming down from the balcony, headed this way. Mike! Of course. Mike standing above the others on the monument.

No need for me to say anything. Mike's friends have seen the men in blue, and move to prevent their reaching him. Linking arms, they shout at him to get lost. I watch Mike as he goes, then see him pause and turn.

For the third time the Mounties are rushing the crowd. This time a club is in the left hand and in the right a gun. Some are waving the guns in the air and shooting indiscriminately. Probably blanks, only blanks. Veterans, strikers, all are hissing and booing.

A gunshot nearby, and from the area of the balcony comes the sound of wood splintering. I wheel around. The mayor! Has the bullet missed its mark?

More shots, and now pandemonium. An elderly man, standing by the side of the Union Bank on William Avenue, drops. Someone near Mike has been hit in the head. Bleeding, the man falls. And in the moment that my attention is given to the victim, Mike disappears. Startled by the shots, the men who have been keeping the handful of policemen away from Mike loosen their hold, and the police break through. But Mike is nowhere to be seen.

Veterans, strikers, wives, and sympathizers are being routed. Jumping down from the monument steps, I follow those who are heading towards North Main. Pray Mike gets away. Pray Mike gets away.

I run until I am well beyond the disappearing remnants of the hysterical crowd, my breath coming hard, my heart racing. But why the hurry? Gedda will be at the House and I will get to her as soon as I can. I sit on the curb, determined to quiet myself. Amid the clutter and odours of the uncared-for street, a lamppost serving as a backrest, I breathe deeply and close my eyes. As the minutes go by my pulse slows and I grow calmer. I try to get beyond the chaos of the past hour, beyond even thought to a point of deep calm. I sit there, oblivious to everything about me. Minutes more pass.

When I open my eyes I know beyond a shadow of a

doubt I must reach Gedda. It's a knowledge and a compulsion that has come from deep within me. I must get to Owen House right away. But how? Few people are about. No streetcars are in sight. As I look anxiously about me I see a bicycle leaning against a store window. One glance, and then without a second thought I'm on the bicycle and pedalling — hard.

Approaching Owen House I can see the smoke. And a fear I have known all my life grips me.

There are people gathered around the burning building. I hear shouts. A woman is screaming. Discarding the bicycle, I find myself for the second time that day forcing my way through a crowd. This time I'm searching for Gedda. As the people give way, some look at me. And though I'm in desperate haste, their expressions register: the compassionate looks of the few, the callousness of some, an expression of excitement, a primitive love of fire and destruction on the faces of the many.

Gedda, hysterical and screaming, is on the grass before the main entrance, a leg curled under her. An unknown man is restraining her. I drop to my knees, trying to understand her words. Seeing me, she clutches for me.

In pain and terrified, her voice is scarcely audible. 'My baby, my little Nikki. He's in there, in his crib."

"No one can get in there, mam," the unknown man informs me. "I tried, but the fire's too much. It's everywhere."

I'm going in and no one can stop me. I run up the verandah steps and in through the door. Hungry flames reach out for me. But I know the way. Up the staircase I go. Tongues of fire are licking at the banisters. It's hard to breathe. Covering my nose and mouth, I rush on. I have a debt to Gedda. Or is it some debt I owe from aeons ago? Has God ordained this baby a

288

necessary link in some chain of events so that His plan be fulfilled? Is this the part I have to play? At the top of the stairs I follow now a fiery path etched in my mind. Through a classroom and an adjoining room, then back into the hallway I weave my way. I can hear the sounds of flames biting noisily into wood. There is a crackling and a crash of beams collapsing.

But I'm no longer afraid. The structure where I walk is holding. Fear has turned to elation. I am doing what I must do.

The door to the second staircase is shut. It's stuck. But I will open it. I struggle with the door and it gives way. The stairway is clear; I climb the stairs and enter the bedroom. I press the crying baby to me and retrace my steps, down the now-smoke-filled stairwell.

Of the rest of that return journey there is no memory, like the negative of a picture left unprinted and filed away. Memory recalls my handing Nikki to Gedda. Mrs. Poleski is with Gedda and I'm insisting they listen to me. Thank God for Mrs. Pole. Taking the second envelope from my pocket, I give it to Gedda.

5

I am forcing my way back to consciousness. I am in bed in the front bedroom on Langside Street. The sun in shining in. It must be morning. Charles is beside me, holding my hand.

He smiles that lopsided smile of his. "Well, good morning, Lady. And how are you feeling this fine day?"

The room is full of flowers. I try to respond to his smile, but it is an effort. I say weakly, "Flowers are beautiful. Is this a funeral?"

"No way. I'm not going to have that."

289

Recollections flood in. "How are Gedda and Nikki?"

"Just fine. Gedda's leg was broken. A Polish doctor set it and put it in a cast. And she and the baby were looked after by that woman the children call Mrs. Pole."

"The one who delivered the baby." Then I ask, "Mike wasn't caught?"

"It seems he got away. Woodsworth and the editor, Ivens, are in the Rupert Street jail for seditious libel. Woodsworth had been writing for the labour paper. It seems Manekowski just disappeared."

Charles pats my hand. Something about that gesture and the look in his eyes makes me suspicious.

"Have you any idea where he might be?" I ask.

"I've no idea. But I'm sure you have."

"Perhaps. Charles, I took your money and gave it to them. A lot of money."

"Why do you think I left the money on the dresser?"

Surprise overcomes my weakness. "But how could you have guessed I'd take it for them? You didn't say..."

"Oh, I've been living with you for a while now. I was pretty sure that if I told you not to go out, and told you that Manekowski was a marked man, you'd figure it all out somehow." His eyes are smiling just a little.

'Why did you do it? I thought you didn't like Mike."

"I never disliked him. And I never considered him to be a knave. A fool, perhaps, like Woodsworth. But I can't fault a man for doing what he believes he has to do. Besides, the Manekowskis are your friends."

I want to cry. I'll phone Sandy as soon as I can.

"Wouldn't it have been easier to tell me, and give me the money? And safer?" Such a convoluted and unnecessary game. 'What if I hadn't taken the money?"

"If I had given it to you, wouldn't you have suspected my game was to smoke out your friend?"

"Yes, perhaps."

"Well, that's enough for now." He gets up abruptly,

in a hurry to get away.

"How about Emma bringing you up a little broth?"

"No broth. Later, maybe."

He turns and moves to the door. I stop him.

"Tell me — Lana?"

But I already know the answer.

Reluctantly he comes back to the bed and grips my hand. "Lana went up the back stairway after her brother. Ethel was there and must have seen Lana go in. She followed her."

Tears are in his eyes.

Lana and Ethel were chosen to die. I was chosen to live.

"Go, Charles. Please, go."

I turn my head away from him. After gently pulling down the window shade, he leaves me.

# PART THREE

# COMING TO TERMS

*Chapter VIII*

# Assessing the Damage

September 1919

Weeks go by. I lie in bed amid the wreckage of my dreams, longing for death. But death refuses to claim me.

When Dr. Winram first examined me there was not much obviously wrong, he said, no permanent damage. A few minor burns, a problem with smoke inhalation from which I soon would recover. He pronounced that safe return through the burning building a miracle. However, there was trauma that must be taken into consideration.

One day when they think I'm asleep, I overhear the doctor whispering to Charles. Mr. Clements must understand that it could be a matter of months, even years, before Mrs. Clements is fully recovered. It will mean patience and understanding on his part and on the part of others. He has heard of a few cases of severe shock with returned soldiers that led to hospitalization and permanent mental problems. Not that he means that will be the case in this instance. Charles is properly upset.

There are no longer terrifying dreams of fire. On the contrary, it's a though fire as symbol has gone from my life. I remain an empty shell. Only the desire to find out about the Manekowskis finally pulls me from my bed and downstairs to telephone Sandy.

I reach Sandy immediately.

"Did the Manekowskis get to your place?"

Surprise in Sandy's voice. "Yes, but I wrote about it. Didn't you get my letter?" Her voice seems so far away.

"No, I didn't. Do you think our mail was being checked?"

"It may have been."

I know very well Charles would not have tampered with a letter addressed to me — he's not that type of person.

"Or maybe it just didn't get through, Bessie, for some reason. Services were upset for some time, you know."

"Tell me about the Manekowskis."

"Mike arrived first, of course. Then came Gedda with Mrs. Poleski to help her. They stayed only a couple of weeks after that. With Gedda's leg it was difficult for her to get around. The baby was fine. Then one day a union man appeared out of the blue and they left with him. Seemed to think our place could be suspect."

"Have you any idea where they are?"

"I don't know where. Mike wouldn't say. Rather, what he did say was he wasn't sure where they'd be. And I've never heard from them since. Bessie, I know they love you for what you did. It was a very brave action..."

"But they've never written."

"Mike was bitter about the ferocious way the strike was put down. Bitter too because the governments paid not the slightest attention to the Strike Committee. He and Gedda were also broken-hearted over the loss of their beautiful daughter. You can understand, Bessie, they weren't themselves. They were suffering terribly. You see, Mike was so sure that fire was set to get him. He had gone home to destroy some papers that would have provided information about the men who had been meeting at the House during the winter. He didn't think he was followed. But it's possible that someone was watching the House and saw him go in and thought it would be a way to settle a score with the union. Anyway, Gedda said anyone could easily have got into the House through the basement door without being seen that day and started the fire. Not many people were around. Mike didn't stay for long. He destroyed the papers and left. Gedda walked several blocks with him. Nikki was asleep. Lana was in the kitchen with Ethel, and when the two of them became aware of the fire they rushed out to get help. They must have thought the baby was with Gedda, for Nikki didn't often sleep at that time of day. Then, when Gedda returned and saw what was happening, in her blind haste she tripped and broke her leg." I say nothing. After a pause Sandy continues, "Mike and Gedda were two different

294

people, Bessie. They'd been through Hell..."

The connection fades. But I am scarcely listening. I, too, had my taste of Hell and am remembering the day Mike and I first made love — his request for a fire escape for the apartment forgotten. Do Mike and Gedda blame me for Lana's death? Emotional strain spills over into physical weakness until I scarcely am able to stand or hold the receiver.

Sandy's voice, coming through to me again. "They spoke of going to the States. Maybe they did write you — as I did. Or maybe they were afraid of making contact with you after all that happened — and what we hear is still happening in Winnipeg. I've no idea about them really. Maybe we'll learn one day."

* * * * *

I'm sure the Manekowskis are all right. Otherwise, why was it meant for me to rescue Nikki? For it was as though that rescue had been a special plan in my life, though I cannot understand the reason. Something which must, because of my limited view, remain an impenetrable mystery, a discordant note which, however, in God's scheme of things is part of one harmonious whole.

And if that is so, was Lana's death too part of God's unfathomable plan? By way of neglect was I meant to be the cause of Lana's and Ethel's death? Surely my negligence and the circumstances surrounding my negligence cannot be condoned. Whatever might be God's long-term plan, I stand forever condemned in my eyes. For I have killed what I have loved and what was beautiful.

My friends and my work are gone. The reason for living is gone. Only a sense of duty to Marty keeps me up and about. But I'm so very tired. I just drag myself

295

about, moving from one necessary chore to the next, my mind centred on the past.

If Lana had gone up the front staircase at the time she went into the House after her brother, she might have made it. If there had been a fire escape! But even then Lana might have headed up the back stairway, because it was natural for her to go to the apartment that way. The fire escape is Mike's fault too, for he never mentioned the matter again. And what difference would it make anyway, if all was destined to happen as it did? Ring around a rosy, around, and around, and around. The guilt is mine.

## 2

1920

Charles and his relatives still talk about the General Strike and how the Red Revolution was nipped in the bud. They talk about the military action as though it had been a necessary and great accomplishment. When I think about that day, that "Bloody Saturday", I want to cry — and frequently do. I can't help myself.

That awful day in June last year when, standing on the steps of the monument, I looked up to discover Fred Hamilton on the platform with Mayor Gray. Fred telephoned the office as soon as he possibly could and suggested to Charles he look for his wife. Charles found me and got me away in time, and saw to it I had the best of attention. Lucky, Charles said, that Fred had notified him. I am not so sure.

Before I regained consciousness I know I was with Lana, Andy, and others. Ethel was there too. Best of all was a wonderful feeling of bliss and I wanted to stay with my friends. But I knew I must return, and forced my way back to consciousness. It was like going back down a long dark tunnel.

Where are the slides and the swings and the roundabout that stood on the grounds of Owen House? Where the laughter of the children? Where the anxious women who stood near me that day at City Hall? I saw those women running. Were they among the many trapped in "Hell's Alley"? Clubbed, beaten, and trampled by horses. Why, oh why?

After all the suffering of the strikers who had work but inadequate pay, and of the veterans just returned from fighting for their country who had no work, the strike was finished by the 26th of June. With nothing gained. Not one measure of a plea granted. When, in July, Mounties raided the homes of strikers and strike headquarters in Winnipeg, no machine guns and no firearms of any consequence were to be found. Still it was said, "A revolution has been nipped in the bud." These words were printed in newspapers everywhere.

When Woodsworth and Ivens were taken to jail for publishing materials referred to as seditious libel, their friend Dixon carried on underground. Finally, when Woodsworth and Ivens were allowed out on bail, Dixon gave himself up. At his trial in January he brilliantly argued his own defence. For sixteen days he pleaded for the freedom of the press in such a faultless and admirable manner that not only were charges against him dropped, but the charges against Woodsworth and Ivens were dropped. Others who had been incarcerated were not so lucky. But it was one important victory.

The General Strike has made Woodsworth more determined than ever to enter the political arena and work for social justice. He said, "It is but the end of round one."

I am not like J.S. Woodsworth. For me it is the end.

297

\* \* \* \* \*

There is no way insurance can be collected on the House. Not that I even care. But Charles and James Reid have tried to get it. There was talk of arson but nothing can be proven. Perhaps the court does not want proof. To Charles and James, who searched the ruins, it is obvious that the fire was started in the basement under the kitchen stairs. But their statements are not accepted in court. They are prejudiced witnesses.

Arson! I immediately accuse Oscar Shaw and become hysterical. When Charles finally manages to quiet me he says that, for all his faults, Oscar Shaw would never do a thing like that. I know that is true. The Shaws are good people, "Doing right as they see the right, as Charles "Abraham Lincoln" Clements is wont to say. Diane seldom spares herself when it comes to helping others and usually was kind to me despite my often ill-concealed contempt for her frills and attitudes.

When I am crying and unhappy over the loss of my friends and Owen House, Charles says, "There's still Diane. I'm well aware that the two of you haven't always hit it off, but you should hear how she extols your heroic action. She's proud of you — as we all are — and wants to be your friend. She can help you get involved again elsewhere. She says you are just the right person to organize and deal with people. Much better than she is. So she says. So there, you see. Why not let bygones be bygones?"

What makes Charles think it's all that easy to forgive and forget? If the Shaws are not to be faulted for the loss of Owen House, with their spying and their prying they certainly had a great deal to do with the disappearance of the Manekowskis and all my misfortunes. Only a saint can forgive and forget that, and I'm no saint. I'll have nothing more whatsoever to

298

do with the Shaws, ever again. Or the North End!

James Reid is devastated by the loss of his wife. No one expected he would take her death so hard. It just goes to show things are seldom what they seem. Everyone considered his treatment of her shabby, and so it was. But evidently he relied on Ethel more than even she knew, for when she died it was as if the ground gave way under his feet. It was James who instigated a search for the arsonist and James who went after legal claims — not for himself, for he had nothing to gain, but because Owen House had meant so much to Ethel. A rather belated show of affection, though sincere nonetheless. But all efforts regarding the House prove to no avail. Now it is as though the House never existed.

Owen House, though among the first of the North End properties to be put to the torch, is by no means the only property to be destroyed. A great deal of damage is done in the period that follows the strike, damage to properties of strike leaders and other union members of high visibility. All in the name of saving the country from the Reds. And still the silent, unauthorized campaign for "freedom" and "democracy" continues. "Foreigners" are deported on the least pretense. Jobs are lost for no good reason. Poor relations between employer and employee continue to destroy the wealth and quality of workmanship. It is a sad legacy, the result being that Winnipeg, which had reached a high level of achievement at the peak of Uncle John's career, has become a frightened, tense city, rampant with hatred and distrust. Completely demoralized.

Charles wants me to go back to the site of destruction, saying that it will be like getting back on a horse immediately after a bad fall. Perhaps he's right, but I can't bring myself to go. I try. I even dress to go one day, but by the time Charles has brought the car around from the back, emotions overwhelm me and instead I go back upstairs and to bed. He has described to me the blackened ruins that once were Owen House. He painted the scene so vividly it will forever remain as a deep scar in my mind.

Miserable, and with the postwar depression continuing, I sell the property for a song.

Now, so I am told, a row of cheaply-built tenements stands there and on the property next door, which was sold soon after I sold mine. That which the Owens fought against so ardently has finally come about. But I no longer care. Charles suggested I hang on to the land until real estate values rise again, which he says they are bound to do. But I had to rid myself of it to clear away the past. But still the past refuses to leave me alone. I'll put the money from the sale in the bank and there it will remain. Maybe someday there will be a use for it.

I bought Owen House for God's work, but God no longer wanted me to have it. I am being punished for my sins. Once more my way has been blocked and I cannot see what lies ahead.

What does anyone know about the scars on my soul, the emptiness I feel in my heart? I have committed adultery. I have put the City of Man before the City of God. I opened the doors of Owen House to all who were in need and freely associated with the Scarlet Woman. And though still a part of me cannot see where is the wrong (for is not God's love all-encompassing?) I must suppress my inclinations and my reasoning. For who am I to set myself against the Church? I must practice the strictest discipline or I will be unable to continue in a life which has become unbearable, divided as I am within myself. For God has forsaken me. How right Richard was about my nature. How right the Reverend Dickinson was about my need for discipline.

300

Charles' concern annoys me. Especially when he fusses over me like a broody hen. And the more he and his cousin Sarah talk about my getting involved at St. Stephen's church, the less I am inclined to do anything. I resent Charles' talking about me to his cousins. I told him Sarah ought to mind her own business.

\* \* \* \* \*

In October Emma and Charlie find themselves a house to rent — "out in the sticks", as they say — on a lot without trees by a mud road and a boardwalk.

"You'll be glad to see the last of us," Emma says. "We came for a month and stayed for well over a year."

"Emma, how could we have done without you? You've helped me and Marty so." I truly mean it, for Emma's buoyancy has kept me going during these past several months. Now I must learn to get along without her. I, who had not wanted them to come in the first place, am sorry to see them go.

"What would we have done without you and Charles when we had the flu? I don't think we've begun to pay our debt to you. Maybe we never can."

"Maybe we shouldn't think in terms of debts and I.O.U.s."

Charlie and his brother, Syd, are building their own homes, having found properties in St. Vital, one behind the other. They are both very clever with their hands but the work goes slowly because it is done in their spare time. The tire business is doing well and keeps them busy.

"We'll move in as soon as the kitchen and bathroom are adequately equipped. It will be like camping for the next several months. Charlie says he intends to build the house around me. I think that will be fun. I mean to help all I can — perhaps I can hold the nails for him.

301

Maybe I'll even learn to do a bit of carpentry."

A baby is on the way.

I will miss the aura of happiness that always seems to surround the young couple. So will Marty miss them, and so will Charles.

## 3

1921

When life appears to have reached its lowest ebb, I find a haven from my unease, a place where I can anchor myself, knowing I will be safe, knowing God has forgiven me. Though I will never forgive myself.

One summer morning I walk to Eaton's, where I buy a length of towelling and order groceries to be delivered that afternoon. Finding myself considerably better for the fresh air and stimulation, I decide to return by way of the Curtis Tire Shop to say hello to Charlie and inquire about Emma and the new baby boy. Both are doing well, Charlie tells me, looking proud as a peacock.

Continuing homeward I come upon a little chapel which I often used to pass by with scarcely a second glance. But today there is a sign on the small square of green grass announcing a visiting evangelist from Detroit, Michigan. I halt, and a wave a nostalgia for my old city and the long-ago overwhelms me. There and then I decide to attend.

* * * * *

Now Charles comes with me to chapel. I know he was loath to give up his Anglican Church, but Charles is adaptable and the change will do him no harm. He said

302

it's for a good cause and I know he is trying in every way he can to get me out from under this awful depression that has settled about me like a heavy blanket.

Charles wears a silk tie and morning suit. Not at all the thing for chapel, but I'll not complain. Marty is appropriately dressed in her Sunday best: her button shoes carefully polished, her beribboned straw hat sitting straight on her dark curls. Marty is fond of clothes. I fear that, for her, pretty clothes are the reason for attending chapel. Whatever can I do with the girl? I have no wish to encourage so active an interest in self-adornment, but I do want to keep her well dressed. The difference is a fine line and I am finding the task a difficult one. Marty is no tomboy. It's a good thing she is not Martha's child, for I'm sure she would be a clothes horse. But then Marty is still very young.

Because the chapel is so close to home, the three of us walk there most of the time. Its proximity is a great advantage, especially for Marty, who will soon be old enough to go to Sunday School on her own in both fair and foul weather. As today is warm, we walk slowly, savouring the good clear air, and when we arrive the little beige clapboard building is almost filled. We are ushered to chairs at the back, to the side of the entrance, and handed hymn books. Several people turn to smile and nod a greeting. The people are all friendly. The pews in the main hall are usually filled to capacity at service time, especially at morning service, while at Sunday School in the afternoon the basement is filled with happy children. They range in age from the very young to adolescents who are students of the Bible. My sincere hope is that it will be here, among these good and dedicated people, that Marty will find her salvation. Charles, for his part, does not know any of the people very well, but is happily sure there is not a

303

revolutionary among them. So he too is content.

The inside of the chapel is painted an off-white, while the wainscotting and trim are dark brown. The whole is bright and spotless and unadorned, except for fresh-cut flowers placed before the pulpit. It suits me very well, for I believe that stained-glass windows, fine paintings, and outstanding music are of secondary importance to the saving of souls, and could indeed, like Marty's pretty dresses, prove to be distractions. The unpretentious simplicity is a proper environment for anyone seeking the spiritual Path.

We stand and sing: "Rock of Ages cleft for me / Let me hide myself in Thee."

The prayer is over and another hymn sung. With a rustling and coughing and clearing of throats the congregation puts hymn books aside and settles down for the sermon. Marty, sitting on her hands and directing her eyes everywhere but where they should be, is already starting to wiggle. It will be wiggle, wiggle, wiggle all through the sermon. Goodness, one would think that girl old enough to sit still for just one hour. Charles is, as usual, regarding her tolerantly, and a kind man seated behind reaches forward to offer her a mint.

Mr. Dunsmore, after standing silently at the pulpit, waiting for the shuffling to end, adjusts his spectacles and gives a cough. Silence falls and he begins.

"Our text today is from Luke, chapter 5, verse 18. 'And, behold, they brought in a bed a man which was taken with palsy; and they sought means to bring him in, and to lay him before Him.'

"Because the multitude was such that the men were unable to reach Jesus, they went up on the housetop, cut away the tilings, and lowered the man in his bed through the roof that he might lie at the feet of Jesus. So great was their faith, they did not care what others might think of this strange action. And, you know, people can become critical when one does God's work. But God had spoken to their hearts and with great joy and holy determination they acted thereon. Anything is possible if one is determined to be a doer of God's holy word. And Jesus, looking at the sick man, did not rebuff him. Instead he said, 'Man, thy sins are forgiven thee, rise up and walk.' And when the man sick with palsy heard Jesus speak to him, he did not say, 'But I can't walk, I haven't been able to stand on my feet for years. I can't be expected to walk.' No. He did what Jesus told him to do. Immediately, and let me underscore the word, immediately he rose up before them and took up that whereupon he lay, and departed to his own house glorifying God.

"The sick man had a choice. As we all have. If you don't want to obey when God speaks to you, you will find an excuse. Any old excuse will do. Was it a miracle when that sick man picked up his couch and walked? Let me tell you, friends, miracles happen. If you are in touch with the Lord Jesus Christ miracles can happen to you. Today as yesterday, as forever, God is the same. He is the same God and God speaks to you today. Don't harden your hearts against the Lord. You have a choice. Say, yes I will, and let the holy determination in your heart bring about a miracle. Maybe you are feeling ill today, maybe you are unhappy, maybe things have gone wrong in your life."

Mr. Dunsmore is speaking to me!

"Say no to the Devil. Say, yes Lord, you gave your blood for me, Lord, I surrender and today receive forgiveness for all my sins. God can turn things around for you.

"Holy determination. Let us be determined to establish a medical mission station in Nigeria. Let us be determined to find the money necessary for that station.

305

Let us be determined go out into the world and preach the gospel of salvation. Does God speak to you? Yes, God speaks. Say, I am going to obey God. When you want to obey God so much that it doesn't matter what others think of you, then you have holy determination and that will bring a miracle. Have circumstances been going against you? Say, now I make a choice and that choice is Jesus.

"If you want to be born again, come to the front and let the words of your mouth be the confirmation of your heart. Will those who wish to come forward come now. Come and say, I confess I am a lost sinner fit only for Hell, I believe Jesus died on the cross to save my soul, I believe in Christ and him crucified. I made my peace with God through the Lord Jesus Christ. Find salvation through the shed blood of Jesus."

As Mr. Dunsmore encourages the few who have stood to come forward, Mr. Yorke returns to the piano and once again the congregation rises to sing, "There is power, power, wonder working power / In the precious blood of the Lamb."

Now is the time for the benediction.

"And may the peace of God which passeth all understanding rest and abide with you now and forevermore. Amen."

Outside, new friends speak briefly before saying good-bye, women nodding and men raising or touching their hats.

"Until this evening or next Sunday." "So good to have you with us." "And will our Helen be seeing Martha at Sunday School?" "Such a dear child."

Such pleasant people.

My mind is full of the sermon. I am sure it was meant for me. Directed to my special needs. I am like the man with palsy who must respond to the command and get up and walk. Was the man's bed one he had

306

made for himself, upon which he had to lie? Just as I have been lying on my bed of problems? Well, Jesus said, get up and walk. But he also told that man to take his bed with him. I want to leave my bed behind. O Lord, must it go with me? I know very well Martha would relate the man's bed to the karma he acquired from previous incarnations, and Jesus's command to walk, she would say means to get on with your living and not let the mind dwell on the past even though the past can never be wiped out — only forgiven. Oh, I know just what Martha would say. But I will not heed that. I will stay within the bounds of this chapel. It is quite enough for me to contend with the omissions and commissions of this one lifetime. I will leave such speculation about other lifetimes to Martha. To know there is forgiveness and understand the command comforts me and is sufficient for me. But can I forgive myself and can I act? How much easier it was to walk through fire!

## 4

1922

Marty has just turned six. She is wearing the beads that Martha sent her for her birthday. How she loves that necklace, insisting on wearing it every hour of the day and taking it to bed with her at night. What a funny little one she is. There are so many birthday presents this year from friends and relatives. Too many. It isn't good for the child; I don't want her to be spoiled. I try to explain how much better it is to give than to receive. I tell her there are so many children in this city who get no presents for their birthdays and have few, if any, toys to play with. Marty listens carefully. But then, without saying a thing, romps away to tuck her doll into bed. So much for that, I think, discouraged. Nothing has registered.

Some days later I am doing laundry. Marty is nearby as I hang out the clothes. She is playing with a stick, pretending to be an old woman walking with a cane. What wonderful imaginations children have. I leave her there as I go to the basement to collect more washing. And upon returning with wicker basket filled, I start pegging sheets to the line, then realize Marty is nowhere about.

I call her. "Marty! Marty, where are you?" But there is no answer. So I stuff the handful of clothespins back into my apron pocket and go looking. She can't be far. Ah, I see, she has managed to slide the heavy bar back from the wooden gates and has ventured into McMicken Lane. How quick and impulsive a six-year-old can be, darting from one pleasure to the next like a butterfly after nectar. There she is talking to a couple with a baby.

Indians! Where ever did they come from? I didn't know there were any in this neighbourhood. I have never seen any around here. I go up to them and smile cautiously. They smile back at me. Marty is chattering away, delighted with the baby's beaded moccasins, showing off her beads in turn, talking about the baby's age and her own age. Talking as if they are old friends! She allows herself a quick glance at me.

"They live — there." Marty points down the lane. And the Indians smile and nod.

Oh, yes, I know. There are two small houses that face onto McMicken Lane. More like shacks with verandahs. Unpainted, like barns with their silver siding. They must have been put up ages ago. How ever does Marty know where they live?

"I've been in their house," she proudly answers my

unspoken question. "They're my friends."

And the Indians confirm her statement by smiling and nodding.

I am upset. I think I keep an eye on my little daughter and always know exactly where she goes. It seems I am wrong. We stand there for a moment, the Indians and I, trying for the sum of one another.

Marty breaks the silence. "Come to my place. I want to give something to the baby," she announces. "This way," she orders them. And they follow us into the backyard and up to the back porch, where sheets hang fresh-smelling and snow-white in the sun's light.

She runs to the back door and opens the screen. "C'mon," she beckons.

But they stand stock still. Just smiling.

"Perhaps they'd prefer to wait outside with me," I counter.

We wait. And in two minutes she is back with that beautiful hinged wooden doll. The one Ma sent her. Offering it to the baby! Maybe the Indians don't even like it but will take it just to please her. And what can I say under the circumstances?

They accept the doll politely. Then she's off again, into the house. I am apprehensive. Another two minutes and she is back again, pushing the screen door open, pushing out her new doll bed full of toys. And again the couple accept the gifts, stoically, politely.

This time the Indian pulls off the baby's moccasins and gives them to Marty. She is thrilled. I feel awkward and don't know what to say, so I just thank them. Actually, I would like to take back the doll bed and beautiful wooden doll. Marty has gone too far. The Indians probably don't even want them and will sell them or give them away.

After that the couple appear in no hurry to leave, but stand quietly by. Should I invite them in? Should I ask

309

them to sit down? Why do I not know what to do? Why am I tongue-tied when once I was so involved with people of all types — with "foreigners"? Is it because I have changed? Or is it because these are not foreigners but the people who belong to this land, that I stand before them pale and embarrassed? I know nothing of native peoples. One seldom hears or speaks of native peoples.

The back porch is draped with sheets and by the steps is the clothes basket. I suggest we move to the stairway that leads from the upstairs balcony. And there I sit three steps above them while the woman cuddles the baby and doll in her arms. Finally I have the temerity to open my mouth and question the man about Cree Indians.

He is soft spoken and intelligent. He tells me he was taken from his parents when he was young and put in a school far away from his home. He hated the school. The ways of the white man were not the ways of his people. They teach how to conquer nature not how to work along with nature as the Indians once did and would again if they were left alone. The white man's greed will destroy the earth, the Indian says. Unless we realize that we are part of the earth and not apart from it, we will all perish.

It is a grim pronouncement, and one that I find hard to understand, for there appears to be an unending supply of land and resources — plenty for everyone. We lapse once more into silence. We sit, and with Marty's discarded cane the Indian draws circles in the sand spilled from the sandbox. I think about the Indians in Winnipeg. They can be seen, if one looks for them, on Main Street especially. Before Prohibition they were to be found outside beer parlours, often drunk by the roadside. Where else? Do they live unobtrusively in other McMicken Lanes? They must be about, so why do

310

we not notice them more? How many times have I mentioned Indians in my letters home? Never. The Métis, yes. I mentioned them once. But not the full-blooded Indians. Foreigners are hated. The French are tolerated if they keep to their own areas. But one seldom thinks about Indians. They are an invisible people. And as Ma says, "What the eye doesn't see, the heart doesn't grieve over."

Finally they leave. We say good-bye. Marty walks with them to the gate and, climbing on it, waves to them, then stands watching as they walk down the lane.

With chin cupped in my hands, elbows on my knees, I sit musing on about the once-proud red man. Returning from my distant thoughts, I find myself staring at a sand circle. As I stare the circle becomes an Indian teepee, which changes to a primitive settlement, to Jericho, the moon, the sun, a planet, a womb, a tomb, the beginning and the end, Alpha and Omega. Plato said the soul is a circle. Martha's friend Carl referred to it as the greatest religious image, and he used the mandala as a device for his patients to explore themselves. I want to discover myself. I'll call the sand circle my mandala and make a picture of me.

I delve inside myself and first in its centre I place a fortress, my symbol for God wherein is my shelter. Then, because I am part of all that I have known, I put the North End of Winnipeg at the top of my mandala. For there, among the underprivileged, amid the turmoil, strife, and suffering, is where once was my mission. It is there where lies a need for change. Then, because I cannot deny security and comfort in my life and so must count myself among the privileged of the city, at the bottom of the circle, in opposition to the North End, I place the South, which represents wealth and all the sound traditional values.

311

But how do Indians fit into my sacred circle? Indians who belong to the past: they too are part of me, a part no longer evident. The unconventional, unrepressed me forced into hiding. A part that must be recognized if ever I am to be whole again.

Security, freedom, even turmoil and pain without which there would be stagnation. All are necessary. All must be recognized. I'll draw a line to join the three and make the city one. I'll make myself whole.

What colours should I use in my mandala? I try to picture brightness but I cannot. Except for the centre, which is white, all is grey. Try as I may my mandala remains dark and gloomy. Until finally a glimmer of yellow and a bit of rosy red appear from the South reaching upwards. From the South? Ah, yes, I know why.

Then comes Marty with a laugh and a shout. Standing before me, oblivious to my thoughts, she obliterates my mandala. I frown. In a way she represents my lack of freedom. But even were she not here, where could I go, what could I do?

"Mummy, there's nothing in their house. No furniture at all. And the baby had no toys. Now he has."

Learning.

**5**

Detroit, Michigan, June 15, 1923

Dear Daughter,

You are wondering why I haven't written for so long. I have meant to but everything has happened so fast you will understand when I tell you there has been no time. Those special lots I hung onto for so long out Gratiot, the ones I put the stores on, they sold for a mint. Much more than I ever expected. I've done all right. And only a few months after the time Pa and I separated. Now I've got it all figured out what to do with my freedom.

Our gray clapboard on Coplin has been a good home for all of us, and a nice one, but with everyone gone I've no need to be rattling around in such a big place with just Pa's nephew Ed Richardson here. He might be only staying for a while, after all, like he has done in the past, though he says he's retired from the Lakes. I had him drive me around a bit as I've been thinking that one of these days with Detroit going on expanding the way it is, that Mack Avenue is bound to be turned into a major throughway with all the automobiles Ford and his like are turning out. There are more automobiles on the roads all the time. So I found this cottage with a nice garden and a garage that will do me fine for a little while. It is an investment and a place to stay until I decide where I want to spend my final time. For in the meantime I intend to take that world tour I've been talking about for the past decade. And now I'm rid of everyone and got my money it seems time to go. Ed says he'll be happy to hold down the cottage for me and help in every way he can until I get back. That was the word I needed so I mean to go ahead and put the big house on the market. Can't say I'll be sorry to see it go for though it was the one house I always wanted to build and live in, it has served its purpose. Its time is over and it's time to move on.

313

Whenever there's an ending there's a beginning and I'm looking forward to what's ahead of me.

I intend to sell most of the trappings and possessions, give much of it to the Good Will, and keep just enough to furnish the cottage. I'll feel good not to be burdened down with so much. Ed says he'll be pleased to work in a garden a bit as it will keep him busy, and he is very good about driving me around. So it all seems as if it will work out well and as soon as I've sold this place I'll write and tell you more.

I was over to see the de Chênes and Martha was there too. Mrs. Schrieter has to have a full time nurse now and Martha says death will be a release. I should think a release for both of them. I told them you were no longer plagued with your nightmares about fire and Martha said that psychologist, Freud, the one who makes his patients lie on a couch and tell him everything, would say it's because you experienced the real thing. Winifred said because the fire materialized it is no longer repressed within you and you are free of it. Though why, I wanted to know was it there in the first place? That got them all talking some more and Minnie wanted to know whatever had Dickinson to do with it all. And Winifred said that after all it was because of the Reverend Dickinson that you stayed in Winnipeg. I find their theories a bit far-fetched but thought you'd like to know and that we are all glad you are not having those dreams anymore no matter what the reason.

I might as well tell you too that though I thank you for the tract literature and am glad you are happy with your new chapel, you will have to allow me to find my own way. And you will not change Martha either nor the de Chênes. They are all following their own paths. If there is only your way up the mountain I think God has wasted a lot of mountain space and the Devil is a good deal smarter than the All-Encompassing One. Which to me

314

*isn't at all a sensible way of handling things.*
*With love,*

*Your Ma*

**6**

*Detroit, July 16, 1923*

*Dear Bessie,*

*I've heard from both your mother and Martha that you are no longer interested in hearing about spiritualism and reincarnation and such matters, and I don't wish to strain our friendship. But I don't quite understand why you feel the way you do. Is it because you wish to keep within the limits of the teachings of your present church? Or because you yourself think it is dangerous to get involved in such beliefs and practices? I know you once were concerned about the source of the information that was coming through you and we tried to explain about that to the best of our ability. We said it was like seeing from another dimension, like being on a mountaintop and able to have an overall view of what's happening below. If I see two trains coming in opposite directions I can tell whether they will pass or crash, But you know about that.*

*I will respect your wishes, for I believe we each must find truth for ourselves. However, I want you to know that spiritualism, clairvoyance, clairaudience, telepathy, and the like are well-established among the most respected of people. I'm sure you know about the Society for Psychical Research that was founded in England in 1882. There are branches in many countries now. And having mentioned respectable people, none could be more so than that most extraordinary man, the classical scholar Gilbert Murray, who among his many honors was awarded the Order of Merit. He is a member of the British*

315

*Academy and of many foreign learned societies. And he doesn't feel it amiss to experiment with thought transference and other such things. He's just one among many eminent persons I could mention. And by the way, there is an excellent group of researchers in your own fair city. A Dr. Hamilton, a medical doctor, has worked with mediums to materialize from ectoplasm the likenesses of soldiers who have passed over to the other side. He has actually photographed the phenomenon in process and I've seen the pictures....*

I'll not read further. I shred the letter and throw it away. Winifred de Chêne, Frances and Minnie will always be my dear friends. But they've no idea of the conflict within me that is tearing me apart. I must obey the teachings of my church. There is only One Way, Frances. It's obvious you haven't been reading the tracts I've sent you.

7

Once her mind is made up it never takes Mary Faris long to act. Within two months her house is sold for a good price along with a few pieces of better furniture. Everything else that she does not wish to keep is bundled off to the Good Will. The cottage out Mack Avenue having been acquired prior to the sale, a moving van carries the remaining bits of her worldly goods to the new home and Mary Faris, along with Will's nephew, Ed Richardson, settles in.

Finally, plans completed, the date for the start of the grand tour set for early spring, Mary Faris sits back in her chair on the screened verandah with Ed in shirtsleeves and braces, smoking his pipe. Both watch the traffic roll by on the highway. It is rather a pretty house Mary Faris has bought, with an attractive well-established garden which one day, in the not-too-distant future, will give way to commerce and cement. The thought doesn't bother her a whit. She is happily anticipating her world tour. She is counting the weeks to the day when she will begin her journey.

"Ed," she says, breaking a long silence, "I'm so pleased with things at this moment, why can't I just leave everything be?"

"Why can't you, Auntie?" Ed asks, rocking peacefully.

"I'm surprised to find I'm over being annoyed with that fickle husband of mine."

"That's sure surprising, Auntie."

"You know Will wants to buy that farm out Grosse Point way and I refused to give him the money for it. I was just being ornery at the time. I've got more money than I can use and Will knows it. There's no reason why I can't give him what he wants and some extra besides. It'll salve my conscience, for what it's worth. Not that there's any reason for that, goodness knows, but he's the father of my children and he's getting on in years. I don't wish to go to my grave feeling I haven't done right by him, and others."

"You always did well by Uncle. No need to worry, Auntie."

"Nevertheless, what do you say if tomorrow you drive me to my bank and I'll write out a cheque — enough to cover that farm — and we'll take it over to Will and surprise him. Then I'll make arrangement for a small income for him, enough so he can manage the place with no worries. After that it won't bother me if I never see the man again."

"If that's what you want, it's all right by me, Auntie."

317

\* \* \* \* \*

The following morning at ten o'clock sharp, with hat and coat on, Mary Faris stands waiting for Ed, who has gone to fetch the Ford from the garage. An automobile drives up and a humourless, bespectacled man steps out and, after inquiring her name, presents her with an official-looking envelope.

Mary Faris has been ordered to appear in court.

# Chapter IX

# Planning Anew

August 1923

**M**artha. How many times have I told you not to flick the dust around like that? Pick it up in the duster. Do I have to show you how again? I've told you how to do it a dozen times if I've told you once. Will you never learn?" My voice has risen to a shriek.

Marty, who has been flicking the duster lightly over the dining-room table, then over the chairs, daydreaming as usual, stops short. Her happy face changes instantly as she starts "picking up the dust", as ordered, now disliking her task, her dream broken, the pleasure of the moment gone.

"You dust these rooms properly or..." Tears fill my

eyes. Unable to continue the tirade, I go into the kitchen.

Whatever is wrong with me? I never used to act like this. Why do I get so upset by such stupid little things as dusting? I return to the dining room in an effort to placate Marty.

"It's my nerves, Marty." A form of apology.

Marty, hurt, pays no attention.

She is a difficult child, mercurial, altogether too sensitive for her own good or anybody else's. I go back to the kitchen to nurse my own wounds, banging my fist against the door frame as I go by, frightening Marty of course. Anything would frighten her. And if I don't calm down she'll be crying as well.

Get a grip on yourself, Bessie. This can't continue. Something is happening. Something awful. And it mustn't go on. What ever can be done? I have spoken to Dr. Winram about my "nerves" and he just said, "Give yourself time, you were through a lot." But that happened four years ago! Then he said, "It could be you're at that age." It is always "that age" if something is wrong with women that can't be understood. What nonsense. Ma was never at "that age", or if she was you'd never have known it. It's something else. Maybe it's everything.

Sometimes my body is so full of pain. Some days it is almost unbearable. The pain adds to the torture of living. Dr. Winram said, "Rheumatism. Try hot baths, get out more in the fresh air." Get out more when there is so much to be done around this depressing place? When some days I can hardly walk?

Another time Dr. Winram said, "Maybe you should have your teeth pulled." Pulling teeth is the latest theory about how to cure rheumatism. I examined my teeth and could find nothing wrong. All good, white, well spaced — and I refused. But one day when I could stand the torture no longer I telephoned Dr. Fremming and made an appointment. When he pulled one tooth I demanded to see it. There was nothing wrong with the root. Not a thing! I was furious. "What is this stupid exercise about anyway?" I shouted. Poor man, it wasn't his fault. He was only doing what I'd asked. He was appalled as I went ranting on about the foolish theories of the medical profession. But how could he have understood that my body was full of pain and my head full of troubles? He stood looking at me. Then I just left. And when I brought Marty in to have her teeth checked a few weeks later, I trust I was myself again.

What can be done? Get out of the house more. Yes, maybe the answer is to get back to office work. Yes. Office work will help me forget myself and my problems. That's the answer. How I wish I could be back with Cedric Wilkins. But work as a stenographer will do to begin with. I really won't mind. That will give me a start, and with my background and capabilities I'll go up the ladder quickly.

Marty? Marty is seven years old and quite capable of getting herself a sandwich at lunch time. Or, here's another thought: maybe Marty can take a sandwich to a friend's!

The planning is already adjusting the flow of adrenaline and I am feeling a bit better.

Charles won't like the idea of my working outside the home. Not one bit. He'll consider it a reflection on his ability as a provider. But he is adaptable and once he sees how much better I am for getting away from the house — for I'll be a better companion and mother, hopefully a different person altogether — he'll understand.

I can't help wondering if Charles still sees Margaret Bradford. I could hardly blame him if he did. How often I have envied Margaret her unmarried state. No smelly socks and germ-filled handkerchiefs to clean on a scrubbing board in a dark prison-like basement. How often I have wished I could exchange roles with Margaret and be the friend and lover — and have a daughter too, of course. Be a kept woman with no depressing house or housework. I find myself relaxing as I fall into the error of my young daughter — daydreaming — enjoying my picture of Margaret, her hair wispy, bent over the scrub board in the basement. Crying, of course, her hands red and inflamed. I look at my own soft white hands. At least my hands never get like that! I picture myself in a bright and cheerful apartment, the "Kept Woman". Marty has been put to bed after having spent a pleasant day in the country with her mother, horseback riding. I am reading, dressed to the nines, waiting for the doorbell to ring...

The front doorbell is ringing noisily, awakening me from my reverie.

Marty calls out, "It's Amy. Can I go out and play?"

"Oh, run along," I reply, resenting the interruption.

Marty skips to the back door with the duster, shakes it briefly, then places it on a hook on the wall behind the basement door. Her face is animated once more. She bounces back like an Indian rubber ball! I begin a more practical line of thought.

Some time ago Charles brought home from the office an old Remington typewriter which I have been using for my letters. Tomorrow I'll check my typing speed. Even if I'm a bit rusty, which I probably am, it won't take me long to get into condition. I was right there at the top before I left Wilkins'. As for my shorthand, I still use it for note-taking, make use of it almost every day for one reason or another. No trouble there. This is how I will "walk" again and forget my "bed" of troubles.

There are signs that the postwar depression is finally easing, and a few more jobs coming available.

322

\* \* \* \* \*

Within a week I have found exactly what I am looking for, an ad in the Help Wanted column of the *Free Press*, asking for a typist able to take shorthand.

I see Marty off to school and Charles off to work without saying a word to Charles of my intention. Then I dress carefully, and completely confident the job will be mine, I set out to be interviewed. To save time I take the Sargent Avenue streetcar, getting off close to the building I am seeking.

After waiting in the outer office for almost fifteen minutes along with other hopeful applicants, I am finally ushered into the inner sanctuary and offered a chair opposite the boss's desk. The boss, Mr. Jeans, has his head down, is writing busily, and does not bother to look up at me. He keeps his head down, writing for fully two minutes. His attitude, which might have unnerved a more sensitive soul, simply annoys me. At last he looks up. Mr. Jeans is a fat man. His cool eyes narrow as he surveys me, then he presents me with a weak smile.

"So, you want a job as a stenographer."

I decide to ignore the attitude, and say quietly, "That is why I am here."

I proceed to give him all the data, the number of years I have done typing, my qualifications, my final years as a secretary in Detroit, and then as —

He interrupts. "Don't you think you're overqualified, m'am? I just want a stenographer."

That flusters me. "How can someone be overqualified? I'm happy to type and take shorthand, and I'll do an excellent job for you."

"I'm just trying to be kind, m'am," he says, heaving a fat sigh. "We prefer the young ones. The young ones are a bit more flexible." He smirks.

323

I know my face is turning pink, and not with embarrassment as Mr. Jeans may imagine.

"Just give me a chance and I will prove that I can match any younger person and more. In work," I add.

He smirks again. "Are you married?"

"Yes."

"Do you have any children?"

"A daughter. She goes to school and is old enough for me to be away during the day."

"Well, I suggest that you go home and look after your family, m'am, and you won't be sorry."

What right has he to suggest what I do! How does the fat man know whether I will or will not be sorry?

My pink flush is turning to red, I can feel it. "I can get you the best of references. I was private secretary to Mr. Cedric Wilkins, here. He managed the large import spice company..."

"Never heard of him. As I said, we prefer younger girls around here. More flexible. More genial. Miss Peterson, will you show this lady out."

Miss Peterson, who has been typing in a corner of the room, gets up quickly and comes over, casting a sly glance at me from a painted eye. Miss Peterson is a peroxide blonde, her skirt is short and her heels high. Mr. Jeans nods briefly and then, head down, interest gone, returns to his writing. Nodding as briefly to the bowed head, I allow myself to be ushered out.

*　　*　　*　　*　　*

At home I take a hard look at myself in the long dresser mirror in the bedroom. Forty-seven years old in November. Dark hair greying, hair that can no longer be done up in the figure eight I was once so proud of — the eight has been reduced to a simple zero. My waist is a little thicker. And glasses: I wear glasses. Bifocals,

324

and still not used to them. The trouble is, I'm too old. Too old and not wanted. I am sorry for myself.

Miserable, I remove my street clothes and put on a cotton dress. There is still time to do some laundry before Marty and Charles arrive home.

I put a load of light-coloured cottons through the washing machine, rinse, wring, and carry them upstairs and outdoors and peg them to the lines. It is a bright sunny day and returning to the basement, facing the gloom of the stairwell, the bifocals confusing me, I miss a step and tumble. Lying there, unable to move, I wish I were dead.

It is Charles who arrives home first at the noon hour to find me a crumpled heap at the foot of the basement steps, my ankle sprained, my back hurting, my flesh bruised, my spirit more so. I can hardly bear to be touched.

## 2

"Marty, what do you think we can do to make your mother feel better?"

Marty frowns, thinking hard. Then she shrugs, "I dunno."

"We've got to think of something. What do you suppose she'd like to do?"

Marty has that one figured out. "Go out."

"But where, that's the question."

She hesitates, thinking again. Her face brightens. "How about taking her for a ride to Assiniboine Park."

"Now that's a good idea; but we go to the parks quite often. However, acting on your suggestion..."

Marty is delighted being made to feel an important part of the scheme.

325

"What would you say to taking her someplace she's never been before?"

"I think that would be better. But where?"

"To Crookston." The idea has just struck Charles. "What would you say to that?"

"Where's Crookston?"

"You've heard me talk about Crookston, where I lived a long time ago with Grandma and Grandpa. It's where I went to school."

"Oh, yes, I remember now, it's in Minnesota in the United States. That's a long way from here."

"It would be a very long day's drive — over two hundred miles. We would have to stay at a hotel overnight."

"That would be fun. Would it be anywhere near Grandpa's farm?"

Now it's Charles' turn to brighten.

"Marty, my fine daughter, though your sense of geography is sorely lacking, you are a source of great inspiration to me. Your grandparents live a long way from Crookston. But what would you say to driving all the way to Michigan? It would take several days to get there and several days to get back. And we couldn't do it until next year during your summer holidays. In the meantime we can travel hopefully, as the saying goes. Do you think your Mother would enjoy going so far and visiting her mother?"

"Let's ask her." Marty is all for a new adventure.

"Well, hold on now. Let's think about it a bit more and ask her in the morning. She's lying down now. You know, Marty, I think we've hit on something. First I mean to look through some magazines. I recall an article on tourism a month or two ago. It was called "From Pine to Palm". I'll try to track it down. In the meantime, how about making some popcorn, and you and I can crawl under the earphones and listen to "The Two Black

Crows" on the radio. Does that appeal to you?"

Marty is enthusiastic. "I'll get the popcorn, and the pan, and the butter, and everything while you're looking for that magazine."

"Good. That's what I like — cooperation."

## 3

When I arrive downstairs Saturday morning it is to find the dining-room table covered with carefully arranged magazines, maps, and brochures; and Marty eagerly standing by, her eyes wide in anticipation.

"What's all this about?"

Charles' voice comes from the kitchen, where he has got into the habit of shaving while starting the breakfast. "Bait!" he calls out.

"You're supposed to be a fish," Marty explains to me.

Curious, I examine the bait.

"Not all fish bite, you know, Marty. It has to be the right kind of bait for the fish."

Marty looks disappointed. "We were hoping you were the right kind of fish."

"We'll see."

I pick up a magazine, then a brochure.

"You're suggesting we go touring?"

Charles arrives from the kitchen, wiping his hands on a towel. "Why not? We enjoy driving. It might be fun and we can visit the parents during Marty's holidays next summer. Your mother has had to postpone her trip because of the lawsuit with Mr. Faris and she won't get away on her world tour before 1925 anyway, no matter how the case goes. A visit from you might cheer her up."

327

How can I refuse? Charles was a good fisherman in his younger days. He knows his fish.

I watch as Marty sidles over to her father and I hear her whisper, "Is she going to say yes?"

As always, conspirators.

Charles shrugs and forms a word with his mouth. "Wait."

Ah, well. I thumb through a magazine. "Would you consider camping out of doors, Charles, in a tent?"

It is not likely he would.

"Well — no-o. Those are just magazines about all the new gadgets for touring. Touring is the latest fad, you know. From palm to pine, from pine to palm. Roads are being improved all the time. More mechanics and garages for repairs about. Thought you'd like to read about it and all the people who are taking to the roads. We might picnic along the way a bit but stay at hotels and have a good hot meal at night and a good breakfast in the morning. Make it easy for you."

"I think if one is planning a tour it ought to be done the way tourists do it. Buy a tent and camp out. It would be more fun."

"Camping doesn't appeal to me. But... hmmm...maybe there could be a bit of a compromise if you really would like to camp out."

I am examining the magazines. How wonderful it would be to get away. I look up. Charles is winking and nodding at Marty who, sensing victory, decides to leave.

"Mummy, can I go out and play?"

"If you've had your breakfast."

"Daddy gave me toast and hot chocolate."

"You never eat enough. You should have cereal and fruit as well."

"I'm not hungry."

"You never are. Well, run along."

While we eat, Charles and I talk about Ma.

"I think you should suggest to your mother that she settle out of court."

"You mean give in to Pa and divide her property with him?"

"That's what I think she should do. Then she could begin her world tour whenever she wishes — next year. She's getting on in years and it's not always wise to postpone travelling."

"You don't know my mother. Ma never gives in. She'd never drop arms in the midst of battle. And the battle's on. You read the letter. She said she had been about to give Pa, not the half of her fortune he demanded, but a goodly sum — 'all he would ever need for the rest of his life'."

"'Including enough for a supply of liquor to finish him off and enough for a fancy funeral to boot!'" Charles finishes quoting.

"Well, that's Ma."

"You know, Bessie, your stepfather could have asked for everything. I hate to say this, but your brother-in-law, Blake Arnold, is right. The chances are the law will be on Mr. Faris's side. A woman's property belongs to her husband."

"And so does the woman," I can't help adding.

"I'm not saying it's right, but that it's legal. So it might be easier on your mother and everyone if she doesn't try to contest it.'"

"But that's not her way. Ma's a fighter. And she's mad because of the way Pa set about trying to get it from her. He never learned how to handle Ma. He should have known, after all those years of living with her that she would have given him the money after she'd simmered down. He's always managed to rub Ma the wrong way. And as Ma added, his timing, as usual, was bad. If he'd only waited one more day. Now she's determined to fight it out."

329

"Even if she loses? Which is likely."

"Apparently. She's angry at Blake, too. It's obvious that Beatrice told Blake of Ma's windfall and that's what triggered the action. It didn't take Pa long to see a lawyer — at Blake's advice. Beatrice told Ma she was sorry she had mentioned anything. But it wasn't unnatural of her to talk to her husband, now was it? Ma doesn't blame Beatrice for that, but she doesn't think Blake had any right to interfere. He's a bit of an autocrat, is Blake. Believes the man should be the one authority in the family and women should be housewives and bearers of children."

I steal a look at Charles who, choosing to ignore the statement, bites into his toast.

Charles, of course, is not like that. He's much too empathetic a person. But if it were not his nature to empathize, I know he would be authoritarian. And in a manner he is. A true but ridiculous thought. But then aren't we all complex characters with paradoxical natures?

"Blake is good to Beatrice, though, I do believe. And Beatrice wouldn't think of arguing with him. Probably enjoys being on a pedestal. She doesn't have to work too hard. But no backbone, that sister of mine."

"Maybe she has backbone — in her way. But rightly or wrongly Blake has interfered, with the result that your mother has a lawsuit on her hands. I can understand her anger, but she's a highly intelligent and reasonable woman and I think if you can get her to calm down you'd be doing her a great service by persuading her not to pursue this course. Instead, settle out of court, then put it all behind her. When she's riding those ocean waves she'll have forgotten all about it."

"I would persuade her if I could, and maybe I should try."

The screen door on the verandah can be heard

330

opening and then shutting. An instant later the sounds are repeated. It is the postman with the Saturday morning delivery. I get up from the table and go to the front door, returning with a letter from Ma I've already opened. Reading it, I sit down.

"Here's our answer."

"Has she lost?"

"She's under no illusion and expects to. She says she realized from the outset that her chances of winning the case in the circuit court were slim. Her lawyer, Mr. Sevald, advised her of that."

"Then why didn't she settle?"

"I've just finished telling you that isn't Ma's way."

I return to the letter and read aloud. "'This — after all I've had to put up with from that man. The court is not concerned with what is rightfully mine but simply that the man is lord and master and can have what he wants. And I don't mean to give in to that sort of claptrap. If such is legal it shouldn't be.' And she continues by saying that she'll fight the case in every court in the land if she loses every penny she has. And, oh Charles, she says she intends to go for entireties."

"Winner take all." There is grudging admiration in Charles' voice. "A real gambler."

"A really angry woman. I understand Ma's feeling about its being so unjust. The money for the original piece of property purchased was hers and came from her mother's estate. Ma's the one who took the initiative and did the work and built up the business. Pa never had any extra money of his own. She tried to make a partner of him once but he botched everything. He got involved with a saloon business, then went into debt and in order to avoid his creditors turned his shares back to her. That was illegal. She kept everything after that because of his drinking and his irresponsibility in money matters. It was the cause of a lot of ill" feeling

331

between them over the years, you can be sure. That was a very long time ago, and since then the business has been entirely hers. Except for that time just before I left home when she allowed him to get involved a bit again and he almost ruined her. But you've heard about that."

I am talking too much. I don't want to be unfair to either Ma or Pa.

"Perhaps we should go to Detroit. I'd like to see my mother. I'll talk to Pa, too. To both of them. Not that it will do much good: my mother's a very determined woman and my stepfather's a stubborn Irishman."

Stubborn like you are sometimes, Charles, I almost add. But I am not unaware that Charles is trying to do something to help me. I really do appreciate his thoughtful ways and his kindness, though I am sure my appreciation does not often show. Why can't I be a little sweeter? Why can't I modify my character and control my temper a bit more? Can Ma change her character? Can Pa? Can a leopard change its spots?

## 4

When autumn comes Charles buys a handsome McLaughlin Buick touring car — dark green with black leather upholstery, yellow-spoked wheels, and eisenglas curtains. A larger, heavier, more solid automobile than the Ford. Safer for touring, he says. Bought well before the date of departure in order to break her in, he says. With it comes a black leather cover lined with red wool, to go over the hood to keep the engine warm during the winter months, along with a few other gadgets and a pair of khaki coveralls. Often during the autumn and the following spring Charles is

332

to be found, if not under the car, then with his head tucked under the hood, close to the engine, listening to its heartbeat so he says. The McLaughlin Buick is his new love, and he cares for "her" almost as much as he once loved Black Beauty.

Charles and I have agreed to compromise and will spend one night at a hotel and the next at a campsite because the gypsy in me yearns for outdoor living and cries out for consideration. So Charles, though still skeptical about the camping bit, purchases an umbrella tent for which I make light mattresses on my treadle Singer sewing machine. An army cot is also purchased because of my rheumatism. And hours are spent making out long lists of bedding and all other necessary paraphernalia.

By springtime one wall of the dining room is covered with large maps supplied by the Automobile Association: maps of Minnesota, Wisconsin, Michigan, and Ontario. Two possible routes have been marked with coloured pencil, and stopovers indicated by thumbtacks holding tiny numbered flags. Closets and corners of the house are stacked with such exciting items as a sturdy dark-green metal table that can be folded to a compact 12" x 36", folding camp stools, compact kerosene stove, and a long trim icebox with a central compartment for ice (to be clamped to one running board — ice to be picked up at ice stations along the way). Then too there is all the necessary equipment for dining: cups, plates, coffee pot, and aluminum cooking ware that neatly fit one inside the other. To say nothing of washbasins, soapbox, towels, and what-not. Where is everything to go in the automobile, I wonder. Charles says there's no problem.

For traveling I purchase for myself a jacket of Donegal tweed with matching knickers and skirt, along with a couple of cotton and silk blouses. And for Marty,

333

bloomers and tops of serviceable khaki. Then, when warm summer days signal the fast-approaching moment of departure, I steal a glance around Eaton's smart couturier shop and add a lovely light afternoon dress to my wardrobe — expensive, not too dressy, and almost as attractive as one Martha might have made for me. And then a hat! I had not planned to buy a new hat. But as the saleswoman says, "A beautiful creation, Madam. Just made for you." Delightfully draped tulle, with the prettiest flowers. It does look good on me. Martha will love it, while my other friends may remark that Bessie has not faded so much over the years after all. And what if one day, as I walk into town, Richard perchance is there to see me! Still a good-looking woman, he will think. Not at all like my wife, Lydia, who has lost her prettiness and become quite fat. Lydia always was on the plump side.

"I'll take the hat, thank you. See that it goes out on this afternoon's delivery."

And when Eaton's red cart, pulled by two handsome chestnut horses, arrives, I am waiting on the verandah to receive a grey cardboard dress carton and a very large round hatbox.

* * * * *

July arrives and two elongated bags of heavy canvas, covered with black waterproof cloth, are strapped at the rear of the car, either side of the spare tire, one containing the tent, pegs, and groundsheet, and the other mattresses and bedding. One running board holds the icebox with food, the other the camping equipment and a can of gasoline, all carefully fenced in and covered with another waterproof cloth. Inside the McLaughlin Buick are the campers and their luggage, including a large hatbox atop all — a real nuisance that must be watched over and cared for in an automobile packed to the limit.

And thus we set off, over flatlands, over hill and dale, over mainly gravel roads which, when dry, throw up dust covering all and sundry. We jounce over the dirt roads, we weave around and through potholes, and once after a heavy rainstorm we are caught in a deep rut. Charles must find boards and then, with Marty and myself pushing and heaving, we try to work the car back to firmer ground. As we struggle away, a lighter car — a Ford of all things — bumps merrily by, the driver grinning and waving but offering no help. Instead of being annoyed we break down and laugh.

We laugh a lot. I, the navigator, with compass and a log book record the details of the tour and make notes on the day's adventures for the sake of family and friends. A tire blows occasionally, the radiator overheats. Once, lost in admiration of virgin forest and lakes, we find ourselves a couple of hours later right back where we started from. When we can, we choose a campsite by a lake and surreptitiously take a cake of soap with us into the water. Hotels are soon forgotten for they prove to be, for the most part, disappointingly primitive. The day comes when, shown to a room, Charles declares it to be a virtual fire trap and insists that suitcases be carried back downstairs. After that we camp, and though Charles blames his outdoor nightlife on the quality of the hotels, it is obvious he does not find the alternative too disagreeable. On the contrary, he is finding it agreeable, perhaps because in every way I truly am much better. The gypsy in me is loving the adventure, the fresh air, the freedom. And under the stars, or the rain, the thunder, and lightning, we feel close to nature, closer to one another, happier than Charles and I have been for years.

335

\* \* \* \* \*

It is eleven days before we arrive in Wilmot, Michigan, where the welcome mat is out and waiting, where the conversation never ceases, and where visits from and to relatives living at nearby Kingston and Cass City seem both endless and pleasant.

Mother and Father Clements talk about the Road Building Machine experience without rancour. They are content to be where they are, used to living with candle and kerosene lamps, a wood stove, an outhouse equipped with a Sears Roebuck catalogue, used to a farm and a lot of hard work, used to being up before daybreak and going to bed some time after the chores are done. Returning to the good earth, as Mother Clements predicted, has proven to be the very best treatment for all that troubled them.

Of course it is not anything like the farms they knew in eastern Canada and Minnesota — just three cows and a couple of horses, a few chickens, a vegetable garden, a few fruit trees and fruit bushes. And a dog named Jack who is their good friend. But then they are not as young as they used to be, either, and this farm is sufficient to keep them in food and above the poverty line — with help from Charles. Not a thing in the world to complain about.

"I wouldn't have known how to be a lady," Mother Clements confesses, blinking both her eyes to tell me she is letting me in on a special secret. "Frankly, I was more than a little frightened at the thought of mingling with all those hoity-toity people. But I wouldn't have let on to Ben for the world."

The farmhouse is spotless. She has hooked rag rugs of various sizes to decorate and add colour to the wood floors. A crocheted afghan covers a couch. Furniture, donated for the most part by friendly relatives, is

336

inelegant but comfortable. One bedroom is filled with the scent of wild roses. Another, offered to Marty, has a homemade mattress stuffed with hay: delightfully aromatic, annoyingly noisy, and guaranteed restful.

"You don't have to worry about us. We're well looked after here."

And that is true. The neighbours, like Uncle Ben and Auntie Chris, check in occasionally to see that everything is all right. I may envy Mother Clements her cheerful farmhouse and country living, where beans are picked and cleaned and readied at the outdoor iron pump. But the housework, the farm work, seem endless. Aren't there other, more important, things to do in life besides constant chores?

"Marty's a worker," grandmother comments with pride.

Worker, indeed! Spending most of the hours jumping in the hay, playing in the sand, riding bareback on a workhorse, collecting eggs with grandfather. Generally being herself, and generally being catered to by the grandparents. Just what she loves: being catered to. Housework is not what I am planning for my daughter. I want Marty to grow up to be a responsible person and do her part in life, but I want her to have an interest in books and go to university. And that is what she will do if I have any say about it. I have no intention of Marty being trapped the way I have been trapped. Marty is going to have a few options in life.

As prearranged, after a week at the farm Charles takes Marty and me to Detroit where he will spend a few days before returning by himself to Wilmot to have time on his own with his parents, while I visit with my special friends in Detroit and have those quiet, well-thought-out talks with Ma and Pa.

337

\* \* \* \* \*

Time in Detroit passes quickly. There is so much to talk about, so many pleasant recollections. Ed drives us around the city with Ma pointing out the many new buildings and development and the huge homes of the *nouveaux riches* in Grosse Point and Grosse Point Farms, along with all the other wonders of a fast-growing city.

As agreed, when we see Beatrice and Blake remarks about the lawsuit are brushed aside and deftly pigeon-holed and we focus on lighter, brighter subjects, such as the growth of Detroit, the new architecture, and the new Henry Ford hospital which Blake helped design.

Marty sits quietly, frowning at her tall, rather austere uncle in his well-cut grey suit as he talks with Charles. Finally she comes over and whispers to me, as her aunt Beatrice moves to the kitchen to make tea, "What do I call him?"

I understand and am amused by her predicament.

"Uncle Blake, of course."

But as she confides to me later, she can't. "Uncle Blake" sounds entirely too familiar and intimate for such a person, who is so totally different from Daddy.

So after much thought, when the moment of verbal action arrives and her mind is made up, Marty says, "Hey!"

"Not quite apt, either," I report to Ma that evening after Marty has gone to bed, "though I appreciate the reason for her difficulty with the formidable Prince. He and the sweet Cinderella appear to me to be well-matched after all. I was too quick to judge Blake when we first met. I thought he was a snob and I recall accusing Beatrice of putting on airs."

"You judged right. That was my opinion then and I haven't changed my mind."

338

"Ah, come on, Ma. I think it wrong of Blake to have interfered in your affairs, but that doesn't mean the man's all bad."

*　　*　　*　　*　　*

My time with Martha is disappointing, and after I had so looked forward to seeing her! At our first meeting, though we greet one another with warmth and enthusiasm and chatter away like a couple of schoolgirls, the conversation inevitably turns to philosophy and religion, Martha making the blunt statement that some Christians are very wrong in thinking they have exclusive rights to salvation — that, to the contrary, there are many paths leading to enlightenment, that Church dogma and wrong interpretation of the Bible have led, for the most part, to persecution and suffering. And on and on. No doubt all this in reply to the booklets I have been sending her, hoping she would get back, as I have, to seeing the light. And she goes on and on, until I am utterly exasperated.

"For goodness sakes, Martha, are you so sure you're not making a faulty job of interpreting what's right and what's wrong?"

Argument is not unusual with us. It has never hurt our friendship, but rather strengthened it. A disputatious pair, Ma used to call us. But we have not seen one another for so many years, and I am changed for I have seen the light. To me argument seems untimely and unfortunate, especially now that it is imperative for the sake of my sanity that I hold firm to the One True Way. But Martha has become so very dogmatic about what she is referring to as a "broad all-encompassing" view of religions. How far can one carry this broad-mindedness, I ask her, and we get into

339

another argument. Then I try to change the subject, but unsuccessfully.

Mrs. Schrieter is dying and Martha is anxious about her. Though her mother is little more than a vegetable, Martha wants to be by her side at the end. Understandably. Perhaps Martha is a bit distraught and consequently more forthcoming in her conversation than she otherwise would be. But then I am not known for holding back the punches either.

By the time I get back to Ma's place, I am sorry and phone Martha. We agree to disagree and not to discuss religion at our next meeting. There are so many other things we want to talk about. I will pray for Martha's soul as I do for Ma's, and maybe someday she will take heed of the tracts I send. The next time we meet, I want to introduce Marty. And Martha is anxious to meet her namesake.

*   *   *   *   *

Martha and Marty take to one another immediately, Martha fussing over the girl and showing her around her workshop, pointing out a few of her paintings and sketches, and giving Marty a small brooch as a memento. In turn, Marty pays Martha the compliment of being sincerely interested in everything. However, before I have time to resume conversation with my friend, the phone rings. It is the hospital. Martha must come immediately. She is upset, and grateful for my offer to accompany her.

At the hospital Marty is left in the corridor, as only Martha and I are permitted to enter the sickroom. I am shocked to find Mrs. Schrieter unrecognizable, the life force fast withdrawing. I stay for a short time, my head bowed in prayer. Then, after holding Martha's hand momentarily, I leave, knowing that Martha prefers to be

340

alone with her mother at the end.

Outside in the corridor once more, hope gives way to hopelessness. I am sad and disappointed, realizing that part of my longing to return to Detroit, to Martha and my other friends, is a longing to return to the past. The folly of it all! Everything is changed.

Marty has been waiting patiently. I hug her, needing her closeness. She puts her hand in mine and we walk silently down the long hall to the elevator.

*     *     *     *     *

The phone is ringing.

"Take it, Bessie, it's probably for you," Ma calls out.

And it is. Minnie de Chêne is inviting us all over for Sunday dinner. "Your Cousin Ed, too," she says.

"How pleasant, Minnie. Thank you very much. However, Beatrice is planning to pick us up Sunday afternoon for a final visit with Pa Faris, since Charles will be returning from Wilmot soon and we'll be leaving for Winnipeg. Then there's the funeral on Monday, as you know. I wonder if I may ask, because we're such old friends, if you could have us over Saturday instead. If it won't be too much of an inconvenience, that is."

"Of course, Bessie. No inconvenience at all. As a matter of fact I had suggested Saturday, but for some reason Mother thought Sunday might be a better day for you. We'll make it Saturday, then. Come for an early dinner, say, 5:30? Because of your young daughter. We want to have a good long talk, yet not keep Marty up forever."

"That's thoughtful of you. You can count on our being there by 5:30 Saturday. It will take longer to get to your place than it used to, now that Ma's moved to St. Clair Shores. Remember when we could just cycle back and forth?"

341

"Yes, indeed. We haven't been seeing as much of your mother lately. I'm sorry about that."

Things have changed. Everything has changed.

## 5

Saturday. The light rain that started about eleven o'clock continues throughout the afternoon.

Ed has gone to bring the car around as I appear in the living room wearing my fine hat of tulle and coloured flowers.

"Bedecked and bedazzling," Ma laughs. "Aren't you afraid of that pretty hat getting wet in this rain?"

"We'll take your umbrella. Thought I might as well wear the hat after carrying it so far. It was very expensive, Ma." I sigh.

"A folly," Ma comments. "But it suits you," she adds generously.

"I thought Martha would take notice of it and enjoy it."

"And what did Martha have to say about it?" Ma is amused.

"Nothing. Just nothing. She was much too preoccupied with her mother to concern herself with hats."

"Not just her mother, I bet. Martha's got interests other than glamour, nowadays. She's after the Holy Grail."

"Indeed! Martha would do well to do a little more searching in the Bible."

Ma, watching out the window, looks relieved to see Ed's Ford has arrived round front.

"Here's Ed. Marty's with him. I told her to sit up front so we can do our blethering in the back. The

342

umbrella's in the stand by the door. Mind you don't forget it."

The gentle rain continues. Saturday afternoon and the traffic is not as heavy as it usually is. Maybe the rain, making the pavement slippery, is keeping a lot of weekend drivers home. Ed, a good driver, is driving carefully and not saying anything; he is not a talkative person at best. Marty is quiet too, looking around, dressing and undressing a small doll with clothes she has been "designing" from scraps of cloth her grandmother gave her from her rag bag, dreaming of the day when she will be a great —

"Mummy, how do you say that word?"

"What word, Marty?"

"Hot coater."

"*Haute couturière.*"

"That's what I said, 'hot coater'. That's what I'm going to be when I grow up."

Once again Marty fastens her attention on the doll.

"Well, tell me what you think of your long-nosed brother-in-law," Ma asks.

"That his nose is not so long after all, figuratively speaking. But I've told you already, Ma. You want me to say that I don't approve of him, but I won't. He's really very nice once one gets to know him. Appearances are so often deceiving. Maybe sometimes when one first meets, both parties are a bit on the defensive. He's very good to Beatrice and he went out of his way to be nice to Marty. Took her, along with Blake Junior, for a ride in the rumble seat of his sports car and gave them an ice-cream treat. Both Marty and I have changed our opinions."

"You're still looking at everyone with rose-coloured spectacles."

"By no means, Ma. That's not the opinion people in Winnipeg have of me. Ask Charles: he would never

343

agree with you there."

Ma needs to be mollified. It seems under the circumstances she would prefer me to dislike Blake.

"Blake had no right to involve himself in my affairs."

"Beatrice said that he was really very sorry when he found out that you were preparing to make that settlement."

"Sorry, indeed. Sorry won't change things. You'll not catch me forgiving him. All the trouble he's caused."

Marty turns and pokes her dark head back over the top of the front seat.

"Can I come and sit with you?"

"Whatever for? Aren't you comfortable where you are?"

"Yes, but I just want to sit with you," Marty insists.

"Oh, let the child sit with us if she wants to. Why on earth not?"

"I think your grandmother would let you do anything you want. Come along."

Marty's long legs straddle the seat. She drops into the back and sits between us, once again concentrating on the little doll and her fashions. Ma continues to apprise me of Blake and his error and Pa and his errors. But I've stopped listening to Ma and her grumbles. I am watching a car in the distance heading our way, coming ever closer. Fascinated — like watching a cobra. As it approaches, one of its wheels slides off the road, then up onto a section of curb. I sit very still. Holding my breath. Waiting.

*  *  *  *  *

I am struggling to stand. Someone is helping me, asking, "Are you sure you're all right? Take it easy now." The voice is unfamiliar but kind. A man's voice.

Ed is nearby, dazed and white as a sheet of paper.

344

We are in a wide ditch by the side of the highway. Ed's car is overturned and in a shambles. Ma is lying underneath, the metal frame of the windshield driven into her forehead.

Unable to speak, I try to go to her, but the man restrains me. "You can't touch her, Missus. Is that your mother? Better not to touch her. We'll try to get the car off her. An ambulance is on the way. Leave her," he warns me sharply as I try to pull away.

Cars have stopped and are still stopping. A crowd of people has already collected. A man is wringing his hands and repeating, "I shouldn't have tried to turn off the curbing." The man who caused the accident?

Marty? Where is Marty?

Marty crawls out from the area of the back seat and stands up. Also in a state of shock, but seemingly uninjured.

The man who is supporting me calls out, "My God, a child! If she'd been sitting in the front she'd have been killed."

Because of the force of Ma's body, propelled forward. The way the car collapsed. What compelled Marty, just moments before the accident, to move into the back seat? Why is Marty saved when Lana was destroyed? Why is Ma lying under the car injured and maybe dying, when I am the one who has so often wished for death? God has a warped sense of humour and life is no more than a cosmic joke. No! It is an intelligent and orderly universe and therefore there must be a reason for everything. Though I can't see it. I can't see it.

Half a dozen men, directed by the man who was helping me, are carefully lifting the car off Ma and moving it aside. Someone puts a coat over her. I should thank the woman, and I want to, but I am numb.

A siren sounds as an ambulance swiftly approaches

345

and abruptly halts. The attendants are gentle and efficient and soon Ma, still unconscious, is on a stretcher and into the ambulance, with Ed, Marty, and myself alongside. People and cars are dispersing as quickly as they gathered. Now the ambulance is speeding for the hospital.

A flowered hat lies where it fell in the ditch, and nearby is a small doll in a crudely stitched dress.

* * * * *

At the hospital Ma is rolled into an examination room. With Marty and I standing by, the doctor checks her over and probes into her skull, lifting up grey matter. Then he shakes his head, bandages the wounds, and orders a nurse to roll Ma to a certain ward and put her into a bed. Too weak to protest so cursory an examination, I follow, holding tight to Marty, with Ed bringing up the rear.

It is a public ward for women, with about twenty beds, and Ed remains outside. The hospital is overcrowded, the nurses and doctors overworked. Those patients in the ward who are able, get out of their beds and crowd around, eager to see what is wrong with the "old lady". They grin, they cluck, they whisper. White faces, black faces, yellow faces, staring.

"The old woman's gonna die, " I hear one say .

I summon up strength and call out, "Go away, all of you. Can't you see she needs air?"

I move towards them menacingly. They go.

The nurse who wheeled Ma in is hurrying by, holding a bedpan, with not so much as a glance at Ma. My surprise turns to concern.

"My mother should have attention," I call to her. "This minute."

The nurse stops briefly and calls over her shoulder,

346

"She's dying . We're short-staffed. I have too many patients to look after."

At least she is frank.

I call back to her, "Then she must be moved to where she can get attention." But the nurse is gone. Something has to be done.

"Marty, you stay right here by your grandmother and look after her. I'll get Cousin Ed and we'll try to find a telephone . "

\* \* \* \* \*

Marty stands guard. Grandma is awakening.

"Water. I want water." The words are scarcely audible.

"My grandmother wants water," Marty says fiercely to the same nurse, now returning with the bedpan.

"I've no time for your grandmother." The nurse is annoyed.

Marty follows her into the corridor, insistent, but to no avail. The nurse is heedless. A doctor comes walking quickly by. Grabbing his white coat, Marty hangs on. The doctor swings around, surprised. Marty is determined.

"My grandmother wants water."

Marty is still holding onto the coat. The doctor is forced to pause. He looks down at Marty momentarily, then he turns. "Nurse," he shouts to the figure fast disappearing down the corridor, "see that her grandmother gets attention."

\* \* \* \* \*

When I return I am surprised to find the nurse giving Ma a bit of attention, helping her drink water through a straw, attempting to make her more

347

comfortable. Ma is in severe pain.

"Marty, Ed is going to take you home. You help him make supper and go to bed as early as you can. Uncle Blake will be here soon. He's arranging to have grandmother put in a private ward at the Henry Ford Hospital, where she'll be well looked after. So don't you worry. I'm going to stay with grandmother as long as she needs me."

I keep vigil for three days. Blake, Beatrice, and I see that Ma is nursed round the clock. She gets the best of care from surgeon and doctor. Ma does not die.

Back at the cottage in St. Clair Shores, undressing completely for the first time since the accident, I discover my body is a mass of bruises containing all the colours of the rainbow. Pain had to be ignored while Ma required attention. Now, relaxing at last, I am overcome with weariness, with a sense of sorrow and of self. Pain surfaces and engulfs me.

**6**

Charles arrives in Detroit and, after doing what he can, decides to drive to Winnipeg on his own. It is time to get back to work. The game is over, the pleasure gone. He had such high hopes that Bessie would recover from her depression, and everything seemed to be working out well. She was like her old self, a mood of the past recaptured for all of twenty-one beautiful days — or was it twenty days, nine hours, and thirty-five minutes before he left to go to Wilmot? Now it is likely she will return to Winnipeg more depressed than ever after this latest traumatic experience. Will she blame him for her mother's accident — on the grounds that had they not gone to Detroit, which was his idea, she and her mother would never have set out to visit the de Chênes? Irrational! But then Bessie in a fit of depression is anything but rational and he becomes the whipping boy. Difficult and unpleasant, both for him and Marty. His shoulders are broad, but he hopes Marty will not remember her mother like that. How can Bessie change so completely, so unexpectedly, and then return to being her normal self? A real Jekyl and Hyde! What in the world can be the problem? A broadminded, well read, top-of-the-line kind of person. Someone to look up to. Then, in a flash, a complete about-face. Is it something physical, emotional, psychological? All three?

He presses hard on the gas pedal and stares down the long road ahead.

*     *     *     *     *

I'll stay at the cottage with Marty until Ma comes home from the hospital and is able to get about on her own a bit. Ed can't care for her while she is still invalid. Marty will miss some school, but I'll teach her long division and grammar and see that she continues with her reading. She's not one to cry her eyes out about losing time at school the way I might have done. But she'll make out. She'll do all right and I'll rather enjoy instructing her. A picture of Owen House and all the little ones and the big people I once helped flashes across my mind. I slam the door on memory.

## 7

When Ma finally comes home, Marty, who has been to the hospital only infrequently, is shocked to see a little old bent woman, a near

349

skeleton with a deep dent in the forehead. Only the bright blue eyes and the quick mind are as ever. At first in a wheel chair, Mary Faris is determined to get back on her feet, and towards the end of October she is walking — feebly — but walking.

I know, and know that Ma knows, that even should she win the lawsuit she will never be able to travel. One morning after Ma starts walking on her own, I notice the travel booklets that were stored so carefully in the bookcase are missing. Discarded? Nothing is said. Perhaps, like Owen House, there are some things that hurt too much for words. But a few days later I find out it is not like that with Ma.

"No use keeping those travel folders around — just extra truck. Those pictures are etched on my mind anyway. And even if I can't travel, I'll go on reading same as I've always done. Don't think I'm not sorry I won't be going and seeing the real thing, but I don't intend to get all worked up fuming over what'll never be."

A part of me asks, why do I live in the shadows of yesterday?

I say, "Ma, before we go, something has to be said about the lawsuit. Please settle with Pa and call it quits. What good is it going to do you anyway, to continue with this fight? You know you've got a chance of losing everything. Besides, look at you! The condition you're in. And you're sixty-eight years old. How ever do you expect to defend yourself in a court of law? Pa's old, too. Why can't you forgive him and give him a bit to live on just as you intended to do?"

"Have you said your piece?" Ma asks, quietly daubing at her left eye with her handkerchief. She is not crying; it is just that since the accident a tear duct continually leaks a bit.

I look at Ma, knowing full well she will go her own

way, and I am expecting a tongue-lashing to follow my bit of advice. Instead she says, "You're not giving your old mother much credit, are you? Sure I'm mad at Pa and Blake Arnold, especially for upsetting my plans and everything. If I'd been on that ship I wouldn't be in this condition now. But who knows. That's just an iffy. The fire's gone out of my anger these past few weeks. However, that's not the point. The point is that I've always admired Emmeline Pankhurst, Susan Anthony, Elizabeth Stanton, and the likes of them and the other suffragettes. You know that, for we used to talk about such things, you and me. And when you wrote about Nellie McClung, how I wished I was there cheering her on, along with you. Well, I haven't been much help to any of them, much as I wanted to be right out there fighting alongside. We're into the twentieth century and in some ways you'd think we were still in the Dark Ages. The reason I'm going on with the case is not just because of Pa but because of a principle. Women have the vote now, but they're still be only chattels if they're not allowed control over their own money. That circuit court gave me no proper chance to say what I wanted. You're right that I'm an old woman with a beat-up body. But I've still a good mind and I can still use my tongue. And if I have to be wheeled into that courtroom, I mean to fight that case as long as I'm allowed to, and I'm betting everything I have on winning it. If I win, though few may ever hear about it or about me, the case will be on record and will make it easier for other women in the future. If I lose — and I may well — I'll manage, for I know how to get along on next to nothing and I haven't far to go. Then, whether I go to Heaven or Hell, or return to this earth — as Martha seems to think I might — I'll have the satisfaction of knowing I tried, in my little way, to make things better for all of us."

A look of smug satisfaction settles on the thin

351

wrinkled face.

My mouth must be hanging open. "Why haven't you explained long before this?"

"I had no intention of telling Beatrice and Blake, and when you and Charles came you were so set on avoiding any mention of the lawsuit, I left it for the time being. Besides, Sevald wanted me to drop it. He's been doing his best to talk me out of it."

"I can well understand."

"He finally agreed to help. Told me so the other week at the hospital. Said if I could pull through this mess I could pull through anything."

She pauses. "I was starting to bring up the matter of Sevald when we were heading for the de Chênes'. But I was shut up. Now I've told you."

"Why, you old curmudgeon," I say affectionately, uncertain whether to hug or shake her. "If things go wrong, I'll look after you, Ma."

"I don't want your help. It's my battle and if I lose, I'll take the consequences. I can manage my own life, thank you."

## 8

January 1925

"Please come in, Charles." Sarah emerges from her living room as the maid opens the front door. "Good of you to bring me the forms. It's such a bitterly cold day."

"I thought it would save you a trip to the office and it so happened I was passing this way." Charles stamps his feet in the vestibule to get the snow off his boots. Then, after removing mitts and boots, bangs one frostbitten hand against the other. "Must be at least

352

thirty below."

"I'm beginning to think Mother and Father have the right idea, spending their winters in Florida.

"Are you still thinking of going to Florida?"

"Yes I am. Father's no better and I've decided to leave in a couple of weeks time. But do have a cup of coffee with me, Charles. It's already made. Have you a few minutes to spare to warm yourself?"

"I think I can spare time for coffee, thank you."

"Take Mr. Clements' coat please, Annie," says Sarah, turning to the maid. "And it's coffee for two in the sitting room." Looking at Charles, she remarks, "You've been wearing that hangdog expression much too long. It's Bessie, isn't it?"

"What makes you think that?"

"She's about the only person I've ever known who can get you into the doldrums. Can I be of any help?"

Charles chooses a comfortable chair. "I can't understand how she can be her old self when we are on tour, or off on any excursion, or playing whist or Five Hundred with Emma and Charlie for that matter, and then frequently be so different and difficult at home. It goes in cycles. She'll go along for a time being rational, and then for a spell depressed and irrational. And it seems those spells are becoming more frequent and lasting longer. I told you what a wonderful trip we had to Wilmot and Detroit. As far as I know she enjoyed herself up until the time of the accident. After that I don't doubt but that she was a real Florence Nightingale, as her mother wrote, completely ignoring her own pains. Then when she returned home, after the stories about the trip and her experiences had worn thin, depression set in once more, and the rheumatism which she appeared to have coped with so well when she was away once again became intolerable. She spends a lot of time in bed, and crying. I don't know

353

what can be done to help her."

"That's what doctors are for."

"They've already made various suggestions — for rheumatism, that is, such as pulling teeth. Nothing she's willing to try seems to help. As for the depression, that's something else again. Though I'm sure constant pain in itself is fair reason for depression, I'm certain that in her case it's not altogether the reason."

"You said that Bessie seems to manage when she's away from home?"

Charles continues his own line of thought. "I'm sure it's not just physical health..." He hesitates, as if wondering whether he should say more to his cousin. "Sarah, Bessie doesn't know this but her mother told me something about so-called psychic abilities that Bessie has, and the trouble she got into with the church because of it. Her mother is sure Bessie is half convinced that God is out to punish her for her misdemeanours. Mrs. Faris said she thinks that bit about God punishing her is a lot of nonsense and I heartily agree. I've always considered Bessie to be a woman of high intelligence, but Mrs. Faris says she can't seem to forget about those past problems. Bessie's become deeply fundamentalist, you know. Sarah, do you think such a conviction that God is punishing her could be the basis for her depression?"

"Why, I've no idea. It must certainly be devastating for someone to be convinced that God is deliberately working against you. But surely that can't be in Bessie's thinking. Maybe there's a much simpler answer to her problems, such as the Owen House mission being destroyed and the two deaths. The trauma she went through then must have been awful. But I had no idea about this psychic bit. Strange how you can know a person for so long and yet not know that person at all."

"I don't go in for this psychic stuff myself, and she's

354

never mentioned anything about it to me. I'm not saying there's nothing to it, mind you, just that it doesn't interest me and I've never inquired into such matters. I know Bessie is highly perceptive — that's another characteristic I've always admired in her."

Sarah is frowning, thinking. "You said she always appears so much better away from the house. Charles, I'm well aware that Bessie never liked that particular house from the moment she moved there. And I can understand and sympathize. A woman either likes a place or doesn't, and a home is very important to a woman. More so than to the average man, who is out of it so much of the time."

"Bessie disliked the place before we even thought of moving there. It was simply a matter of economy at the time; we never intended to stay. Just one thing after another has prevented us from moving."

"Well, what's preventing you now? It could ease the situation, though I'm not suggesting it's the answer to everything. The postwar depression is finally over. Real estate is going steadily ahead. Witness those forms you just brought me to sign." Sarah indicates with a wave of her hand the large manila envelope lying on a nearby table. "What's to prevent your buying a nice house, or building one of her choice? Bessie never chose to live in your parents' place, so do give her the opportunity to choose and make her own home — and see that there's enough money left over to get her a little help. She is not the housewifely type."

"You've noticed that? I admit a new house did cross my mind when I was driving back from Michigan. Guess I haven't been able to see properly through this all-pervading gloom."

"There are a few attractive houses around here up for sale."

"Bessie wouldn't care to live in this area."

355

"Really!"

Putting his cup down, Charles sends her a wry smile. "I know what you're thinking — that I married the wrong woman. I've been aware from the beginning that's what Ray and the others have thought. Ray has said as much. Now I'd like to set the record straight once and for all. I know that if I'd married Margaret I wouldn't be up to my neck in trouble — not like this, anyway. Margaret is a pleasant person. I doubt if she ever has, or ever will, raise waves or tread on other people's toes, and I've never known her to have a fit of depression. But compared to Bessie she's colourless. I've known a great deal of happiness with Bessie, despite all our differences over the years. She's a wonderful person, and she's my responsibility. And Marty and I intend to stand by and see her through her problems."

"Are you sure you and Marty aren't taking on too much?"

Charles, getting up, says nothing.

## 9

T hought we might begin planning our house," Charles states bluntly, dumping four magazines on the table in the kitchen as I am putting the finishing touches to the evening meal.

He is looking at me as though he's not at all sure how I'll react. But he needn't worry. I am thrilled. At last. After all this time: eleven years, or more than eleven years.

"Do you think we can afford it?"

"I think so. The market is picking up and it looks like clear sailing ahead, for a while at least. We can either buy or build. Whichever way you'd like."

"I think that will depend on where we decide to go."

"I could be happy almost anywhere as long as the property is large enough for a good-sized vegetable garden. At one time I wanted to be near Sarah and Ray, but I know you're not keen about that part of town, and it really doesn't matter to me anymore. What would you say to that lot of mine in Wildwood across from the river? It's a few miles out of the city, lots of trees, wild roses, berries at the doorstep — and enough land to grow whatever we want. Only a scattering of houses about. A country atmosphere. I could enjoy that if you could."

"Sounds appealing. But that would mean building a house, wouldn't it?"

"Which would mean you can design just the house you want. And if that's what you want, you give me the details and I'll try drawing up the plans."

That is something Charles will enjoy doing. He is a bit of an artist.

During our spare time we drive around the snow-banked city, looking and commenting on the various styles of houses. In the evenings we search through magazines, making notes. Then, after we have decided to build in Wildwood, out Fort Garry way, Charles arrives home one day with a drawing board, a T-square, a set of architectural tools in a velvet lined box, rulers, squared paper, and other necessary items. We set about our planning with zest. By now I have settled on a colonial-style home.

"It's a style that's easy to live in. It will be bright and well balanced."

"Whatever you say, Lady. I'll take your word for it."

For weeks the dining room table is the architect's domain and each day all three meals are relegated to the kitchen. First plans show a large house of the magnitude of the Shaws'.

357

"Impossible, Charles. Not only do I not want such a large place, but it'll cost a lot of money to build a house like that. And think of the upkeep, of the heating cost alone during the winter!" I know all about costs involved in looking after a large house.

Charles is a practical man. "Put it all down to enthusiasm," he says cheerfully. "I'll scale it down to a reasonable size, and you can check the footage carefully."

I know the house will be attractive. By the time Marty and the other neighbourhood children are busily chopping drains to allow water from the fast-melting snow to run to the sewers, by the time the crocuses are poking their first green spikes above the moist earth, the design is finished to the satisfaction of both of us, and blueprints have been made. By that time, too, Sarah has returned from Tampa, Florida.

*　　*　　*　　*　　*

Greeting Sarah at the office, Charles asks about Uncle John.

"Mother said he brightened up considerably during the time I was there, but I'm afraid it was only a temporary respite. Father's frail. But, tell me, how is Bessie? I've been thinking a lot about her, and you."

"House plans proved to be sound therapy. She's considerably cheered up, and as you can see, so am I. We're both looking forward to the move. I think you know it's to be that lot in Wildwood, and in another few weeks I'll begin cutting down trees to clear for the foundation."

358

# 10

1925

As soon as the ground is sufficiently dry, we go to Wildwood for a few hours each weekend carrying a picnic lunch, relishing first the clean spring odours of the woods and fast-greening trees, then the perfume of June's abundant wild roses. Marty and I walk along the tar-lined road, go down to the river, speak occasionally to the friendly interested people who will be our neighbours, while Charles chops trees. Then we help him a bit by dragging the lighter logs and branches aside. The outings are good for all of us, especially for me, despite the mosquitoes, and the woodticks which have to be picked from Marty's long hair.

\* \* \* \* \*

When summer's days are over and the ground readied for excavation, a growing disquiet clutches at me. But what can I say? What can I do after all this? These past months I have been hoping, just hoping and dreaming...

\* \* \* \* \*

"I've been checking on construction companies," Charles announces cheerfully, "comparing prices and so on, and I think I've found the crew who will do a proper job for a fair price."

Now I have to say something. Now is the moment I have been dreading.

"Charles, let's put it all aside for awhile."

"Put it aside!" he repeats, unbelieving. "But why?"

"I've been thinking... Wildwood is so far away from

359

everything," I end lamely.

"But I've told you, as soon as we can afford it, you can have your own car. You can learn to drive. Eight miles is not so far from town."

That is not it. I know he will find me unreasonable.

"Marty has some good friends on Langside. She might find it lonely out there."

"Not Marty, she's quite self-reliant."

He is frowning. He knows that is not the reason.

"The chapel is so close. Marty walks there on her own."

"Couldn't you have figured that one out long ago?"

Now he is growing angry, as I knew he would. And Charles is slow to anger.

Now comes an attempt at patience. "Would you prefer to build on that lot of yours on Florence Avenue? Marty can come in by streetcar. That's not a problem."

"The chapel is so close. She can walk." I am repeating myself.

And the chapel is important. I would not want Marty to have an excuse for leaving it. But that too is not the reason. I am stalling.

Now Charles is really angry. "Are you trying to tell me that you don't want to move? Damn it all, why couldn't you have said so in the first place and saved all this trouble?"

"No. I do want to move." I am crying now. Tears again, for I do so want to move. I do, I do. More than he can ever guess. "It's more than just Marty and the chapel. It's Ma. I'm worried about Ma. What if she loses the lawsuit? She'll have nothing. Who will look after her?"

"If it's concern about your mother that's behind this change of heart, then your mother can come and live with us. More reason than ever for building the house."

"She's too independent. She would never agree to

360

living with us."

"Then why can't your well-to-do sister and brother-in-law help her out, if — and I repeat, if — she were to lose?"

"You've been insisting she's bound to lose. And Ma would never accept money from Blake after what he's done. She's too proud. And Belle and Joe haven't a cent. We must wait and see what happens. Maybe it won't be too long to wait now."

"For God's sake, Bessie, it could be years."

"Don't you dare swear at me and take God's name in vain!"

"Why do you seem so sure she's going to lose? Has all this something to do with that famous sixth sense of yours?"

"Don't say that. I don't know, I don't know. You were the one who said she has every chance of losing, that the law is against women. I'm so worried for Ma, she's so thin and crippled. You asked me if I would refuse to help my mother when you wanted to give to your parents. And if you think you had the right to send money — and initially it was my money, and I've had to contribute a lot of my money to them all these years — then I have every right to consider sending money to my mother should she need it."

"I don't deny that — should she need the money. But Bessie, control yourself and try to be reasonable..."

Control myself! Just look at who's talking. He's acting like a volcano about to erupt.

"It could be a long time, years even, before a decision is handed down. Should real estate continue its upward trend, we could have enough money by that time to keep her comfortably wherever she wants to live. Besides, I can't imagine a court in this day and age throwing an old lady out on the streets, even if Mr. Faris refuses to provide for her — and in the first place

361

he asked for only half —"

"If! If! I asked Pa, and he wrote that if he gets his hands on the money she can go whistle. And I don't know what the court will do, nor do you. I can't and I won't let Ma down. If you felt you had the right to impoverish Marty and me by sending all that money to your parents — buying them a home and all, and forcing us to live in this rotten place — well, you can just stay here for another three or four years until we find out what has to be done."

He has no right to get angry with me like this. I'll tell him a thing or two.

"No way have you and Marty been living in a state of poverty. You've both had everything you've ever needed — if not everything you've wanted."

"I have not!" It is a statement without meaning.

"I give up. If you can't even be rational..." He moves towards the hall. "I'm going over to see Uncle Walter."

\* \* \* \* \*

What's the use. Hope gone again. There's no dealing with Bessie when she gets that way. Childish and unreasonable. Or just plain off her head. His spirits have sunk to the level of his boots. The McLaughlin Buick, *en route* to Uncle Walter's, takes a wrong turn and finds itself parked in front of Margaret Bradford's apartment. Margaret, comparatively colourless, but pleasant. Reliable. No shouting.

\* \* \* \* \*

When, finally, I calm down, I am frightened and ashamed of myself. I know it was wrong to make that statement about Ma at this late date, and I had no business saying what I did about his parents. After all, I

362

do not resent what has been given them. And about being impoverished! That was wrong. Our needs are taken care of. What makes me say such ugly things? Sometimes after such an outburst I cannot even remember what has been said, or the cause of it all. Charles works so hard at being good to me. He is a better man than Richard in many ways. Richard would never bother to be so concerned about others — completely detached, the impartial lawyer. Still, despite his many fine qualities, Charles constantly annoys me — because he is not Richard.

I want desperately to move from here, but I must consider Ma.

My head is aching, my body is aching. Slowly I get up from the chair into which I dropped when Charles left me and, clinging to the wall for support, slowly I walk up the stairs to my room. The house is whispering, laughing at me. Holding me.

## 11

Charles, at the office finishing the accounts, caps his fountain pen and applies blotter to paper; then, closing the ledger, tips back in the swivel chair, linking hands behind his head.

Uncle John dead — eighty-six years of age, would have been eighty-seven come October. His was a good life and a rewarding one. Now is the end of an era. Things will never be the same with J.R. gone. Always very good to his nephew. A penny-pincher in so many ways, yet very generous in other ways: a philanthropist. That penny-pinching must have been a habit built-in since youth which made him able, in the first place, to invest at the right time. Charles would have liked to

363

have succeeded, even in a small way, but things just have not worked out for him. Perhaps there was a fair amount of luck that went along with the careful calculation that J.R. was noted for. Shrewd man. That huge sum of money that Uncle John gave him just disappeared — except for what was turned back into the Company. There are numerous reasons why it disappeared and Charles has counted them over and over many nights, unhappy that he has not managed to do what he wanted to do for Bessie. But knowing too that, given the circumstances, it could hardly have been otherwise. He is still feeling raw about Bessie and that house. So damned unfair, after she had been fussing and fuming about the place on Langside for years. Always putting him in the wrong. And after he has tried to do his best by her and Marty. In the end it is always back to her bouts of depression — worse than ever.

Well, there is almost nine thousand dollars set aside, waiting for her to say when she wants to start building — when and if her mother wins that lawsuit. Fat chance. For the most part the cards are stacked against women in this world, the very reason of course that Mary Faris is engaged in her gamble and Bessie so adamant about the building bit. Well, good for Mary Faris. But what about us?

Would it be wise to invest that $9,000 and have it working for them in some way, rather than just sitting in the bank at three percent interest? Charles has been wondering about that since Bessie's most recent bombshell.

At this point in his thought the office door opens and a tall, untidy, though not altogether unprepossessing man walks in.

"Mr. Clements?" he asks with an engaging smile.

"Yes. C.H. Clements. I'm holding the fort for a while. My cousin, L.R., is in Florida."

364

"Of course, the senior Mr. Clements has recently died. I read the news in the paper."

"That so? What can I do for you?"

"John Jones is the name." The tall stranger holds out his hand. "Call me Jack."

"All right, Jack."

"I'm here from Flin Flon, selling shares in a gold mine. Geep Gold Mine. Heard about it?"

"No."

"Thought you might have, being in investments and that sort of thing."

"Sorry, but no."

"Let me tell you about it before the news goes too far, 'cause it's a sure thing and shares are selling fast. Limited amount."

"Don't think I can do anything about it with the other Company members absent. Against Company policy."

"Why not invest on your own?"

"Not in a gold mine, thank you. Haven't that kind of money."

Jack's face falls. "Look now. What say I leave you some literature and you can think about it. And here's my telephone number. I'll only be around for another day or two, so you'll have to make up your mind fast."

"I've already made up my mind. Sorry."

Jack Jones leaves. "Thought I was doing you a favour," he calls back over his shoulder.

Scoundrel, no doubt. Lots of his type around. Probably reads the papers to find out about business men and their associates. Read about Uncle John and decided to stop by the office. Charles sits glancing at the pamphlets. Gold in Flin Flon is big news these days. Father headed down to California in his youth in the early days of the gold rush there, and all he got out of it was a handful of small nuggets, one of which he had made into a tie pin. And he brought back some Mexican

365

spurs, Charles recalls. There was gold in California and there is gold in Flin Flon — somewhere. If only one could be sure of where.

The door opens again.

"Oscar! Good to see you. I haven't seen you for ages."

Getting up, Charles shakes Oscar's hand. "You're looking well."

"Doing well. Saw the news in the paper yesterday about your uncle and wanted to stop by to offer my condolences. I had great respect for J.R., as you know. A fine man and a good friend."

"Yes. But you probably were aware his death was not unexpected. Still, when the news comes it's not easy to take. We'll miss him."

"We all will." Shaw glances down with faint amusement at the literature scattered on Charles' desk. "What's this you've got?"

"This? Some villain was just in, trying to sell me shares in a gold mine."

Shaw picks up a pamphlet. "Not the Geep Gold Mine in Flin Flon?"

"The very one. You know John Jones-call-me-Jack? I wondered if Geep should be spelt g-y-p."

"Hold on. Not everyone's a crook, and I happen to know about that gold mine. A geologist, friend of mine, was in Flin Flon recently for the purpose of checking it out. The owners have struck a vein of gold that looks most promising. I've invested $20,000 on the strength of my friend's observation and report."

"$20,000, whew! You think it's a sure thing, then?"

"As sure as anything of that kind. Enough for me to bet on it."

"At that rate, why does Jones have to go out of his way to look for investors?"

"He's not, as far as I know. Just happens he's here

366

seeing our mutual friend at the moment. Maybe he was at a loose end and thought he'd do a little business. Come to think of it, I may have mentioned J.R. in his presence."

"Said he saw the write-up in the paper."

"That's it. He was with us when I got the paper and I mentioned that we'd been friends."

That matter having been cleared to his satisfaction, Charles asks, "Would you advise me to invest in that mine?"

"You know me, Charles, I wouldn't give a good friend advice on anything as uncertain as a gold mine. I think it a fair gamble, that's all I can say. You have to do whatever you think best. Well, I must go. How's Bessie?" A conventional inquiry.

"Just fine, thank you." The conventional reply. "Nice of you to stop by. And my best wishes to Diane."

*     *     *     *     *

Charles leans back in the swivel chair once more. Then, straightening his spine, he collects the scattered literature so carelessly thrown aside, and starts reading.

Hmmm... If Oscar Shaw has put $20,000 down, and the mine has been checked out by a geologist he obviously trusts... Oscar is like Uncle John was, seldom ever been known to be wrong. A Midas touch there. Might not be a bad idea to take half the savings and sink it into the mine, and put the other half into something very safe — slow, but safe. Or maybe something more than half into the mine. After all, it could bring a quick return and then there would be money both for the house and Ma Faris in the not so distant future. And besides that, with the market moving along as nicely as it is, by the time the lawsuit is

367

over there might even be the same amount of money in the bank as would be invested in the mine. How could he lose? Given today's market with everything on the up and up and everybody investing and some people making money hand over fist! He has been altogether too cautious after that 1913 fiasco. It's hard to understand Bessie's attitude and her reluctance to build, when everything is on the move again. Bessie can get a notion into her head and then she can be just plain ornery. Why shouldn't he take a flyer? After all, it's his money, no matter what Bessie might think.

If Oscar Shaw has put all that money down...

# Chapter X

# Renovating

**B**elle is coming to Winnipeg! Waiting on the train platform along with Charles in the morning cold of late March, oh how I am looking forward to seeing my young sister. Young? It has been seventeen years since I last saw Belle, and what a lovely girl she was. Hard to believe, but Belle will be thirty-five this year! Things did not go too well for Belle and Joe in Dallas. Joe had managed to make a living as assistant manager in a large hardware store. But they put aside every penny they could to realize his dream of running his own store. Then the store he purchased and stocked never did too well. And last year they decided to return to Detroit, where industry continues to thrive. Taking Ma's advice, Joe invested in a building with living quarters above. A good area for business. All this, just as the baby they wanted so very much was finally on the way.

Belle wrote, "Joe won't allow me to pack or do a thing. He's put me on a shelf as though I were an expensive figurine, insisting that he and the movers will do everything. But the doctor says it's okay for me to travel."

All went well. They were nicely settled in the new quarters when the baby arrived, a fine healthy boy, Ronald Alexander. And with the hardware store off to a good start, the future was looking rosy until the day Belle went to check the baby in his basket. And found him dead.

"It wasn't my fault, so why does Joe have to blame me?"

Belle left Joe and moved in with Ma.

"An impossible situation," Ma wrote. "Joe isn't blaming her, they're blaming themselves. And what good does it do? Of course they're broken-hearted but these things happen. She's just moping around here saying she never wants to see Joe again. Fiddlesticks! What she needs is a vacation until she can get herself in hand."

So I invited Belle to stay with us for an indefinite period. And Charles is pleased. Charles likes having people around.

Charles reported one day that he had mentioned Belle to his cousins. Told them, he said, that Bessie's sister Isabel was coming to visit, a good-looking woman from her pictures, and someone that Bessie has talked about over the years, frequently and fondly. So Sarah and Ray have offered to introduce Belle to a few people,

370

which is very good of them. And it is my intention to have Belle meet people at the chapel. I haven't many friends the way I once had, but there are always Charles' relatives. There's Emma. Belle is sure to like Emma. What Belle needs is chapel and cheering.

Down the line the mournful cry of the train announces its arrival.

We've fixed up the east room next to Marty's, bought a new bed, new blankets, and placed three hyacinth bulbs, soon to bloom, in a shallow bowl on the dresser. Oh, I hope Belle will like everything. Charles even suggested I update my wardrobe. My cloche hat is new, my long-line mid-calf coat is new, as is the dress underneath which is one inch shorter. The latest fashions show off the legs to advantage and my legs are not bad. But what I approve of is the freedom the fashions bring. At last, how sensible! What will Belle think of me?

The train rolls slowly, clanging its way into the station, and comes to a squealing halt. A black monster, hissing hot steam. A powerful creature worthy of respect. Along the line porters swing down from coaches, placing stools in readiness for passengers about to be disgorged. And here they come, one after another, the red-capped porters taking a small suitcase, an overnight bag, offering a hand in help.

Everyone is off the train now.

"But where's Belle?" We are walking towards the quickly dispersing passengers. I am sick with disappointment. "I don't see her, Charles."

"Who is this?"

A slim young woman is running towards us, coat to the knees, galoshes unbuckled and flapping, smart cloche hat well down on bobbed head, bright lipstick evident even at a distance. A wide brilliant smile — the smile I recognize.

371

"Belle!"

"My sister Bessie!" Belle drops her small case, throws her arms wide in the air and then around me. A big hug and a kiss. Next she turns to Charles. "And this is Charles!" She gives him a hug, her left leg kicking up behind like a stylized picture from a fashion magazine. And depositing a kiss, she leaves lipstick on his cheek.

"Now look what I've done." Taking out a lace-trimmed handkerchief, she carefully wipes red stains from both our cheeks.

I glance at Charles, whose expression might either be translated as amusement or pleasure. Maybe both.

Still somewhat startled, I turn to Belle. "I didn't recognize you at first. You've, well...changed."

"And so have you, sister Bessie. But I'd know you anywhere, just the same." And with a laugh Belle threads one arm through mine, the other through Charles', and walks us towards the station, chattering brightly, galoshes buckles flapping, flip-flop, flip-flop.

"Hold on." Charles stops abruptly. "How about your luggage? And have you a trunk?"

"It's all being taken care of by a porter. The suitcases will be delivered this afternoon and my trunk, tomorrow. Don't worry. I've tipped, and all is well."

Belle, efficient as ever.

"Then we can go right home and I can get you sorted out and we'll have time for coffee before Marty arrives for lunch. There won't be much chance to talk when she's around. When she's excited she chatters like a magpie."

And she'll be excited about this flapper aunt. I steal a look at Belle, noticing now her plucked eyebrows, carefully rouged cheeks. Just how much does Belle require sorting out?

\* \* \* \* \*

"How do you like me, Bessie?" Having just been introduced to her bedroom, Belle has taken off hat, coat, scarf, and thrown them on the bed, disclosing straight bobbed hair shingled at the back and a smart two-piece, long-waisted dress with a short pleated skirt, and high-heeled shoes. She does a twirl, revealing silk stockings rolled above the knees.

"Very modish," I say hesitatingly, still wondering about all that make-up.

"You don't like it! Why, Bessie, a girl has to cut loose, you know."

"Cut loose from what or from whom? From Joe?"

"That isn't what I mean. But you may as well know right now that I'm not going back to Joe. And I want you to promise never to talk about Joe or our problems, or I'll pack up and leave."

"I promise." I may as well. "But first you'll just have to tell me why and then we won't say another word."

"Because he accused me of murdering my own beautiful baby boy." Belle's eyes fill with tears. She bites her lip to keep it from quivering.

I am thunderstruck. I can't believe it.

"You mean Joe said that to you?"

"Well, no, he didn't use those very words."

"What did he say then?"

"He didn't really say anything. He just looked it and I knew what he was thinking."

I can't help drawing my breath and then emitting a sigh like the final bit of steam from the black engine. "I'll just say one word and then I'll say nothing more, for I promised."

"What, Bessie?" Belle's voice is querulous.

"A word we're both very familiar with — fiddlesticks!"

How right Ma is. Then, knowing Belle's anguish is

373

real, I hug her. "Come, let's have that coffee. Charles has probably made it by now."

*  *  *  *  *

"I don't think Bessie likes my get-up." Belle does another whirl for the benefit of Charles before sitting down for coffee.

"I never said I didn't like it," I protest. "I do."

"I think it's cute." Charles winks at me.

"Well, I must say I'm glad to hear you say that. Bessie, you of all people. I thought you'd understand, for weren't you working to get freedom for women?"

"Political freedom, Belle."

"I'm for personal freedom and don't tell me you're not interested or you're not the sister I once knew. See, it's a protest against male domination. We girls have flattened our chests." Belle rolls her eyes from Charles to me. "And given up our femininity," she explains, crossing her shapely silk-encased legs.

"You've got me fooled there," says Charles, obviously delighted.

"Bessie, now you'll remember the time Richard took us to Belle Isle and you let me take off my bathing stockings? And you took yours off too. Now that was really daring, then."

"Just a little ahead of the times."

I look quickly at Charles. Will he ask, who is Richard? But he doesn't. Richard is my memory and I do not wish to talk about him.

"Belle, I think you look very chic."

"Chic, that's the word," Charles agrees.

At which Belle's slightly worried expression gives way to a charming smile.

374

\* \* \* \* \*

I think your young sister will prove to be a good tonic for you," Charles remarks at bedtime. "For both of us," he adds hastily in case I might take it amiss. "For all of us, Marty too."

"I'm afraid to think what turn Marty's admiration for her Flapper Aunt will take. She's a regular copycat, that one."

"At which rate her flapper era could possibly be a short one."

"I can only hope so," I sigh. "She's already asked for a compact and lipstick like her Aunt Belle."

"To which you said?"

"No."

"And if I catch her plucking her eyebrows like Aunt Belle, I'll skin her alive. You'd better warn her. What do you really think of your sister's 'get-up', as she put it?"

Busily brushing my hair, I answer, "I meant it when I told Belle I thought her outfit chic, and I know you did too. It's today's fashions among the young people, although quite a few are going to extremes. But she's not that young anymore, even if she looks to be in her twenties. The thing that bothers me is why she's doing it. When people are unhappy they tend to react in different ways according to temperament. Haven't you noticed how some women will go on a buying spree when they're unhappy? Some buy clothes and paint and powder their faces until their faces look like masks, attempting to be other than who they are. Well, that's what I think this is with Belle. A masquerade."

A thought strikes me. I put my brush down. "I wonder if it's a deliberate and conscious role she's playing, or if it's an act outside her control — something welling up from the subconscious as a sort of safety valve for the hurt within."

375

Charles is not given to such reflections. Saying nothing, he turns down the sheets and crawls into bed.

## 2

Wow! Look at that, will you. An electric icebox. Well, isn't that the cat's pajamas!"

"Our new General Electric refrigerator, Belle. No more need to empty water pans. No more waiting for ice delivery in the summer months. Someday, maybe, there will be no more ice man for Marty and her friends to chase after, begging a sliver of ice."

"Oh, mummy, I don't do that sort of thing anymore. I'm much too old. That was years ago when I was little."

Belle is patting the gleaming white "beehive top" which houses the encased machinery atop the enameled box, opening the refrigerator, oohing and aahing.

"Must be expensive. Did you get it on the never-never?"

"Indeed, no. We're pay-as-you-go people. Charles won't even consider so much as a small loan. After his father's problems in 1913, when we were all hurt so badly and so many people went broke because of too much borrowing, we've been very wary. There is too much installment buying nowadays. People have gone quite mad, and Charles thinks if such buying doesn't slow down this present economic utopia could turn into something very unpleasant. It reminds us too much of 1912 all over again."

"Another depression on the way, you mean?"

"Oh, we don't know and of course we hope not. There are so many other factors besides buying without money that go into the making of a depression. The Prairies, the whole of Canada for that matter, are very

376

dependent on wheat and the farmers have been producing some wonderful crops for the past year or two and now are busily replacing their horses with horsepower, using money they haven't got..."

But Belle's interest in economics is lagging. She has pulled a compact from her pocket and is busily powdering her nose. In the kitchen! Marty is regarding her enviously.

"Marty, off to school before you're late. You can see your Aunt Belle this evening."

* * * * *

In the evening Belle admires the piano, an upright Heintzman Grand. "Another recent purchase, this time for Marty," I inform her. I got it at an auction and it has excellent tone. One of Marty's friends has been taking piano lessons, so she decided she must take lessons too."

"Music lessons will be good for her."

"I wonder. But Charles prodded me a bit. Marty too often just wants, then doesn't have much stick-to-it-ness."

"Come on, Bessie, let's hear you play. How about, 'Yes sir, that's my baby, No sir, don't mean maybe...'"

"I don't know the music."

"Come on, you can improvise, you've done that before. It goes like this."

Belle gets up and sings a little and does a little dance.

"Come on, Bessie, you're good at that."

"It's my bifocals. I can't see the music and the keys too well." I am flustered and fumbling.

"Whatever have bifocals got to do with improvising? You don't want to play the piano? What's the matter with you, anyway?"

377

Charles raises his hand in a futile gesture to Belle, who is looking at me, not at him. I am about to cry.

"Why, Bessie, don't you play anymore?"

I can only shake my head without speaking and leave the room.

"Housewife's Syndrome, that's it," Belle calls after me. "Bessie, you've got Housewife's Syndrome."

"She used to play a lot," I can still hear Belle's puzzled voice explaining to Charles.

And his quiet answer: "I thought the piano would be good for Bessie. But if she ever uses it, it's not when I'm around. Maybe she associates music too much with her mission house, and that period seems to be a raw spot in her life. But I'm sure I don't know."

So, the piano was another of his little conspiracies. What does he think I am, anyway? I am sitting in the kitchen, trying to hold back the tears, and I can hear them talking.

"Housewife's Syndrome," Belle is repeating. "It's very common."

"Sounds like a disease," says Charles.

"Believe you me, it is. Starts to surface when a housewife becomes afraid to do something she really wants to do. Probably due to a feeling of inadequacy or uselessness. I have no intention of being a housewife any more, thank you. When I get back to Detroit I'm going into the beauty business. Then I'll be providing a service of a kind and communicating with people. Keeps the old brain oiled. I refuse any longer to be involved in a repetitious round of tedious tasks. The brain dries up, you know. All these newfangled electrical appliances won't help change the housewife's lot much. You still have to push a vacuum cleaner. I mean to have a talk with Bessie, believe you me!"

So Belle thinks she knows what's wrong with me! Indeed, my girl, that's not the half of it. If I were so

378

unkind I could tell you a thing or two about yourself. You with your painted mask.

She is coming to the kitchen. I must not quarrel with her; she needs my help. I get up and busy myself with making hot chocolate and putting out biscuits, pretending the piano bit has not bothered me, pretending I have not been listening.

And when Belle explains her theories to me, I tell her about my efforts to get work outside the house.

"I've tried, Belle. I've applied several times for a position. I'm well qualified but it's always the same old story. I simply can't compete with youth. I've given up trying. Besides, some days my nerves and my rheumatism are so bad I can scarcely get out of bed. Some days, maybe, I wouldn't even be able to get to work if I did find employment."

I tell Belle too that I even thought of getting involved in real estate, like Ma, but Charles is jealous of his family turf and anyway the times were against it. And now my health.

Everything is against my bid for freedom.

*     *     *     *     *

The evening we are invited to Ray and Cora's, I beg off. "I'm not feeling very well. Think I'll go to bed early." It is an excuse and Charles and Belle know it.

"Have a good time, Belle."

Belle has a good time and acquires several young friends. But I am not too happy about it. I am worried. Belle seems quite unlike her old self. She is, well — a bit wild.

"It's not Ray and Cora's friends who've been taking Belle out lately." Charles is always quick to come to the defence of his cousins. "I asked Ray who they are and it appears they're friends-of-friends who've been escorting

379

her around. Young people who seem to have nothing better to do in life than have a good time."

"I don't like it. She's been coming in at all hours and sometimes it's obvious she's had a bit too much to drink."

I have been wanting to introduce Belle to the ladies at the chapel, but she's not interested. And to tell the truth, the way she paints herself — and it isn't that I mind a little rouge and lipstick if it makes a woman feel better, but, well, her slang and her flippancy, really! It's a bit too much.

Why not try a little strategy to keep her home more?

*   *   *   *   *

The strategy is Mah Jong. All the rage. Belle enters into the game with enthusiasm and becomes quite adept with Flowers, Winds, and Bamboos, as do we all. She buys silk kimonos for Marty and herself, which they wear while playing — "to help get into the mood." Emma and Charlie often play with us.

One evening when the game is over, Belle goes to the radio, puts on earphones, adjusts the dials, shouts "Whoopee, this is it!", and starts doing the Charleston.

Marty, earphones on as well, follows suit.

"I'm practicing," Belle announces brightly. "How about giving it a try, Emma?"

Emma protests, laughing.

"That's right, Marty, you're getting it. Now, bend your knees a little more, like this." Then she adds as an afterthought, earphones still on, "I'm going to a dance tomorrow night with Derek." She tosses out the information as though she believes that with Emma and Charlie here neither Charles nor I will mind.

380

\* \* \* \* \*

"You can't expect to play Mah Jong or table tennis or do jigsaw puzzles all the time. That won't keep her 'down on the farm'."

"He just drove up in his roadster, honked the horn, and she went running. She doesn't even consider introducing us to the young man. I never did think much of chaperons, but this is going too far."

"It seems it's the way it's done nowadays. Belle probably knows we wouldn't approve of him."

"It's called 'emancipation', but it could be called 'stupid'."

"Do you want me to grab this Derek chap and haul him in for a talk next time he comes honking?"

"You can't do that, it would just antagonize her. Once when he came around there was another young couple in the rumble seat. The young man was playing the ukulele and making quite a show of himself — seemed to enjoy drawing an audience. I neither know nor care what the neighbours think of it all, and I'm not about to ask. But I just hope she comes to her senses before something unpleasant happens. Why, she's old enough to be Derek's mother: that young man can't be more than twenty!"

\* \* \* \* \*

"Stop worrying, Bessie." Belle is annoyed. "Sure he's only a kid, but what's the diff? He's harmless, really. We're just having fun."

\* \* \* \* \*

Spring moves into summer and I help Belle pass the time by visiting the chautauqua, bringing home ideas for

381

patterning and stringing small glass beads into necklaces, fashioning glass flowers. Filling the moments with rainbow-coloured soap bubbles to ease the pain. Diversion, simply diversion.

Summer's flowers fade and autumn comes with its multicoloured leaves. Soon there is a nip in the air and a few snowflakes fall lazily. The mellow days are over.

Belle is my project and the aim is to cheer her up, scrape off some of the paint, uncover the real person — and in the process help save her soul. Belle appears impervious to all attempts. She will go to chapel on Sundays as she goes along with my many suggestions for games such as crossword puzzles and newspaper contests. Even gaily will she enter into meaningless games, but all the time I can see she is restless and that her mind is elsewhere. She opens Joe's letters, which arrive regularly and occasionally include a cheque. But if Belle reads the letters, she never says anything. The cheques are spent on new clothes and on quite unnecessary presents for me, Charles, Marty, and her new friends.

"A silver cigarette case for Derek. Isn't it smashing!"

"The case is pretty. The cigarettes are abominable. I hope you won't try smoking, Belle."

"Don't you tell me what to do and what not to do. If I want to smoke, I will."

Miserable, I launch into a monologue describing what I consider to be the many evils arising from cigarette smoking. My project is not doing too well.

The next time Derek arrives, the little roadster has its top up. Belle is waiting impatiently, featuring a new long-line coat with a fox-fur collar.

Gloomily, I say to Charles, "I can almost picture a flask of 'hooch' in her garter."

"As the province dropped Prohibition last year, any liquor she consumes is at least government-controlled and hopefully uncontaminated."

"Small comfort, that. I'm afraid I didn't help when I lectured her yesterday. I shouldn't have, but I'm at my wits end and it's hard to stand by and watch my sister making a fool of herself."

"That's her business — or considered to be her business in this day and age."

* * * * *

Just before dawn Charles and I are awakened by a call from the police.

When we arrive at the station, we find Derek is still sobering up in a cell. Belle, scared, the scent of liquor and cigarettes still clinging, tries to explain.

"Derek was driving me home, we'd been dancing and, oh well, maybe we'd had a bit too much. Snow was falling and it was hard to see. I can't imagine where this guy came from. You see, suddenly this old man was right in front of the car. I think Derek slammed on the brakes, because the car skidded and hit him. Bessie, it's awful! Will that poor old man die? And Derek's in prison. Will he be charged with manslaughter?"

We are given permission to take Belle home. No charges are laid against her.

* * * * *

Derek, the son of a wealthy clothing manufacturer, is shortly allowed out on bail.

Luckily, the man does not die.

The Winnipeg court excuses the "high-spirited youth" — "an unfortunate incident due to low visibility." But the newspapers refuse to let the incident die. If it were the son of a working-class family who got himself drunk and ran down an old gentleman, what would one

383

suppose the verdict would be? Jail, not bail. A good long term in the clink, and a charge of manslaughter if the man died.

. Belle, her name coupled with Derek's and splashed over the newspapers, described as "an older woman coming to Winnipeg to have a fling", is completely sobered.

"I've disgraced you, Bessie. And you've been so good to me. I'm ashamed of myself. I honestly don't know why I acted as I did."

"It's all right," I try to comfort her. "We all do things we wish we hadn't."

Don't I know!

Later Belle tells us, "I've decided to go back to Detroit. Before Christmas."

"Home?"

"I'm going to stay with Ma."

*     *     *     *     *

Saying good-bye at the train station a couple of weeks later, Charles says, "I'm really sorry to see you go, Belle."

He means it. I am sorry too. She has been a breath of fresh — even if turbulent — air.

### 3

Entering Ma's house in St. Clair Shores, Belle says, "Bessie has changed."

Ma sighs. Looking at her reflection in a small mirror as she removes her hat, taking stock of her white hair and wrinkles, she replies, "It seems we all have. Bessie probably thought you'd changed a bit too,

384

with your flapper dresses, rolled stockings, rouge, and all."

"Oh, Ma, don't evade the issue. You know what I mean. Bessie's changed inside. I'm just the same underneath the decorations." She adds, "At least, now I am."

Ma says nothing for a space, then she remarks, "Joe phoned before we went off to collect you. He's coming over."

"I told you, I don't want to see him. Ever again. I'm staying here and looking after you. I'm going into the beauty business and I'll have a shop of my own one day. I won't be any trouble to you, honest."

"That's what I told Joe you said. And he said he was coming here to take you back where you belong."

"He did?" Belle's face brightens. Then, quickly, concern is apparent. "Ma, do you think Joe will like my new look?"

"How do I know? But didn't you just tell me you were the same as ever underneath? In all the years I've been on this earth, one thing I've learned about men is that it's what's underneath that interests them most."

## 4

Chiropractic: Chiropractic is a science. It is the science of the restoration of health and well-being. It is the science in which you should be interested more than any other science, as it deals only with the normal healthy activity of the mechanism of your own body, which you cherish and prize, but which causes you so many aches and so much suffering. It is a science which is loved and revered by countless multitudes who have passed from disease to health, through the application of its principles. It is the science through which throngs of people are being liberated from pain and suffering, almost daily. And it is the science which like a great wave has passed from the little room 12 x 12, in the city of Davenport, Iowa, over almost every civilized country in the short period of 15 years.' Et cetera. 'In Winnipeg, your own city, Chiropractic is being practiced by several doctors, some of whom are highly proficient in the science, and through whom cures have been effected that savor of the miraculous. In evidence of this is the case of...Mrs. Finucan, Brooklyn St., St. James, who had suffered from Rheumatism for approximately 19 years, "Rheumatic cures" and "Rheumatic no-cures" having equal effect. Chiropractic Adjustments ousted the Rheumatism — stiffness, pains and all — in 14 days.' Et cetera. 'Alfred Walton, M.D., ex-President and Chief of the Surgical Division of the Essex Co. Hospital, Essex Co., New Jersey, also author of many books on Hygiene and Medicine, writes: "Chiropractic does away with treatment by expectancy or guesswork. It is a method of procedure that is at once direct, scientific and certain in its operations, producing results that in the light of orthodox methods are almost miraculous." Dr. H.J. Munroe, 360 Portage Ave., Winnipeg, Man. Telephone Main 234.'"

I finish reading the pamphlet out loud and hand it to Charles. "I've made an appointment with Dr. Munroe," I tell him.

"Chiropractor! Sure he isn't a Quackopractor?"

"No, I'm not. But at this point I'm willing to try anything. Whatever he does can't be any worse than pulling teeth, or gold treatments."

"Gold!" Charles is startled, as though he has a guilty conscience.

Whatever is the matter? What has he been up to?

But he continues good-naturedly, "Have you read

about the foot treatments offered by one Dr. Locke, who is convinced that almost every ailment is a result of fallen arches or a foot defect of some kind? Now just look at me as an example — poor feet and sound body."

"There's always an exception to the rule. Dr. Locke is a graduate of that outstanding medical college at Queen's University. Besides being a Fellow of the Royal College of Surgeons, so he must be well qualified. He's taken care of thousands of people and they can't all have had the wool pulled over their eyes."

"There's a fool born every minute."

"Including such people as Lady Eaton and Mrs. Franklin D. Roosevelt, who have been treated successfully by him, as well as Robert Borden and MacKenzie King?"

"Include the last two named."

"I'm going anyway, no matter what you think. Maybe you think I'm just imagining my pains."

His Christian Science tendencies.

"You do what you think is best, Lady."

\* \* \* \* \*

Returning one day after a treatment, I say, "I imagine I'm feeling somewhat better. Or maybe it's just that I hope I'm a little better."

It is a year of hope and achievement. Only a few weeks ago, twenty-five-year-old Charles A. Lindbergh made a solo non-stop flight of 3735 miles across the Atlantic from Long Island, New York to Paris, France in 33 hours and 39 minutes. That was in May. Charles' father knew the young Lindbergh's father in Little Falls, Minnesota. Imagine, one can be as close as that to sheer courage!

The sun is bright. Everyone is doing a little better.

It is a year, too, to indulge in fantasy.

387

"Dr. Munroe has a little black box, Charles. It has a dial on it like a radio. He calls it a medical dowsing machine."

"Dowsing as in water dowsing? All good country folk know about dowsing for water."

"Exactly. It's similar to water dowsing, so I understand. Even some of our provincial governments have their official water dowsers. But in this case Dr. Munroe takes a drop of blood, which he says is part of one's whole system and therefore can give a picture of everything in that system, and he dowses it to find out what is wrong with one."

"Did he discover you were crazy to go to him in the first place?"

"Do try to be serious for a moment. He told me a number of things that are very true. Then he said there is a possibility of my having diabetes and cancer sometime in the future."

"Bessie, now I am serious. That man had no right to say that to you. There is such a thing as putting an idea into your head..."

"Don't worry. It doesn't bother me. I find it interesting — an intriguing theory — and wonder if there could be something to it. All of you depicted in a drop of blood. Just imagine. Macrocosm and microcosm. However, my concern is my present problems. I intend to take a few more treatments and see if there is further improvement and if he really is helping."

\* \* \* \* \*

Healers, quacks, and gold mines. There were no dividends last year. Absolutely nothing — not one red cent. He could have taken a flyer on just about anything other than the Geep Gold Mine in Flin Flon and made a

388

small fortune. As with the Gene Tunney—Jack Dempsey fight the other night, he bet on the wrong man.

## 5

1928

You've had a letter from your mother?"

"No, this one's from Belle. Belle and Joe are getting along very well and she's going to have a baby."

"Wonderful news."

"As you know, Belle's been working at a beauty shop and she says the baby will interrupt but not prevent her from continuing to work outside the home in the future. Joe has given her a Chrysler roadster which she 'absolutely adores'. She says it's 'smashing'."

"I hope we're not meant to take that last too literally."

"The hardware store is doing well but they won't be purchasing their 'castle' for a while yet. Joe likes her new marcelled hair style and she wants us to know she's using only a very little paint and powder, and that mainly because of the beauty business. And her dresses are decently short as would suit the mother-to-be of a modern child. She goes on to say that Blake forbids Beatrice to get her hair cut. 'I think he's an old fogey, don't you?' I'm quoting from her letter now, Charles. 'But then I'm beginning to think that some women actually like the domineering type of male. And do you know, Bessie, Beatrice actually told me she enjoys cooking and cleaning. Imagine that! I should have known. I've seen it with my own eyes over the years but couldn't believe it. It just goes to show it takes all kinds of people to make a world.

389

"'Blake gets these simply awful migraine headaches — perhaps Beatrice has told you — so he's decided to resign as one of Henry Ford's architects and set up a private practice. It's mainly so he will be able to work at his own pace without so much pressure. And that's probably a good idea. They will be leaving Detroit and moving to Chatham, Ontario, where Blake still has his family. And he means to design their own home with offices attached. How about that! But I'm sure you'll get all the details from Beatrice soon. I'll miss Beatrice, and so will Ma, but I'm sure it's for the best for them.'"

"That all sounds good."

"Yes, though Belle will have her baby instead of her own beauty business. She'll probably work in someone else's shop when the baby gets older."

* * * * *

Beatrice will have a custom-designed home. And what about Bessie? Charles is thinking. One day Bessie will be standing calmly, thoughtfully, maybe stirring a pot of soup at the stove. Then she will turn and ask, right out of the blue, "Whatever happened to the money for the house?" For that is the sort of thing Bessie does. Sort of uncanny, as though suddenly she knows what went wrong. Then there will be hell to pay. Well, it was his fault, not consulting her. All that money!

* * * * *

"I'm glad things are turning out so well for Belle. Even though it was an unfortunate accident that brought her to her senses. That young Derek — his family settled a sum of money on the victim. I understand it wasn't much but the man recovered completely and was pleased."

390

"What pleased me were the newspaper articles."

"How could you have been pleased about those write-ups and what was said about your sister?"

"Do you realize that not so long ago the press wouldn't have taken the slightest interest in a working-class man? For a change it was the rich man's son who was taken to task, and for Winnipeg that's a step in the right direction. Though it's my opinion the city still has a very long way to go."

"Oh, come now, Bessie, I think Winnipeg's doing all right."

"Well, I don't think so. What about that design for the war memorial? You may recall that the contest was won by an Emmanuel Hahn, two years ago. A beautiful design he had. Then when it was discovered he was born in Germany, even though he came to Canada at the age of seven, he was disqualified. In my opinion that was a most immature attitude on the part of this city. But much, much worse is the fact that the Ku Klux Klan were able to establish a base in Canada and turn their hatred against French Canadians, Catholics, and Jews. We see and hate in others the wrong we refuse to recognize in ourselves. And the entry of the Ku Klux Klan into Canada shows that along with the many fine people in this country and in this city exists a bigoted lot who project the ugliness within themselves onto innocent people."

"True, true. We all have a lot to learn and a long way still to go."

## 6

Charles hands me architectural blueprints, a mangled version of the house we were so long designing. I look at them, puzzled. The rooms are small to the point of being useless. A lot of storage space is omitted. The roofing and siding are about the cheapest obtainable.

"What's this?" I ask.

Charles appears uncomfortable.

"I'm aware the house is not just what we want. It's small — a compromise for the time being. But it means you can move from here and we'll build a larger version in a few years time."

I am suspicious — something is afoot — but I continue to examine the plans and do not voice my thoughts.

"Really, Charles, what would be the use of building a place like this and then having to build again? The house we're in has more space. If we go to the trouble and expense of building a house, it should be built properly. I can't see the reason for making two moves."

"I want to get you out of here. Besides, we could build that house and likely sell it at a profit. There, now, I've given you two good reasons."

"I'm against it," I say flatly. "We'll get out of here if Ma wins the court case. And if she doesn't, we can review the matter then and see what can be done. Everything's wrong about these plans and I refuse to have anything to do with them. Why didn't you consult me first?"

My irritation is because something is rankling at the back of my mind, something that refuses to surface. I regard him coldly as my suspicion grows. Why has he gone to all this trouble when he must know the plans are unsatisfactory? He surely must know that. A way to

392

make a little money? Well, maybe. But just think of the work involved and the condition I am in with my rheumatism. It is all so unnecessary.

*   *   *   *   *

Unhappy about the way I acted over the blueprints — after all, Charles was trying his best to be kind to me — I reluctantly agree to his suggestion that we repair and redecorate the house on Langside. There is no doubt that the house requires an overhaul, and I don't have to be convinced that it will increase the sale price. Another way to make a little money? Oh, well.

But I have no idea, when I agree, what work is involved.

It is total upheaval. The work continues for months. Paint inside and out, new flooring, new wallpaper. Even new electrical wiring, which Charles does himself to save a little money. Furniture, boxes, books, everything shunted from one room to another and back again. It is worse than a move would have been. I deplore the time, the effort, the upset. It gets on my nerves and I am continually protesting.

"We're spending too much money on this old place. For what? Whoever buys the house will prefer to choose their own wallpapers and do their own decorating."

But once started, Charles, bullheaded, refuses to stop.

"The place will look much cleaner and better in every way. It'll fetch a better price," he repeats, as though now to convince himself.

And it pleases him when I buy a chesterfield and chair and a few other pieces of furniture from Leslie's Furniture Company. They are for our future home, along with the drapery materials and other linens I have

393

stored in trunks.

Altogether it is an exhausting experience and my health deteriorates further.

So Charles arranges for Marty and me to go to the beach at Gimli. It is pleasant for both of us and he does not seem to mind our being away. I am sure he gets along very well without us.

* * * * *

The snows of winter melt, spring brings colour once more, summer fades into autumn. Time passes, and still no word from Ma about her court case.

## 7

One morning toward the end of June 1930 word finally comes about the court case. It is after the crash of 1929 and Ma has lost a lot of money.

The postman must have arrived early. Charles is leaving for the office and I am on my way upstairs when I hear him say, "Thank you. Ah, yes, this is what we've been waiting for."

"Good news, sir?"

"I hope so."

I go to the verandah. I know what it is.

Charles hands me a letter from Ma's lawyer, Sevald. I tear open the envelope and hastily scan the contents.

"Wait, Charles. Listen to this. 'I am enclosing herewith the opinion of the Supreme Court which was filed on June 22nd 1930 in the case of William Faris vs. Mary Faris. ... My only comment is that it absolutely and positively fixes the ownership of all property with

394

your mother. ... Your mother is to be congratulated in the establishing of her rights to the property, for the Court...substantiates every claim she ever made. ... Yours very truly, Frederick J.S. Sevald.'

"Ma has won!

"Against all odds, Charles, Ma has won. You never thought she would. Now what do you say to that?"

"I think it's wonderful."

I know. He is thinking about the stand I took towards the house he planned. Why doesn't he say 'I told you so'?"

"I had to be sure," I tell him, answering his thoughts.

He pats my shoulder, letting me know that bygones are bygones. "Congratulate her for me, won't you. That mother of yours is a fighter. It's good news."

I nod. My eyes are blurred. "She won't let Pa down, Charles. She'll see that he's looked after. I know my mother."

These are hard times.

A thought strikes me. "Charles! You remember it was because Ma wanted to do something for women, wanted to help set a precedent. And this year the Alberta Five, including Our Nellie, Nellie McClung," I emphasize the name, "have also won their case in court. Now at last women are persons."

Charles chuckles. "Well, good for you." The screen door swings to with a click as he leaves.

Is "good" what he really means?

Well, anyway, good for all of you, Ma.

\*     \*     \*     \*     \*

The letter still in my hand, I sit on the verandah. Ma lost a lot of money, but as she never believed in keeping all her eggs in one basket, she has still a fair bit left.

395

She's no longer rich but she'll get along. Those years before the end of 1929, when most people appeared to be living the good life and giving no care for the morrow, were simply a pleasant prelude to the worst economic slump the country has yet known. Even nature conspired during that period of plenty by supplying an abundance of sunshine and an abundance of wheat. Wheat, the weathervane of the Canadian economy, finally glutted the market and prices dropped abruptly, as they had in 1913. But this time there was added a disastrous crash on Wall Street: on October 24 people panicked and rushed to withdraw their money from banks so that a great many banks were forced to close. Many people lost everything.

If Charles never managed to make much money during those vintage years, neither did he incur debts. So we'll manage somehow. It won't be easy but we'll manage.

But we'll not be moving now.

The lot on Wildwood was sold for back taxes as were our other properties.

My home is within me and of my own making. So wrote Martha. If I could find peace within me, would this house on Langside Street seem otherwise?

What have I accomplished in these past many years? But then what could I have done considering sickness and circumstance?

The Alberta Five, Ma, and Woodsworth, all were fighters. Woodsworth did not let problems stop him in his quest for a better deal for the underprivileged. Now he has a seat in Parliament. His party, the Canadian Commonwealth Federation, was born in the dust-bowls of the west. But there is much still to be done.

So many people in need.

Winnipeg's relief offices cannot cope with the homeless and the hungry. The breadlines grow longer.

I see a man, looking tired and half starved, coming slowly along the sidewalk. He notices me, hesitates, then fumbles with the gate latch and, opening it, comes up the walk. I wonder if he will turn away and run as did the man yesterday, overcome by humiliation at having to beg for food. I open the door.

"Would you like to come in?"

He nods. Forcing himself to speak, he asks, "Have you something...?"

"Sit down. Here." I indicate my rocking chair. "I'll see what there is."

I leave him and force my aching body into the shadows of the house. My morning reverie has faded, replaced by pity for this man and pity for myself. Replaced by repugnance for all injustice. By anger at myself for my mistakes and missed opportunities. There is confusion and despair in Winnipeg and within me.

Taking what is left of yesterday's stew from the refrigerator, I pour a large helping into a pot and put it on the stove to warm. What else can I give? Bread and butter. The bread box is on a utility table under the west window, the wooden work surface littered with this, that, and everything. Everything cluttered and heaped. The rubbish of my life. As this house is my prison, so this is my protest.

Charles and Marty don't understand. They try to clear away the surface mess when I'm not looking. How can I explain there has to be chaos and pain before there is transformation. Mike, Woodsworth, Ivens, and Dixon — they would understand. Sometimes I scream and scream. I am not myself. And I am frightened. Then, depressed and exhausted, I lie in bed for days. No doubt, Charles and Marty consider me slightly mad. But — perhaps this too, will pass.

I take out the bread, pull out the breadboard, cut three thick slices and butter them.

397

Then I carry the food to the man and place the tray across his knees.

"Would you like tea?"

Again he nods, raising his eyes to mine. They are faded eyes and in them, a declaration of defeat. My pity is watered with contempt: I understand him all too well.

# Chapter XI

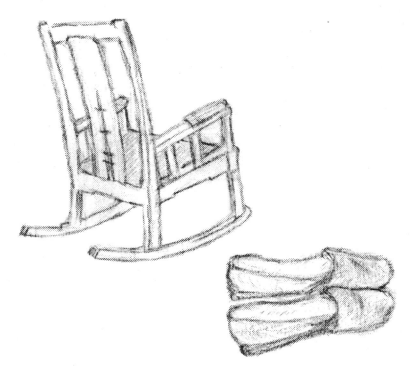

# Maybe Another Time

One day I search for a receipt in my cherrywood desk. Not finding it where I expect it to be, in my fumbling annoyance letters come spilling from an overstuffed cubbyhole. One is an old letter from Martha which I thought long discarded. I seldom hear from Martha anymore, our correspondence having dwindled to a mere exchange of Christmas cards. We have gone our separate ways. Still, I love her and regret the chasm that lies between us. About to put the letter away, I hesitate. The fondness for my old friend is too great. With a certain reluctance born of sadness, I open the letter and go to the verandah to read it.

\* \* \* \* \*

She stands before me, an attractive young woman with quiet ways. I want to greet her as was my wont with a hug and a kiss, and link my arm with hers. Then we'll walk up the steps, past the heavy oak door and into the house, talking nineteen to the dozen as we head for the studio. But wait, Martha. First I want to look into the drawing room to see if Richard is there. If he's waiting to tell me I'll not make a good Christian missionary for I'll declare an "open city" and fraternize with the enemy, I'll tell him that is so. I'll tell him I've met people from many countries and learned of their creeds and cultures and loved and understood them all. But I failed the course I set myself.

And if Richard begs me to stay...will I?

The letter holds my horoscope — like a mandala, Martha said. I look at the symbols that show me in this lifetime, and I read Martha's interpretation of those symbols in juxtaposition one with another. And I think about my life and all that happened from the day I visited Martha to tell her I was leaving for Winnipeg. And still I wonder, if I could have willed myself more strength and courage, would my life have been otherwise?

I did what I knew I must do. Surely in that there was no wrong. Then where lies the fault if not in me? I am the one who wove the web that trapped me. I am the spider and the victim. But I will not accept responsibility for all circumstances that impoverish me and others. Surely this economic depression can be no making of mine!

Memories come rushing in and I no longer repulse them, but count them one by one like beads on a rosary. My beads are not easy to hold, for too many have rough edges and many are jagged and hurt me.

But with deliberation I count them all.

## 2

Stew again for supper. Served at the harvest table in the kitchen. We eat without speaking until Marty shatters the silence.

"There's to be a street dance tonight on Langside."

"Is there? I hadn't heard."

"Wondered what all the commotion was about when I drove up. So many people on the road, thought somebody'd been killed."

"Oh, Daddy, you didn't. The street's to be cordoned off and the dance will be right out in front of our house." Marty is excited.

"Then I'll have to move the car. I'm going out anyway. A few accounts to look after."

Always something. "

Everybody will be there," Marty continues.

"Where's there?"

"At the dance, of course."

"Who's everybody? Does that include all the riff-raff? Some dance."

"And why not, Charles?" I interject. "People have to find some way to have fun without going to a lot of expense nowadays. What's wrong with that, anyway?"

"I'm not against people having fun. But there's no way of controlling who'll be there. That's what's wrong."

"Including a lot of nice people and some of my friends." Marty is vexed.

"I don't want you to mix with the wrong type of people. There's no telling who'll be on the street. Or what will happen. I saw you with some young people the other day. That family's not your sort at all. A bunch

401

of working-class Reds."

Bolshevik phobia still. Reds under the bed. How much can people change? How much have I changed? I focus on my tea while Marty pouts.

Noticing her unhappiness, Charles says more kindly, "Now, Marty, one of these days we'll hire a hall, a proper place for a dance. Maybe a room at the Royal Alex or the Fort Garry. A proper place where you can invite your cousins and your friends. We'll do it up right. What do you say to that?"

Marty does not think much of that. More pie in the sky.

The front doorbell rings and Marty jumps to answer.

"It's a man asking if you'll please move your car, Daddy."

"Tell him I will, soon. It's only seven. When does this shindig start, anyway?"

"Eight o'clock and the dance is to go on until well after dark. They're anxious to get the street cleared now."

"Well, I may as well get ready and go. See that you wash up for your mother, Marty. And remember what I said."

After Charles leaves, taking his biases with him, Marty looks at me slyly. "He didn't say I couldn't go to the dance, Mother, now did he?"

"I don't think he got the chance. I think he was interrupted." For pity sakes, it won't be long before the girl is fifteen. I say, "I didn't hear him."

*   *   *   *   *

Wearily I sit on the verandah, glancing at the evening *Free Press* but more interested in the people as they gather outside. A few youngsters are already trying out dance steps, laughing, whirling, chatting, clapping, singing. A man from down the way strolls by, strumming his ukulele. Someone is warming up with a piano accordion. That's better. Now I can hear a violin or two, and brass instruments. What is that — a saxophone? Perhaps a street band has been hired for the occasion? I know so little about these affairs.

Now they start. Dancing in the street — how I'd love to be out there with them. There's Marty dancing with that girl from the terrace housing. What's the name of that piece? Someone's singing. Quite a good voice, really. I can't hear the words too well. There, now I've got it.

*"Falling in love again*
*Never wanted to*
*What am I to do?*
*Can't help it..."*

A new tune.

Go to it, Marty, go to it. No, Charles, there's nothing posh about this dance. Nothing fashionable about the dresses. Many of the women are wearing housedresses. I see short skirts left over from the twenties. I see one woman with a long dress in style about fifteen years ago. Some hair looks home-cut, bowl-cut maybe. Most of the men are in shirtsleeves and braces. A few of the young fry are wearing sneakers. They're having fun, so what does it matter?

A collie with its tail wagging insists on getting in the way. Max! I wish you were Max. There's a young boy all legs and arms who reminds me of someone. Awkward. He is really awkward. Oh, my! Why, it's Martin. Wipe your nose, Martin — no, not on your sleeve — and come over and say hello. You helped me on my way, Martin, do you know that? It was because of you I met Martha. And I never thanked you. I hope one day I can do you a

403

favour in turn.

I dream along, still listening to the music.

*"Gone is the romance I once found divine*
*'Tis broken and cannot be mended*
*You must go your way and I must go mine..."*

Over the beat of the music isn't that someone calling "Bessie Robinson!" Who's that? The voice sounds like Richard's. It surely can't be Richard.

"Come on, Bessie. I've never known you to sit out a dance."

I'll dance just a little with him. Out of my painful body, I'm out on the street dancing with Richard. He holds me close and the voice sings on:

*"What"ll I do when I am far away*
*And I am blue, what'll I do?*
*What'll I do when I am wondering who*
*Is kissing you, what'll I do?*
*What'll I do with just a photograph*
*To tell my troubles to?..."*

"I kept your photograph, Richard, did you know that?"

*"When I'm alone with only dreams of you*
*That won't come true, what'll I do?"*

I'm young again. We dance lightly as once we did. Another score. Another song.

*"I'll be loving you always,*
*With a love that's true always..."*

"I still do love you, Richard. Have you always loved

404

me?"

"You shouldn't have left me, Bessie. It would have worked out."

"But I had to go. It couldn't have been otherwise."

I put my head on his shoulder. But I'm resting it not against fine wool but against a working man's rough-cut jacket. It's not Richard I'm dancing with but Mike! Where's Richard?

"You left me," I say accusingly, looking up.

Mike's face is grim. I'm wearing the blue silk Martha made for me and Mike is in worker's clothes.

*"Remember the day you said you loved me..."*

"I know it had to be. But why couldn't you have told me what happened to you and Gedda and little Nikki?"

He won't answer me.

Look. There's Uncle John. I didn't know he could dance.

And there's Ma. Ma loves a dance. And Belle and Beatrice with their beaux.

"Andy! Where are you, Andy?"

"Naw, I don't want to dance. I'm going over to the ballpark."

"Don't go, Andy. Please, please, stay here. It's growing dark. I don't want anything to happen to you." I panic.

Andy's gone. The band plays on. The people dance.

I'm back on the verandah, trapped by my chronic pain.

A woman, a stranger, standing by the gate notices me and calls out gaily, "Join us. Won't you join us?"

I wave.

"Another time," I call back. "Maybe, another time."

405

# APPENDIX

# BESSIE'S MANDALA

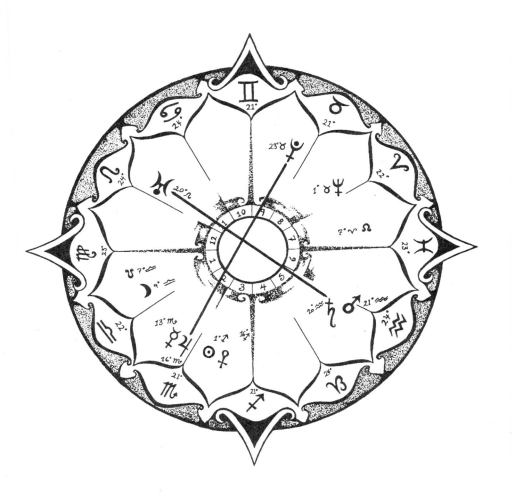

ELIZABETH ROBINSON
November 23, 1875

**Elements.** Fire, Air chart. Highly developed both intuitively and intellectually. Exceptional mind linked to intuition and strong sense of value. Able to see things in terms of relationships and wholes. Grasps things instantaneously. Don't fence me in — love of travel. Better comrade than traditional wife.

**Grand Cross and Fixed Dominates Chart.** Chart represents a psychological confinement. Zest for life, yet she is in a psychological wheelchair. Great frustration, as circumstances do not allow her to develop enough. The fixed Grand Cross is a most trying and testing one to bear.

**Problem: Sagittarius and Uranus** on one side of chart are strongly developed and North Node is in Aries. These are right up against Saturn conjunction. A lot of physical energy — a caged tiger. **Animus in chart conjunct Saturn.** Male archetype is linked up with shadow archetype which brings a Saturn quality to life. Also may indicate a loss of father at early age. **Uranus opposite Saturn.** Anytime Uranus interests appear (Uranus in Eleventh House: radical social ideas), Saturn archetypes rear up to say, "This is wrong." Also guilt feeling experienced from authority figures.

**North Node in Aries.** Integration would come through forging path of her own. Self assertiveness. But problems of Grand Cross provide no outlet for energies. Pressures internalize in deeper levels of psyche. Pent-up and turning inward, they result in enduring blockages and inhibitions.

**Venus trine Uranus.** Humanitarian chart, concerned about welfare of humanity. Strongly developed social sense. Interested in people who are not just status quo.

407

**Sagittarius Sun and Mercury and Jupiter square Uranus.** Tomboyish quality when young, and interested in unorthodox people. Yet through force of will she keeps the lid on.

**Sagittarius Sun; Moon in Libra.** Harmonious relationship, both well aspected. Great vitality despite everything. An underlying buoyancy.

**Well-aspected Venus sextile Saturn.** Can willingly give up personal happiness through a sense of duty.

**Virgo Ascendant.** A desire for improvement, also a wish to serve and help others. Under stress it can mean a tendency to be very critical of other people and situations. Worry — to relax is difficult.

**Sun and Venus in Third House in Sagittarius.** A real love of learning, and travelling; wants to explore far horizons, whether foreign countries, foreign people, religions, philosophies.

**Uranus in Eleventh House, conjunction Twelfth House Cusp.** (Uranus ruler of Sixth House.) Someone who wishes to serve society and is attracted to social movements that are somewhat radically inclined. But as there is a **Square from Uranus to Pluto** it indicates that this can at some time come in conflict with a more conservative belief system.

**Sun and Venus in Third House trine Uranus Eleventh-Twelfth House.** A great deal of vitality and energy when travelling or engaged in helping others.

**Jupiter conjunct Mercury in Scorpio in Second House.** A very perceptive mind that can dig deep. Perceptive of other people. As Jupiter rules the Fourth House, indicates she would do very well in real estate.

**Pluto in Ninth House.** Wants to help transform the world through religious and philosophical connections. When under stress can become highly dogmatic.

**Mercury and Jupiter square Saturn-Mars conjunction in Fifth and Sixth Houses.** The wish to explore new horizons intellectually is frustrated by early responsibility and sense of duty. Education cut off prematurely, resulting in a feeling of insecurity. In later life looks for security in conservative and authoritarian forms of knowledge, as shown by Pluto in Ninth House.